But the LORD said unto Samuel, Look not on his countenance, or on the height of his stature . . . for the LORD seeth not as man seeth; for man looketh on the outward appearance, but the Lord looketh on the heart.

1 Samuel 16:7
Holy Bible – King James Translation

THE GUARDIAN OF HEAVEN

By Mark H. Barratt

Book 1 - *ONE*
Book 2 - *David*
Book 3 - *Shannon*
Book 4 - *Israel*
Book 5 – *Galaedael*

www.guardianofheaven.com

Revision 1
Copyright © 2006 Mark H. Barratt
All rights reserved.
ISBN: 1-4196-5890-5
BookSurge Publishing
North Charleston, South Carolina

DAVID

Book Two
of
The Guardian of Heaven

Written by
Mark H. Barratt

Cover Art by
Adair Payne

To friends old and new . . .
for the priceless treasure that is experience.

Preface

When the Children of Israel cried for freedom from the brick pits of Egypt, God sent ONE — a babe bundled in a basket and set into the Nile River.

When all the world was lost to sin and the bands of death loomed everlasting, God sent ONE — His only begotten son — a babe wrapped in swaddling clothes and laid in a manger.

And at the end of our world, when the Enemy of Life unleashes his armies, God will send —

ONE.

JOHN

Chapter 13

David ran out of the hospital into the cold November night. Minutes later, he felt the first drops of rain touch his face. It was cold. Still he ran. The cold rain gradually grew in strength and intensity. Soon it washed over him, soaking his clothes and penetrating his skin. He never slowed his pace.

David ran down the boulevard and through a park. He ran past some large buildings and a school. He was not fully cognizant of the world around him. He was running from something inside of himself. His body began to ache, crying out for him to stop. His chest and his legs were on fire, but he hardly noticed the pain. The darkness and the emptiness drove him on.

The dark cloud that shrouded his mind was obliterating his feelings. It was the cauldron, the cauldron that had been in the rec room of his school. It was in his mind now. Every time he closed his eyes, he could see it pressing against him, pressing on his mind, on his memories, crushing the little boy he had always been. He couldn't escape. It was part of him.

It was all wrong, everything was wrong. Even though the cauldron burned with the fire of an intense heat, it was covering him in darkness, absorbing him in coldness. He couldn't concentrate on anything else and no matter how hard he ran or in which direction; it was always there, creeping across his heart, closing off his feelings. David shut his eyes again and it exploded in his mind, looming, hovering, waiting for him to stop so that it could catch him and engulf him in darkness. David shuddered in fear, his eyes flinging open. The cauldron threatened to sever him from the love that burned in his heart, threatened to destroy that tender place where he had always thought of himself and . . . his mother.

There was only one way to push it back. He had to run. It was the pain. If he kept on running his lungs and his legs would ache. Then he could feel something and he would know that a part of him was still alive, still capable of feeling.

David ran until his body reached its limit. He stumbled to the ground and panted, trying to catch his breath. Still, he had to move. He couldn't let the darkness cover him. Shaking, he rose to his feet and stumbled forward. He loped for hours through the darkness. Directionless, he traveled as far and as long as his little legs would carry him. When he finally crossed a small plaza miles from the hospital, he was hardly able to place one foot in front of the other. He tripped on the edge of a sidewalk and tumbled to the ground.

His mind screamed. Like a cornered animal his instincts told him to get up and run, but when he attempted to lift himself, his body only trembled in agony. He gulped down several ragged breaths before rising to his hands and knees. His body spasmed, but he was able to crawl. At least he was moving again. He tried desperately to push the cauldron from his mind, the black abyss, but his thoughts were drawn to it. There was no escape.

He crawled through the wet grass and across the sidewalk to a park bench that faced the plaza. Pulling himself up onto the bench and peering across the park, he finally noticed the rain. It was then that he realized he was lost and alone, soaked to the bone and cold. He shivered and it drew his concentration away from the cauldron. A new thought burst into his mind. *Cold is good!* Cold was like the pain in his lungs and in his legs; it helped him push back the shroud covering his mind. David concentrated on the cold, but the cauldron stole his thoughts again engulfing him in darkness. It was drawing closer. There was nothing he could do now. The tentacles of darkness were reaching into his heart. Fear exploded anew. He had to run!

Urgency seized David. He tightened his muscles to stand, but before he rose six inches, his body locked in refusal. Pain arched through his legs and chest. He fell back onto the bench in agony. He bent his knees up under his chin and wrapped his arms around them. The sight of his arms tightly holding his legs triggered a memory. *Just like my mother held me.* The memories erupted inside of him and with them came haunting questions. *Where is my mother? Why is this happening to me?* David avoided closing his eyes and instead, concentrated on his arms and on the tiny specks of dirt on his jacket, anything to keep him from seeing the cauldron and feeling the black death that boiled from it. He began to rock back and forth on the bench. It was the way his mother used to rock him.

The sun broke through the gray, bleak sky on the eastern side of the park. For a second, hope raced through him. *Maybe the light will push back the cauldron. Maybe I'll be all right if the sun shines on me. If only the clouds would go away.* David concentrated on the eastern sky. He willed the sun to make him feel better. He remembered the warmth of it on his face and arms. He needed the sun.

With the sunlight bathing his view, David absorbed his surroundings. He was somewhere in a big city at the edge of a small plaza that covered a single block. The park was mostly a flat, grass covered field, except for the playground in the middle. The playground reminded him of his family. Suddenly, the deadness burst back upon him. It was the cauldron closing him off. *Run!* His mind screamed. But he couldn't move. His heart pounded.

David concentrated, trying to distract his mind. It was hard to see anything in the early morning dimness, but close to him, on the adjacent side of the park, he noticed an old man lying on another of the park benches. He had a newspaper draped over his head to protect himself from the rain. *Probably a poor person, no one else would be out in the rain.* He peered intently through the darkness. He couldn't tell for sure, but he thought the old man was watching him.

* * *

Mason Alburton woke groggily that dreary Sunday morning and wiped the drool from his mouth. He had fallen asleep on the floor in front of his couch and his mind was disoriented and sluggish. It was early, too early; he peered at the clock in the kitchen. It was barely 5 o'clock. Then he remembered. He had stayed up late watching movies. They were his special movies and they had created a craving. It was a terrible, all absorbing craving. It had been too long since he had been up to the cabin. It was time to go back. But he couldn't go alone. No, he needed "a little friend" to go with him. Mason had cruised the poor neighborhoods for weeks now with no success. He just couldn't seem to find the right child. But this morning was different. He had an impression. He needed to go to the old part of the city now. Time was critical. There was something there for him.

Mason rose slowly, rubbed the sleep from his eyes, and donned his jogging suit. He ambled lazily down the steps to parking lot. He stumbled on the bottom step and nearly fell on his face. He thought momentarily about going back to bed. *No!* He felt his blood burn with urgency from the voice in his head. *Something . . . someone is out there waiting for me.* A cruel smile crossed his lips.

Mason started the car and pulled out into the early dawn. He had seldom seen the city at this time of the day. He was amazed at how quiet it was, even for a Sunday morning. He had a vague idea of where he was going, but as he closed in on his destination, his senses seemed to intensify. When he pulled down a long broad street near the edge of town, his vista opened to a small plaza and his heart quickened. *This is the place.* The voice in his head was practically screaming.

Mason cruised slowly up the western side of the park and peered through the darkness. When he turned onto the northern side, his eyes filtered across to a boy on a bench. It was hard to make out the details in the dim morning light, but as he studied his victim, he felt the connection. *Too young,* he thought dismissively. *He's too young.* Mason liked his friends to be about twelve to fourteen. He reasoned that the boy on the bench couldn't have been much older than ten. He would have kept on driving, but the hunger seized him again. It was just that it had been so long. He shook his head in consolation. *No matter.*

The easiest way would be to draw the child to his car from the curb. He stopped, rolled down the window, and called softly for almost a minute. The boy never looked up. Frustrated, Mason circumnavigated the plaza, finally parking on the nearest side street. Avoiding any onlookers, he ambled nonchalantly to the plaza while making a mental note of his surroundings. *No people. That's good and, of course, no cops, even better.* It suddenly occurred to him that even though he was in the suburbs of Sacramento, he was in the middle of nowhere.

Mason knew from experience that he couldn't approach the boy directly or bully him. *No,* he thought menacingly, *I'll just take my time this morning, promise the boy whatever he wants, and then . . . take him to the cabin.*

A tiny smile touched Mason's lips. In the end it would all come out the same. *I'll be gentle with this one because he's so young. Still, I'll have my way and when it's over, there will just be a smaller hole to dig; one more grave to match the other two in my little mountain retreat.* His lips pulled back in a full smile as he felt a flush of heat and desire wash over him.

Mason crossed the southern side of the plaza and headed slowly up the eastern walk toward the boy. He contrived his little speech as he approached, something inviting and caring but not too friendly. Suddenly, a pang of fear rippled though him. Something was wrong! Someone was watching! Mason stopped in his path.

A ray of sunshine broke through the clouds and Mason searched his surroundings more carefully. There was another person just a few yards short of his target. He stared in concentration and frustration as light exposed the obstacle. It was an old man. He was lying on the bench, apparently sleeping. Mason cursed to himself. He hadn't noticed him before. If he had, he would have walked up the western side of the plaza and crossed to the boy on the northern end.

He paused for a moment and calculated his options. *Just an old drunk,* he reasoned to himself. He shook his head. *He'll never wake up.* Mason lowered his eyes and muttered another curse. Then slowly, careful not to make any noise, he continued his approach.

When he was a few feet away, the old man stirred on the bench. Mason slowed and measured him from the corner of his eyes. *Now what?* He thought bitterly. The old man slid his legs off the bench and sat up. Mason froze. The last thing he needed was a witness. He knew he should just turn around and walk away, but his blood was on fire; he couldn't stop now. He dropped his eyes to avoid the obstacle and continued.

As he closed in on the old man's position, Mason surveyed him without turning his head. A feeling of disgust washed over him. He was dressed in a ragged coat that fell nearly to his ankles. Mason cringed in disgust, imagining the smell of the liquor and body odor on the old man. His lips curled into a sneer. The old man's hair and beard were medium length, somewhat scraggly, unkempt and gray. He had a sturdy build but was short and hunched over. He couldn't have been taller than five feet four.

The old man lifted his head as he approached and Mason could tell he was being watched. He ignored him, but the old man rolled off the park bench and, holding it for support, gradually straightened to a stand. His eyes were on Mason now and he could feel that gaze. Mason slowed and adjusted his course. Avoiding eye contact, he took a step sideways to evade the bench and its unwanted inhabitant.

Too late, Mason cursed in his mind. The old man took a few steps until he was directly in his path and then, slowly, pathetically, he held out his hand and opened his palm. Mason's mind revolted. *He wants a handout!* Nothing could have infuriated him more. He hated beggars. His mind raced with what to do. He didn't have his wallet or any money for that matter, but more importantly, he didn't want to delay or make himself conspicuous in any way. An angry thought filled his mind. *If you and I were alone, I'd teach you a little lesson about begging . . . begging for your life.* But Mason remembered that he wasn't alone. Instinctively, he glanced up at the child. He was still there, still rocking himself on the bench.

Seething, Mason reconsidered his feelings and checked his anger. He needed to be in control. He couldn't strike the old man and it wouldn't do to raise his voice either. He glanced again at the filthy vagabond and shook his head.

Still avoiding eye contact, Mason quietly sidestepped again without slowing down. He gave a deliberate wave to discourage him, but the old man was quicker than he looked. He stepped in front of Mason with his hand still held out.

Mason's frustration boiled into rage. He was not going to stop. This old man had no right to block his path. Mason never broke his stride. Without so much as a glance, he pulled his left arm across his stomach and balled his fist. When he reached the old man, he pushed his arm out with enough force to swat the disturbance out of the way. He believed the blow would knock the old man to the ground, but that was a chance he was willing to take.

He was wrong.

When the back of his hand touched the odd stranger, it was met with absolute resistance. The old man never budged. Mason stopped just before they collided and lifted his head. He was startled. That face may have been old, but that body was one of strength, muscle and sinew. Mason sagged in bewilderment. The body belonged to a man in his prime, twenty-five, maybe thirty years old, and strong. A tiny sliver of fear slipped into his mind as he examined his nemesis. His face was weathered with age and wrinkled from years of experience, but his eyes told another story. Those ancient eyes were filled with sadness and something else far more invasive: intelligence, wisdom . . . power.

A spasm of fear seized Mason. It felt like his soul was draining from his body. Those burning eyes transfixed him. Mason's mouth dropped open and his muscles locked. This was no ordinary old man. He was filled with power. Mason could sense it. He thought of running, fleeing those burning eyes, but he couldn't move. He was a caged rabbit now, staring at the open mouth of a lion.

The old man peered deeply into Mason's eyes, gazed upon his soul and found something terrible. The expression never changed on his face, but Mason knew his secret had been discovered. Strangely the old man did not react. Instead, he slowly extended his hand and terror shot through Mason, terror as he had never known it.

Something inside of Mason screamed at the thought of that hand touching him. He felt panic echo throughout his body. Miraculously, the old man stopped short of touching him. Instead, Mason watched in apprehension as he slowly turned his hand over and brought it across in front of Mason's face, in front of his eyes.

Everything went dark.

Mason fell to the ground, stunned. For a moment he just lay there. Then he turned to see if the old man was still there. Nothing, there was nothing. He felt his way along the sidewalk. He touched his fingers to his face, opening and closing his eyes over and over, but it was no use.

Mason Alburton was blind.

* * *

David didn't notice how or when, but at some point, the old man who had been lying on the bench made his way toward him and sat down next to him. He sat there silently for several seconds and then he spoke. His voice was soft and David could feel the warmth in it, but what surprised David most was the word the old man spoke. It was a single word and even in his confused state he recognized it. It was his name . . . "David."

At first he couldn't believe his ears, but when he heard it a second time, he lifted his eyes. The voice seemed familiar. There was something soothing about it.

"David," the old man spoke a third time. This time David concentrated, focusing outside of his mind and onto the face beside him. He didn't speak because his mind wouldn't work, but as he gazed into the eyes of the stranger, he found something far different from the old man who was sitting next to him.

The old man smiled weakly. "Your mother sent me to help you." Then the smile disappeared from his face. "We need to go, David. It's time for us to go."

Slowly, the old man slid off the bench and knelt in front of David. He lifted his gnarled hands and rubbed David's arms. Warmth from that touch flowed through him. It seemed to calm the storm that raged inside of him. David loosened his grip and lowered his arms from his legs. The old man never stopped. He stretched David's legs until his feet were on the ground in front of the bench. Then he started rubbing David's legs. Each touch felt like penetrating fire, but David made no expression.

Soon David's legs loosened to the point that he could walk again. The old man seemed to understand. He stood and, taking David's hand, helped him off the bench. Together they began walking a single step at a time. It felt good to be moving again. *Maybe,* David thought hopefully, *in a few more steps, I can run.*

They hobbled down the sidewalk together for several feet until David turned his head to gaze more intently at the person who had been so kind to him. When he looked up, he noticed that the old man was staring down at him. There was something familiar in those old eyes. It was sorrow; it was understanding; it was tenderness. David wasn't sure how, but those eyes reminded him of someone. When the old man noticed David's eyes on him, he smiled and gently squeezed his hand.

"My name is John."

THE VALLEY OF WINTER WIND

Chapter 14

The next ten days were a blur to David. From the park, John took him to a bus station and from there they traveled to bus stations day after day. Sometimes at night they stayed in small hotels and sometimes they just slept on the bus.

David liked traveling on the bus. It was a lot like running. He stared out the window and imagined that he was getting away, that the cauldron was too far behind, but always, when he thought about it, it was right there in his mind, waiting to destroy him.

Even though he was exhausted, David couldn't sleep at night. He did his best sleeping on the bus where he could lay his head in John's lap and imagine another time, another place. The security of that touch and the droning of the engine reminded him that he was getting away. That thought brought peace to his heart and he slept.

His worst nights were when they stayed in the small hotels. John fell asleep quickly and David just lay in bed avoiding his thoughts. It seemed that a thousand noises pervaded the night. He could hear cars and trucks constantly, occasional trains, and sometimes music or people talking. Sometimes he felt like running. On those long nights, he eyed the dark door and wondered what was out there, wondered if there might be a place, somewhere, where he could outrun even the cauldron.

Between bus rides they walked to grocery stores or small restaurants. Once they walked to a strange store that had racks of clothes, toys and other things, with no shiny advertisements. John said it was a thrift store and he bought

David a plethora of items: shirts, pants, socks, pajamas, boots, a winter coat and a suitcase to carry them in.

When they reached the motel that night, David felt especially bad. They had dinner and John said prayers with him, but it didn't help. The cauldron was heavy in his mind. After tossing and turning in bed for two hours, he was ready to run. He slipped out of bed and crept silently to the door. He stretched out his hand to open it when suddenly, John spoke. "David." The sound of his own name startled him. "We need to rest. If you can't sleep I will tell you a story."

David felt guilty, like he had been caught trying to do something wrong. He took his hand off the doorknob and answered slowly. "No . . . I'm okay."

David went back to bed, but an hour later he was still awake. He sat up in frustration and peered longingly at the dark door. Finally he sighed softly and as he lowered his head in defeat. He resigned himself to not getting any sleep when, suddenly, an idea flowed into his mind. Slowly, quietly, David took the pillow and coverlet from his bed and crept across the room to the floor right under where John was sleeping. Making every effort not to disturb him, David lay on the floor and listened to the comforting rhythm of John's steady breathing. Minutes later, he lapsed into a fitful sleep.

The next morning he was lethargic and tired but not completely dysfunctional. As they prepared for the day's journey, David's thoughts drifted to his family. *Where are they?* Whenever he thought to ask John about them, his hands shook and his throat tightened into a knot. *No,* he finally decided, *it's better not to think about them.* But he couldn't avoid it. Everything reminded him of them: a car similar to their old minivan, a girl whose hair was the same as Rachael's, a mother taking her child to school the way his mother used to take him. He couldn't stop them; the images kept coming, creeping into his mind and when they did, they always awakened the cauldron. Only running helped or at least the feeling of getting away.

The bus rides snaked through random cities on random roads, but every town seemed a little colder and every forest seemed a little darker. One night they reached a city that was very cold. David had slept for hours on the bus and he couldn't sleep when they reached the hotel. He rolled and fidgeted in bed and visited the bathroom twice. On his way back to bed after his second trip, he wandered to the door and touched the doorknob. It was cold. His mind drifted outside as he remembered the path that had brought him here. A part of him needed to open that door, needed to run, but it was too cold. He didn't want to be cold, not right now. When he turned to go back to bed, he noticed John sitting up in bed watching him.

"David, come here."

David quietly walked across the room and sat on the bed next to John. John leaned back against the headboard and helped David up next to him. He threaded his arm behind David and gently squeezed his shoulders.

"David," he began, "many years ago in a place far from here, there was a woman who had great faith. Her name was Hannah and although she was not especially beautiful her husband loved her because she held so much love in her heart for others. Her husband's name was Elkanah and he was a good man. Unfortunately, Hannah could not have children and this was the great desire of her heart. After Elkanah's other wife had many children and she had none, it made Hannah very sad."

David peered up as John's eyes drifted down towards him.

"Every year they would go and worship God in a place called Shilo. Here they would pray for special blessings, but in this certain year, Hannah would not eat or go worship with her husband because she was so ashamed about not having any children.

"Elkanah loved Hannah very much," John paused, shaking his head sadly. "He loved her so much that it broke his heart to see her suffer. To show his love for her and his other wife, he made special gifts for both of them, but to Hannah, he gave the best gift of all.

"When Elkanah gave his beloved wife her gift, he hoped that it would lift her spirits and give her joy, but his gift did not make her happy. When he realized that she was still troubled, he tried to reason with her.

"'Am I not better than ten sons?' he asked. 'I love you more and I would do more for you than any son would.' But this only made Hannah sadder because more than anything else, she wanted to bear a son for her kind husband.

"So Hannah went to worship by herself that year. She prayed to God and poured out her heart to Him. She promised God that if He would help her have a baby, a boy baby, that she would give the boy back to God to be His servant."

Something rang familiar about this story to David. He had heard it before but not like this. David's thoughts swirled around the image of a woman who was sad. He knew that image all too well, but it wasn't the woman John was describing. David concentrated on John without saying a word, his eyes pleading to hear the rest of the story.

"David," John paused as if remembering the story, "God heard Hannah's prayer and her promise. He blessed her with a son. Hannah was so very happy that she never forgot her promise. When her little boy was about four years old, she took him back to Shilo and gave him to the priests to serve God and to be their helper.

"She named him a special name. His name was a lot like yours. She named him Samuel. That name means 'heard of God' because God heard her prayer and answered it." John stopped talking and smiled at David.

David pondered John's words until confusion crossed his face. *Is that the end of the story?* David formed a sour conclusion and frowned. *That wasn't a very good story. What happened to the little boy? Did he have any friends? Were the people nice to him or were they mean? And what about his family?* There was no smile in David's eyes as he looked at John. He just glared intently at him for almost a minute before asking his penetrating little question, "Did his mother ever see him again? Did she just leave him?"

John lowered his head in defeat. He paused before continuing.

"Hannah came to see her son as often as she could. She brought him clothes and other gifts and no matter how far apart they were, she always loved him."

David's eyes drifted from John to the door across the room. He was silent for several seconds before asking his final question. "Will my mom ever come see me?"

John exhaled slowly and closed his eyes. It took him almost a minute before he whispered his quiet answer, "Yes."

The next day John told David that they weren't going to travel because it was Sunday. John's announcement upset David. He hadn't slept much that night and he was anxiously anticipating lying on the bus and sleeping. David frowned but never voiced his feelings.

John brought out a loaf of bread he had purchased the night before. He took some cheese and cut it, making a simple sandwich for each of them. He poured two glasses of milk and they ate their meager breakfast together in silence.

When they finished, John glanced out the window. It was snowing. "Would you like to go for a walk?"

David nodded his head in approval. Anything that felt like travel was always a relief.

When they opened the door, an amazing world of white burst upon David's senses. The ground and sky were filled with cold white powder. It was snow! He had never seen snow falling before. He stepped outside and absorbed the view for several seconds while the snowflakes licked his face. It was heaven. Seconds later, he bent down and scooped a handful up in his glove. It was so cold that it felt dry. David rubbed his gloves together and the snow sifted through like fine sand at the beach.

Walking out onto the parking lot, David felt the snow crunch under his shoes. He ran a few steps and the powdery substance billowed up into tiny clouds with each step he took. David was thrilled. What a great thing it would be to tell his friend Kevin about this or show his mom. The thought stopped him. That was a different world. He could never go back. As suddenly as the thrill had overtaken him, it disappeared. The little boy that would have run and played in the snow was gone.

Still, David gave it his best effort. He stooped again and attempted to make a snowball, but the snow was so light and powdery that it wouldn't stick together. Then he ran out on the sidewalk and tried to slide with his boots. That was a mistake. David's feet caught on the sidewalk beneath the snow and he fell face forward on the hard cement. He held out his hands in time to keep the damage to a minimum, but he still managed to bump his forehead on the sidewalk. It hurt and, for a second, the fear that always comes with an injury flared in his mind. Then something strange happened.

David closed his eyes and the cauldron exploded upon him. It flashed briefly in his head and threatened to consume him. But this time the pain anchored him to reality and, by concentrating on the pain, he was able to hold the cauldron at bay. David concentrated on the cauldron and the flames burning to heat it. Those flames were meant to destroy him, but he couldn't be destroyed because the pain pounding in his forehead told him he was alive.

He didn't cry out or move. He just lay there on the sidewalk, face down in the snow. A moment later he felt John's gentle hands roll him over. He could feel something warm and wet running down his forehead. It was blood. He didn't speak. John examined him carefully. He stared at the wound in his forehead before catching David's eyes.

"David, are you alright?" John questioned him in concern.

"Yes, I'm fine." David responded flatly. There was no emotion in his answer, only information. Part of David wanted to cry out, wanted to say how badly it hurt so John would feel sorry for him and help him, but instead, he simply gazed up and spoke with a strange steady disaffected voice.

John pulled a handkerchief from his pocket and gently wiped David's forehead. It was only a scrape. It stopped bleeding immediately. Then John patted David's hand and squeezed it; it made him feel better. John released him and held out his hand. "You'll be alright, David. Come on, we have a long walk."

They walked in silence after that. At first it seemed to David that the snow was like a beautiful white blanket, but as their walk went on he noticed the stark contrast between the snow and the gray buildings that lined the streets. It was like the world had become black and white, like the snow had drained all the color from it. It was still pretty, but after the second hour he was relieved to see a McDonalds with its bright colors and covered playground.

The cold was starting to seep into David, mostly in his face. Although his coat had a hood, his nose was freezing and runny. About fifteen minutes after passing the McDonalds, John stopped at a church. It was a large gray building with lots of little carved things on the outside. There was a gate in front leading to the sanctuary that stood open and beckoning. David thought they were going inside, but when he made a motion in that direction, John didn't follow.

Startled, he looked up at John and followed his eyes to a lighted glass-covered sign whose little white letters on a black background announced the times of the meetings. Next to that was a picture of Jesus. John stood fast, examining the placard. David could tell that it was the picture that held his interest.

Finally, after almost a minute of motionless staring, John peered down at David and spoke with a smile. "We are almost there."

From the church they turned down a narrow street that led into another narrow street and, for the first time that dreary morning, David saw a crowd of people. They were lined up and waiting to get into a warm building. But these weren't normal people. Their clothes were dirty and you could tell that they had been worn a long time. Some of them had shopping carts and some were carrying or dragging their possessions. There were no children.

John stopped across the road from the building and, reaching into the pocket of his coat, drew out a worn envelope. It wasn't very thick and it only had one word written on the outside of it in beautiful cursive writing. John knelt down next to David and placed the letter in his hand.

"David," he spoke intently, "I need you to do something for me. Inside you will find people eating at long tables lined up together. Toward the back of the room on this side," John motioned with his right hand, "you will see an old woman about my height. She has long gray hair and very sad eyes. When you see her, call out her name and she will lift her head. Then give her this letter." David examined the letter apprehensively. "This is very important, David. Her name is Lilly."

John glanced across the street to the crowded doorway. Something inside of David told him that he should be afraid, that he should complain or cry, but something else told him that it didn't matter how he felt. So in the resolute, emotionless way that he was coming to see himself, David just walked across the street and edged his way through the crowd and into the building.

It was warm inside. David enjoyed the warmth letting is soak into his skin as he made his way. The room was large and filled with people. There was some conversation, but mostly he could hear trays, dishes and utensils clinking, as people ate their meals in silence. He made his way to the back of the room on the side that John had indicated. Several people stared curiously at him as he squeezed past them, but no one spoke to him. Keeping his head up and peering intently through the crowd, he finally found Lilly. She was sitting by herself at the last table in the corner of the room, exactly where John said she would be. He stopped in front of her table. She never looked up. Then he remembered John's instructions and called out her name. It surprised him how clear and steady his voice was.

"Lilly?"

Slowly, the old woman lifted her head to find the odd little boy addressing her. She seemed very tired. Her hair was a mixture of different grays and hung down past her shoulders. She had dark brown eyes that were filled with sadness, but there was also kindness in those eyes. They reminded David of Grandma Helen's eyes, but he didn't have time to think about that because just as her eyes met his, she smiled and spoke.

"Yes, little boy. Can I help you?"

David didn't speak, but held out his hand with the letter in it. Lilly stared at him for a moment and then reached across the table and took the letter. Confusion crossed her face when she found her name on the front of it. She carefully opened it and took out the note. David stood mesmerized by the scene.

Lilly read her letter and as she reached the end, her head fell to her chest. David couldn't see her eyes, but he did see the tears that streaked down her face and dropped onto the table. Embarrassed to be watching someone cry, David turned quickly and headed for the door. Within seconds he was through the crowd and outside. He found John standing on the opposite side of the street staring at him. John held out his hand and David crossed the street and took it. Together they started back the way they had come.

Although it was the same distance, the trip back seemed shorter than the walk there. They walked in silence for most of the way, but as they approached the hotel, David peered up at John and spoke emotionlessly. "She cried." Then realizing he hadn't explained what he meant he added, "When I gave her the letter and she read it, it made her cry."

John only nodded his head. When they entered their hotel room, John retrieved the bread and cheese they had partially eaten for breakfast and David filled their glasses with water from the sink in the bathroom. They sat together at the little table under the swag lamp as John blessed the food before they ate.

"David," John spoke softly. David stopped eating and gazed up at John. "One of the great purposes of this life is to come to know exactly who we are. This process takes experience and our reaction to each experience tells us something about ourselves." John concentrated on the morsel of bread resting on his plate. "The most difficult experiences teach us the most about ourselves." He ate the last of his lunch. "Because of agency, or the freedom people have to make choices, things sometimes happen to people that are so devastating---" Realizing that David did not understand that word, John corrected himself. "---things happen that are so bad that it can shatter a person's life, just as this plate would shatter if I dropped it on the floor."

John lifted his eyes to meet David's gaze. "It is not God's will that people should suffer and languish without hope. So, every once in awhile, he takes their hand and lifts them back to a place where they can be happy again." John could see from David's confused face that he had no idea what he was talking about. He smiled at David's expression.

"Many years ago Lilly had a husband and a little girl. She was very happy until the day her little girl wandered away from her in the grocery store. Eventually her daughter went out to the parking lot searching for her mother, but she couldn't find her. After being outside and alone for several minutes, she finally saw her mother exit the store. When she recognized her, she yelled excitedly and ran toward her. Unfortunately, a car came into the parking lot just as the little girl crossed it. There was no time to stop. There was nothing anyone could do. The little girl was killed."

John gave David a chance to comprehend his story. "Lilly never forgave herself. Her life was shattered and things just kept getting worse for her. Her husband was also brokenhearted and the dark feelings that drowned Lilly, hurt their marriage. One year later, he left her; the sorrow was just too much for both of them.

"Lilly gave up then. Instead of going back to her family and trying to start over, she just started wandering. She tried a few jobs, but she just couldn't forgive herself. Finally, she ended up a homeless person, disturbed and unhappy. In spite of all this, David, she has held kindness in her heart for all people and even though the world has forgotten Lilly, God remembers her and He still loves her very much."

John studied David's worried eyes. "The letter you gave Lilly was from her sister, Emily. Emily was never able to have children and her husband passed away three years ago. She is a wonderful person, but now she lives by herself and is very lonely. She wants Lilly to come and live with her. They were such happy little girls when they were children and so close. So Emily wrote that letter for Lilly and kept it on her fireplace for many years, wondering where to send it. She tried every way she knew to find her sister, but it was as though Lilly had vanished. There was no way to find her."

John lifted his head, focusing on the door behind him. "But Lilly's daughter is still alive, David. She lives in another place now. It's a beautiful place of peace and rest." David was listening intently. John glanced at David's serious little face and smiled. "I met her," John said thoughtfully, "her name is Holly. She asked me to help Emily find her mother, Lilly. She asked me to help her mother forgive herself and be happy again."

John paused. "So I went to visit Emily and I told her that I knew where Lilly was. Emily was happy just to know her sister was alive. She gave me the letter from her mantle, the letter you gave Lilly this morning."

John broke off another piece of bread. "Because of that letter, Lilly will find her way back home. She will see her sister again and they will both find peace."

David lowered his head in concentration. It was a strange story and David could tell from John's serious face that he had carefully measured the words he had spoken. Finally he finished. "And one day, not too long from now, Lilly will see her little girl again." David stopped eating as those words burned in his heart.

"David," John went on, "what you did was a good thing. Lilly cried because she felt hope for the first time in many years. She knows now that she has a place to go and that in all this difficult world, there is someone who still loves her."

* * *

The next day they were back on the bus. David enjoyed it much more than staying in the room, but it was getting boring. Not only that, the scene never seemed to change. Day after day they traveled through forests that must have contained millions of scraggly Christmas trees. Eventually they arrived at a small bus station in a little town surrounded by those trees. They waited at that bus station for over twelve hours. It seemed like forever to David and since John didn't look like he was going anywhere, David lay down on the bench and put his head on John's lap. At six o'clock the next morning, they boarded another bus and traveled all day again. David slept most of the journey until they arrived in a town where everything was silent and blanketed in snow.

John shook him awake. "David, we're here. We're home." It was a dark and moonless night and to David, it could have easily been the surface of another planet.

Everything was covered with a thin layer of blown snow and although the town was similar to some of the places he had seen with his father in California, no place had ever been as cold as this place. The only visible light was where the streetlights lit the road. Beyond that, dark forests swallowed everything.

David wanted to ask a million questions, but he was so tired that all he could do was hold John's hand and follow. About fifty feet from the bus station, John unlocked the door of an old, faded blue and gray suburban. After loading their suitcases, David pulled open the heavy door and slipped inside. The door closed with a creak and the frigid seat seemed to crack under his weight. Seconds later, he felt cold penetrate his pants. It made him more awake than he had been in days.

John inserted the key in the ignition and the engine ground to a start. He shook his head as if he hadn't necessarily expected that to happen. He jammed the old suburban in gear and it lurched forward. Soon they were out of town, turning from one winding road to the next. Within minutes David was completely lost and after thirty minutes of confusing dark roads, John pulled down a long driveway and the forest opened to reveal a small log cabin in a large clearing.

David stared at the cabin in silence before speaking with some trepidation. "Is this your home?"

John nodded in confirmation. "This is," and John paused for effect, "*our* home David."

David absorbed the view. It was so lonely. There were no streetlights, no cars, no other houses, not even any animals that he could see. The dark forest looked menacing and seemed to consume light. David swallowed hard and repeated John's words in his mind, *our home*.

Slowly, but with some curiosity, David retrieved the suitcases and trudged through the snow toward the cabin door. It was obvious that no one had been here for days.

There were no foot tracks in the snow and a small drift had formed in front of the door.

When John reached the door, he didn't unlock it; he simply turned the knob and pushed it open. Inside there was a large room for cooking and eating and some furniture for sitting. A large picture window in the front room held a view of the unbroken forest. There were two doors off the main room and David soon learned that one went to the bath/laundry room and the other to the only bedroom in the house. David was relieved to discover that it was warmer inside than outside, almost livable. John went into the bedroom and turned a dial. An instant later, the drone of a heating system answered.

John wandered to the back of the living room and pulled a board down on the wall. It was a large table that was hinged at the wall and had chains connecting the far corners to the wall. John unrolled a foam pad on the table and then added a sheet, a blanket, and finally a heavy quilt. He glanced at David, "This is your bed. You'll have to use your clothes for a pillow until we can get one from the store." John beckoned David to come closer.

David glanced at the doors in the back of the living room. "Is that your bedroom?"

"Yes," John nodded. And then, reading David's thoughts, he continued. "I'm going to tidy up a bit and stretch my legs. Why don't you go ahead and try and sleep. I will be right here if you need anything."

David didn't feel much like sleeping. He had slept most of the day on the bus and this whole place was fascinating to him. He wanted to protest, but John started unpacking and putting things away, so David watched him instead. Soon the foam pad and the ability to stretch his legs made him very comfortable. Minutes later, he fell fast asleep.

The next morning he woke with a start. He had completely forgotten where he was and the strange cabin disoriented him. Light was filtering in the windows, but it didn't seem like sunshine. It was a cold white light. John was up cooking something and, in all truth, that was what woke David.

David sat up slowly and took in his surroundings. It didn't seem real because it was so different from any other world he had ever lived in. David stared at John until he caught his eyes. "Good morning, David. Why don't you go wash your face and hands and then join me for breakfast?"

"Okay," David mumbled as he rolled out of bed. On the way to the bathroom, he glanced out the window again. He noticed the same frigid scene he had seen the night before, but this time it was bathed in harsh white light. The snow and dark spruce trees which seemed so foreboding the night before were still there, but behind that, he saw a ring of snow-covered mountains cascading into the sky. He had seen mountains in California and on the trip west from Atlanta, but these mountains were more primitive and more dangerous. David gazed at them for several seconds before remembering that he was supposed to wash up.

A few minutes later he was sitting at the table with John, eating the first good meal he had had in what seemed like weeks. As he wolfed down his pancakes and eggs, John spoke sternly. "I let you sleep in today, but tomorrow you'll have to get up for school." David peered up at the clock. Even though the sun was just barely up, it was well past ten. John continued his explanation. "We'll have to go over there this afternoon and get you registered."

After breakfast David grabbed his coat and gloves. He desperately wanted to go outside and explore his new world. Instead, he received and unwanted surprise. Just as he reached for his coat, John spoke abruptly. "David, I do the cooking, but you have to do the dishes." David glanced back sheepishly. He had never done the dishes before. He supposed he would have eventually, but with three sisters his turn hadn't come yet.

It took David the better part of an hour to clean the few dishes that John used for breakfast. It wasn't so much the difficulty as his unfamiliarity with the task. His shirt was soaked by the time he finished, so John insisted that he take a bath. With all the morning chores behind them it was almost noon before they went outside. When David took his first step out of the cabin, he was amazed. The windows of the cabin faced southwest and the mountains he had seen earlier were the Chugiak Mountains, but as he turned to the north his eyes found the distant towering Talkeetna Mountains and far to the northwest, the Alaska range that brandished Mount McKinley at its center. David had never imagined a place that was surrounded by so many mountains.

They made their way to the car and as they wound down the road, David noticed an old sign that read "Matanuska Valley, Home of Matanuska Maid." There was a faded drawing of a girl wearing a short coat with a thick hood and ice skates. The girl in the drawing reminded him of Helen. Suddenly, he was back in the old trailer and Helen was helping him with his Halloween costume. *Helen was always so kind to me.* He missed her, but he only had a second to remember her before the cauldron flared to life. David focused his attention on the scene in front of him.

The Matanuska Valley, David thought. He examined again at the towering mountains on all sides and then he reached a conclusion. *We are the same. This frozen valley is trapped within these mountains and me,* David hung his head in sorrow, *I'm trapped inside myself.* The thought made him sad, but he didn't say anything to John. Instead he just stared out the window and watched the trees whisk by. In a way, it was like running.

THE KINGDOM OF GOD

Chapter 15

Winter dragged by slowly for David. He didn't make many friends until late in the year and the darkness and cold were always there. For a long time, he thought of the Matanuska Valley as a cold prison, but when winter finally ended and he was able to watch spring explode into summer, he began to love the valley and think of it as his home. This was his world now. He rarely thought about his other one. It was a lifetime away.

David was busy anyway. Every morning he was responsible for taking care of himself and doing the dishes. In the evening he had to do his homework, clean part of the house, fold clothes, and help John with other things that needed fixing from time to time. That summer he discovered he was responsible for a large garden. Though the growing season was short, it was intense and David managed quite a harvest from the field surrounding the cabin.

The only break in this rhythm was Sunday. On Sundays, they mostly read and studied. When summer arrived, John began taking him into the rugged mountains behind their cabin. Eventually they would find a pristine spot and sit down. There, in those secluded magnificent settings, John told him story after story after story.

These stories included people like Moses, Abraham, Noah, Joseph, Peter, Paul, and, of course, Jesus. Over time David came to realize that these were stories from the Bible. They were the same stories that his mother had read to him in the other world. David never tired of hearing them. Whenever John told them, they seemed so real. It was almost as if John knew the people in those stories, knew how they felt, how they struggled---and mostly, how they loved God.

The most precious stories he told were the ones about Jesus. One resplendent Alaskan summer day, they hiked to a particularly beautiful spot next to a pool of water formed from a cold mountain stream. There, John made David build a large fire before starting in on his sermon.

"David, if you remember, the last time we talked I told you about how Jesus taught in the temple in Jerusalem when he was just a boy." David nodded as he sat down next to the fire. "The Bible doesn't say much more about Jesus until many years later. Then, when He was a grown man, He went to visit His cousin, John the Baptist." David peered up at John when he heard John's name, but John was concentrating hard, his eyes focused on the fire.

"John was called the Baptist because he lived outside the cities and he taught people that a Savior was coming to redeem the world. When people believed enough to express their faith openly, John would take them into the water and baptize them so that their sins would be forgiven and by doing so, they would become Christians, heirs to God's kingdom. Many people believed in John the Baptist and in his message that the Messiah would soon come." John glanced up from the fire to see David staring back at him. "The Baptist's words carried great power because they held the truth and when people hear the truth, it rings in their hearts."

John paused for a moment giving David time to absorb the importance of his point. "David, those people who seek after righteousness are given a light. When they hear truth, that light burns inside them and guides them to do what is right. This is the way that God teaches men to find truth in the world and to know the truth when they find it.

"One day as John was baptizing in the River Jordan, Jesus came to him to be baptized. Jesus was John's cousin and John recognized the Savior, because he had taught of His coming. He also knew Jesus was perfect and did not need baptism. So John told Jesus that he was unworthy to baptize him. But Jesus had not come to be baptized for the remission of sin, but to fulfill all righteousness. He was baptized so that all men would know, by example, the way to His Father's kingdom. Jesus called to John and told him these things and John, recognizing the truth of the Master's words, baptized Jesus.

"John took Jesus and immersed him in the river Jordan. When He came up from the water, the Holy Ghost descended upon Him as a dove and light filled Him. Then a quiet voice spoke from heaven and filled the hearts of all those who were there that day. It was the voice of God and these were His words: 'This is my beloved Son, in whom I am well pleased.'

"David," John peered across the fire, "John loved Jesus. He spent his entire life preparing people to receive Him and helping them to understand the purpose of His mission. He knew that Jesus was the greatest of all who would ever live, so after John baptized Him, he sent all his followers to Jesus.

"Some of John's followers were upset and wanted to continue following him. But John understood that each time the Messiah comes, a messenger is sent to prepare the world for His coming. John knew that he was that messenger and he was faithful in his calling, even to his death.

"Many of the followers of John became great followers of Jesus. In fact, two of Jesus' original apostles were among the followers of John the Baptist. They were Peter's assistants. Their names were James and John and they were brothers. They were the sons of Zebedee."

John stopped talking and concentrated on David who was staring intently back at him, trying to understand every word he spoke. Then John turned slowly to face the stream beside them. "The time has come, David. You are old enough to take responsibility for your life and your actions and you are old enough to decide if you want a place in the Kingdom of God. So, if you are ready and if it is your desire, I will baptize you here in this stream . . . today."

David was taken aback. He hadn't expected this. Still, there was no decision to it. John was his world now and while he didn't understand everything that was going on, he understood enough to know that if John, in his soft-spoken way, asked, then he should probably obey. Without ever truly comprehending the path he was choosing, he nodded yes and followed John to the stream.

They entered the frigid waters together and John blessed David and baptized him. The water was shockingly cold. When it penetrated his clothes, the cauldron flared for a fleeting moment before he pushed it away.

When David came up out of the water, John embraced him in approval. Then they headed for the fire to warm themselves. After they were partially dry, John placed his hands on David's head and blessed him again, giving him the gift of the Holy Ghost. It was a long blessing and after he finished, he embraced David again and whispered quietly into his ear. "Welcome, David. Welcome to the Kingdom of God."

David felt something surround him. It was a strange and soothing warmth. He recognized the feeling. It was the way he had always felt in his other world, the world before the cauldron. David laid caution aside and opened his heart to the warmth that enveloped him. It filled his whole body. Soon it burned with such fervor that he stopped trembling; his partially soaked clothing having lost its effect. David marveled. He stared up at John and, for the first time in all their days together . . . he smiled.

TOMMY

Chapter 16

The years passed quickly for David after that first summer. Soon, the long cold winters were no longer strange but a part of his life. David grew to love the fresh smell of the air and the invigorating cold. During the summers, he loved to be outside and cherished the task of coaxing life out of the ground by planting a few seeds in the short spring.

Because David was new to the area and spent so much time at home, the process of finding friends was a slow one. To aggravate the situation, he was at least a foot taller than most of his classmates and he was painfully shy and introverted. But of all David's strange characteristics, it was his distant eyes that haunted people the most. Even at such a tender age, there was a disconnection in his eyes that made people think he wasn't listening to them or wasn't interested in what they said. His best friend ended up being an odd little loner like himself. He was the only boy who seemed unaware of, or indifferent to, David's debilities. His name was Tommy Anasogac.

Tommy was a native Alaskan, an Eskimo to people from the lower forty-eight states but Athabascan by his own admission. He was short with a medium build and a dark complexion. His straight, jet-black hair fell to his shoulders and his dark eyes were penetrating. Tommy and David shared few common character traits, but the one that led to their isolation and ultimately to their friendship, was the fact that they were both very quiet boys. David and Tommy were so much alike in this regard that, left to themselves, they would sometimes spend the entire lunch period just sitting at the table together in silence.

They shared one other common trait. Both greatly loved nature and while David had his garden, Tommy had his pets. Because of the attendant duties each of these hobbies imposed, they didn't spend much time together outside of school.

Their lives would have passed in obscurity if not for the third member of their group, Camille Magelby. Camille was exactly the opposite of both these boys. She forced her way into their amazingly boring lives by way of pure imposition. Born into one of the oldest, well-known families in the valley, Camille had relatives and acquaintances everywhere she went. She had long blond hair and a pretty face and would have been a beautiful girl except for one unmistakable blemish, her girth. She was, in fact, a large girl, but mostly she was just fat. This made her an outcast among those who would normally have been her friends and a candidate to consort with David and Tommy.

What was most remarkable about this trio was the lack of any other common characteristics. David, in his quiet, invisible way, was extremely diligent and intelligent. He never missed an assignment and was generally graded 100 on everything he turned in. If extra credit work was available, he did all of it.

Tommy was the worst student in class. He had a hard time focusing on school and usually didn't hand in his homework. Many a teacher had called him aside and lectured him on his lack of effort. It was obvious that he was capable of far better performance, but he rarely applied himself. Tommy understood the situation perfectly well; unfortunately, school just didn't interest him. He loved his animals and he cared more about raising them than any school could ever teach him. So, year after year, he did the minimum he could to still pass.

Camille was an okay student, but she had the heart of a warrior. Underneath her corpulence was a flash temper that could be ignited by the slightest irritation. Anyone who kindled her wrath usually got to unkindle it by having Camille knock them down and sit on them. Camille was bigger and meaner than any other kid in her grade and she knew it. She wouldn't tolerate anyone making fun of her or any of her friends. By the time she reached sixth grade she had been in so many fights with unsuspecting children that few dared to speak to her.

The combination of these three strange people and their unique characteristics earned them a title. Somewhere in the middle of their fifth grade year Marty Kenley, the class clown, labeled them "the good, the bad, and the ugly" after Camille threw his backpack on the roof of the school. Camille threatened to throw Marty on the roof if he ever said it again, but it was too late. The moniker was so close to the truth that it stuck and behind their backs everyone abbreviated it to "the GBU."

Every day at lunch, David and Tommy would sit down and begin eating together. After three minutes, neither had spoken a word. Then Camille would join them and begin rattling off the local school news and politics. She often asked them if they had seen such and such on TV, but even after repeated explanations, she refused to remember that David didn't have a TV and Tommy never watched his.

It was during one of those lunchtime monologues that Camille was babbling on about her farm, how hard her life was, and all the chores she had to do, when she happened to mention that one of her chores was feeding her dad's horse, Raven. Both boys stopped eating as Tommy stared up at her with his mouth open. Amazingly, Camille actually stopped talking when she felt Tommy's glare. It irritated her. "What?"

"Your dad has a horse?"

"Yes," Camille said mockingly, shaking her head like he was stupid, "haven't you been listening?"

Actually the answer to that question was "no," but Tommy perked up. For the first time in weeks, maybe ever, Camille had said something of real interest to him. "I've never seen a horse up close. What's he like? Can you ride him?"

"Of course I can ride him. It's hard this time of year because it's so cold and gets dark so early, but in the summer we ride him all the time."

Camille could tell that she had finally seized Tommy's attention. His eyes were open wide and he had an amazed expression on his face. She guessed what he was going to say next, but she waited just to hear it.

"Can we come see him?"

Camille loved it. She had finally stumbled upon a subject that elicited a reaction from her friends. "Sure, anytime."

"How about after school today?"

"That's fine with me, but don't you need to tell your folks?"

"No, it won't matter to them as long as I get home before dinner." Tommy turned to face David. "How about you?"

David shook his head without giving it a thought. "No, I can't go tonight . . . maybe Saturday."

"Why not?" Tommy furrowed his brow and glared sternly at David. David read Tommy's mind. It was one thing for the three of them to hang around school together, but it would be quite different for Tommy to go home with Camille by himself.

David shrugged apologetically. "John waits for me every day and expects me to be home by four-thirty, five at the latest. I can't just go to Camille's house and not tell him."

Camille piped up at that point. "Just call him and tell him you'll be a little late. I can have my dad drive you home."

David shook his head. "We don't have a phone."

Camille's mouth dropped in disbelief. "What is it with you and technology? You don't have a computer, you don't have a TV, and now you're telling me that you don't have a phone. It's like the stone age."

In his heart David had to agree. At first it didn't bother him too much, but as he progressed in school he noticed his peers doing an ever increasing amount of homework on the computer. It made him jealous. He tried to bury the conversation. "I have all these chores to do and, well, we don't have much time for it anyway," David muttered more to himself than his friends.

Camille piped up. "You do way too much homework. You should watch more TV." She glared menacingly into his face. "That's why people think you're so weird, you know." She gazed across the lunchroom as if to emphasize her point. Then her face twisted into a smile as a solution popped into her mind. "Wait a minute. If you don't get home until five, your home must be one of the last stops on the bus. My bus stop is the first one, so we could be at my house by three-thirty, you could see Raven, and I'll get my mom to take you home by five for sure."

David considered Camille's solution and realized that for once, she had a point. He was about to concede when something tugged at the back of his mind, telling him that it wasn't right. David peered over at Tommy. It was obvious that he wanted to see Camille's horse and, to be honest, David did too. Horses were rare in Alaska, something of an extravagance with the long cold winters. When Tommy found David's eyes fixed on him, he nodded vigorously and mouthed "yes" out of Camille's glare.

"Okay," David surrendered, "but you have to get me home before five, Camille. I mean it."

Camille smiled. "No problem."

At the end of the school day, David and Tommy stood silently in the bus line with Camille. A few feet away from them stood Marty Kenley waiting for his own bus. He pulled the pigtail of the girl in front of him and then stared casually in another direction. When he noticed Camille staring him down from her bus line, a wicked smile crossed his lips.

"Hey, Camille," Marty shouted. "We were studying hurricanes today and guess what? You have a hurricane named after you." Marty broke out in a snorting laugh before continuing. "I guess they needed something really big to name it after."

Camille went bright red. She dropped the backpack she was holding by one strap and launched herself across the sidewalk to take Marty out. Suddenly, a strong hand landed on her shoulder bringing her to a halt. It was David.

Camille turned and lasered David with her eyes. He never flinched. "Don't listen to him, Camille. Nobody else does."

Camille took David's hand off her shoulder. "I'm going to kill him once and for all. He can't run away right now or he'll miss his bus."

"Yeah and we'll miss ours too." Tommy practically shouted at her.

David picked up the conversation from there. "Tommy and I want to see your horse so don't run off chasing Marty right now." Camille stood there debating David's advice until bus number six pulled up and opened its door.

"Okay," she said, picking up her backpack, "but some day I'm gonna get him for real. He will never say a word to me again after that." The terrible scowl on Camille's face punctuated her remark.

David's mind drifted for a second and suddenly came to focus on a point just behind Camille. There was an image floating there. It was a strange phenomenon, but it happened to him once in awhile. Concentrating, he realized that Camille was at the center of that image. She was much older, maybe twenty or twenty-five. She had lost most of her weight and she looked great. She was dressed in white and a beautiful smile filled her face. It was a strange vision. Camille was holding someone's hand and staring at him. He was a tall handsome fellow with brownish-red wavy hair and freckles. He was dressed in a long black suit. For a moment, David couldn't tell who it was and then he recognized that unmistakable crooked smile. There was only one person who smiled like that. It was Marty Kenley!

David closed his eyes and shook his head in disbelief. *Marty and Camille?* The strange thought echoed in his mind. David peered at Camille and muttered softly, "Oh, you'll get him, alright."

The ride from the school to Camille's house was uneventful except for its brevity. It was amazing to David that Camille only rode her bus ten minutes each way, while he often spent up to an hour and a half getting home. Of course, he spent most of the time doing his homework, so he didn't really mind the ride.

When they stepped off the bus at Camille's house, it couldn't have been any later than three forty-five, but the sun was already nearing the horizon. Although David had been to Camille's farm a couple of times, he had never been inside any of the great barns that dotted her property. He swept his eyes across the flock of buildings and imagined which one held their prize.

They started with Camille's house. She said hello to her mother as she dropped off her backpack. Then Camille led them across the property to one of the smaller barns at the back of the lot. It was mostly filled with equipment, but in a stall at the end of barn, David and Tommy caught a glimpse of the head of a giant, pure black horse peering down at them.

Camille piped up when she saw Tommy's mouth hanging open. "That's Raven." Raven neighed and bobbed his head up and down as Camille approached. "Usually I walk him for a few minutes before feeding him, but if you want, I'll let you two ride him instead."

Tommy couldn't believe his ears. "We can ride him?"

"Yeah, sure. I'll feed him afterwards." Camille slipped through the barn and opened a paddock next to Raven's. Inside was a variety of saddles and long leather straps with strange metal pieces, which Camille explained were reins and bits. She took one of the bits down and told David to get the saddle. Then she opened Raven's paddock and led him to the center of the barn.

David gawked in awe at the beast. Raven was the most magnificent animal he had ever seen. He was huge, solid black with a long, flowing tail and a short clipped mane. His back was as high as the top of David's head and his neck and shoulders were solid muscle. His long muscular legs ended in powerful hooves.

Camille gave Raven a handful of grain and then slipped the bit into his mouth. He seemed perfectly content to stand there placidly while she looped the bridle over his head. Then she placed a small blanket on Raven's back and told David to throw the saddle on top of the blanket. Raven stiffened at the saddle's touch but soon relaxed and concentrated on Camille.

"Raven is a Thoroughbred and he's a big one. Dad says he's sixteen and a half hands, but I think he's bigger than that. Raven's gelded so he's easier to manage."

"What's gelded mean?" Tommy asked.

Camille rolled her eyes. "I thought you were the expert on animals."

Tommy responded by shrugging his shoulders.

Camille shook her head. "A gelding is a boy horse . . ." Camille was about to say something crude, but her eyes caught David's innocent gaze and she was suddenly embarrassed. She paused and rephrased her explanation. "A gelding is a boy horse that can't have babies."

"Oh," Tommy nodded, "like a dog that's been neutered?"

"Yeah, exactly."

David didn't have any idea what they were talking about, but he didn't want to appear stupid. He decided to just keep his mouth shut. When Camille finished tightening the girth, she grabbed saddle horn and motioned to Tommy.

"What?" Tommy stood stonily.

Camille snapped at him. "Come over here and give me a leg up." Tommy's face melted to confusion. Camille let go of Raven, grabbed Tommy's hands, and placed them together near the side of the horse. "Just hold your hands together right there and I will put my foot in them like a stepping stool. When I get up on the saddle, push my foot up and help me on."

It took Tommy a few seconds to get the hang of it, but Camille was finally able to get her leg across Raven and Tommy pushed her up into the saddle. From there they walked to the end of the barn and David opened the door. Camille nudged Raven and he walked out into the frigid air. The sun was hanging low in the sky and the moon was already up. It was a strange site to see both of them together.

Camille walked Raven up and down the farm road several times before coming to a halt and climbing down. Then she motioned to Tommy. "You climb on and I'll lead him up and down the road for you. It's too slippery to canter. We'll just do baby rides today."

This time David gave Tommy a leg up while Camille held the reins. When Tommy sat on Raven's back and felt the horse's muscles lurch forward carrying his weight, a smile lit his face from ear to ear. It was as if he had discovered a new heaven where man and animal did more than just observe each other.

Camille could tell that Tommy was in bliss. She walked him up and down the road for twenty minutes before finally getting tired. "You've had enough," she growled up at him, "now get off and let David ride."

David stepped up to Raven and Tommy held his hands cupped together to give him a lift. He threw his leg over the saddle and lifted himself up. Once he was settled, David peered out across the snow-covered valley surrounding him. He only had a moment to admire the view before Raven's muscles flexed beneath the saddle as Camille tugged at him. The giant horse slowly ambled forward and David was in bliss. This was freedom, a kind of freedom that he had never before imagined.

David thought about all the pictures he had seen and all the books he had read about horses. A wild thought raced through him. *What would it be like to feel the strength of those massive legs flying through the valley at full gallop?* It was impossible this time of year, but his imagination carried him to a time and place where it was possible.

Camille huffed and puffed while walking David and Raven up and down the road for the next ten minutes. Unfortunately, she was so tired from dragging Tommy around that she was soon spent. "Okay, you can get down now." David peered down at her with longing eyes, but it was a lost cause. Camille's cheeks were flush and sweat was beading on her forehead.

Slowly and obediently, David slid down off the horse and walked beside Camille as she led him back into the barn. Camille sensed his disappointment. "You and Tommy can come over again some other time. You don't have to ride all night tonight. Besides, aren't you supposed to be getting home?" That brought David's attention back to reality. He gazed anxiously at his watch. It was half past four.

Camille walked Raven into the barn and Tommy held his reins while she took off his saddle and handed it to David. She pointed to a sawhorse in the near paddock, then led Raven back into the far paddock and hung a bucket of grain in front of his stall. After that, she broke off a large flake of hay and pushed it up over the stall into a strange- metal feeder hanging there. Camille was just closing the paddock when Tommy stopped her.

"Just a minute." Tommy went over to Raven, who was munching his grain while keeping an eye on Tommy. Tommy wrapped his arms around Raven's great neck. He hugged him for a long moment until Raven turned his head and sniffed Tommy a few times.

Camille laughed. "What are you doing?"

"Just saying thanks and . . ." he paused, imagining how crazy this would sound, "and getting one last smell of him."

Camille rolled her eyes and headed for the door, but David only stared at Tommy. He knew exactly how Tommy felt. Raven had an earthy smell like dirt and hay and sweat and fresh air all mixed together. It was wonderful.

It took about three minutes to navigate the frozen road and reach Camille's house. The second they set foot through the front door, Camille bellowed. "Mom! Mom!"

"Back here, honey," the answer came filtering in. David and Tommy followed as Camille trundled through the house shedding coat, hat, and gloves along the way. They reached the laundry room and found Mrs. Magelby busy folding and sorting clothes. When she saw Camille, she stopped and looked up. "Yes, dear."

"Mom," Camille started in, whining from almost the first word, "David and Tommy came to see Raven and they need a ride home now or they'll get in trouble. Can you or Dad take them?"

Camille's mother was a pleasant woman. She was about five feet eight inches and, while a little heavy, had a calm and loving countenance. Her hair was brown and cut about shoulder length. She wore blue jeans, tennis shoes, and a salmon-colored shirt. She peered behind Camille to David and Tommy.

"So these are your friends that you talk so much about." Camille blushed. "Perhaps you should introduce me to them."

Camille whipped around and pointed to David. "This is David Samuelson, he lives at the Hanson's old cabin, and this is Tommy Anasogak. You know his mom, Amethyst, from the restaurant."

Mrs. Magelby sized up both boys and greeted them. "Hello, boys. Did you enjoy seeing Raven?"

Tommy spoke before David could say anything. "Oh yes, and Camille let us ride him. I'm gonna raise horses when I get older."

Mrs. Magelby smiled. "That probably won't be in Alaska. They are pretty much a luxury up here."

Camille tugged on her mom's shirt. "David said that he had to be home by five, so can you give him a ride?"

Mrs. Magelby frowned. "Your father is fixing the brakes on the car. He took the truck into town to buy parts and last time I looked, the car was in several pieces in the garage."

Camille glanced at David and, seeing the concern in his eyes, she frowned, realizing that her plan was coming apart. "When will Daddy be back? David really needs to get home."

"I don't know, dear, but as soon as he gets here I'll take both your friends home. Why don't you make some popcorn and watch TV until he gets back?"

That sounded like a great idea to Camille until she noticed that David's eyes were more distant and concerned than usual. It made her mad. "Just chill out, David," she scolded him. "There's nothing you can do now but wait. I'm sure my dad will be home soon and besides, wouldn't you like to see TV for once instead of doing homework?"

David's expression melted to sickly guilt and Tommy shook his head. Camille herded them into the living room and turned on the TV. She slipped off to the kitchen to make popcorn.

David slumped in the sofa, worry and concern written all over his face. Tommy felt bad as he sat next to him. Then his face lit up. "We could walk, you know."

David shook his head. "That's crazy. It must be miles from here. It takes at least sixty more minutes to get there on the bus."

Tommy pulled off his gloves and set them on the coffee table in front of him. "That's because the roads go all over the place, but your cabin is just over that ridge at the north end of Camille's farm."

"How do you know that?" David peered at Tommy in disbelief.

"Because there's a little stream over that ridge and my brother and I go there all the time in the summer. Sometimes we even hike down through your place when we are hunting rabbits."

"How long would it take?"

Tommy screwed up his face in concentration, "Less than forty-five minutes, I'm sure. The snow is frozen over so we can walk on top of it and there's a full moon so we won't have any trouble seeing." Tommy bit his lip as he studied David. "I promise I'll get you there if you want to go."

David wanted to go. Hiking through the mountains behind his cabin was something he loved to do anyway. He had never seen it in winter, but he had a pretty good idea which stream Tommy was talking about. But David's real motivation for considering the idea had nothing to do with Tommy's plan. David needed to do something. He was worried about John and the cauldron was starting to gnaw at him. The best way to quiet it was to run, but hiking was almost as good.

"Let's go." David stood and grabbed his backpack.

"Yeah," Tommy agreed, "this will be a piece of cake and if we're lucky, John will just think the bus was a few minutes late."

Tommy stood up and grabbed his backpack. He picked up his gloves and both of them headed out the door. When Camille came back from the kitchen, the living room was empty. She wasn't sure where Tommy and David were, but she assumed that her dad had come home and her mom had taken them. It seemed a little rude to her that they would leave without saying goodbye, but since they were both in such a hurry she understood. *Losers,* Camille thought disgustedly. Then another thought struck her. *Oh well, everything worked out after all.* She sat down on the sofa and picked up the TV remote. Her favorite show was on now and she had a fresh bowl of popcorn to eat.

* * *

Tommy and David ran across the Magelby farm on top of the crusted ice. It was invigorating to be outside in the cold. The sun was down now, but moonlight reflected brightly off the snow, giving perfect definition to the surrounding trees and bushes. When they reached the foothills, however, the journey became more difficult.

It turned out that the snow had not melted and refrozen under the dense forest at the edge of the Magelby farm. As a result, they broke through the surface of the snow and had to slog their way through the deep powder beneath. This made the going much slower and very tiring at times. With each delay David felt that tiny voice in the back of his mind shouting louder and louder. *Go back, go back, this is not a good idea.*

Forty-five minutes into their adventure they finally cleared the first set of hills. To his discouragement, David realized that there was a second, higher set of hills behind the first. The little stream Tommy was talking about was another mile away.

As David's face fell in disappointment, Tommy voiced his thoughts. "It's right over that ridge, David. It's a little farther than I remembered, but I'm sure that's it." David didn't say anything, but Tommy read the worry in his eyes. They pressed on in silence.

The Magelby farm disappeared behind them as they trudged over the first ridge and down into the valley that separated it from the higher one. Soon they were swallowed by the forest. The only sound was the soft crunch of their boots in the snow and their labored breathing. It was an eerie setting, almost as if they were the only two people in the world.

Between the first and second ridges, they found a clearing where they could walk on top of the snow again. This accelerated their journey and lifted their spirits for a while, but it didn't last long. They soon found themselves slogging up the steep slope of the second ridge, hanging onto trees and dragging themselves up the hill instead of hiking.

When they crossed the second ridge it was already past six o'clock. David had a lost look in his eyes and his deep unspoken concern was beginning to wear on both of them. As they came down off of the second slope, Tommy made David stop for a few minutes while he caught his breath and got his bearings. He knew that the stream was somewhere in this tiny valley. He needed to find it in order to know where they should cross the final ridge close to David's house.

Tommy carefully studied the mountain and the orientation of the peaks surrounding them. He soon recognized the place. They were close, but they needed to travel east and deeper into the mountains. Without speaking, Tommy led out in that direction and parallel to the ridge they had just crossed. David dutifully followed and they again found a clearing where they could travel quickly across the top of the snow.

Fifteen minutes later they broke into a line of thick Alder bushes. Once they penetrated the first layer, they reached a clearing that was hemmed in by another line of Alders. Tommy stopped between the two rows and smiled. "This is it." He exclaimed excitedly, tapping the snow at his feet. "This is the stream."

David examined the setting. It was different in winter than summer, barely recognizable, but as he imagined the snow gone and the trees decked with foliage, he could see it. He nodded in recognition and both boys shared a smile. David laughed inside himself, *Tommy may not be the best student, but he sure knows these forests.* From that vantage point, Tommy pointed the way home up over the last ridge and David nodded in agreement. Then, another comforting thought filled David. *At least we're not lost.*

They crossed through the line of Alders on the other side of the stream and headed off through the clearing beyond it. After trudging through several hundred yards of powdery snow, David suddenly stopped. Tommy stared ahead of David into the forest to see what was the matter. There was nothing. Confused, Tommy turned and peered into David's face. Something was wrong . . . dead wrong. David's eyes were closed, but Tommy could see his teeth clenched and the muscles flexed in his jaw. He was trembling, almost convulsing. It was like he was having a seizure. Tommy took a step forward and was about to shake him, when he felt it.

It was like nothing Tommy had ever felt in his life. It was as if a cold wind had blown through his soul, freezing everything inside of him. An uncontrollable shiver ran through him as light began to close in around him. Tommy was rarely afraid, but that cold feeling terrified him. Panic seized him. There was something here, something unnatural, and it was stalking them. Tommy looked around in desperation to see something, anything. He tried in vain to identify their predator, but nothing was visible, only penetrating, freezing fear.

Both boys stood frozen, immobile, and then . . . David bolted. He opened his eyes and flew. In all Tommy's life, he had never seen anyone run like David. He ran straight across the clearing on a course directly to his home. Realizing that he would be left alone, Tommy followed. He ran behind David as quickly as he could, but with his short stature and delayed start, David soon outdistanced him.

Tommy didn't want to be alone. He redoubled his efforts in an attempt to keep up. Luckily, David reached the edge of the clearing and broke through the crusted snow. The deep powder slowed him and gave Tommy time to catch up until he too broke through. Even in the powder, David was still outdistancing him. Then Tommy heard a sound. It was the sound of soft feet rushing lightly through the snow. There, to the right, he traced the sound and saw two soulless, pale blue eyes staring back at him . . . wolves.

Tommy knew what wolves could do to game. He had seen the carcasses of moose that wolves brought down in the winter. He also knew they didn't travel alone but in packs of six or seven. This was their element and they were hungry. Tommy shouted at David and tried to stop him. They couldn't outrun wolves in this environment. Their best was to stand and fight together, hopefully scaring them off. But David never stopped or acknowledged him. Tommy recognized David's reaction. He was blinded by terror, bounding full gait through the deep powder that held him.

The heavy fear that had descended on them clouded Tommy's judgment. Still, he managed to identify the real danger. Wolves always took down the straggler, the smallest, least healthy, and easiest prey. Slowing for a moment, Tommy dropped his backpack and snapped a frozen limb from a tree. He was still running, but he used the limb to push himself up over the powder and keep up with David. It was hopeless. He was falling farther and further behind, but it was better than before and now . . . he had a weapon.

David was at the top of the small hill they were climbing and about to cross over, when Tommy saw the wolf lunge. It was surreal. The distance between the lead wolf and David disappeared instantly. Tommy watched in slow motion as the huge animal's jaw gaped open and then snapped powerfully shut on David's right thigh.

Confusion clouded Tommy's mind. Wolves almost never attacked so quickly. They usually ran their prey longer, wearing them down before they killed. But what failed all logic was the fact that the lead wolf had attacked David instead of him. From the left, Tommy caught sight of two more dark shapes racing through the forest beside him. Suddenly, he realized that they were not coming after him. They were focused on David. A single, self-serving thought penetrated him. *I can escape! I'm safe. The wolves will only kill once today.*

Tommy reasoned that the wolf that reached David was the largest of the pack, no doubt the alpha male and probably over one hundred pounds. Its lunge had been perfectly timed and deadly accurate. At the end of that short leap, it sank its great bare teeth into David's thigh, crippling him. Both David and the wolf went down in a puff of powdery snow.

Tommy gazed to the east, passed the hill, to his route of escape. The window was there. He had a way out . . . but it wasn't right. Tommy peered back at the wolf snarling and tearing at David's leg. The snow was turning dark with blood and David was still frozen with fear. It was then, in the maelstrom of fear, that a space cleared inside of Tommy. Strangely, his perspective lifted until it was as if he were in the sky looking down emotionlessly on the impossible situation before him. Something snapped inside him. A single word boiled in his mind. *No.*

Rage surged through Tommy and energy filled him. With four incredible bounds he crossed the distance between himself and his friend. He stared down at David who was face down in the snow, frozen with fear, while the huge wolf twisted and tore at his leg. Tommy raised the branch and with the yell of an Athabascan warrior, he brought it down on the torso of the wolf. There was a sickening thud and Tommy saw the wolf spasm and release David's leg. Unfortunately, Tommy was still running when he landed his blow. The momentum of his attack carried him past the melee and into the snow bank.

Tommy pulled his stick back and attempted to rise, but his left arm was caught in the snow. It was then that his eyes met David's. It startled Tommy. David's expression was blank, emotionless. There was no fear---no feeling in those eyes. But when David's eyes followed Tommy's terror-stricken gaze to the wolf roiling in the snow, Tommy witnessed something he had never before seen in man or beast. David changed. Something seemed to wake up inside of David . . . something powerful.

David lifted himself and lunged for the wolf. He tackled the great beast and wrapped his arms around its neck. The wolf's head swung back, his powerful jaws snapping and biting. Tommy shuddered, the wolf's gleaming teeth came within an inch of catching David's throat. But David held the beast fast in his arms. Then, he stood up, pulling the wolf toward him and trapping its throat with the inside of his arm. The wolf exploded in fury, snapping its jaws and flailing its talons wildly.

Struggling with all his might, Tommy finally freed his arm and rolled over to gaze upon the terrifying sight. David was standing now, the wolf caught under his right arm. David's left hand was over his right arm applying pressure, ever more pressure. The wolf was struggling. Twice Tommy saw its talons connect with David's arm, releasing a puff of goose down from his coat and tearing into David's flesh. But David never flinched. His eyes were on Tommy. He held the wolf fast.

Then, in a flicker of moonlight, Tommy saw David's face. He was shocked! The lonely distant look was gone. David's countenance was filled with pure immovable purpose. There was no fear. It scared Tommy. David was gone. In his place stood a warrior locked in hopeless battle, but destined to win with nothing more than the determination to imagine no other course. And in the wolf's pale blue eyes, Tommy recognized something far more critical . . . fear.

The wolf had gone from predator to prey and now fought with the ferocity of a cornered animal. It was too late. With its air cut off, life began to ebb. Soon the struggles stopped. Its tongue lolled to the side of its mouth and everything went silent.

David held the animal and searched deep into the forest around them. Those eyes seemed to be hunting. Tommy knew enough about animals to know they could sense fear. They had sensed it before in David and they could not have missed it in their own kind. The huge male wolf who led the pack had broadcast the silent siren as he expired under David's relentless grip. Tommy stared in awe at his friend. No animal would attack a warrior like that. No animal in this world.

Tommy tore his eyes away from David and examined his surroundings. It was silent. Only the blood stained snow remained to testify that something unusual had happened here. Everything else was frozen in the Alaskan night.

Then from beyond the hill, Tommy heard a voice, a human voice. Somehow John had found them and was calling David's name. David didn't respond, so Tommy turned toward John's voice and shouted. "Over here."

When John arrived his eyes traced over David before finding Tommy. David was standing motionless where Tommy had last seen him, transfixed and seemingly unaware of the dead wolf that he held under his arm. His eyes were still scanning the forest. David spoke quickly.

"John, I'm sorry I'm late, we went to Camille's house to see her horse and we couldn't get a ride home. We tried to walk, but it took longer than we thought." David's voice was level, void of emotion. It was as if the wolf trapped under his arm didn't exist.

John walked swiftly to David and put his hand on David's shoulder. "Its okay, David." John stared down at David's blood-soaked leg. Urgency filled his eyes. "Let it go, David. Let the wolf go and I will carry you home."

David appeared puzzled for a moment and then realized that he was holding the dead animal under his right arm. Confused, he slowly lifted his arm and the wolf slid silently into the snow. It was a lifeless heap now, its tongue hanging to the side of its great teeth-filled mouth. Its head was soaked with blood, David's blood. David looked up at John. "I'm okay."

But John, who was almost the same size as David, picked David up like a sack of wheat and began trudging home through the snow. David didn't protest. Tommy picked up his stick and then, remembering his backpack, ran back to get it before running to keep up with John. None of them spoke for the fifteen minutes it took to reach David's house. A long trail of blood marked their path. By the time they reached the cabin, David's skin had turned grayish white.

* * *

Caren Abernathy had been a teacher for almost thirty years. She had taught in some of the remotest parts of Alaska in her younger days before settling down in the Matanuska Valley, or Mat Valley, as everyone abbreviated it, for the bulk of her career. She was fifty-four years old and in all her years as a teacher, she had never taught a student like David.

Every paper he turned in was a 100 and the detail and care with which each answer was written suggested the boy was spending hours on what little homework she gave him. Not that she wanted to complain about a child who was the most dedicated, conscientious student she ever had. It was just that it was so far from normal that she knew, from sad experience, that something was wrong. When he was in the fifth grade the previous year, Beth Holmstead had mentioned it to her. At the time she didn't seriously consider it because David wasn't in her class and wasn't under her watchful eye.

She wanted to talk with someone about the situation, but she really didn't know enough to make an informed decision. In consolation, she convinced herself that she would take some time and visit with David and his parents within the next few weeks. However, even that proved to be complicated. To her disappointment, she discovered that David and his family did not have a telephone. That wasn't an uncommon situation in Alaska, but it was unusual for someone who had a child in school. She sent home a note with David on Tuesday, but she didn't get a response. She stewed over what to do all week, trying to convince herself that she shouldn't go, but by Friday, she realized that she had no choice.

It seemed rude to her to visit someone's house without an appointment. She was also unsure of the implications of asking perfect strangers why their perfect child was so unusual. After reviewing it in her head all week, she finally decided to justify her visit as "exploratory," to find out if David was interested in doing some special assignments. Caren wasn't good at lying, but she was old enough and experienced enough not to be intimidated by anyone.

She left school late Friday and managed to get lost for about a half hour along the way. Finally, she rolled slowly into the driveway and found John's old suburban in front of the cabin. She had second thoughts about the whole thing when she realized that it was dinnertime, but she shook them off.

She parked her jeep, gathered up her belongings, and headed to the cabin. She was careful not to slip on the frozen walk. She knocked on the door and after a moment's hesitation, an old man opened it. He was nothing like Caren had imagined. David was a large, brown-haired, brown-eyed boy with a light complexion. The man who answered the door was short, maybe five feet four, a little stooped over, and had a dark complexion with graying hair. Since she didn't see David, she wondered for a second if she was at the right house.

"Excuse me, I am trying to find the Samuelson residence." Caren spoke clearly and distinctly so the old man would understand. He didn't speak at first. Instead, he studied her face and she peered into his ancient weary eyes. It startled her for a moment. There was great intelligence in those eyes and something else, something unexplainable. It was unsettling.

The old man gestured to Caren. "Please come in. My name is John."

Once inside, Caren quickly deduced that John had been making dinner until something stopped him and caused him to delay. She examined her strange host and wondered for a moment if he was David's father or just some relative. She followed him into the living room and sat on the couch. John closed the door and sat in a wooden chair across from her.

Caren swallowed hard and began. "Excuse me, Mr. Samuelson, my name is Caren Abernathy. I am David's homeroom teacher."

John's face melted to concern at the mention of David's name. "Miss Abernathy," John spoke softly, "have you seen David this evening?"

"He's not here?" Caren asked in confusion.

"No." John answered frankly. "He's usually home by now and I'm worried about him."

"Maybe the bus is late."

"I don't think so. The bus has never been this late and the roads are clear today."

Caren read the concern in those penetrating eyes. She wanted to ease his mind and make him more comfortable, but there was little she could do about the situation. *How,* she thought to herself, *am I going to find out anything about this child?*

Taking time to organize her thoughts, Caren slowly removed her coat and gloves and laid them on the couch next to her. "Mr. Samuelson, I wanted to talk to you about David's work in school. He's one of the hardest working students I have ever taught." She reached into the satchel by her feet and pulled out some of David's work. She laid it on the wooden coffee table in front of her. "Look at these scores and the care with which this work was done." Caren peered up at John and smiled. It was a stiff smile. "David is quite a student."

John never spoke and he never examined the papers that Caren placed on the table. Instead he stared into her eyes and listened intently. Caren could feel those eyes on her. It was frightening in a way. Those eyes seemed to be reading her, reading everything about her and her purpose for being here today. She shook her head and continued. "I just wanted to see if David was being challenged enough. Perhaps he needs more difficult schoolwork or some special projects."

That was a lie. It felt terrible leaving her lips and the moment it was out, she could tell that John wasn't buying it. This should have been easy, but it was becoming terribly difficult. John never spoke. His silent stare only intensified her uncomfortable feeling. After a few seconds of listening to her conscience twist and squirm, she had had enough. She was old and impatient, and suddenly, she no longer cared about politeness.

Caren shook her head and started again. "Mr. Samuelson, I'm sorry, I don't want to be intrusive, but I need to find out more about David. It isn't that he needs any special homework, it's just that he's too careful with what he does and I'm concerned that there may be some other problems in his life." There, it was out. Caren found her emotions rising. She wanted to help David, but she wasn't getting anywhere with John.

Suddenly she felt something like a cold mist settling in on her shoulders. She shivered and the hair on her neck tickled. It took her breath away and caused her to lose track of what it was she was talking about.

John's reaction was far more intense. His eyes widened in terror and then he sprang to his feet. He muttered a single word. "No." He took his eyes off Caren, took one look at the door, and bolted. He never touched his coat or his gloves. He left the door wide open in his haste.

Caren was left alone and bewildered in John's cabin. When she realized what was happening, she tried to follow him, but he was long gone before she could ask any further questions. For a moment, she just stood there confused. This whole experience was far stranger than anything she could have imagined. She knew she should just gather her things and leave, but that would leave all her questions unanswered.

Maybe this is all a ruse to avoid me. The idea made her mad until she thought it through. *No, there was deep concern and urgency in John's eyes. Something's wrong . . . terribly wrong.*

Caren thought again about leaving, but now she was more intrigued that ever. Maybe it wasn't what she thought she was going to learn, but something was happening and she wanted to know what it was. With a determined scowl on her face, Caren closed the front door, sat back down on the couch, and waited. John was out there in the cold without a coat. He would be back soon. One way or another, she was going to figure this thing out.

The minutes began to stretch out as Caren sat silently on the couch. She was not good at waiting and she was not in a good mood. Finally, she dug some schoolwork out of her satchel and attempted to review the quiz her students had taken that day. It was no use. She couldn't concentrate on anything in this strange environment framed by even stranger events. Instead, she let her mind wander and she watched the clock. Ten, fifteen, twenty minutes went by. She began to worry. It wasn't an especially cold night, but it was too cold to be out that long without a coat. From all her experience in Alaska, she knew John would be in trouble by now. Caren worried. Then finally, after twenty-five minutes, the front door burst open.

Caren jumped up with a start, her silent reverie shattered by the bang of the front door. There in the dark entryway stood John holding David in his arms and, right behind them, Tommy Anasogak. Something was wrong with David. His face was deadly pale and he appeared to be unconscious. It was then that Caren saw the blood. David's right leg was drenched in blood. It was dripping on the floor.

She stared at John and practically shouted. "I'll call 911."

"There isn't time," he answered abruptly, "just take Tommy and get him home. I will take care of David."

The order wasn't bitter or filled with any emotion other than urgency. Something inside of Caren made her want to comply, but reason wouldn't allow it. David's situation was dire. He definitely needed professional help and Caren's instincts told her he was dying. She just did not believe that John had any idea what he was doing.

Caren was about to argue, when John cut her short, "Caren, you must leave . . . now!"

It was an order and Caren didn't like it. She glared at John. She didn't trust him and the life in his arms was far too precious to gamble, but something in those penetrating eyes made her comply. Without saying another word, she grabbed her coat and gloves and stomped out to her jeep. Tommy followed dutifully behind her. He too was in shock. *Well,* Caren thought flatly, a*t least I'll get some answers out of Tommy.*

Caren unlocked the passenger door and placed her satchel and purse on the back seat before she let Tommy in. Then she walked around and climbed in the driver's side. Tommy set his backpack on the floor of the jeep and climbed in next to her. Caren glared at him. He was a hard child to read. He had always been quiet and respectful in class and while he wasn't a good student, she knew he was an intelligent boy.

Caren backed out of the driveway and headed towards town. She smoldered in silent anger and worry until they reached the main road. Then, before turning left to head out to Tommy's house, she turned and fixed him with a stare. "What happened out there?" Her words were sharp and harsher than she had expected. Tommy flinched and squinted his eyes at her. He wasn't afraid, but Caren could tell he was trying to read her mood. She started over, "I'm sorry, Tommy, I'm just upset because David was so badly injured and his father just kicked us out. What a stubborn old fool! I'm terrified. I hope David makes it. He looked pretty bad."

Tommy just studied her in silence. She wanted to shake the boy and get some answers out of him. Finally he spoke. "I need to get home, Miss Abernathy, my folks will be upset if I'm much later than seven."

Caren didn't budge. "Tommy, I need to know what happened. You aren't going to be in trouble any worse than you would be if you didn't tell me, so please let me help you and David."

Tommy still seemed undecided, but eventually he relented. "David and I went to Camille's house after school to see her horse. Have you ever seen it? He's a big beautiful black horse named Raven and Camille let us ride him. Anyway, Camille's mom was supposed to take us home before five so that David wouldn't be late, but Mr. Magelby was in town getting car parts so there was no way to get David home on time. Mrs. Magelby told us to wait, but instead of sitting there waiting, I told David that we could walk to his house."

Caren recognized the flash of guilt in Tommy's eyes. She was so busy concentrating on what he was saying that she didn't try to discern why he was so upset. Finally Tommy's explanation registered with her. "You can't walk from Magelby's farm to David's house. They are miles apart. It would take four or five hours to walk that."

"Not if you go over the mountain."

Caren shook her head, *Of course, Tommy has probably hiked every inch of this valley in search of animals to hunt or adopt.* She glared sternly at him again. "Well, that wasn't a very good idea but go on."

"It was farther than we thought and we were slowed down by the snowdrifts. Still, we would have made it except for one thing." Tommy paused and considered his words carefully. "When we reached the stream that's about a mile behind David's house there was a . . . a . . . cold wind." Tommy shook his head realizing how inadequate his description was. Then he went on. "David froze for just a moment and then he started to run."

Caren was spellbound. Tommy had felt it too. She shivered involuntarily as the memory of that cold feeling flashed in her mind.

"Anyway," Tommy continued, "David had only run for a few feet when I saw them." Tommy's eyes widened as he looked up at Miss Abernathy. "A wolf pack, probably about six or seven, but I only saw three. I thought they would get me because I'm smaller and I was behind. I couldn't keep up with David." Tommy stopped speaking, rethinking the impossible events of the day. "But that didn't happen. The lead wolf went right past me and took David down."

Caren sat stock still, her mind racing. *Wolf attacks are rare, but not unheard of. Children have been killed by wolves and never seen again, but David is much larger than most of the children who were victims of such attacks. Still, two boys out there alone in the night, if the wolves were hungry enough* . . . She closed her eyes in an attempt to squeeze the terrible images out her mind.

"How did you get away?" Caren's sharp eyes focused back on Tommy.

Tommy was uncertain how to describe what happened next. His face filled with confusion. "When the wolf took David down, it went down with him. It tried to tear David's leg off, but I caught up with them and managed to clobber it with a stick." Tommy paused. "That got its attention and the wolf let go. Then David . . ." Tommy stuttered a little as he thought about his next words, ". . . David woke up."

Tommy shook his head as confusion filled his face, but Caren never spoke. Instead, she peered at him with her sharp eyes, commanding him to continue. "David saw me and he could tell that I was afraid. He rose up out of the snow and lunged for the wolf. He caught it and . . ." Tommy's eyes were wide open and Caren could see the confusion and disbelief there. ". . . and then he strangled it to death."

Caren's mouth fell open. That couldn't be. David was only a boy. It would take superhuman strength to wrestle a full-grown wolf down and kill it like that. "What about the rest of the pack?"

"When they saw David kill the lead wolf, they were scared off."

It just didn't make sense. When wolves started in on a kill they rarely quit. Hunger usually drove them to frenzy. Something else must have frightened them away.

"Tommy, I can't believe that David killed a wolf." Before Tommy could say anything else she thought about the wound in David's leg. It was large and deep; only a big animal could have done that. Her mind was in a swirl as she muttered her thoughts. "David is just a little boy."

Tommy peered up at her. "Miss Abernathy," this time his face was clear and she could see he was thinking hard, "there's something inside of David that isn't a little boy."

Those words penetrated Caren's heart like no others. There it was, from the mouth of a child. That's what had bothered her about David's homework, his demeanor; everything about him really. Whatever he appeared to be on the outside, there was no child inside of him. Caren thought again about her wounded star pupil and the strange events that surrounded him. She shook her head in grief and anxiety. Finally, she peered up at the roof of her jeep and prayed in her heart.

Please, dear God, help him, and help his father . . . help him to save that precious little boy.

* * *

The next two and a half days were the longest of Caren's life. She worried and stewed over David's fate from Friday evening until Monday morning. She called every hospital. There was no record of a David Samuelson. *If only David had a phone,* she lamented over and over. Three times she trudged down to her jeep to visit him, but each time she remembered John's stern command and decided against it. She was angry at John. She was terrified for David.

When Monday morning finally arrived, she was at school an hour early. She had slept less than six hours the entire weekend. Her eyes were bloodshot and her face was puffy.

She was in a bad mood and there was no guessing what kind of mess she would make today.

All her stewing finally distilled down to a single plan of action, *If David doesn't show up today, I'm going straight to his house. If he shows up injured in any way, I'm taking him to the school nurse and getting some professional advice. If something terrible has happened to him . . .* she bit her lip unconsciously whenever her mind tortured her with this alternative, *I'll never forgive that deranged old man . . . never.*

The minutes ticked off slowly until the first period bell sounded and her students began filing in. Most of them could tell that she was not in a good mood. They avoided her and just slipped silently to their desks. Tommy Anasogak glanced at her as he came in, but she never acknowledged his presence. Two minutes before the tardy bell rang, David came into class and sat down in his seat. Caren raised her head and stared at him incredulously. He seemed to be in perfect health. Tommy was also staring at him.

Nothing made sense. Absolutely nothing made any sense at all. Emotions swept over Caren like the waves of a hurricane tossing a tiny dinghy up and down. She was so relieved to see him and see that he was alive and well, that she wanted to cry. On the other hand, she was angry with herself for stewing all weekend over nothing, apparently. She gawked at David in a stupor until remembering again what she had seen on Friday. She shook her head in disbelief, "It can't be."

She kept staring at him until his eyes met hers. He was unchanged. There was only that dreamy disconnected look about him. There was nothing different, nothing unusual. Caren's emotions exploded inside of her. She stood up angrily and knocked her chair over behind her. "David," she shouted, "come with me!"

The class exhaled an anxious "uh-oh" as Miss Abernathy came down the aisle to collect David. Camille turned around and whispered smugly to Tommy. "Ha ha, it looks like Mr. Perfect finally got in trouble." Tommy never uttered a word.

Caren Abernathy took David's hand and marched him silently down to the school office. There she cornered Elizabeth Wellington, the school nurse. "Liz, I want you to examine this boy. He was mauled by a wolf on Friday and his father never took him in for treatment. He appears fine now, but I would like to be sure."

Liz gaped at Caren in surprise. "Mauled by a wolf?" There was disbelief in her eyes because of how rare and devastating those incidents were. David, on the other hand, seemed to be in perfect health.

Caren repeated her request. "Just check him for me, please. I'll feel a lot better getting a professional opinion."

"Where's the wound?" Liz questioned honestly. Then seeing how serious Caren was, she clarified her question. "Where is it you think he was injured?"

"His right thigh. Friday night it was shredded and bleeding profusely."

"Okay," Liz shook her head incredulously, "I'll take a look." Liz took David into her tiny office and closed the door. A moment later Caren heard Liz's soft exclamation. "Oh, my!"

It was too much for Caren. She burst through the door into Liz's tiny examining room. David was sitting there with his pants off and a towel draped across his lap. Liz was staring at David's right leg in deep concern. It took only a second for Caren to find the wound. There, from the top of David's leg to his ankle, was an angry white scar.

Liz rolled David's leg from side to side searching for any new wounds. Seeing nothing on the right leg, she checked the left as well. After a examining him thoroughly, she turned to Caren, "He's had a terrible accident at some point in his life, but none of these wounds are recent. Did you see the wolf maul him?"

Caren sat down on the stool next to the examining table. Her mind was spinning. She had seen the blood, seen the injury, there was no doubt in her mind. David had been drenched in that blood, even the color had drained from his face. *Maybe it was the wolf's blood. Maybe David was only faint.* She rolled through every plausible explanation, but in her heart, she knew the truth. David had been mortally wounded and now he was fine. He had an old wound, but nothing lingered from the incident on Friday. Slowly, by degrees, she recovered. Finally, she decided to go right to the source of her confusion.

"David, what happened to your leg?"

David glanced at his leg and then up at Miss Abernathy. "I was in an accident on my bicycle several years ago. I was hit by a car."

Caren examined the scar again. "What happened Friday when you and Tommy walked home from the Magelby's?"

David's face melted into dark puzzlement. "I don't remember exactly. I remember Tommy and I were walking home and something scared us really bad. The next thing I remember was waking up in John's house."

Caren sighed and shook her head at Liz. Liz returned Caren's bewildered stare. They didn't speak, but after a few seconds, Liz patted David's shoulder. "Go ahead and get dressed, honey. Everything's okay."

Both Liz and Caren stepped out of the examination room and Liz read Caren's face. "Not what you expected?"

"No, I could have sworn he was bitten by a wolf, but I must have been mistaken somehow."

Liz tried to cheer her up. "Well that's a doozey of a scar on his leg. It's probably good that we are aware of that in case he has any problems in gym or on the playground." Liz continued thoughtfully, "That must have been a terrible accident." Caren nodded without speaking.

A minute later David came out of the examination room fully dressed. Caren gazed at him from head to toe before putting her hand on his shoulder and walking him down the hallway. As they reached the classroom, an idea came to her.

"David," she questioned, "would you let me give you a ride home from school today?"

David looked up at her with those trusting but distant eyes and shrugged. "Okay."

The rest of the day went by slowly for Caren Abernathy. She was tired and had trouble concentrating on events around her. Whenever her mind wandered, she thought about David. Nothing made sense about the entire situation and the more she thought about it, the less she could come to a logical conclusion.

Thankfully, at half past three, the bell rang and school was over. Everything was quiet in her room and she was exhausted. What she really felt like doing was laying her head on the desk and taking a nap. By quarter to four the noise in the hallway had subsided and she began to wonder if David had forgotten. She was about to go search for him when she heard a light knock on the door. "Come in," she responded and David sauntered cautiously into the room. He was bundled up in his coat, hat and gloves, and carrying his backpack. Caren smiled to herself. *Of course he didn't forget. This is David.*

"Hello, David." Caren greeted him politely and then she began the process of getting her coat on and her things together. She asked David to carry her bulging satchel as she fished in her purse for her keys. They walked down the hall in silence. Caren thought about making conversation with him, but he seemed content to just amble along behind her.

The trip to David's house took less than thirty minutes. The direct drive from school was a far cry shorter than the ninety minutes he usually spent on the bus. When they arrived at the cabin, Caren left her satchel and her purse in the jeep and marched David to the door of his house. Removing her glove, she knocked loudly on the door.

Seconds later, John answered and, seeing Miss Abernathy, smiled and spoke warmly. "Hello, Miss Abernathy. Thank you for bringing David home." John stood there for a second as Miss Abernathy studied him and then he continued. "Please come in."

John was so polite and cordial that it threw Caren off. It was as if they were meeting for the first time. This time, however, she was more interested in John than David and she noted the slight accent in his voice. It sounded Greek or possibly Italian. It was something Mediterranean, of that she was sure. It distracted her for a moment and then her mind began turning again, trying to unravel the puzzle, but it was no use. It was just another absurd clue to a riddle that no one could make sense of.

Caren quickly followed David into the cabin. She took off her coat and gloves and laid them beside her as she sat on the couch. John sat on the chair facing her. When she was ready, she turned to face him. She had rehearsed this conversation in her mind all day and she wanted to be polite, but she was tired and confused and still a little angry at John for the way he dismissed her. So it just spilled out when she started.

"What is going on here?" Caren hadn't meant for it to sound so abrupt, but there it was. She softened her voice a little, "When I was here Friday you came in carrying a very injured young man. At the time, it appeared to me that David might bleed to death unless he received immediate medical attention. Tommy told me on the way home that David was mauled by a wolf. I checked every hospital and doctor that I know of and none of them have seen you. Then today, David comes into class and there isn't a mark on him, he has no signs of any attack, and he doesn't even remember being injured."

Caren stopped and stared at John. She expected an answer and she expected it now. But John did not answer immediately. Instead he stared unflinchingly at her and, those cursed ancient eyes of his, made her nervous. *For heaven's sake,* Caren thought to herself, *I'm fifty-four years old. I'm not going to be intimidated by this man.*

It was a stare-down, but Caren Abernathy was determined not to flinch. The longer John looked into her eyes, the more she held her ground. But while she was staring at John, John seemed to be looking through her. It was a very unsettling feeling as his eyes peered deeper and deeper, like they were exposing her soul and everything that was hidden inside of her. Finally, John took a long breath and spoke, but not to her. He spoke to David.

"David, since you are home a little early, could you help me with the laundry? Please go in the laundry room and fold the clothes for me. Thank you." David never questioned the command. He dropped his backpack onto his fold-down bed and went into the bath/laundry room. Understanding that John wanted privacy, he closed the door behind him.

John turned slowly to face Caren, but this time his eyes did not linger. After only a moment, he turned his head and stared out the window. His eyes were distant and Caren thought in relief, *At least they aren't focused on me.*

John spoke slowly. "Do you remember the day that Cody fell through the ice?" John paused, turning his head to face Caren. His eyes were filled with compassion.

Caren's heart stopped. She stopped breathing as time froze. No one knew that! There was not another soul on the planet who knew what happened on that bleak November morning almost forty years ago.

Seeing that he had her attention, John finished his revelation. "Sometimes . . . there are miracles."

Caren's mind swirled as the memories poured through her. She had been such a lonely little girl. When she was three years old, her father left them. Her mother carried on best she could, but she was lonely and miserable. Her mother finally married after years of solitude and Caren resented it. She resented it because it wasn't her real father and she resented sharing her mother. Looking back with the years of experience she now had, she couldn't believe that she had ever felt that way. At the time, she thought her mother was so weak.

Then Cody was born. Caren was six at the time and she detested him from the day he came into her world. Her mother stopped focusing on her and took care of Cody all the time. It was always, "Cody needs this and Cody looks so cute in that." Caren remembered her bitterness, but she was always careful not to offend or distance her mother over the situation. To make matters worse, as they grew up together Cody loved her and idolized her. He would follow her everywhere she went and it drove Caren crazy, especially when her friends teased her about him tagging along.

Then one dreary November morning, when Caren was twelve, she took off to her friend's house, seemingly by herself. It was Saturday and she had a new book and her favorite music with her. As she left the house she noticed Cody dressing to go outside as well. Afraid that he might follow, Caren quickened her pace. She darted out the back of the house and around the north side of the small lake that lay along the shortcut between her house and her friend's.

Caren remembered giggling as she ran, reasoning that Cody would never be able to keep up. She heard him yell at her when he came out of the house and waddled down the trail behind her. He kept yelling at her to wait, but Caren ignored him with a smirk on her face. When she reached the other side of the lake, she couldn't help stopping for a moment to see how far he was behind.

She didn't see him on the trail. Her eyes swept up to the house and then back down across the lake. It was there that she found him. To her horror, Cody was trying to catch up to her by crossing the lake. Caren knew instinctively that it was a mistake. The ice had only covered the center of the lake a week earlier. It couldn't have been more than an inch thick. Caren dropped her purse and ran back to the edge of the lake.

"Cody," she shouted, "Cody go back! The lake isn't safe!" She was too late. As Cody glanced up at her, the ice gave way beneath him and he plunged through. Caren ran with a speed she had never before possessed to the closest point on the shore to where Cody had gone through. When he bobbed back up to the surface, he reached out his stubby arms to grapple the ice and pull himself out. It was no use. He couldn't get a hold on the ice and the weight of his soaked clothing was too heavy. In spite of all his efforts, Cody slowly sank back into the freezing lake. His trusting little face was filled with shock and fear. It was an image that Caren would never forget.

Caren's heart filled with silent desperation, she crawled out spread eagle onto the ice and tried to make her way to Cody. As she moved onto the lake she heard the eerie tin sound of the ice cracking under stress and then she felt it start to sag. Instinctively, she rolled back onto the shore. Fear froze her heart as a single thought paralyzed her. *Cody is going to die!*

Cody bobbed back up again and she heard him sobbing. She stared at the tiny hooded figure clinging to the edge of the ice, clinging to life. A sickening, foreboding fear filled her. If Cody died here, a part of her would die with him. Her mother would never be the same.

Caren searched desperately for a tree branch, anything to reach out with, but the spruce trees surrounding her only offered short, bushy branches. She thought about running home to get help, but it would be too late. There was nothing she could do but watch in horror. Out of options and out of time, she did that last thing that she could conceive of; she dropped to her knees in the snow and prayed with all the fervor of her tiny heart. She remembered crying so hard that she could hardly utter the words.

Then it happened. As she watched in agony from the shore, Cody just popped up out of the lake and landed spread eagle on the ice. Slowly, ever so carefully, he began crawling to shore. Each tiny motion terrified both of them, but Caren shouted encouragingly to him. She could see that he was having difficulty because his clothes kept freezing to the ice. When he was four feet of shore, Caren stepped onto the lake and grabbed him.

She immediately went through the ice and so did Cody, but this time she caught his hand and with superhuman strength, she pulled him to safety. He was blue, soaking wet, and heavy. Caren tore his coat off and flung it on the ground. Taking off her own coat she wrapped him in it. Then she picked him up and carried him running, to the house.

Luckily, no one was home. Caren guessed that her mother had gone out to get groceries. She carried Cody upstairs and filled the bathtub with warm water. Then she tore most of the rest of his clothes off and made him get in. His teeth were chattering and his color wasn't good.

Caren just sat there watching him. She couldn't take her eyes off of him. Slowly, the color returned to his face and his teeth stopped chattering. When he peered up at her, she saw the tears streaming down his face. He was terrified. Caren felt sick. Neither one of them spoke.

They stayed in the bathroom together for almost an hour. Caren was worried that her mother would return and find them, but she never did. When Cody's color finally improved, Caren retrieved a change of clothes and stepped out of the bathroom. She gathered all their clothes and carried them down to the laundry room sink. Then, another thought occurred to her.

They would both be in serious trouble if their parents found out. Worse yet, her mother would worry herself sick, sick the way Caren felt. *No,* Caren remembered reasoning, *I don't want mom to worry.* She made a decision that day, a decision that would end the ordeal right then and there. They would never tell anyone.

That was it; once Cody was dressed, she dragged him into her bedroom and they made their pact. Neither one of them would ever mention it to anyone. For once in his annoying little life, Cody understood. He never broke his promise.

Years later, when Cody was a teenager, Caren asked him how he was able climb out of that lake. He said he didn't know for sure, but all of a sudden his feet caught something, maybe a log or a rock, and he was able to push himself up. That answer never made sense to Caren. Logs were generally on the surface and those boggy Alaskan lakes never had any rocks in them.

Cody's near death was a defining moment for Caren. From that day on, she took care of Cody and the two brothers that followed him. Years later they would all come to think of her as their second mother and from that experience to becoming a teacher . . . Caren had been taking care of children ever since.

Caren felt sick. She felt like someone had kicked her in the stomach. She was staring down at the carpet when she came back to her senses. She barely remembered she was at David's home talking to John. Tears were streaming down her face betraying her feelings. She shook her head in exhaustion. She just wanted to go home. She glanced up at John who was studying her. Again the questions rang in her heart. *How did he know?* But she felt like such a fool, crying in front of him, that she just couldn't ask today.

Caren slowly gathered her things and stood to head out the door. As she donned her coat, she felt John staring at her with those penetrating eyes. He was standing now. He reached across the table and took her hand in his. That got her attention. She looked up at him.

John's eyes were filled with a tenderness she hadn't noticed before. He caught her eyes and spoke softly. "Teach him how to live in this world." As he spoke, John gestured toward the laundry room where David was folding clothes.

Something warm washed over Caren. The feeling was indescribably, but it left her more balanced and filled with peace. She smiled a little and nodded her head.

"Thank you," was all John said as he led her to the door.

Caren's mind was spinning as she methodically made her way home. So many memories, so long ago, and still, they were as poignant as the day they happened. Worst of all, she just couldn't stop crying. "Grown women don't cry like this," she muttered out loud to herself, but it was no use. She now knew, for certain, what she had believed all her life . . . it was a miracle that saved Cody that day. God had answered her desperate prayer.

The next day Caren stayed home and enjoyed a rare day off. She called Darrell Wright, the school principal, and told him she would be out for the day. He understood. One day every twelve years wasn't too much to ask. That day Caren thought about her life and the twists and turns it had taken. She had only one regret. *Why didn't I get married? Why didn't I have children?* It just seemed like there was never time, that she already had too many children to take care of, but that had been a mistake. She was old now and there were very few problems in her life, but there was also nothing to look forward to. She would just get older and older and finally, she would disappear, but there was one consolation.

She had gained a prize this week. It was the most powerful knowledge that the human heart could ever possess. She knew that God lived. At last, even in death, there was something to look forward to, something . . . amazing.

The next day she returned to class refreshed and clearheaded. Everything was as she had left it. David was there watching her attentively. Tommy was gazing distractedly out the window and Camille was talking to him, even though he wasn't listening. Caren taught her class with the same structure and vigor she always had, but there was just the slightest feeling of peace in all that she did. She seemed to see a little deeper into the minds and hearts of the children in her care.

At the end of class, David lingered after the rest of the students left. Caren finally noticed him. "Yes, David?"

"Miss Abernathy, yesterday Mrs. McCreary, the substitute, gave us an assignment to research the bears of Alaska on the Internet." David fidgeted nervously.

It took her a few seconds, but Caren finally thought she understood. She dipped her head to study at the work on her desk. "So you did the assignment, and you want to turn it in?"

David shook his head. After pausing for a moment, he continued. "She said we didn't have to turn it in. But . . . but I couldn't do the assignment because we don't have a computer."

"David," Caren smiled, "don't worry about it."

Caren was about to return to her desk and shuffle through the papers she needed to review when she noticed David turn slowly and reluctantly headed for the door. His downcast demeanor caught her attention and she followed him with her eyes. *Something's wrong.* She was confused. She tried to imagine David's thoughts. *Why does he care so much about this assignment?* She shook her head. *He wants to do the assignment, but he . . . can't.* Caren was staring at David now, reading the intangible clues that swirled around him. *He can't do the assignment because he doesn't have a computer. He doesn't have access to the Internet.*

"Just a minute, David." David stopped and turned around to face her. "You said you couldn't do the assignment because you don't have a computer. Is that what's bothering you?"

David nodded sheepishly. Caren smiled to herself, pleased that she had penetrated another layer of this complex boy. "Well," she thought quickly, "if you need to use a computer or the Internet, you can just come home with me and use mine." David's face brightened and she almost laughed. "Just tell your father that you'll be coming to my house after school to do homework."

David's expression suddenly darkened. Caren observed him in silence, wondering at the emotions that seemed to seize him. He finally looked up at her with confusion in his eyes. He spoke slowly. "Miss Abernathy . . ." David's eyes were unfocused. He seemed almost lost in his thoughts. "John isn't my father." He paused for almost a full minute. Caren could see that his mind was working, but his eyes were cloudy and confused. Finally, he finished his revelation. "My mom and dad are gone."

Those words flattened Caren like a steamroller. She wanted to reach out and take him in her arms, but she knew it would embarrass him. She checked her voice and continued. "Tonight, David, just tell John that you'll be spending the next evening at my house to study on the computer. I'll bring you home afterward." David smiled and, recovering to a degree, sped out of the room and off to his next class.

Caren bit her lip in concentration. It all made sense in a sad and sobering way. John wasn't David's father. They didn't look anything alike anyway, but the confusion in David's eyes when he spoke of his parents told the rest of the story. A part of David was missing. The little boy that should have been inside the little boy who sat in her homeroom class, wasn't there anymore. He had no doubt disappeared with the loss of his parents. Caren felt the tears begin to build in her eyes, but once again, she checked them and redirected her thoughts. This wasn't the time to get all teary-eyed. She had a class to teach.

CAMILLE

Chapter 17

School was a lonely experience for the GBU. They pretty much stuck together, apart from their peers, through middle school and into high school. Life would have passed without incident for David and Tommy had Camille not brightened their existence. She ate with them every day and alluded to being the center of all school activity, though the truth was far from it. She dragged them along on half a dozen adventures, strengthening their friendship in spite of a few mishaps. Now it was the middle of their 10th grade year and today was the first school day after Christmas break.

Camille was a little nervous about her new classes, but she was excited about all the people she was meeting. At lunch she searched the cafeteria for Tommy and David. Sure enough, they were eating at a table at the far end of the lunchroom. They were by themselves. Camille sighed and waddled over to their table.

"Happy new year," she called out sarcastically. Both David and Tommy glanced up. "You would think that you two could have called me or come over at least once during the vacation. I never heard from either one of you; what did you do that whole time?" David smiled at Camille and shrugged, but Tommy just continued eating his lunch in silence. "Well, I have a new plan for this spring." Tommy groaned and rolled his eyes at that statement. Camille's schemes usually landed them into a lot more trouble than anything else, but Camille acted like she didn't hear him and just plowed ahead.

"My Dad says that I need to get into better shape so we're going to join the track and field team." Tommy couldn't help it. He snickered at the thought of Camille hobbling around the track. David didn't say anything. He riveted his eyes to his lunch tray and tried to avoid the battle that was brewing.

Camille glowered at Tommy. "I'm serious. It'll do us good to get in shape and who knows? Maybe one of you will turn out to be an athlete."

Tommy had heard enough. He glared up from his plate and caught Camille's eyes. "I'm not going to stay at school any longer than I have to. I can't stand this place."

Camille frowned and switched her attention to David. "What about you?"

The idea touched a strange chord inside David. He rubbed his chin thoughtfully. "Are you serious about this?" Camille nodded. "Actually, I would like to run on the track team." That made Camille happy. Rare was the day that she had a suggestion that either Tommy or David liked, but David frowned after considering it for a moment. "But I don't think John will let me."

"Why not?"

"I have so many chores at home and John won't want to pick me up after school."

Camille ate a French fry. "I'm sure coach would love to have you since you are the tallest tenth grader in the school. Besides," she shrugged, "I'll be in track too so I can give you a ride home if that's a big deal for John." David didn't respond. Camille needled him. "At least ask him."

David relented. "Okay."

That night David and John ate dinner and talked some about David's new schedule, classes, and teachers. John didn't say much but nodded supportively as David described the new courses of study. David thought about asking if he could join the track team, but somehow the opportunity never presented itself.

The next night was Thursday. David usually went to Miss Abernathy's home on Tuesdays and Thursdays after school.

Miss Abernathy was like a second mother to him. She had practically adopted him after the sixth grade.

Miss Abernathy lived in a modest trailer that had been converted to a house over a period of several years and several upgrades. The trailer that had once gleamed with aluminum siding was now covered with wood panels and trim. A pitched roof had been added and shingles now covered the top. There was even a small deck with a rail on the back that overlooked a clearing and the dense spruce forest behind it. With the exception of the metal doors, it was hard to tell it was a trailer.

The living areas were modest and crowded due to her collection of books that rivaled the library's. Over Christmas she insisted that David read several of them. But the real attraction to Miss Abernathy's house was the computer with Internet access. As a result, David often did homework there. That night, while they were discussing his new classes, the thought suddenly came to him to ask her about going out for the track team.

"Miss Abernathy," Caren peered up thoughtfully from her reading, "Camille wants to go out for track this spring and she wants me to try out with her."

A puzzled expression crossed Caren's face. "Camille Magelby?"

"Yeah, Camille said that her father told her she should get more exercise, so she decided to go out for track and, of course, she wants Tommy and me to join her."

"It might be good for you, David. You are big and tall enough to be quite an athlete." Then Caren remembered the scar on David's right leg and concern crossed her face. "What about that scar?"

David followed her stare. "It doesn't bother me anymore. I don't think it will matter."

"Have you asked John?"

"No. I wanted to hear what you thought first."

Caren smiled. "It's a great idea. Tell John that if he can't drive you to the events, I'll help."

David smiled. "Camille said her parents would drive us."

"What event are you going to try out for?" David's face fell in confusion. Caren explained, "There are lots of different events in track and field. You can do dashes, or distance running. You can do high jumping, pole vaulting or shot put. Have you thought about any of those?"

"I just want to run," David answered, "probably long distance."

Caren nodded. "The longest distance events are one and two miles."

"Then I guess I'll do those."

Miss Abernathy wrinkled her forehead in concentration. "I wonder what Camille will do? She should probably try something like shot put or discus."

The next day Camille cornered David before he reached his first period class. "Did you ask John about track yet?"

"No, but I did talk to Miss Abernathy and I promise I'll talk to John over the weekend." Then, remembering about what Miss Abernathy said, he asked, "What event are you going to try out for?" Camille hadn't really considered that and her expression showed it. David continued, "Miss Abernathy said there are different events in track and field, like dashes, high jump, distance running and shot put. She suggested that you try shot put or discus."

Camille's expression fell and she wondered if David was making fun of her, but no, she could see in his eyes that he was sincere. That was what she liked most about David. He was always kind. He hated to see other people get hurt and big as he was, she had never, in the six years she had known him, seen him tease or bully anyone. It was obvious that David had issues, he was considered a little weird and quiet and didn't make many friends, but she just didn't care. He was the only boy who had ever been kind to her and that was enough.

Camille remembered David's question and reconsidered. She had forgotten all about field events and had been concentrating on track. Joining the running team was no small concern to her. She really couldn't run more than about a hundred feet. Tommy's little sneer when she told him her plan hadn't helped. Sometimes she hated Tommy, but he was an outcast like her and, "beggars can't be choosers."

Miss Abernathy thinks I should try out for shot put. Camille mused. *That sounds great! I can just throw a big steel ball around without running a step.* "Yeah," Camille stuttered, "I'm gonna throw the shot put."

David was quiet that night as they ate dinner. He peaked up at John from time to time to read his mood. As they were clearing the dishes, he finally made his point. "John," David waited for his full attention, "Camille wants to try out for the track team next week and she wants me to join her. She said that her family would help me with rides, but I need your permission to be on the team."

John slowly peered up at David and something flashed through his eyes. David had seen that look before. It was worry. *What could go wrong with this?* David wondered, but he didn't say anything. He just kept his attention on John and waited for his answer.

John placed the dishes he was gathering back on the table and sat down in his chair. He was silent for several seconds before speaking. "David, could you give me a little time to consider this? I know it seems like a simple request, but I want to be certain."

David nodded. Nothing more was said the rest of the evening. When night fell, John told David that he was retiring early and David watched as he went to his room and closed the door. Then he heard, as he had so many times before, the faint murmurs of John saying his prayers. On rare occasions, he had listened in on those prayers, but they were in a language that he had never heard anyone else speak. There was no way to understand any of it. John prayed for a long time that night.

The next morning John woke David early. "If you want to join the track team, I will support you."

David was surprised at John's answer. Usually when John deliberated on something so long, the answer was no. Like time he pleaded with John about getting a computer.

A big smile crossed David's face and John also brandished a rare smile. Even so, David could tell that John was worried. He tried to reassure him. "I promise I'll get my chores and homework done, no matter what."

John stared intently at him. That stare always unnerved David. It was as if John could read every thought in his head. Finally, he spoke. "Be careful, David, and remember your limits."

Although those ancient eyes bore into him with absolute certainty, David had no idea what John was talking about and therefore, no way to comply with his stern request. What made him nervous was the fact that John had a way of seeing things way before they became issues. Still, he didn't want John to reconsider his decision so he nodded his head and agreed quickly. "Okay."

The weekend seemed to pass slowly for David. He couldn't wait to tell Camille that he would be joining her. When Monday arrived he was off to school early with a smile on his face. He scoured the halls for Camille all morning, but he didn't see her until lunchtime. When he finally found her, she was sitting at the table with Tommy. David waved at her and smiled as he approached.

"What?" Camille asked suspiciously as he set his tray down on the table.

David blurted out his good news, "John said I could join the track team."

Camille was shocked. "That's amazing. It's about time that the guy who never gets to do anything, gets to join track." Then she turned her attention to Tommy. "What about you?"

Tommy screwed up his face. "No way!" He sneered at David and back at Camille and then he shook his head. "And I'm willing to bet that you quit before the season is over." The barb was aimed at Camille and she felt it.

"Bet what?" Camille frowned at him a second time.

Tommy hadn't actually meant to bet anything, but now that Camille was staring him in the face, he wasn't going to back down. "Twenty bucks."

Now it was Camille's turn to get nasty. "You've never had twenty dollars in your whole life." This was true and it hurt Tommy's feelings. His family was not exactly well off. Tommy frowned. Both of them glared at each other in contempt until David interrupted.

"Camille, Tommy doesn't have to join the track team. Not all of your ideas work out." That focused Camille's scowl on David. He instantly regretted his indiscretion. "Okay, okay, let's just forget about this. You and I can do track without Tommy."

"I want animal boy to bet me something," Camille snapped.

Tommy clearly was not going to talk at this point, so David attempted to negotiate. "Okay, how about this? If you don't quit the track team then Tommy has to do your chores for a week."

Tommy almost objected until he thought better of it. The only chore that he was aware that Camille did was to feed her father's beautiful horse, Raven. He would gladly take over that chore. But he didn't want to give away his position, so he simply frowned at Camille. "And if Camille quits?"

David thought again. "If Camille quits she will give you twenty bucks."

Camille liked that idea. If she did end up quitting, and she had to admit it was a huge possibility, she could just get twenty dollars from her mother and give it to Tommy.

"Deal," Tommy blurted out quickly while Camille nodded.

Camille then proceeded to review all the news of the weekend while Tommy and David ate their lunches in silence. At the end of the monologue, she told David that they would have to stay after school Wednesday to meet with Coach Morrison and the rest of the track team. David could tell that Camille was nervous and he understood why. She was deathly afraid that people would make fun of her and she was probably right. One thing about Camille though---something that David had always admired---she loved to be in the middle of things, no matter what the personal costs. *No doubt,* David thought, *this is going to be an adventure.*

The first meeting on Wednesday was all about forms and physicals and schedules. David must have collected ten pieces of paper, trying desperately to remember exactly what to do with each of them. Camille and her mother filled out and returned most of their forms that night. Coach Morrison made a special effort to meet each of the new kids and their families. He told them that there would not be any tryouts. Not many students wanted to be on the team, so he took everyone. When he met Sarah Magelby, Camille was surprised to find that they knew each other. Coach Morrison took a few extra minutes to ask about Camille's grandfather, Allen Magelby. Camille's grandfather had moved off to warmer climates about five years earlier, but a lot of people remembered him. Camille was worried that Coach Morrison might say something about her weight, but he seemed not to notice.

Coach Morrison did notice David, however, and asked him several questions. David mumbled a few answers but pretty much just kept his head down. It embarrassed Camille that he was so shy. *Why doesn't he just act normal around people?* She thought angrily. She could tell from Coach Morrison's expression that he was surprised to find out that David was only a sophomore. He was so tall for his age. The meeting finished and everything was settled. They were on the track team and practices would start, in earnest, on Monday.

Camille was feeling uncertain about the whole track thing when she and David arrived early Monday morning. Everyone seemed to know each other and nobody knew them. She figured out later that most of the track team did cross-country running or cross-country skiing in the fall. They also had gym bags with their gym clothes inside. She thought they were going to exercise, but Coach Morrison started them out in class. The first practice was a lecture.

Coach Morrison explained the practice schedule: Monday through Friday, one hour before school. Everyone had to be at the practices and dressed to work out by seven o'clock. There was a block of gym lockers reserved for team members and they could keep a set of clothes in there. The first two weeks would be spent getting in shape. Every training session would begin with running. No matter what event you competed in, you had to run every morning. Everyone groaned on hearing this. Coach Morrison explained that they would begin individual event training and technique after the first two weeks.

The rest of the first session was dedicated to the science of good health. Camille really wanted to turn it off and watch TV. All the mumbo jumbo about protein, carbohydrates, fat, and exercise was more than she could process. She stared annoyingly at David who was, of course, listening carefully and taking notes. When Coach Morrison finished speaking, everybody made a beeline for the lockers and the ones who were prepared stowed their equipment. At that point she realized that David and she were supposed to have combination locks, unfortunately, nobody told them.

Tuesday morning was the first workout. Camille hated it. She showed up in a new blue and white jogging suit with matching shoes. It was no coincidence that her outfit matched the school colors. The attire would have looked great on almost anybody else, but her bulk prevented her looking good in any type of gym clothes. David, on the other hand, came in his gray standard-issue school gym shorts and gym shoes. His tall and gangly appearance in those shorts was startling, not to mention the scar down his right leg. Standing together, David and Camille made an odd couple. No one said anything, but Camille scowled at everyone. She was absolutely sure they were laughing at her.

There were few conversations. Everyone was tired. The experienced team members started stretching before slipping out onto the indoor track to jog. Camille and David followed suit with one exception. After the first hundred feet, Camille thought she was going to die. She ran her heart out, but that only took her around the track once. David stuck right beside her even though he was almost walking. After completing the first lap, Camille drifted to the outside of the track and walked. She was already sweating and feeling very conspicuous. David slowed down to join her, but she waved him on. The magnitude of her mistake suddenly struck her. She felt so alone. Everyone was running but her. It was humiliating. *How did I ever let my dad talk me into this?*

So it went for the next two weeks. No one said anything to her, but she heard a few conversations come to an abrupt end when she entered the gym. Coach Morrison only prodded her to do more each time and by the end of first two weeks, she could actually run four laps before having to walk.

After the first two weeks of practice, they broke into separate groups for the events. To her mortification, Camille found that only two girls were in the shot put and discus group; she and Louise Komahuk. Louise was huge. She was a senior that year and easily reached six feet, most of it muscle. The first time Louise picked up and threw the shot put, she set a school record. Now she was a senior and she was one of the best female shot putters in the state.

Because of Louise, Camille decided right then and there that she would go for discus. She thought it would be like throwing a Frisbee®, but when she picked it up the first time, she realized that it was solid lead. Needless to say, her first toss was a different kind of school record.

David, on the other hand, decided to run the 3200, which was the fancy way of saying two miles. When he lined up on the track with all the other runners, he looked just like the rest of them and fit in like a glove. He was far from the best, but he had a respectable time, so he was accepted and liked.

This is not working out, Camille grumbled inwardly. *I am becoming more isolated and weird and David is finding new friends. I hate track.* The realization bludgeoned her to reality. She mulled her terrible position over for a few seconds and then her anger flared as the truth surfaced in her mind. *I would quit today if it weren't for that sneering snot of a Tommy Anasogak.* Camille refused to lose that bet. But things were getting worse. She found out in the third week of practice that she had to lift weights. Now she was in the weight room sweating it out with a bunch of smelly boys and Louise Komahuk.

The first meet of the year was scheduled for the beginning of March. The two months it took to get there almost killed Camille. The only upsides were the facts that she hadn't yet lost her bet to Tommy and she had actually lost ten pounds. She was still miserable at the discus, but at least she could throw it without making a fool of herself. David was doing well and was about the fourth fastest person in the school. He had experimented with a few other events, but the 3200 was the one he enjoyed the most.

The day of the first big track meet finally arrived and in spite of her sour attitude, Camille was excited. The first meet was with one of the bigger high schools in Anchorage, so it was a sure thing that they would lose. This actually worked to Camille's advantage, in her mind at least, because she knew she would lose and if everybody else lost, she would fit in.

It was a bright, cheery morning when they arrived for the track meet. The kids from Anchorage seemed like Olympians compared with the motley crew from the valley. *Oh well,* mused Camille, *at least I won't be the only loser today.*

For most observers this would have been a strange event. The ground was covered with snow, but the red rubber track had been cleared and was actually dry. The Astroturf field for discus and shot was also cleared but was surrounded by snow mounds over four feet high. Camille arrived in her usual matching outfit with a winter coat on top. She warmed up by jogging a couple of laps and then doing some stretches. After a few minutes, Louise joined her and she took to glaring at the Anchorage girls like she would like to hurt them. The Anchorage girls, for their part, mostly ignored the valley kids. Camille couldn't help but notice that the Anchorage kids had four girls in each event compared to her and Louise for the valley. Most of the girls were big and well built like Louise. Once again, Camille felt like an outsider.

The first three field events were the shot put, discus, and long jump. Louise Komahuk nestled herself in the ring and picked up the put. Since Louise held the state record and everybody knew it, the crowd was mesmerized. With a mighty grunt she hurled the put out and away. The first throw was over forty-two feet and, although they didn't know it at the time, the competition was over. Louise's second toss was forty-one feet and her third was a mind boggling forty-four feet. The nearest the Anchorage girls came was thirty-seven feet.

When Camille lined up for the discus, all eyes were on her. The Anchorage team had been intimidated by Louise and they were wondering about Camille. Camille steeled her nerves. She set herself in the pit. After several seconds of concentration, she whirled around and hurled the discus with all her might. Up, up and away it went and down, down it came. It landed short of the marking lines by at least ten feet. There was a ripple of laughter from the Anchorage girls and Camille hung her head in humiliation.

When they measured the toss, the throw was a disappointing sixty-three feet; just a little more than half the distance the other girls threw. On the third throw, she managed to get up to seventy-two feet, but none of these were in the competition. The winning throw came from a beefy Anchorage girl who threw the discus over one hundred ten feet.

Feeling dejected and humiliated, Camille consoled herself to watch the rest of the meet in silence. She donned her coat on and stood across on the opposite side of the track with a few of her teammates. The bleachers across the field from them were lightly populated with the hardiest of fans, including Camille's mother. For the most part, it was going the way she had expected. Louise had the only win for the day. They had a couple of second places, but essentially they were getting trounced.

Finally it came down to the last event, the 3200-meter race. David was on the track with seven other runners. He had one of the poorer starting positions and seemed outmatched by all of them. Still, Camille was excited for him. There was no chance he would win, but at least she had somebody to root for.

The starting gun sounded and they were off with a cheer. As they left the gates, David fell into the pack and it was hard to find him. When they passed her side of the track, Camille finally found him. David was running hard, harder than she had ever seen him run, and concentrating too. Camille waved and shouted his name, but David never looked up.

* * *

David had been anxious all day about running his race. It was one thing to run with his friends at school, but the kids from Anchorage were bigger and better athletes than most of the valley kids. He had watched in disappointment as they lost event after event. He lined up on the marks, caught his breath, and bang! They were off.

It was a fast race. David realized in the first hundred meters that the pace of this race was faster than any other he had ever been in. It took tremendous effort just to keep up. He didn't want to fall out of the pack or let his new friends down, so he concentrated and ran his heart out. After the fourth lap, he was in trouble. His chest was aching and it seemed like he couldn't get enough air. He panicked a little as fear touched him and then, his mind betrayed him and the cauldron flared to life.

It was always there, always just out of reach, haunting him, stalking him. Fear rippled through David and threatened to end his race. David faltered for a moment, falling behind a few steps before a strange idea burst into his mind.

There was a way to fight the cauldron. Something he had learned when he fell on the sidewalk years ago. It was pain. David remembered the pain that stabilized him and gave him power to face the cauldron.

The cauldron expanded in his mind. It threatened him, threatened to destroy him, threatened to engulf him in darkness. David accelerated. The cauldron burned brighter and closer with every step David took, but the pain brought power and clarity. David opened his senses and let the pain flow through him. With each wave, his mind grew stronger and his thoughts clearer. Then an idea burst into his mind. *If you can touch the cauldron . . . you can destroy it.*

The thought exhilarated David. As he moved closer and closer to the burning cauldron it glowed brighter and brighter. Pain was the key. If he ran long enough and hard enough, if the pain became great enough, he could reach the cauldron and . . . he could destroy it.

By the seventh lap, he was near enough to the cauldron to see the embers burning inside and feel the pain piercing his heart and chest. His feet were moving, falling in rhythm over and over as the rubber track disappeared beneath him, but the race was far away. The only concentration he needed was to place one foot in front of the other.

He poured his soul into that run. Each step brought him more pain and the pain allowed him to move closer to the cauldron. He accelerated again. He was so close. The eighth lap came and went and he heard a noise, but he was lost within himself. He was close now, so close. He could see the cauldron right before him and now, if he reached out, he could touch it. Surprisingly, the cauldron was not hot. No, it wasn't heat that flared from that eternal furnace. It was fear; fear and . . . sorrow.

David hesitated, *Will it destroy me?* He had never been here like this before. He had never been able to stand so close to the cauldron with so much strength. It was the pain, David realized, the burning agony in his chest and lungs that gave him strength. He was on fire with pain.

This was his chance, maybe his only chance. Fear abated in David's mind and he reached out to touch the cauldron when suddenly . . . the world exploded into white.

* * *

Camille could tell that David was in trouble. She measured the terrible exertion on his face and the concentration in his eyes. The race was a blistering pace and already half the contestants had dropped from the lead. But David was still there, still keeping up. When they reached the sixth lap she couldn't believe it. He was one of three boys left in the race. The other two boys were seniors from Anchorage, but David was right behind them, close enough to be a threat. When David came by her on the sixth lap, Camille knew there was something wrong. Her heart filled with sickening worry.

In all the time she had known David, the only look she had ever seen in his eyes had been that distant, sleepy, disconnected look. But when he passed her on the far side of the track, she was confronted with an image of David that she had never seen before---his eyes were clear and burning with concentration. It was a different person than Camille had ever known. Instinctively, she knew that David would win the race, but she also knew that he was in trouble.

In the seventh lap David pulled ahead of the final two serious contestants. It was clear that they were running the hardest race they had ever run, but David's blistering pace was too much. Everyone was on their feet, everyone was screaming at the top of their lungs. But Camille wasn't cheering. She was afraid. Was it her imagination, or did it seem like David was speeding up? She couldn't tell. But the distance between him and the other competitors was increasing.

When David crossed the finish line, he was in a lonely first place. The valley team erupted in a cheer, but Camille was transfixed. David didn't stop or even slow down. He didn't even acknowledge the race. He just continued running. By the first one hundred meters after the finish line, everyone thought David was just showing off, but by the time he reached the opposite side of the track, they began to wonder.

Camille was terrified. David's skin was red and he was flushed, but his eyes were still burning and powerful. She couldn't stop herself. She had to help him. She bolted. Camille came up out of her chair and raced onto the track to intersect him. Normally she would have gotten in front of him, but he was going so fast that she just barely caught the back of his shirt and hung on for dear life. It nearly yanked her fingers out of her hand, but she managed to pull David off balance and both of them tumbled into the snow bank on the inside of the track. It was a spectacular tackle. They rolled for several feet before coming to a stop, buried in the snow. When Camille finally came to her senses she heard people laughing. She searched desperately for David then and found him face down in snow, his breathing was ragged.

I've killed him! She almost panicked until she noticed David lifting himself up on quivering arms. His flushed face came out of the snow and he stared at her in surprise. Camille then witnessed an astonishing transformation. The clarity and strength drained from his eyes and the old and distant David returned. She could tell that he was confused and in pain, but Camille didn't care. She was acutely aware that the crowd was laughing, laughing at her. Her anger flared.

"You won," she shouted, peering into his confused eyes. "Why didn't you stop? You stupid moron!" She felt bad the instant she said it, but she was so angry at being embarrassed in front of all those people. Her temper raged and her teeth clenched in humiliation, but David was still distant and she could tell he didn't understand.

Finally, David shook his head and recognized Camille. Remembering the race, he gazed beyond her and heard the crowd laughing and clapping. When his eyes fell on Camille, he calculated the reason for the anger in her eyes and the blush of embarrassment covering her face. Suddenly, it all coalesced. He shook his head apologetically and peering at his old friend, spoke softly. "I'm sorry, Camille."

Seconds later the team surrounded David. They pulled him out of the snow and dusted him off. Everyone congratulated him, shaking his hand and patting him on the back, but Camille had had enough. David watched her as she headed across the track toward her mother.

On the ride home, Camille sat in the front seat and let David sit by himself in the back. The journey would have been completely silent had it not been for Sarah's adulations. She congratulated David and told him what an exciting finish it had been. She said it lifted the whole team's spirit. He smiled at Mrs. Magelby and thanked her, but his acknowledgement held no celebration.

David's lungs ached and the muscles across his body spasmed and quivered from time to time. He had injured himself, but he didn't know how badly. It worried him. He couldn't quite understand what had happened, but he was acutely aware of the fact that he had embarrassed Camille and damaged their friendship. David wanted to tell her again that he was sorry, but he sensed from her demeanor that she didn't want to hear it. He guessed that she probably didn't want anything to do with him. *Who could blame her?* He thought sadly. *I'm a freak.*

When David walked into the cabin, John was waiting. He measured him with his piercing and all-perceiving eyes. "How was your event?"

David glanced up somewhat startled. *Did he know somehow?* "I won." David smiled weakly and then quickly went into the bathroom. Nothing was right. His chest still throbbed and his legs were on fire. All this should have passed by now, but he had barely been able to get out of the Magelby's car. He tried to brush it off again and again, but there was no doubt, he was injured.

It was only five o'clock when he stepped out of the shower, but David was through for the day. He limped over to his pull-down bed and prepared it for the evening. He felt John's eyes upon him, but David never looked back. "John, I don't feel very well. Would it be okay if I skipped dinner and just went to bed?" David finally glanced over at him. John simply nodded, concern etched on his face.

David climbed into bed instead of kneeling and saying his prayers that night. After rolling onto his back, he thought a quiet prayer before sleep overcame him. He slept on and off for about twelve hours, waking every hour to try and adjust to a new position that would be more comfortable. His lungs hurt and by the early hours of the next morning, he was breathing with a wheeze. When his eyes fluttered open at 5 A.M. he realized he was done sleeping. He needed to get up and use the bathroom, but he couldn't move his legs. He just lay there in fear, wondering what would happen next.

An hour and a half later, John's door creaked open. He came immediately to David's bed and stared down at him. "Feeling any better?"

"A little." This was true. The burning in his chest and muscles had pretty much passed, but he still didn't seem to be able to move his legs.

John reached over and touched David's forehead. David thought how good it was to feel the touch of another human being, even if it was just John. Then John pulled up a chair and sat down beside him. Slowly and gently, John began massaging David's legs. At first it felt like the fire was returning. Then they started to respond as David felt the blood flowing back into them.

John studied David's face as he worked. "David, it's probably not a good thing for you to be on the track team." David thought for a moment and then nodded in agreement. Whatever had happened to him at the meet was not normal and it would not be good if it happened again.

John spoke tenderly. "Long before the world was created, we lived as spirits with our Father in Heaven. We loved Him and wanted to be like Him. We are His children, David, and He loved each of us so very much that He wanted to share His kingdom with us. Unfortunately, we lacked experience and understanding and the gulf was so vast between us, that it seemed impossible to bridge.

"But in the reaches of His infinite intelligence, He knew a way to help us cross that chasm. He knew that if He created a mortal world and set us in it with our agency, that we would come to understand good and evil and their consequences.

"At the center of that plan, David, is this mortal body." John stopped massaging and patted David's knee. "Designed from the infinite knowledge of a God who has created worlds without number, it is a wondrous gift composed of the materials of this world and created for us by our mortal parents. It is a precious gift. Every day that we spend with these mortal bodies gives us experience and every one of those experiences are priceless.

"As a part of this gift He shared with us the greatest of all His powers; the power to create life." John's demeanor changed to a more serious tone. "It is in the creation and nurturing of life that we learn the most about God." David focused on John's serious expression and recognized the sorrow and compassion in his eyes.

"You must cling to life, David, until your mission is finished, you must never give up. And in your case, you must take special care to keep this body safe and whole." John stopped. David could tell he was weighing carefully his words. He finally spoke distractedly, as if he were seeing something in the distance, something in his memory. "Your spirit is very old, David, very old and . . . very powerful."

John massaged David's legs for almost a half hour. By 7 A.M. David was able to get up and use the restroom. After breakfast he was feeling better and by the afternoon he was able to walk, though he was slow and stiff.

* * *

That weekend was the longest of Camille's life. She was more than frustrated with the track team. She was disgusted with her entire life: she was fat, she was ugly, her friends were losers, she was terrible at track, and she had to work out with Louise Komahuk. When her mother attempted to wake her for track early Monday morning, she rolled over and spoke in discouragement. "Mom, I'm quitting the track team. I'm terrible at it and everybody just laughs at me." She spoke to the wall. "David can just miss practice and ride the bus today."

Sarah Magelby squeezed her daughter's shoulder. "Dear, I know you are discouraged, but I believe that track is a good experience for you. You've made some wonderful new friends and you get to be with David every day. He is such a fine young man. I can tell that he really cares about you."

Camille scowled at the thought of seeing David again. Sarah continued, "Just think it over before you make a decision, that's all I ask." But Camille had made up her mind. Her only regret was the bet with Tommy. She hated to admit he was right. That was one of the strange things about him.

He could hardly get an answer right in school, but when it came to real life, he was hardly ever wrong. He had known it wasn't practical for her to be on the track team and he had been right. She decided she would give him the twenty dollars quietly on the side. She would tell David that she had joined the track team for him, and, now that he was the team hero, he didn't need her any more. She had it all worked out in her mind.

Unfortunately for Camille, the tiny peace of mind that she had artificially created came to a catastrophic end five minutes before first period. Marty Kenley, her dreaded nemesis, flopped the newspaper on her desk and pointed to a large, full-color picture of Camille tackling David on the track. It was on the front page of the sports section. Camille never had a chance to read it. Her face flushed red with the realization that her moment of shame had been captured for all eternity.

Marty knew he had her. When Camille's cheeks blossomed with color, he let out a wicked laugh and chortled. "Coach Whitaker says that you're on the wrong team. He wants you to try out for football next fall."

Before Camille thought to snatch the paper away, Marty was up and halfway across the room, showing it to everybody who would listen. Camille dropped her head. Anger and frustration flowed through her. She wanted to disappear so badly that she froze in silence, hoping no one would see her, but it was not to be. As part of the morning announcements, Principal Boyle congratulated Louise and David for first place in their respective events and then he congratulated Camille on her flying tackle.

All morning long Camille felt eyes upon her. People snickered when she walked by, but nobody spoke to her. She avoided everyone that day, didn't answer a single question. Normally she would have reacted by getting angry and letting a few people have it, but this time her humiliation went beyond anger. What could she say when even the teachers were commenting on it? Her goal was invisibility, but that was impossible when you were fat. At lunchtime she stayed in the library. She didn't want anyone to see her and especially to see her eating. She couldn't face Tommy and David either. *Those two are the root of my problem. They're such losers.*

At the end of the longest day ever, Camille crept down to Coach Morrison's office and waited by his door. When he came in from teaching his last class, he acknowledged her with a smile. "Camille, we missed you this morning."

She studied his face to see if there was any deception in his eyes, but no, he was sincere. "Coach," she said as sternly as possible, "I need to talk to you."

His face drooped as he guessed at where she was headed. He quickly unlocked the door and waved her in. To her horror she noticed a copy of the newspaper lying on his desk. It was open to the page with her picture on it. Her cheeks flushed red. She wanted nothing more than to grab that paper, wrinkle it up, and throw it in the trash.

"Coach Morrison. I'm quitting the team. I'm no good at discus and I just make a fool of myself out there." She couldn't help but notice the lines harden in his face as his lips compressed into a line. He sat there glaring at her with that hard expression for almost thirty seconds before she heard his flat answer.

"No." It rolled slowly through his mouth and came out in a rumble.

Camille couldn't believe her ears. She was caught completely off guard. She had been through one of the most difficult days of her life and she wasn't prepared to have a fight with this stern coach. She didn't say anything, but her mouth fell open a bit. It was too much, she couldn't stand it anymore, the frustration and humiliation were overwhelming. Finally, without a sound, her eyes filled and huge crocodile tears began to roll down her checks.

Coach Morrison sighed and spun his chair around. From the bottom shelf of his cabinet he pulled out a box of tissues and plopped it on the desk in front of her. Camille never moved. His face softened a little. He picked up the paper and studied it. "Did you see this, Camille?" She nodded. "Did you know that I am in the process of cutting it out and framing it?" She stared up at Coach Morrison in horror. "I'm framing it so that I can put it on the 'wall of fame' over there, right next to the picture of Donny Hellwig breaking the state record in the hundred-yard dash, Louise Komahuk setting the shot put record, and Brenda Wells winning the state championship in the long jump. There are three others up there, but I won't go into detail. They all exemplify something: discipline, perseverance, and personal victory. They all achieved a type of excellence." Then Coach Morrison paused and seemed to change the subject. "Let me ask you something, Camille. Why did you tackle David?"

Camille hadn't really thought about it, but when she did, she knew the answer. Still, she took her time because she didn't trust her voice. Finally, she squeaked out her answer. "He was out of control."

"How did you know?" he drilled her.

She sucked in another breath. "I've known David for a long time. He's not a competitor or a showoff. When I saw his face, I knew he was in trouble."

He smiled a little. "If you had to do it all again, knowing how people would laugh at you, would you still tackle him?"

That hurt. When Coach Morrison mentioned people laughing at her, she visibly flinched. Still, there was no doubt about her answer. David had to be stopped no matter what. In spite of the humiliation, in spite of the terrible picture in the newspaper, she knew she would have done it again. Camille didn't answer out loud this time but just stared at the floor and nodded.

"Camille, you are a true friend. What you did for David is the stuff that legends are made of." She didn't raise her eyes. "David came into my office after lunch and told me that he was quitting the team."

That got Camille's attention. She looked up at Coach Morrison with shock on her face.

"You didn't know? He was walking with a limp and wheezing like an asthmatic. When he told me he was quitting, I told him I understood. In all my years coaching, I have never had a young man win a race, apologize for winning, and quit the team. And," he added with hesitation, "I have never been so glad that he did."

Coach Morrison stared at Camille like he was looking through her. "Did you know that David ran the last four laps at a record pace for the mile? It's no wonder that no one could keep up with him. The last lap was close to a sixty-second lap. When he failed to stop running at the end of the race, I also knew that he was in trouble. I would have tackled him myself, but I was at the finish line. I have never been so grateful for any student as I was for you, Camille. When you brought David down on the opposite side of the track you probably saved his life."

Coach Morrison leaned back in his chair. Both of them sat in silence for almost a minute. Camille hadn't thought of it that way. It scared her. It couldn't have been that serious.

Coach blew out a long sigh. Looking past her and speaking to no one in particular, he resumed. "A long time ago I was a pretty tough kid. I got into trouble with the law and I thought I knew where I was going. My father was an alcoholic and not much of an example. The summer that I graduated from high school, your grandfather gave me a job when nobody else would. I worked with him all summer building one of those cow barns of yours and I found in him the example of a father I never had." He leaned back into his chair again. It squeaked loudly as it tilted under his weight. "Now I owe both of you something."

He stared back at Camille and bit his lip. "Stay with the team, Camille. I will help you and it will change your life. Just," he swallowed hard, "just give me a chance, like your grandfather did."

Camille was confused and hurt, but she was thinking clearly now. *Maybe Coach Morrison is right. Maybe there is something good about me.* She threaded her hand into her pocket and felt the twenty-dollar bill her mother had given her. She crushed the bill. A tiny smile touched her face, the first smile that had graced it in days. *Maybe Tommy won't get this after all.*

THE IMPOSSIBLE DREAM

Chapter 18

C aren Abernathy was in a hurry. It was always a busy time of year for her. There were only two weeks of school left and she had a dozen tasks to complete. In order to get ahead of the onslaught, she had stayed at school later than expected, grading some of the projects her students were turning in. Normally, she would bring them home and grade them, but they were physical things this year, like volcanoes and islands, so transporting them was a problem. The accompanying essays were already in her satchel.

As if life wasn't hectic enough, it was Tuesday and David would be coming over soon. He was working to complete a large research paper on Lake Victoria and the Nile River. She knew from experience that he would be there in about twenty minutes to use the computer.

Caren sped home along the long-memorized path without thinking about a single turn. She had lived in the same house and commuted to the same job for over eighteen years. She often drove that path even when she wasn't going to school. Out of pure habit, she once found herself at school on a Saturday morning when she had fully intended to do the grocery shopping. It had been a disorientating experience.

Caren was happy to see that John's old suburban wasn't there when she pulled into her parking spot at the edge of the valley where her house was nestled. *Good*, she thought. When the car came to rest, she reached over and grabbed her satchel. As her head came up, she caught a glimpse of something strange out of the corner of her eye. There was a large brown blob at the edge of her property. Her mind almost dismissed it until she remembered that it hadn't been there that morning. Caren stopped, turned her head, and stared down at the far corner of her clearing.

There, standing in the center of her budding garden, was a giant bull moose. It was huge. The gangly fur-covered creature was one of few species that survived the ice age. The tips of its ears were over seven feet from the ground and it weighed well in excess of a thousand pounds. Its antlers reached up to the sky like a giant set of groping hands and it was in the process of rooting and eating her new garden.

Fury filled the wiry elementary school teacher. Dropping everything, Caren hurled herself out of the jeep, ran behind her house and down the hill to the northeast corner of her lot. In all her life, she had never weighed more than one hundred twenty pounds and, at five feet three inches, she was not a big woman. The Bull Moose who was eating her garden that afternoon could have easily deflected her attack with the tiniest flick of its antlers. But size didn't matter to Caren. That moose was stealing something from her and it was wrong. As she sped around the side of her house, she raised her arms and started screaming at the top of her voice. Many a medieval berserker would have been impressed; few military charges have contained such fury.

When the Bull Moose looked up from his savory dinner and saw the tiny parka-coated ball of screaming rage descending upon him, he did the only sane thing imaginable. Leaping from the garden, he took off for the woods at a furious pace. Whatever that terrible noisy beast was, he didn't want to be bitten by it.

As her intruder vanished into the woods, Caren stopped and surveyed the damages. The cabbage and lettuce were eaten, the rhubarb was trampled, as were the carrots and the potatoes. It was a blow, to be sure, but most of it was recoverable. The flimsy mesh fence made of woven orange plastic and T posts was another problem.

Caren was concentrating hard on her wounded garden when a terrible grinding crash startled her. Jumping a few inches from the scare, she glanced up the hill to the source of the noise. The sight that filled her eyes was something from an alternate reality. She watched in awe and horror as the top of her house leaned inexplicably toward her. It seemed like some terrible invisible giant was sitting on it, causing the entire structure to creak and groan from its horrendous weight. She furrowed her brow in confusion, when suddenly, the wall closest to her exploded outward and the roof collapsed into the rubble.

Caren was in shock. *What in the world?* Slowly, she made her way up the hill to the front of her house where she found the perpetrator of her disaster. Her jeep was parked in the center of her house, pinned by what use to be the roof. The engine was still idling. She stood there dumbfounded, studying the mess, until she pieced together what had happened. She had left the jeep in gear. When she ran to chase the moose out of her garden, she had forgotten to put it in park. It had crept over the edge of the driveway and cascaded down into her house.

A wave of nausea spun Caren's head as the sickening realization of what happened settled upon her. She sat down heavily on a boulder at the corner of her driveway and absorbed her situation. It was a personal disaster of unrecoverable magnitude. She had some insurance, but not enough to build a new house. She only had liability insurance on the jeep.

Fire! She thought with a jolt. She needed to shut off the electricity and the fuel oil! *I should call 911.* But her cell phone was in her purse in the car. She thought about trying to get to it, but the whole mess made that too precarious. Finally, in absolute surrender, she stood slowly and started for her neighbor's house. When she reached the top of her driveway, she turned and surveyed the wreckage again. *What a mess. Of all the dumb things I've done in my life well . . . this has got to be the topper.*

* * *

David was late getting to Miss Abernathy's house. He had to run several errands for John and when he finally arrived, it was after six o'clock. He was completely surprised by the chaos that confronted him. The normally placid clearing was alive with activity. The first thing he noticed were the flashing lights of two police cruisers sitting in the spot where he normally parked. At the end of the driveway sat a huge fire truck. There were police and firemen everywhere.

Miss Abernathy! Fear struck David, but as he scanned the site, he found her standing next to one of the police cruisers, talking with an officer. She was distressed, but not injured in any way that David could tell. He parked John's old Suburban along the gravel road, stepped out, and walked over to her. Miss Abernathy noticed him and nodded, but didn't break her conversation with the officer.

David could now see over the hill to the pile of rubble that used to be Miss Abernathy's house. The roof was collapsed on her old jeep and the exterior walls were pretty much lying on the ground. It was a disaster. Firemen were climbing all over the house. Since Miss Abernathy was busy, David wandered down behind the house and realized what they were concentrating on. The fuel oil tank was pinned under the back wall.

The house was a mess. It was as if someone had turned it inside out. It was strange to see all the things that Miss Abernathy had arranged so neatly and carefully now scattered throughout the rubble. Almost everything was bent, broken, or damaged. The computer was crushed, smashed to a triangular shape by the file cabinet that had stood next to it.

David stared at the conglomeration for several minutes before he felt a tap on his shoulder. When he looked up, he found Miss Abernathy beside him.

"Quite a mess, isn't it?"

David nodded. "What happened?"

Miss Abernathy rolled her eyes in exasperation. "It's all my fault. When I got home this evening, there was a moose eating my garden. I jumped out of the jeep to chase him off and . . . well, I forgot to put the jeep in park. It edged up over the end of the driveway and crashed down into the house. My poor little house couldn't take it. The walls blew out and the roof collapsed." She gazed forlornly down the hill. "Oh, David," she sighed in despair, "I'm just a foolish old woman. Can you believe I did this? That house wasn't much, but it was almost everything I had in this world. I don't know what I will do now."

Both of them stood in silence. David felt the sorrow and loss in Miss Abernathy's voice. He knew from years of experience what a strong woman she was. She was devastated. He could read volumes just from the way she was standing; stooped over, shaking her head in regret. For the first time in all the years he had known her, David realized just how old and frail she was. She had always seemed like such a bastion of strength before tonight.

Miss Abernathy finally lifted her head. "Would you stay a little while? I know you have homework to do, but I guess I'll be staying at a hotel tonight and," she paused glancing at her jeep, "I think I'm going to need a ride."

About an hour later, the last of the policemen drove away and Caren finished talking with her neighbors. David waited patiently and when she finally approached, an image materialized in the mess behind her. David recognized it immediately. It was something that no one else could see.

Miss Abernathy slowly climbed into the Suburban and shut the door. She clung to her purse, which the fireman had been kind enough to retrieve from her vehicle. "Well," she said, "I guess you can take me to the motel in town." Then talking more to herself than to David, she continued, "I hope my insurance will cover some of these incidental living costs."

David didn't start the Suburban, instead, he turned and faced her. His demeanor was serious. "You could stay with us for awhile. I'm sure that John wouldn't mind after all that you've done for me."

Caren smiled at that. "Thank you, David, but I don't believe this town is big enough to have a single old spinster like me, staying with two handsome men like you and John." She smiled when she said it, but it was a forced smile. Then she fell silent for a long time. David still didn't start the car. Miss Abernathy continued, "I just don't know what I'm going to do, David. I have some insurance on the place, but it isn't enough to build a new house. I'm not wealthy enough to retire and I'm too old to start over." Caren was too experienced to become emotional over this, but David realized that she was suffering. It broke his heart. "Well," Miss Abernathy smiled bravely, "at least I wasn't inside when it happened."

They both sat in silence, staring at the wreckage in front of them. Finally David spoke. "Miss Abernathy . . ." He wondered how to say exactly what he needed to say. Finally he just spoke the words. Those words came directly from his heart in a matter of fact tone, as if they were nothing of consequence. ". . . I will build you a new home."

That surprised Caren. Her mouth dropped open as she turned to stare at the young man next to her. "David, you can't build me a house. You're just a . . ." She stopped herself. David was almost eighteen years old, six feet four inches tall, and had a strong build. He was a bit skinny and had the acne typical of many teenagers, but he was most assuredly not a boy. He had never been just a boy. Still, Miss Abernathy knew David and she knew he had no idea of how to build a house. She was sure he was underestimating the task.

Caren regrouped, "David," she took his arm and patted it gently. "Thank you ever so much for offering, but you don't know the first thing about building a house." She gazed into his eyes and shook her head. "I just can't let you do that."

David turned his head and faced her. His words came slowly, filled with the full power of his will. He spoke solemnly. "I will find a way . . . I have already seen it."

Caren felt in those words the finality of what David said. In his solemn, powerful, revelation it was obvious that he had spoken the truth. Of all the children she had ever known or taught, this was the one who could do it. Caren's mind raced into a tailspin until the realization overpowered her. *He can do it.* She examined her star pupil in a light she had never seen before. It all came flooding back; his dedication and attention to detail, the care and research that he invested into every assignment. In all the years she had known him, he had never failed to complete a single task that he had set his heart on.

Caren was dumbfounded. She stammered to find the right words. *Even if he can do it and even if he wants to do it; it isn't right.* Finally her mind organized her thoughts. "David, this isn't your problem. I just can't allow you to do that for me. It's . . . it's too much."

David's head slumped to his chest. He closed his eyes in sorrow. "Miss Abernathy . . . please let me help you."

Caren felt that. In all the years she had known David, she had witnessed little emotion from him. Today had been no exception. But behind that plea, she felt David's sorrow. He was suffering because someone he loved was suffering. *Empathy!* The word tore open her heart. It *was* his problem, more so than she could ever imagine. He would suffer more if he could not stop her suffering.

Caren smiled weakly as a silent tear streaked down her face. *How I love this boy!* She gazed forward into the waning sunlight at the mess that used to be her home. Then she shook her and surrendered. "Okay."

* * *

Although David, Camille, and Tommy had changed significantly during their high school years, some things never change. They still ate lunch together every day and spent most of their summers together, but David had kept growing until he towered over both of them. His hair and eyes were dark brown and his skin was pale due to the weak Alaskan sunlight.

Tommy stopped growing in the tenth grade. He was still five feet six with jet-black hair and a dark complexion. He grew his hair down past his shoulders in twelfth grade so that he now greatly resembled an ancient Athabascan warrior. He had filled in over the last couple of years and had a strong body with a set of shoulders that many football players would have envied.

Camille, however, was the one who had changed the most. Under the tutelage of Coach Morrison, Camille lost most of her excess weight and replaced it with muscle. She did track in the winter and cross-country skiing in the fall. Her waist wasn't exactly slim, but she had substantial shoulders for a girl, so it gave her a figure of sorts. She was about five feet four with golden braids that came out of the sides of her head. Her face was a little small and round, but she always had a beautiful smile. When they studied Norse legends, Tommy found an image of one of the Valkyries and they teased Camille for weeks because she was the spitting image of that picture.

The day after Miss Abernathy's accident, Camille and Tommy were seated at a table just finishing lunch when David sauntered up. "Where have you been?" Camille asked intrusively.

"I was in the library."

"Tommy and I were just having a discussion about what adventure we should plan for our summer this year. Since this is our final year in high school, and we only have one week of school left, we're going to do something incredible."

Tommy glanced up from eating his dessert and gave David one of his *help me* looks. David sat down quietly without saying anything.

"Anyway," Camille continued, "I think we should train all summer and climb Mount McKinley in August. Wouldn't that be a great story to tell our kids?"

Tommy couldn't take it anymore. "Camille, last year you made us take that float trip and nearly got me killed. I'm not going anywhere dangerous with you again."

David clearly remembered that day. It had started off rather casually on a large, slow river. Unfortunately, and unknown to them, the river was at flood levels. Two miles into the trip, they found themselves floating through the center of a thick forest with torrents of water rushing around, through, and under the trees. The three of them did a great job avoiding obstacles until they were sucked into a whirlpool that swept them under a fallen limb. Within seconds, the raft capsized, landing David and Camille on the tree. Tommy landed in the water and had to fight for his life to keep from being sucked under. It was only with the help of adrenaline and sheer terror that they had managed to pull Tommy out from the heavy current.

In the meantime, the raft and Camille's five-course picnic lunch sailed down the river without them. It took the rest of the day to find the raft and walk back to the car. The tiny craft was beaten to a pulp and Camille had a lot of explaining to do to her dad.

"Oh yeah," Camille sneered, "what about marmot hunting? We spent twelve hours down in Eklutna trying to rig Tommy's ridiculous traps in front of marmot holes only to find out that marmots have about fifty entrances and exits to their hovels."

"At least nobody got hurt," Tommy shot back.

Camille noticed that David was not participating in the conversation. "What about you? Wouldn't you like to climb McKinley this summer? It's probably the only chance we'll ever have."

David wrinkled his forehead in concentration. "I can't," he stated matter-of-factly. "I have to build Miss Abernathy a new house."

Both Tommy and Camille gaped at David in confusion. "What?" they chimed in unison.

David stopped eating and studied their shocked faces. "Miss Abernathy needs a new house and I promised her I would build it."

Camille still couldn't imagine it. "Miss Abernathy already has a house. You mean a greenhouse, a storage shed, a garage, a play house---what?"

David pressed his lips together. "Didn't you hear?"

"Hear what?" Tommy asked, clearly intrigued at this point.

David sighed. "Last night when Miss Abernathy got home she saw a moose in her garden. She immediately jumped out of her jeep and ran down to chase it off. While she was inspecting the garden, she heard a crash and realized that her jeep had rolled over the end of the driveway and down into her house. Since her house is basically just a trailer, the whole thing sort of collapsed."

Camille gasped, whipping her hand to her mouth, but Tommy smiled. "No kidding?"

"I'm not kidding. Her house was destroyed and I promised her I would build her a new one."

Tommy couldn't help himself, he blurted out his retribution. "You see? You see what happens to people who are mean to me? Miss Abernathy was the meanest teacher I ever had. She needled me about every assignment I didn't turn in and if I ever did a rush job on something, she would stick it right back in my face. No offense, David, since you were the teacher's pet you didn't notice, but she was awfully hard on a lot of kids."

David's mind traced back to the sixth grade. "If I remember right, you got the best grades of your life in Miss Abernathy's class. Miss Abernathy believed in you and you know what? She was right. You are far more capable than you let people know."

The smile faded from Tommy's face.

Camille butted in. "David, you don't know anything about building a house."

That was true and Camille had touched on David's greatest reservation. David slowly bent over and took a book out of his backpack. He laid it on the table in front of them; *The Fundamentals of Homebuilding.* "That's why I was late to lunch. I was checking this book out of the library."

Camille and Tommy gazed at the book in disbelief. They both knew that David would finish what he started no matter what. They had seen him do assignments, reports, and projects in detail that would give a college professor goose bumps. But they also knew that there was something a little wrong inside of David. They knew he was capable of working himself to death in the process.

Camille had a sick feeling in her stomach. She wanted to object and point out to David that he was crazy and that this wasn't his problem, but she knew it would be a futile effort. Whenever that strange clarity glowed in David's distant eyes, it was hopeless. It was like trying to stop a locomotive. Worst of all, she knew that she would be sucked into it. There was nothing she could do. David would need her help. *So much for climbing McKinley*, she mulled in annoyance.

No one said another word for the rest of the lunch break.

* * *

School ended with a whimper for Caren Abernathy. She lived out of a hotel room while trying to grade papers and finish school. Meetings with insurance and construction people ate up the little spare time she had. Her life was a disaster.

When Principal Wright heard about Caren's predicament, he called her into his office. They shared a quiet chat and then he offered to bring his old RV over, so that Karen could get out of the hotel and live on her land. He also loaned her his truck. Caren spent hours hauling her belongings from her home site to the storage unit she rented in Palmer. She couldn't lift anything, but David came over every day and helped. She enjoyed his company. She felt bad that he was there instead of being off with his friends. She attempted several times to persuade him otherwise, but he wouldn't hear of it. He knew that she needed his help and that was it.

Finally, after weeks of consideration, the insurance people gave her the estimate: $87,000. *Nothing,* Caren thought in discouragement. Her home was worth nothing because it had been built on the shell of a trailer. The insurance people had also been unwilling to release funds until she had the old house bulldozed and hauled away. It cost her $8,000 just to have it hauled off.

Adding everything up, Caren believed she would need about $160,000 to build a modest home, maybe more. She was going to have to get a loan. *A home mortgage at my age.* The thought almost made her cry. It just seemed ridiculous. She toyed with the idea of giving up and retiring, but, without selling her home, she really didn't have enough to retire on. And now she didn't have a home to sell.

* * *

The first week after school finished, Camille did nothing but enjoy her freedom and indulge in all the pastimes she hadn't had time for during school. In her mind, she had graduated from high school and she was queen bee for the summer. She loved it. The only cloud on her horizon was David.

The last week of school had not been the best for the GBU. Tommy and David had been especially quiet as David concentrated on finishing his homework during every break and focused all his spare time into studying about home construction. The more Camille thought about it, the more she doubted it would ever happen. David asked everybody about everything and the more he asked, the more she realized how much he didn't know.

Most people would have admitted they were in over their head and given up. But David just kept gathering information. It was like a tidal wave rising from the seabed before it hits the shore. David was so absorbed that she avoided the subject and avoided David, but there was this little sensation in the back of her mind that just kept telling her she needed to help.

Today was the day she finally surrendered to that irritating little voice. The worst thing about Tommy and David was that you never saw or heard from either of them unless you went over to their houses. So Camille pried herself out of bed that morning, did her morning run, took a shower, changed clothes, and headed over to David's house. It was no surprise that David was gone and John was nowhere to be seen. Camille climbed back in her car and headed for Tommy's house.

Tommy was home feeding some mountain sheep he managed to get his hands on. Camille hated Tommy's house. His collection of stray dogs always barked at her when she drove up. She parked the car, hopped out, and made a beeline to Tommy so that he would make the dogs shut up.

"Tommy," Camille yelled over the cacophony, "have you seen David?"

Tommy turned around when he heard her voice. "A little," he shouted.

"Where is he?"

"He's over at Miss Abernathy's place," Tommy rolled his eyes, "every day."

That makes sense, Camille thought flatly. "Come on, let's go see if he needs some help." She finally reached Tommy and the dogs stopped barking once they realized that he recognized her.

"Can't go," Tommy stated matter-of-factly.

"Why's that?"

"Because I'm busy building stuff and feeding my animals."

Camille noticed the beginnings of a new cage of some sort: chicken wire, nails, and boards scattered all over. A cross expression blossomed on her face as she caught Tommy's eyes. "You do that stuff every day. You need to come with me and see if David needs our help."

Tommy set down his project and glowered at Camille. "I'm not working on Miss Abernathy's house, no matter what!"

But Camille was not in the mood to retreat. "We're not doing it for Miss Abernathy, we're doing it for David. How many times has he saved your bacon in school? How many reports has he helped you start and finish? I don't really like spending my summer working on Miss Abernathy's house either, but we're going to help David."

Tommy glared at her with fire in his eyes. She was right; she was usually right; he hated that. But the real truth was that Tommy was bored and every time he was around Camille, things got interesting. He already knew he was going. Still, he had to at least protest. It wasn't a good idea to let women boss you around. "What about feeding my animals?" Tommy swept his hand behind him.

"I'll help you feed your animals." And then with a little smile she added, "After all, you did feed Raven for me that summer."

Tommy flinched at the remark. *How did I lose that bet?* It was the surest bet he ever made, but as it turned out, David quit the team and Camille ran track for years. *Oh well,* Tommy consoled himself in silent victory, *Raven was worth it.*

Tommy groaned. He laid his hammer down and trudged over to Camille's car.

"What about your animals?"

"I already fed them."

Camille unlocked the door and both of them climbed in. As Camille started the car, Tommy glared at her.

"You know, I'll probably never get married because of you."

Camille scowled back. "What are you talking about?"

"I'm damaged goods now. For years I thought that women were like my mother, hard-working, quiet . . . let their husbands do pretty much what they wanted, but you have changed all that. I now realize that some women bully people into doing all kinds of things they don't want to do, so I sort of have this aversion to women now."

"Anasogak," Camille chuckled, "you are soooo lucky to have me as a friend."

Tommy studied his menagerie of animals as they backed up. Then he smiled a little, but not enough for Camille to see. Camille was right. The best memories of his life were the ones that included her and David.

When they arrived at Miss Abernathy's house, they were surprised how much it had changed. The old house was completely gone and there was an RV parked up near the driveway. There was a level bald spot where the house used to be and David. He was digging some kind of trench around the edge of the bald spot.

When Camille climbed out of the car, she waved her hand and yelled at him. David stopped digging and looked up. When he recognized her and Tommy, his face transformed into a big toothy grin. That was unusual for David.

As they walked down to meet him, they could see that he was drenched in sweat. He had taken off everything but his T-shirt and pants and it was only sixty degrees that morning. Camille led the march with Tommy behind her. When she reached the edge of the pad she called out. "I bet you thought we'd never come."

David was still smiling. He nodded his head. "I was hoping."

"Well, we're here, so what do you want us to do?"

David jammed the shovel into the bottom of the trench. "Come here and I'll show you."

Camille and Tommy followed David to a tent on the side of the building site. Inside were a table and some chairs and on the table was a blue three-ring binder. David opened the binder and Camille smiled. On the first page inside the binder was a drawing of a house. It showed everything: walls, doors, windows, roof, porch, etc.

Camille studied the picture. "Is this what it will look like?"

David nodded without speaking. He turned instead to the first tab in the binder. On that page, Camille noted a rectangular step with dimensions all over it. The image was hand drawn with the aid of rulers. David explained. "This is the footing. We need to make a trench eighteen inches deep and twelve inches wide. Inside of that, we'll have to build a form, about two feet high, all around the base of the house. We'll fill it with concrete when we finish and the house will sit on it."

Tommy and Camille couldn't really tell what David was talking about, but they could see from the picture exactly what he was trying to do. "So what do you want us to do?" Camille grimaced, peeking out the door of the tent at the shovel stuck in the dirt.

David glanced sheepishly at Tommy. "Well, I was getting a little tired. I was hoping Tommy could finish digging the footings while you and I start making the forms."

That sounded pretty good to Camille but Tommy remained unconvinced. "I have a better idea." He smiled at Camille, "Why don't we have Camille dig the footing while you and I trap those little arctic foxes we saw last winter?"

"Tommy boy," Camille pointed out the tent door, "your shovel awaits you."

After about two hours of working with David, however, Camille wished she had chosen the shovel. David was so careful and picky about every little detail that it was driving her crazy. By the end of the day, Tommy had finished the digging, but they only had one side of the forms up.

Miss Abernathy brought them some cookies in the evening and they all talked about going out to dinner. But when seven o'clock rolled around, and the forms were nowhere near completed, David informed them that he was going to keep working until dark. Camille and Tommy shook their heads and silently trudged back up to her car. Once inside, Tommy, who had been increasingly silent as the day wore on, finally spoke. "Maybe climbing Mount McKinley wasn't such a bad idea after all. I think I would rather die from a quick fall than be tortured to death by David."

Camille nodded in agreement. "He's never going to finish. He's so picky that it drives me crazy to work with him."

Tommy smiled for the first time all day. "Good, so it's settled. We will avoid David all summer or however long it takes him to get over his insanity."

Camille didn't respond right away. She knew what she should say, but something about Tommy's plan appealed to her. She drove to the end of the driveway in silence and then changed the subject. "I'm too tired to go out to eat. Can I just drop you off?"

"Fine with me."

When Camille arrived home that evening she was tired, hungry, and discouraged. For the first time since David came up with his crazy idea, she began to understand the scope of what he was trying to do. "How did I get involved in this?" She mumbled to herself as she made her way into the kitchen for a late dinner. Her mother was cleaning the dishes.

"Camille, where have you been? We missed you at dinner." Sarah Magelby studied her daughter for the first time that evening. Camille's face and hands were dirty and the knees of her pants were black with mud. "What have you been up to?"

"Tommy and I went to help David today. You know he's trying to build a house for Miss Abernathy. Anyway, we had the immense pleasure of digging foundations and playing in the mud all day. It was a real picnic." Camille finished in a sarcastic voice. "He'll never finish, you know. He's so picky and careful . . ." Camille shook her head. "I thought I was going to go crazy today."

Sarah wrapped her arms around her discouraged daughter. "So what are you going to do?"

"I don't know, Mom. I honestly believe that if I try to work with David every day, I'll end up killing him." Camille smiled at the morbid thought. "Not much of a friend, huh?"

Sarah changed the subject. "Coach Morrison called today. He wanted you to call him back no matter how late you got home."

"Coach Morrison," Camille wondered out loud. "Doesn't he know that I graduated?"

"I don't know, sweetheart. Maybe you left something at the gym."

Camille chuckled and mumbled under her breath, "Yeah, about sixty pounds."

"What dear?"

"Nothing, Mom, nothing."

Camille walked gingerly to the telephone. She was sore already and she hadn't even gone to bed yet. She made out the telephone number scribbled on the pad next to the phone and dialed Coach Morrison.

"Hello, this is Frank Morrison," came the stern voice that Camille had come to learn was not really that stern.

"Coach, this is Camille."

"Camille," his tone lightened, "how are you doing?"

"I'm okay."

"I guess the real question is what are you doing?"

Camille was tempted to tell Coach all about David and Miss Abernathy's house, but she decided to avoid the subject. "Not much."

"Well," Coach sounded excited, "I'm putting together my annual two-week training camp starting next week and I want you to help me. You can come here tomorrow and help me with the preparations. I'll even pay you for your time."

Camille's mind raced. It would be something to be one of Coach Morrison's trainers. She had always admired those glorious seniors that ran all the new recruits ragged. It was the perfect excuse. David would understand and it was only for a few weeks. She would have the rest of the summer to work on Miss Abernathy's place.

Just as Camille was forming her answer an image flashed across her mind. It was David. He was stooped over in that trench digging it by himself. Something melted inside her. David needed her help. It made her angry that he didn't really understand that he needed her help and that he probably didn't even appreciate it, but that didn't change the fact that he needed her.

Camille sighed in defeat. "Coach," she took in a deep breath, "I can't."

Coach Morrison was silent on the other end of the phone. Camille knew from long experience that he did not like to be told no. Finally she heard him grumble, "Why not?"

Camille felt the heat in his question. She blurted out her excuse. "Because I told my friend David that I would help him build a house for Miss Abernathy this summer. It's his crazy idea and it's going to ruin my senior summer, but," Camille paused in frustration, "he's my friend. You remember David, don't you?"

There was a long pause. "Oh yes, I remember David Samuelson. And I remember Miss Abernathy, too. She was my sixth grade teacher, you know."

Camille's mouth dropped open. "You're kidding."

"No, she's been around for quite a while, and yes, she was just as tough on kids back when I had her. I read that article in the paper about her house collapsing. I thought she would just get the insurance to build another one."

Camille had never thought of that. It made her mad to imagine that Miss Abernathy might be using David. Then she thought better of it and shook her head. "I don't think she got much money because David is building a pretty small house and they are both really careful with the money." Camille hesitated before finishing, "She isn't paying David anything either. She would if he'd let her, but he's really stubborn about that."

"Does David have any idea what he's doing?"

"No, and he's driving me crazy."

"After I worked with your grandfather to build that barn, I worked the next few summers building houses. I know a few things about building, so maybe I should come by and see your project sometime."

"That would be great! You could check David's work and give us some pointers." Then she thought for a second and a mischievous smile lit her face. "You could even tell him that every tiny detail doesn't have to be perfect." Camille paused for effect. "That is, if you *really* wanted to help me."

Frank Morrison perceived Camille's intent. "Aw yes . . . I think I understand. I'll be by this week sometime. But please reconsider my offer to help with the training camp. I don't have anyone else who knows anything about discus and shot put."

"Okay," Camille responded flatly, but she already knew her answer.

The next morning Camille arrived at Miss Abernathy's place sometime before ten o'clock. David was already there of course. Tommy was nowhere in sight. Camille parked, put on her dad's tool belt and trudged down to David. He smiled up at her. "I didn't know if you'd be back today."

Camille didn't return his smile. Instead, David heard her mumble caustically, "Neither did I."

Tuesday went a little better than Monday. They were both used to each other now and Camille had a better idea of what needed to be done. Still, it took them all day to set up the forms on two more sides. The pace was excruciatingly slow with David.

On Wednesday morning, Coach Morrison showed up. He examined the project and then David took him into his little tent and showed him the notebook of drawings. Coach Morrison studied David's plans and smiled. There was a complete drawing of the house and drawings of every detail. "Inside Wall" showed the placement of all the studs, electrical, and plumbing, while "Outside Wall" showed the finished view. Each page included dimensions and notes. The same was true for the floors, roof and attic. There were even drawings for sidewalks, porches and stairs.

Coach Morrison gave David a few tips on how to order the concrete for the footings and how to place the rebar. Then he perused the site on last time before writing an order for lumber on a slip of paper. He told David to have that lumber on site by Wednesday of the next week. David absorbed the information. As Coach Morrison was leaving, he noticed Camille giving him the 'look" and he remembered what she had said in their phone conversation. Coach Morrison smiled and gave David one last bit of advice.

"David," he said, patting him on the shoulder, "don't try to make everything perfect when you build it. Most things aren't that critical and if there's a problem, it can usually be corrected later. Right now I would say that speed is more important than precision." Frank Morrison winked at Camille and she beamed back at him.

The advice helped. Every time David wanted to redo something, Camille would remind him of Coach Morrison's message and usually talk him into moving on. By Thursday they had finished the forms and on Friday they were filling them with rebar. Then, just before noon on Friday, David told her that something was wrong. He collected up his level and his ruler and some string and did all sorts of calculations before finally giving her the bad news. "The foundation is off by an inch. We're going to have to redo one of these walls."

Camille tried to keep the murder out of her voice, but she was not completely successful. "Every foundation in the world," she shrieked, "is off by one inch. We are not redoing anything!"

The ferocity of Camille's rebuttal caught David by surprise. Camille could tell that he hadn't fully realized how badly he was frustrating her. She felt bad about yelling at him, but if he touched those forms, he was going to have a fight on his hands.

Just then Tommy's old car rolled in the driveway and came to a stop. After much rummaging inside his car, Tommy opened the door and stepped out. He was carrying a workman's belt with some tools in his left hand. He wore a new black hockey jersey with a giant silver "L" on the front of it. He wore an expression of complete disgust on his face.

Camille shouted, "What's the L stand for?" Tommy stopped where he was and slowly turned around until both David and Camille saw the word "Loser" across his shoulders where the hockey player's last name was normally written.

Camille couldn't help it. She let out a great peel of repressed laughter and clapped her hands together. David just shook his head. "Where did you get that?"

"Oh," Tommy answered casually, "my big brother bought this for me at college. He said it was perfect for me." Tommy sat down on a pile of lumber and wrapped his work belt around his waist. "Anyway, since I was coming out here to work with you two building Miss Abernathy . . ." and Tommy's face soured as he pronounced her name ". . . a house for free, I thought it was appropriate."

"Tommy," Camille taunted, "you don't really need a shirt, you know. Everybody already knows." She kind of whispered that last statement like it was a secret.

"Hey," Tommy retorted, "they don't call us the GBU for nothin'." That made Camille mad. She hated that moniker and she hated Marty Kenley even worse for giving it to them.

David smiled. "I'm glad you came."

"To be honest with you, I'm not really here to work. It's just that my mom and dad keep bugging me about getting a job and moving out. I would much rather be here than have to listen to them nag."

Camille couldn't stay quiet for that. "It doesn't matter why you are here, Anasogak, you still get to work. Besides, you know you missed me," Camille smiled slyly, "life is just no good without me."

Tommy gazed up into the sky. "Why me, God? Why can't I just have normal friends?" He stared at David's perfect forms and the hopelessness of the situation sank in. He knew a little about building from the cages he had made and from repair work his father had bullied him into. "I can't believe I'm doing this." Then Tommy stopped for a moment as an expression of disgust filled his face. He slowly lifted his head and stared up at the RV where Miss Abernathy lived. "You know what the worst thing is?" Tommy shook his head in disbelief. "I don't even like Miss Abernathy." Tommy said it with such confusion and surrender that both Camille and David laughed.

They worked together on the forms and rebar till early afternoon. When they were finished, David borrowed Miss Abernathy's cell phone to call the cement company. He attempted to order 9.7 yards of concrete, but the lady at the office informed him that they only delivered by the half yard, not by the tenth of a yard. So David told them to bring ten yards. They informed David that they couldn't deliver until the next day.

Realizing they would have extra concrete, David made Camille set up the forms for part of the sidewalk. After that, there really wasn't anything else to do so they left early. Tommy went over to Camille's house to ride Raven, but David just went home. It was the first time he had been home before dark all week. When he arrived, John was nowhere to be found.

David had an idea. Although the budget didn't allow for it, he was hoping to include a fireplace in Miss Abernathy's place. So, just in case some extra money turned up, he wanted to know how to install a fireplace that wouldn't burn the house down.

David went into the laundry/wash area and pulled down the attic steps. Then he went up inside and began to study the chimney pipe that drew the smoke from the fireplace to the outside. After a few minutes, he heard John call.

"David, are you up there?"

"Yes."

"What are you doing?"

"I'm trying to figure out how they installed your chimney so that I can make a fireplace for Miss Abernathy." David paused before asking his question. "John, do you know anything about chimneys?"

John smiled. "No, I'm afraid not." David climbed down the stairs and folded them back up. John observed him in silence. "You're home early. Is something wrong?"

"They won't deliver the concrete until tomorrow so Camille, Tommy and I quit early. By the way, where were you? I didn't see you when I came in?"

"Ah," John nodded his head, "I was out in the garden trying to get something to grow. It hasn't had much attention this summer since you started your project."

David grimaced. "Oh."

John shook his head and smiled. "Don't worry about it. This year it's my turn to grow the garden." Then he studied David thoughtfully. "Perhaps you are growing a different garden this year."

David sighed. It was always scary when John made such statements. He knew from years of experience that there was tremendous meaning in everything John said, but you usually didn't figure it out until after the catastrophe. He stared at John suspiciously and probed. "What do you mean by that?"

John's penetrating eyes pierced David's as he spoke solemnly. "Where men of vision lead in righteousness, the people prosper."

David narrowed his eyes in concentration. *Is he talking about me? Well, at least it doesn't sound too bad this time.*

John reached up and patted David's shoulder. "Come on. It's time to eat. Since you're home early and I'm doing the gardening, you get to fix dinner." David smiled. That meant they were having toasted cheese sandwiches and tomato soup.

* * *

They were all there Saturday morning when the cement truck arrived. The driver instantly identified where he was needed and backed his truck up to the foundation. Thanks to Coach Morrison's advice, David had a wheelbarrow handy in case they needed to run concrete to the edges of the footings.

With his vehicle in place, the driver exited and made his way to the back of the truck. When he started breaking out the shoot, he whistled to himself. Camille noticed his strange expression and wandered over next to him. "What?"

The driver smiled. "Did you put these forms up?" Camille nodded, waiting to hear what was wrong with them. The driver let out a chuckle. "I've never seen forms like that before: mitered joints, braced and cross-braced. It looks more like cabinet work. Those are probably the most beautiful forms I have ever seen."

Camille's face instantly went red. Her eyes traced the forms until she found David fiddling with one of the braces. A mean little voice in head told her to march over and yell at him, but she didn't have time. After the concrete hit the first form, they were busy tamping and vibrating the forms to get concrete into every last crack; not to mention, wheel barrowing and shoveling cement to the corners that the shoot couldn't reach. It took the rest of the morning, but the work went quickly. David, of course, had calculated the amount of concrete out to the last shovel full. There was just enough left over to make a big cow pie at the end of the driveway.

By one o'clock, everybody was beat. Camille and Tommy took the rest of the day off and David ordered lumber for the next week.

On Monday and Tuesday, they finished the piers and beams and added the floor joists. Wednesday they started in on the floor decking. Camille almost enjoyed that. Progress was much more visible when you were laying down four-foot-by-eight-foot sheets of plywood.

Wednesday morning, a camouflaged truck drove up. Tommy and Camille stopped working to see who it was, but David just kept cutting plywood. The vehicle parked at the end of the driveway and after a few seconds, Frank Morrison stepped out. Camille waved to him and Coach waved back. She stepped over the footing and wandered up to his truck.

"What are you doing here?" Camille asked. "I thought you had your training seminar this week."

Coach Morrison ducked inside this truck and studied his odometer. "Did you know it's 4.2 miles from here to the high school?"

Camille shook her head. "No, I didn't know that. Is that important?"

"It will be," Coach laughed.

Eying the back of his pickup, Camille couldn't help but notice it was filled with tools, three five-gallon water jugs, and three large coolers. She was about to ask more questions when she heard the sound of footsteps. As she traced the sound to the head of the driveway she found three joggers racing toward the house. Coach Morrison was staring at his watch when Wayne Bysby, Allen Hendrix, and Jimmy Compton all panted up to his truck.

"Not bad, boys," he shouted as they came to a halt. "I see you haven't lost your edge in the two weeks since school let out. I expected to see Randy with you and Pam not too far behind.

Wayne smiled and let out a little laugh. "Randy had to slow down a little so that he could run next to Marci." Allen and Jimmy both snickered at that. "And Pam," Wayne continued, "Pam stopped to make sure a couple of the newbies didn't get lost."

Jimmy noticed Camille on the other side of Coach Morrison. "Hey, Camille, how are you doing?"

"I'm surviving," Camille frowned, glaring over at David. "It's a little hard working for 'Don Quixote.'" That was a little inside joke that Tommy and Camille had fostered. They would lip sync the song "The Impossible Dream" to each other whenever David wasn't watching them. Camille also liked to point out to Tommy that it made her Dulcinea while he was resigned to the part of Sancho.

"So, Coach Morrison, are you just here for a country run?" Camille questioned, eyeing the tools in the back of his truck.

"As always, Camille, we are here to work."

He turned to face his students. "Boys, take a minute to rest and get a drink and then find the tool you brought this morning and meet me down on the building site. I'm going to talk with David."

Camille watched as Coach Morrison walked down to where David was working. She was enjoying listening to Wayne, Allen and Jimmy talk about the track team and training when two more boys straggled in. Camille nearly laughed out loud at David's expression of dumb wonder as Coach Morrison no doubt told him that thirty to forty people were here to work on his project. She speculated menacingly what he would do about quality control now.

David and Coach Morrison walked from the home site to the tent then disappeared inside. When they were out of sight, a few more members of the track team straggled in. Pam finally showed up. She instantly found Camille and gave her a little hug. It was then that Camille realized how much she missed being with the team. Tommy stopped working and watched the parade. Within minutes, all forty-two track team members were gathered around Coach Morrison's truck sipping water and talking. Camille was ecstatic.

A smiling David and Coach Morrison emerged from the tent. The coach took one look at the crew surrounding his truck and started shouting orders. It was like watching a tornado swirl to life. Tommy, who was now standing next to Camille, brandished a rare smile.

The next three hours were a miracle. The track team finished the decking and began framing the walls for the house. It was like watching ants working. They assembled the walls on top of the decking and raised them into place with the help of many hands working together. David kept measuring the walls and showing Coach Morrison drawings from his book, while Coach Morrison kept shouting orders and making adjustments. Even Miss Abernathy came out to witness the excitement. At one o'clock, they sat down for a thirty-minute lunch and by three o'clock, they were finished. The team quickly loaded their tools back into coach's truck and began the jog back to high school.

Before leaving, Coach Morrison found David. "David, we will be back on Friday and again on Wednesday and Friday next week. Don't worry about keeping us busy. I'll figure out what they need to do when I get here.

When the excitement was over, Camille approached David and Tommy and needled them. "See, I told you that joining track was a good idea."

Tommy shook his head in disgust, but David smiled as he watched Coach Morrison's truck disappear up the driveway. "You were right Camille. You were right."

The next two weeks were fabulous. With the help of the track team, they were able to finish all the framing and even the roof rafters. The progress continued at breakneck speed and when Camille saw the roof joists going up against the gray Alaskan sky, she was excited.

On Friday of the second week, they had a special visitor. Sam Swenson from the local newspaper arrived at Coach Morrison's request and interviewed almost everyone about the project. Sam wrote the local school sports section in the newspaper and he and Coach Morrison were pretty good friends. Sam was also the one who had taken that terrible picture of Camille tackling David two and a half years earlier.

At two thirty that afternoon, the rain that had been threatening all week finally arrived. Coach made the team members run back to school before it got too bad. Since track camp was over, he said his goodbyes to David, Tommy and Camille. Miss Abernathy came out of her RV, thanked him and gave him a little hug. Camille almost burst out laughing when Frank Morrison blushed. It was a sight she had never seen before.

By half past three, the rain was coming down in sheets and David decided to call it a day. The house was actually starting to look like a house. The 2x6 walls were up and the roof trusses were in place. The roof decking was partially completed on the back of the house.

Saturday it was still raining, so Camille called Miss Abernathy on her cell phone. "Miss Abernathy, this is Camille, is David over there?"

Miss Abernathy peered out her window. "He's not and if he does show up, I'll send him home. It's too cold and slippery to work in this weather."

Camille called Tommy then and told him that they weren't going to work because of the rain. She was happy for the break. She made herself a bowl of oatmeal and sat down in front of the TV to watch cartoons. It felt great.

Camille stayed up late Saturday night and when she finally lumbered out of bed Sunday morning, it was half past ten. As she walked downstairs, her mother smiled at her strangely. It was one of those "I'm so proud of you" kind of looks.

Camille was immediately suspicious. When she reached the bottom of the stairs she noticed her father staring at her the same way. That really made her nervous. He was smiling. She gritted her teeth and practically shouted at him. "What?"

No one said anything for a few seconds and then, her father stood up and put his arm across Camille's shoulders. "Have you seen the newspaper today?" Camille's heart sank. She suddenly remembered that Sam Swenson had interviewed her Friday. She shook her head as the image of her picture mounted on the wall of fame flashed through her mind.

"Oh no," she exhaled in exasperation. "You better let me see it."

Ben Magelby handed Camille the paper and she slowly opened her eyes. There, on the front page of the sports section, was her face in gigantic full color. David was standing in the distant right of the picture and Tommy was standing in the distant left. Both of them looked very stern with their arms folded in front of them. Camille on the other hand was radiant. She had a smile that stretched from ear to ear and her golden braids glowed like defiant sunshine against the gray Alaskan sky. It was probably the best picture she had ever taken.

Camille read the headline, "Track Team Tackles Housing Project." The rest of the article was even better. Camille Magelby said this, Camille said that, blah blah blah . . . Coach Morrison . . . the track team All-stars . . . It just had a tiny mention of David and Tommy. Oh it was soooo perfect. David wouldn't care, but Tommy would be absolutely disgusted with how she got all the credit. Camille couldn't help it. She hoisted the paper high over her head and hooted a victory laugh.

* * *

Caren Abernathy gazed out the window of her camper and absorbed the view of her new home materializing through the rain. When David first began the project, he showed her the final drawing and each of the detailed drawings that followed. She tried to believe, but it hadn't been until Frank Morrison raised the walls and roof that she found her faith. It just seemed too good to be true.

Over the last three weeks, she had also come to a better understanding of what it would take to build that house and how much time David would have to invest. To be honest, she felt terrible about it. She had approached David three times about compensating him, but he wouldn't discuss it.

It was now Tuesday and it had been drizzling steadily since Friday. The only work that had been done on the house over the weekend was the article in the paper by Sam Swenson. It was a great article and she had received about a dozen phone calls from people who wanted to wish her well or help in some way.

That morning, however, David arrived to work on the house alone. Everything was wet and the weather was miserable. When Caren heard the first hammer blow, she grabbed her slicker and ran outside. She found David on the slippery roof dragging sheets of plywood up there and hammering them in place. She scolded him for working in the rain and more so for subjecting himself to a dangerous situation, but she couldn't dissuade him. He simply informed her that he didn't have much talent and no experience, so the only thing he had was time, and he was going to need all of it to finish the job.

Caren had attempted to help on occasion, but she was just too old. She did what she could, but the little real help she had rendered had cost her dearly in terms of arthritis, back problems, and sore muscles. So now she just sat in her RV and listened to the sound of David working on her house. It was a gift so great that she could never repay it and with each ringing blow of the hammer, Caren felt her fiercely independent soul slipping away.

Finally she bowed her head in surrender and pleaded. "Dear God, how did I get into this mess? How can I ever repay this boy?" She sat silently at the tiny camper trailer and remembered. She remembered the first time she had seen David and the year she had been his homeroom teacher. She remembered all those perfect assignments he handed in and that distant look in his eyes. Then there was that vivid night when she had visited his home and John had carried him in half dead. And the next Monday when he had come to school in perfect health. Caren thought about that for a long time. It was easy to concentrate with the soft rain as a backdrop. She thought about David, his life and his accomplishments. She thought about John with his strange knowledge and his ancient penetrating eyes.

Those memories swirled in Caren's mind until they congealed in a single blinding insight. *David is someone very special to God. His life will change the world, just as he is changing mine.* It was just a thought, but it was so powerful and so personal that Caren knew it was true.

What can I do? It was more of a prayer than a thought. *How can I help David? How can I repay, in some small measure, this tremendous gift?* Her mind raced until her thoughts came to rest on the words John had spoken to her the night he revealed that Cody's escape from certain death was a miracle. "Teach him to live in this world."

Caren pondered those words. What did that mean? Maybe she had already done that by letting him use her computer and by coaching him with his homework. But really, to live in the world, David would need more. Suddenly, a second thought came to her. This one came with such force and certitude that she knew exactly what she needed to do. A warm sensation washed over her as goose bumps rippled down her arms and back. Then, for the first time in several days, Caren Abernathy smiled.

* * *

Ben Magelby was a busy man. Most people thought of him as a dairy farmer, but he knew better. He was a repairman. From the moment he woke in the morning until he lay down at night, he fixed things. There were cars, trucks, tractors, fences, machinery of all kinds, and . . . buildings. *Oh yes, buildings,* Ben mused to himself. There was not a day where one of his buildings didn't need some form of repair.

He was also a father, but those responsibilities had taken a back seat to the farm. Sarah was such a great mother that he never worried about it. He loved his kids, but he just wasn't very involved with them.

Camille was his youngest child and she was, in some ways, the most difficult of the three. When she was younger, she had been heavy and ever so opinionated and obnoxious. Many were the times that she had given her monologues at the dinner table, talking and talking about things she didn't really know anything about. It had been a long hard lesson in patience, but Ben had learned to pretty much tune her out when she spiraled into one of her random dissertations.

During her tenth grade year, he finally suggested that she join the track team. At the time, he was worried that she needed to lose some weight and take care of herself, or she might never graduate from living at home. Amazingly, she joined and Coach Morrison really helped her. After that, things improved somewhat. Camille still talked just as much, but at least she started talking about things she knew something about.

Unfortunately, that also meant they had to go to track meets. Ben shuddered involuntarily. He had only attended three. It was an agonizing experience to sit there and waste half a day only to watch Camille throw the discus half the distance needed to win. Ben often wondered how she ever stuck with it.

But when Camille's picture came out in the paper, along with the article on Miss Abernathy's place, it changed everything. Camille Magelby was the toast of the town. Everywhere he went, people showed him the article and asked him about his daughter. She was the town hero and Ben eventually realized that the town needed a hero. It was strange to him how so many people could work together so closely without ever really knowing or caring about each other. Then, with a single sweeping stroke, Camille had captured the interest and concern of the entire valley. It was like the world suddenly woke up from a long winter's sleep. Ben smiled and shook his head every time he thought about it.

What surprised Ben the most, however, were his own feelings. He realized it when Alvin Miller bumped into him at the auto parts store. After discussing the article for several minutes, Alvin patted him on the back and said, "You must be proud of your daughter."

Ben answered honestly. "Yes we are." And, for the first time in his memory, it was true.

So Monday morning, a week after the article came out, Ben Magelby decided to do something that he rarely did. He decided to get involved. He had already been up for a few hours taking care of the morning milking and now that that was underway, he figured he would steal a few minutes and visit Camille's project.

"Camille?" Ben shouted up the stairs to his daughter's bedroom.

"Yes, Daddy?" Camille answered poking her head over the railing at the top of the steps.

"Are you going to work on Miss Abernathy's house today?"

"Yeah, I'm going just as soon as I get dressed. It hasn't really dried out yet, but at least it stopped raining."

A puzzled expression crossed Camille's face. "Why?"

"Because I'm going with you."

Camille's faced melted to shock and then she smiled broadly before ducking out of sight.

They took Ben's work truck that morning instead of Camille's car. When they reached Miss Abernathy's house, David and Tommy were already working. Camille noted that somebody had finished the roof decking and Tommy and David were working on siding. When Ben lumbered out of the truck with Camille, both of them stopped and stared. Ben was a stern man and they were both a little nervous until they noticed Camille's broad smile.

David walked over and shook Ben's hand. "Hello, Mr. Magelby. What brings you here?"

Ben examined David's project and nodded in approval. He could tell it was good work even from a distance. "David," Ben almost laughed at the concern written on his face, "this is a great thing. I'm here to help."

Tommy and Camille continued with the siding while David took Ben into his tent and showed him the extensive plans for the house. Ben studied David's plans carefully, but when they walked through the house together, Ben looked around worriedly until a grim expression crossed his face. David read his mind.

"What's wrong?"

Ben scratched his head. "Where's the plumbing? Usually the plumbing is roughed in before the floor decking gets completed."

Ben's concerned revelation crashed down on David. He countenance fell as he answered sheepishly. "I haven't hired a plumber yet. I thought we could add the plumbing the same time as the electrical, just before we sheetrock."

Ben's brow furrowed with worry. He hated to ask the next question. "What about the sewer line---you know, the pipe that goes to the septic tanks."

"When they leveled the trailer house they left a sewer stub up on the pad. They covered it with a plastic garbage bag. It comes up about right here under the house." David walked over and tapped his foot on the floor at a certain spot.

Ben Magelby breathed out a sigh of relief. Then another concern crossed his mind. "What about the septic tanks and lateral lines? David, do you know where they are?"

David swallowed hard. "What's a lateral line?"

Ben bit his lip. He wasn't really a religious man, but he thought a prayer in his heart, *Please, God, don't let the septics be under the house.* Then he smiled. "I tell you what. Let me take care of this. Everything is probably okay and if it isn't, well. . ." Ben paused for a second and rubbed his chin, ". . . it can be fixed."

Ben went back to his truck and retrieved a long black metal probe. *It should be okay. Caren's new house is only a few feet larger than her old one and they are almost in the same spot.* Then he thought again, *Never assume anything.* He crisscrossed the back yard for several minutes, poking and probing until he finally found what he was searching for. He stopped and shouted up to David. "It's okay, David, the septics are out here."

David smiled, although he didn't completely understand what Mr. Magelby was talking about. He was still feeling a little sick about the plumbing when Ben popped back into the house.

"I'll tell you what, David. If you'll cut an access hole in the floor for me, I'll plumb the house. I'll also get Brian Summers over here to do the electrical work. You'll have to pay him, but he's a pretty straight up guy. Maybe he'll give Miss Abernathy a break."

David nodded and Ben could see the worry drain out of his face. "Just tell me where you want the access hole and I'll make it, Mr. Magelby."

Ben picked out the guest bedroom closet. "PUT it in there, David. Make it twenty-four inches by thirty-six inches and save the board you cut out so that you can make a little door out of it later."

Ben Magelby hated working in crawl spaces, but at least this was new construction. There wouldn't be as much dust, nor as many critters as his buildings spawned. He pulled the tape measure from his belt and took several measurements within the house. Jotting down his dimensions, he waved to Camille and headed out to his truck. On his way to the hardware store, he called Brian Summers.

"Hello, this is Summer's Electric," said a young female voice.

"Yeah, is Brian there?"

"No, Brian's out on a job right now. May I give him a message?"

"Tell him that Ben Magelby called and tell him to give me a call back."

"Phone number?"

Ben gave his cell phone number and hung up. Thirty minutes later he was at the hardware store. It took him about an hour to gather all of the copper and plastic pipe he thought he would need and then he had one of the boys working there help him load it into his truck. Ben tilted his head when he saw the load. It was a good thing it was a small house.

On the way back to the house, his cell phone rang. "Ben Magelby," he answered automatically.

"Ben, this is Brian Summers. What electrical nightmare have you created for me this time?"

Ben heard the mirth in Brian's voice and he couldn't blame him. Ben wasn't much of an electrician. Oh he could fix little problems, but every once in awhile he would end up in such a pickle that he had to call Brian. Brian scolded him every time and told him to call before he messed things up, but Ben would never do that and Brian knew it. No matter what the problem, Ben would try to fix it himself before calling in help, so if Ben was calling him, the problem was probably pretty bad.

"Brian," Ben practically shouted. "Did you see in the paper where the kids are building a house for Caren Abernathy?"

"I didn't read it," Brian answered truthfully, "but I heard about it."

Ben continued. "I want you to wire it for us and . . . I want you to do it at cost."

The other side of the phone went silent and Ben guessed the problem. Brian was a good electrician and a pretty good guy, but he liked to collect for his services.

After a long pause, Brian finally responded. "Well, I don't know, Ben, we're pretty busy this summer."

That made Ben mad. Brian bought a new truck every year and he had purchased a new five-bedroom home three years ago. Rumor was that it was already paid for.

Ben snapped back. "I tell you what, Brian. You wire the house for cost and any profit you think you need to make, well . . . you can just send that bill to me."

The phone was silent again and Ben could tell he hit a nerve. Finally he heard Brian mumble back. "Ben, you are the slyest old . . ." Brian's voice trailed off for a second and then he finished his thought. "You know I would never do that!"

Ben smiled. There was a heart in there after all. "Come on, Brian, it's a small house, everybody's donating something, you need to ante up."

Ben heard Brian sigh on the other end of the line. "Okay. I'll send some of my trainees over. And don't worry, I will personally check their work."

Ben almost chuckled out loud. You could just hear Brian squeak when he talked. He was such a tightwad. But Ben wasn't finished. "One more thing, Brian. Do you have a trencher?"

Brian responded worriedly. "Yeah, I have one. Why, does this place have a buried power feed?"

"No," Ben answered, "but I'm doing the plumbing and I need to get the water line trenched in. Do you think your boys could do that for me?"

"I guess so," Brian's voice was flat. "What else do you want me to do, milk your cows?"

Ben could tell that he had reached the end of Brian's good will. "No, I can take care of that." And then Ben thought for a few seconds before hanging up. "Brian?"

"Yeah, Ben," came the flat voice back to him.

"Thanks."

They said their goodbyes and hung up. The only thing that was left was the furnace and heating equipment, *But,* Ben thought calculatingly, *that can wait awhile.*

When he returned to Miss Abernathy's house, David had the decking cut out of the floor and was hand sawing the joist he had crossed. Ben took over and finished that job and then he worked two more hours roughing in the plumbing and connecting the sewer. He was finishing up the kitchen when his cell phone rang. It was Sarah.

"Ben, one of the tractors won't start and Matt says that one side of the milking machinery is acting up. You probably need to come home." Ben sighed. They were small jobs, but they were urgent. He would have to take care of them now.

He dumped the rest of the pipe off his truck and sped home. On the way, he made a few more phone calls trying to drum up more contributions for David's project. Ben knew he was calling in a lot of favors that people didn't owe him, but he figured it was for a good cause.

On Thursday, Camille and Tommy arrived together. Tommy's van had broken down and he had to call Camille on her cell phone. Once they arrived, they started by setting the windows that had been delivered a day earlier. At a quarter to eleven, a beat-up noisy Ford Bronco pulled into the driveway and a scruffy-looking man exited. Camille and Tommy kept on working while David went over to greet him.

"Hello," David said, sticking out his hand. "Can I help you?" The scruffy man gazed past him to the house and then back at David. Finally he spoke.

"Who's in charge here?"

David had never really thought of himself as in charge. He answered timidly, "I guess I am."

The scruffy man studied David and quickly sized him up. "Aren't you a little young?"

David decided to get back to the point. "So what exactly did you want?"

The stranger drew a sharp breath. "I'm looking for work. I've been in construction all my life and I heard you were building a house. I thought you might need some help."

David studied the man. He wasn't as old as he had first thought and he was in good shape, although the beard and mustache made him appear older than he was. The wrinkles around his eyes didn't help either.

"Well," David responded slowly, "there's plenty of work here, but none of us are getting paid. This is sort of a charity project for our teacher who lost her home."

The scruffy man leaned back against his jeep and sighed. "I guess I knew that. I read that article in the paper last Sunday and thought maybe you could use a little paid help."

"I am paying a few professionals, but the rest of the budget is very tight. By the way, I never did get your name."

"Bill Robertson," he answered as if David would know it. He paused for a second before continuing. "I uh . . . just got out of prison in March. I had to do one year for drunken driving. I haven't been able to find a job since and it's been pretty rough. I've been living with some friends in their apartment, sleeping on the floor, but I would really like to find a job and get my life started again."

David didn't know what to say. He hated to see people suffer, no matter what the circumstances. He changed the subject. "What kind of construction do you do?"

"Roofing, but I can do anything. I was a foreman before I got in trouble. I helped build the Ponderosa Apartments and I worked on the Carr's grocery store as well."

David had an idea. "Well, you're here and we need the help. How about donating a day's work with us and we'll buy you lunch."

Bill scratched his head. "I don't know. I really need to make some money."

"It's just one day."

"Ah, you're right," Bill surrendered. "It'll do me good to be busy for awhile."

Bill followed David to the house where David introduced him to Tommy and Camille. Then David set him to work measuring up the roof and ordering the roofing materials.

When David was alone, Camille grabbed him and dragged him into a corner of the house. She had a harsh expression on her face. "Who is that guy?" she demanded.

"I don't know," said David. "He said he was having a hard time finding a job. I told him that we weren't paying anything, but we could sure use his help. He decided to stay for the day."

Camille glared at David. "You don't know anything about him. He could even be a criminal or something. He's probably here to steal all our stuff."

David glanced around. There were a few hammers, saws, nails, boards, piping, and other construction materials but nothing really worth stealing. He was about to point that out to Camille when Tommy interrupted.

"Hey, what's with the secret conversation we're having here? How come I wasn't invited?"

David piped up. "Camille is worried about Bill. She thinks he might be a criminal and that he's just here to steal our stuff." David didn't have the heart to mention the fact that Bill actually was an ex-convict.

Tommy shook his head at Camille and smiled. "I don't think you need to worry too much about that, Camille. If Bill is a thief, he isn't a very good one. Look at that Bronco he's driving."

That made David laugh, but Camille just gave Tommy one of those "very funny" glares. That did, however, settle the argument. It was two against one. Bill could work out the day.

Bill worked beside David most of the day and at lunch they all had a few laughs as Bill told them story after story about construction mistakes and pranks he had seen. Even Camille laughed when he told them the story about the guy who was asleep in the port-o-potty when they picked it up. Bill showed up every day after that, except Mondays, when he said he was searching for work.

As it turned out, Bill was only the beginning. On Monday the next week, two young guys from Summer's Electric appeared. They didn't know quite what to make of David's detailed drawings until he explained his own particular symbols for electrical sockets, switches and fixtures. Once they got the hang of it, they started drilling, hammering and jumping all over the house like monkeys. David was worried when they started drilling holes through all his studs until Camille noticed him staring at them. She tossed a piece of insulation board at him and when she had his attention, she gave him the eye. "Chill out."

On Tuesday Ben Magelby showed up again and climbed back under the house. He was only there for three hours before his phone rang and he had to go home and take care of another emergency. He told David before he left that the plumbing and electrical were roughed in, but they needed the heating system roughed in before closing up the walls. Then Ben winked at David. "I have a surprise for you."

"What?"

"I think it will be here this afternoon."

Four hours later, David was starting to run out of things to do when a truck rolled up from the hardware store. A big guy with coveralls rolled out and walked over to the project. "Is there a Mr. Samuelson here?"

Tommy and Camille both snickered at the thought of David being addressed as Mr. Samuelson.

"That's me." David came out to meet him.

"I have a fireplace for you. Just sign here." The deliveryman handed David a clipboard and David signed for it. Then David, Bill, Tommy and Camille carried the fireplace into the living room and set it down.

"This is great!" David exclaimed. His original plans hadn't included a fireplace because of the cost.

Upon examining the carton closer, Bill whistled. "This is a circulating fireplace and a pretty pricey model. How much did it cost?"

"I think it must be free." David commented slowly and then he stared at Camille. "Your dad promised me a surprise and I'm sure this is it. Every time he does anything he tells me exactly how much it's going to cost. He never mentioned anything about the fireplace, so I'm guessing he talked somebody into donating it."

Camille clucked in acknowledgement. "He's been on the phone all week twisting people's arms. I wonder what else will show up?"

David sat down on the floor in front of the fireplace. "Now I have to figure out how to incorporate it into the house." Camille and Tommy just rolled their eyes.

* * *

By nine o'clock that Sunday evening, Ben Magelby was in a bad mood. He tried not to work as much on Sundays, but he had wrestled all day with an obstinate little pump and it had been a huge waste of time. He would have to buy a new one. It wasn't the cost that upset him. It was the fact that he wasted an entire day working on it and that he would have to order the special part. It would probably take a week to get another.

Ben was just getting ready for bed when his cell phone rang. He debated whether to answer it but couldn't resist the temptation. If it was a problem, it would be better to nip it in the bud rather than wait until the whole forest was on fire.

Expecting the worst, he barked gruffly into the phone. "Ben Magelby speaking."

The phone was almost silent. Ben could just barely hear the soft murmur of a television playing in the background, so he knew someone was there. Realizing how gruff his original response had been, he started again and answered more civilly. "Hello, this is Ben Magelby, can I help you?"

"B . . . Ben," the voice stammered uncertainly. "This is Mary Faber. I'm sorry it's so late. I hope I didn't wake you."

Ben glanced up as Sarah entered the room. He noticed her mouthing the word "problem?" and shook his head "no."

Ben adjusted his voice. "No, we hadn't quite made it to bed yet." Then, worrying that he had been too brusque, he apologized. "I'm sorry if I startled you, Mary. It's been a long day. Did you want to speak with Sarah?"

"No . . . uh . . . well," Mary continued, "I was wondering if my girl scouts could come and help with Caren Abernathy's house. We've been searching for a service project all month."

Ben frowned, regretting his earlier demeanor. "That would be great, Mary. When were you thinking of coming?"

"We would like to come on Thursday morning around ten if that's okay. We'll stay until two and have lunch there." Then Mary added quickly, "We'll bring our own lunch so you don't have to worry about feeding us."

"Mary, you don't have to make a reservation. Just show up and ask David how you can help. He'll find something for you to do."

Mary answered uncertainly. "Are you sure, Ben? There are a lot of us. Sometimes it's a little confusing."

"How many?" Ben asked, truly curious now.

"Well . . . there are twenty-four girls and four leaders in the troop. Most of them are Brownies, we have twelve this year, but there are also seven Daisies and a few older girls. Would that be too many?"

Ben paused as the image of two-dozen little girls fluttering around Caren Abernathy's house filled his mind. He hadn't really been thinking about the conversation until that moment and then, it all came into focus. Initially, he had started the ball rolling, but so many others, like Mary, had just come out of the woodwork and asked if they could help. Ben's mind shifted as face after face, name after name, paraded through his memory. He could see all of them now, working on Caren's house, donating time and energy and smiling, they were all smiling. The process only took a few seconds, but it was a powerful vision. Ben's throat knotted as a wave of emotion washed over him.

Sarah Magelby saw Ben eye's mist before he turned to face the wall. She knew he was embarrassed and didn't want her to see him. She also knew that he had had a hard day and that things were a little tough on the farm right now. Fear touched her heart. This had to be something terrible. In twenty-six years of marriage, she had never seen Ben so emotional. She walked across the room to see if she could eavesdrop on the rest of the conversation.

Ben cleared his throat a couple of times. It was a long pause. Finally he sniffed and answered in a strained voice. "No, that's fine Mary. I'll try to give David a heads up so that he'll be ready for you." They finished their conversation and Ben hung up the phone. He never turned around. Instead, he stood there frozen, one foot from the wall, just staring at it.

Sarah couldn't stand it. She had never seen him so upset before. "What is it Ben? What's wrong?"

Ben hesitated for some time before his shoulders sagged and he turned and faced her. When she saw him, she was truly alarmed. There were tears streaming down his weathered face. She could tell that he was self-conscious and when he looked into her eyes, she started crying too. Finally he took a deep breath and got control of himself.

Sarah couldn't stand it. She re-iterated her inquiry. "What is it?"

Ben shook his head as he answered slowly, his voice laced with emotion. "The Brownies are coming."

Confusion rang in Sarah's mind. *The Brownies are coming? What kind of a problem is that? What Brownies?* Panic struck her and her thoughts swirled wildly. *Maybe it's the bank, maybe we're behind on the mortgage---or worse, maybe it's the IRS.* Sarah shook her head in confusion and fixed Ben with a stare. "What in the world are you talking about, Ben?"

Ben took off the rest of his outer clothes and climbed in bed. Sarah hadn't moved. She was still staring at him. He took another deep breath and sighed. He had to finish this.

"Sarah," he started, "when I went to help Camille and David with Miss Abernathy's house, I called a few people to see if they would help out. I didn't think much about it at the time, but those people rallied to the cause and more. Since that first week, people have been calling me all the time. I get two, maybe three calls a week." Ben took another long breath.

"Jim Petersen from the hardware store donated a fireplace. Riley carpets donated all the carpet and the labor. They said that it was new home carpet removals from people who had changed their minds, but it was beautiful, high-quality carpet. Sergeant Miner from the state troopers offered to donate the labor for sheet rocking, and the fire chief, Stan Monson, volunteered his crew to do the roofing. All the grade school and high school teachers have called me."

Ben stopped speaking and Sarah could tell he was struggling with his emotions. Finally he continued. "And now the Brownies are coming. Mary Faber asked if her troop of Girl Scouts could come and help." Ben paused for a long time, consolidating his thoughts. "They have rallied to the cause, Sarah. These are the best people a man could ever know. I will never speak ill of anyone in this valley again."

Sarah couldn't believe her ears, her mouth hung open in disbelief. "You're crying over that?"

Ben nodded.

Sarah gazed dumbfounded at the husband she thought she knew. "Is this the same man who can work forty-eight hours straight without a sigh of complaint, the man I saw lift a cow out of the mud single-handedly, the man who worked half a day with his arm broken because he was too busy to see a doctor, the guy who never cries? Now . . . now you're crying because . . . the Girl Scouts are coming to work on Caren Abernathy's house?" Sarah was practically shouting, her face a mask of incredulity. "I can't believe it."

Ben just shook his head in defeat. "I can't believe it either. I guess I'm getting old."

Sarah shook her head too, but she wasn't crying. She was smiling from ear to ear. She took off her outer clothes and climbed into bed. Then she scooted over next to Ben, rolled to face him and put her arm across his chest. She chuckled softly as she whispered in his ear, "You're not just getting older, Ben . . . you're getting *better*."

A DEBT REPAID

Chapter 19

C aren Abernathy found herself sitting in a rather uncomfortable chair next to a rather ordinary looking office. The sign on the door read, "Phillip Barrington – Professor." The office assistant had offered her coffee at least three times and Caren could tell it made her nervous to have an older woman sitting in a chair where students usually sat. Caren had waited for almost an hour. In hindsight, she should have called ahead, but she didn't realize that Phil was even here until she recognized his picture hanging in the hallway. It was then that she realized what she needed to do and it began with waiting for Phil.

Phil had been one of her first students when she started her career in Anchorage. Although it was years ago, she remembered him well because he was such a bright and energetic boy; she knew he would go far in life. Caren thought for a while about those times. She was so young and so convinced she could change the world back then. Over the years she had come to understand that she could only make a little difference, but that knowledge was as liberating as it was discouraging.

Caren's reverie was broken by a man in blue slacks, white shirt and tie standing beside her. He stooped over slightly and spoke, "May I help you?" It was Phil.

He was in his early forties and handsome, even though he was a little heavy and his blond hair was beginning to thin. He had the same knowing smile on his face that had graced it thirty years earlier. Caren examined him carefully. She could still see the energy in his bright eyes.

"Phillip, is that you? It's been so very long."

Phil Barrington froze. He furrowed his forehead and studied his visitor more closely. "I'm sorry Miss . . ." he said, then paused, hoping she would fill in the blank.

Caren stood. "Phillip, I guess I shouldn't expect you to remember me, but I still remember you. You were always such an energetic young man. I can see you've done very well."

That voice, Phillip thought. *I remember that voice.*

"It's me, Phillip. Caren Abernathy. I was your fourth grade teacher."

A smile of recognition flowed onto Phil's face. "Miss Abernathy," he took her hand. "It has been so long, what, over thirty years now. I can't believe you're still in Alaska. Are you still teaching?"

Caren nodded. "Believe it or not, I have been teaching in the Mat Valley for over twenty-five years."

Phillip took a step back and examined at her from head to toe. "Oh, how you made us all work that year. You were one of the toughest teachers I ever had. I don't think I'll ever forget the fourth grade." Phillip's expression melted to curiosity. "So what brings you here to Fairbanks? Surely not just to see an old pupil."

She smiled. "Not just any pupil, one of my star pupils. But you're right, I didn't come here just to see you. I came here for a very special reason, actually for a very special person and . . ." Caren gazed into Phil's eyes, ". . . I need some help."

He nodded thoughtfully. "It must be something big to get you all the way up here." Opening his door he gestured for her to go in. "Come inside and tell me. Let's see what we can do."

Caren glanced around the crowded office. The desk was clean, but there were books and papers stacked in the back of the room. She noted that in front of the desk were two wooden chairs and behind the desk, a brown leather office chair. She sat down in one of the wooden chairs in front of the desk. Phil closed the door and sat down in the office chair. He spun around to face her and then he clasped his hands together and interwove his fingers. Caren smiled at the expression on his face. He was really curious.

"Well," Caren began, "six years ago I met this young man in my homeroom class . . ."

* * *

When Ben Magelby came in for breakfast, Sarah was waiting for him. She was dressed in her jeans, a t-shirt, and cowboy boots. Ben noticed, which was rare, and scowled at her. "Why are you dressed like that?"

"Because," Sarah concentrated on the pancake she was flipping, "I'm going to work with you today."

"Hey, that's great," Ben smiled. "I could really use a little extra help today. I finally decided to fix that southern fence and add a gate down there. With your help, I'll be done by ten and I won't have to take Matt off the milkers."

Sarah took a platter of pancakes to the table. "Oh, we're not going to work on the farm today. We're going to help Camille."

"What?" Ben's eyes flew open, "You want to work on Miss Abernathy's place? You don't need me for that," Ben protested, "just take Camille over and talk to David. He'll put you right to work." Ben smiled at the thought of David bossing Sarah around. David had enough trouble telling Camille what to do.

But Sarah wasn't finished. "Ben, we're going to Miss Abernathy's house and you're going with us."

"But they don't have the flooring in or the walls finished. I can't do the finish plumbing until they get the walls in and the floors done."

"Well, I'm sure you can find something useful to do. Besides, don't you remember what day it is?"

That statement was one of the most feared and ominous in Ben's life. The truth be known, Ben hardly every remembered what day it was. His thought plummeted into a tailspin. *It's not her birthday. It's not our anniversary. It's not a holiday. No, as a matter of fact, I don't remember what day it is.*

Sarah read his mind. She arched her eyebrows in mock alarm. "Today is the day that the 'Brownies are coming.'"

Ben groaned. Sarah had been teasing him about that for days. He furrowed his brow and thought sullenly. *A guy makes one little slip out of character and he has to hear about it forever.*

Camille bounded down to the table. She noted her father's frown and didn't say anything. She could tell her parents were having a "discussion."

But Ben wasn't about to give up. It was a rare sunny day in Alaska and that fence was crying for him to come and fix it. "Well, Sarah, then they certainly don't need me with all that help around."

"Wrong," Sarah practically shouted at him, "David will really need our help today; he won't have any idea what to do with two dozen Girl Scouts."

Ben hissed. He could see that she had made up her mind, probably days ago, and he wasn't going to get out of this. Still, he couldn't surrender without a fight. "Well, whatever help he needs, I'm sure that you can manage it without me."

Sarah frowned. "When was the last time you took me on a date?"

It had been years. They had tried to go on a date once a month when they were first married, but when the children came and he took over the farm, the both lacked the time and energy. Slowly the tradition had died and they hadn't been on a date or a vacation together in almost ten years. Ben realized he'd lost. He wasn't very good with personal relationships, but he understood enough to know that if you were going to lose a fight, it was better to lose it quickly before any real damage was done.

Ben peered down at his pancakes and nodded. "Okay. Just let me have a word with Matt before I leave. We've had a few problems with the mixers and I want him to keep an eye on them." Then he murmured to himself, "I guess I'll fix the fence tomorrow."

Halfway to Miss Abernathy's house, Sarah told Ben to pull into the shopping center. Ben queried her, "I thought we were going to help David."

"We are," Sarah answered with a little smile. "Can you make some room in the back of the truck? I'm sure David won't be able to keep those little girls busy all day, so Camille and I are going to buy a few flats of flowers. When they run out of things to do, we'll have them plant flowers."

Ben nodded. "That's a good idea." He said it more to himself than Sarah. "It'll keep 'em out of the way."

Ben piled his tools and equipment toward the front of the truck and made room for the flowers. He chuckled to himself as he worked. *Of all the things this truck has carried: broken toilets, dead carcasses, newborn calves, cattle feed, even manure . . .* He couldn't remember a single time it had ever carried flowers.

Ben, Sarah and Camille arrived at Miss Abernathy's house by half past ten that morning and there were already several people there. Most were donating their time, but some were professionals whom David would have to pay. David and Tommy were inside setting doors. Ben went straight in and found them. "Good morning, boys."

Both Tommy and David were a little startled to see Ben. David finally spoke. "Good morning, Mr. Magelby. Are you here to help or just look around?" David thought for a minute and then added, "We're not quite ready for the final plumbing."

Ben shook his head. "That's okay, David. Mrs. Magelby wanted me to be here today because the Girl Scouts are coming. It's uh . . . kind of a joke between us, but if you have something you'd like me to do, let me know and I'll get started." Then Ben added a final punctuation. "I hate just standing around."

Ben almost laughed as David's face brightened. "Well, since we had a little extra money, we decided to add a rear deck to the house."

Ben couldn't help but notice Tommy rolling his eyes.

"Anyway," David continued, "we poured the footings last week and if you could get started framing the deck, it would be a great help."

Ben had to ask the next question even though he knew from experience that it was like throwing a bone to a rabid dog. "Do you have a plan for the deck?"

David smiled and nodded his head. "Oh yeah."

"Don't tell me," Ben read David's thoughts, "there's a drawing in your book in the tent."

David didn't speak, but nodded and then headed for the door. When Tommy realized that he was going to get a break he spoke up. "Mr. Magelby, did Camille come with you?"

"She's here, Tommy. She's out helping her mother with the flowers."

At eleven o'clock, a large van pulled up with three mini vans behind it. Once the caravan came to a stop, the doors opened and the sound of laughter and dozens of tiny voices exploded from the vehicles. They ranged in age from six to eleven, but the bulk of them were seven or eight. They wore a cacophony of colors to match the noise they were making. Tommy, who always wore black, gray, or an occasional pair of blue jeans, later swore that he almost went blind from color exhaustion.

Both David and Tommy stared up just in time to see a slightly harried mother emerge from the first van with a little three-year-old girl in tow. She weaved through the crowd of girls that had accumulated on the sidewalk in front of the house. As she walked, she gave instructions and answered questions. David noticed Miss Abernathy emerge from her camper and give two of the older girls a hug.

Tommy gave David a disgusted look. "You know what? I'll just help Bill with the kitchen cabinets. You obviously need to take care of the circus out there."

David nodded in agreement as the front door creaked open and Mary Faber stepped in. "Hello, I'm Mary Faber. Do you know where Mr. Samuelson is?"

Tommy snickered loudly every time he heard that title, but David just ignored him. "I'm David Samuelson." David stuck out his hand and shook Mary's. "Mr. Magelby told me you were coming today."

"Yes," Mary continued, "thank you for letting us come. I'm sorry we're so late. It takes a while to get these girls moving in the morning. How can we help?"

David glanced over Mary's shoulder to the crowd of girls behind her. "Well," David began, "if they don't mind picking up trash, I brought two boxes of garbage bags and there is a lot of construction debris around the house and blown into the woods. Could your girls could start with that?"

Mary spied the box of trash bags and nodded. "That would be perfect."

David handed the trash bags to Mary. "Once they get the bags filled they can leave them by the dumpster. It's quite tall so Tommy and I will throw the bags in later."

So the day began. From the picture window at the back of the house, David observed the two dozen girls meandering around the house and down into the woods. They must have been using some kind of buddy system because there were always two of them together when there weren't of eight or ten of them talking and chatting. It was a strange sight indeed. It reminded David of a flock of huge colorful birds as they bobbed up and down picking up trash, flittering across the lot and through the forest.

The sound of their voices filled the air. It didn't really look like they were doing that much work. It seemed like there was a lot more talking and playing, running and jumping, but by and by, the old shingles, blocks of wood, paper, insulation, plastic, piping and electrical wiring that cluttered the house and field, began to disappear.

A little after noon, they all disappeared from the back yard and converged on the front sidewalk to eat lunch together. When they were done, Sarah intercepted Mary and gave her a box of spoons. Then Mary lined the girls up while Camille handed out flowers. Sarah and Camille had been preparing several flowerbeds all morning and now the brightly colored bouquets of pansies, geraniums, petunias and begonias were finding their new homes.

Phil Barrington arrived that afternoon just as the sun reached its zenith. He had a hard time finding a place to park amidst all the workers and their equipment. When he stepped out of the car, a broad smile crossed his face. The sound of hammers, saws, drills and voices filled the air. There were girls dressed in every color of the rainbow planting flowers in three different beds. He grabbed his camera and started taking pictures. There was so much commotion and activity that it was hard to focus on any single thing.

Instead of going to the building site, however, Phil headed to the tiny camper on the other side of the driveway. There he knocked on the door and when Miss Abernathy opened it, he smiled and greeted her. "Good afternoon, Miss Abernathy. It looks like the whole town's here today."

Caren smiled and stepped out of the camper. "Thank you for coming, Phil. Please call me Caren. I'm not your teacher anymore." Phil nodded and together they walked over to the building site. They went through the front door and wandered into the living room. David was there with Tommy shimming and hanging doors. Caren interrupted them.

"David, I want you to meet an old student of mine. This is Phil Barrington. He's a professor at the University of Alaska and he wanted to meet you."

David smiled and stuck out his hand. "Mr. Barrington, it's a pleasure to meet you. This is my friend Tommy Anasogak."

Tommy stuck out his hand and shook Phil's, but he didn't speak. He was amazed. With his balding head and paunchy stomach, Phil appeared to Tommy like he was at least fifty. It just seemed impossible that he was one of Miss Abernathy's students. Tommy screwed up his face and stared at Miss Abernathy. *How long has she been teaching?*

David spoke to Phil. "If you'd like to work, I'm sure Mr. Magelby could use some help with the deck."

A look of surprise crossed Phil's face and David suddenly realized that he wasn't really dressed for working. He was wearing a pair of pressed slacks, a dress shirt and loafers.

Miss Abernathy chuckled at David's assumption. "David, I told Phil about my house and he just wanted to stop by and see it for himself. I don't think he was planning to help out today. Would you mind just showing him around? Why don't you start with your plans?"

"Sure," David said and then he glanced at Tommy sheepishly. He had been in and out of the house all day directing people. He hadn't been much help getting the doors hung.

Tommy waved him off. "Go ahead, I'll just work by myself for awhile."

David led Mr. Barrington out of the house to the now-weathered tent where the book of plans lay on the card table. Phil leafed through the pages. It was an incredible piece of work. David explained each page and finished with the appendix showing the fireplace and back deck additions. Phil nodded in approval and took several pictures. Then David showed him the rest of house. It really wasn't that different from any other house Phil had seen, with one very special exception.

"So David, Caren tells me that lots of folks have helped with this house. Could you tell me anything about that?"

David smiled. "Every day somebody comes by to help. When we first started, it was just the three of us: Camille,

Tommy and me. Then Camille's track coach brought the track team over and that really got things started."

Phil remembered the newspaper article Caren had shown him. It wasn't hard to figure out who Camille was.

"After that, Camille's dad called a lot of people. I think everybody in town must owe him a favor because a lot of stuff got donated. Mr. Magelby did the plumbing for free, he even donated the materials. The firemen came and shingled the roof and the state troopers did most of the sheetrock. The electricians did their work at cost and the flooring company volunteered to do the carpet and linoleum for free. Lots of Miss Abernathy's fellow teachers from school pitched in to help with things like taping and bedding, texturing, siding, trim and so on.

"The hardware store donated a fireplace and we got the roofing material at cost thanks to the firemen. Today the Magelbys donated those flowers for the Girl Scouts to plant. Every week we get something from someone."

Phil was truly impressed. It was a remarkable story and the results were even more remarkable. Then an idea came to him. He reasoned that it would be a travesty, really, to come this far, hear this story, and not make some kind of contribution. "Actually, David, if we're done with the tour, I have a few extra minutes. Is there anything I could do to help out?"

David's face melted to surprise as he examined Phil's clothes again. "Well, uh, I guess you could help Mr. Magelby on the back porch." Then David tilted his head and added quickly, "But you might get a little dirty."

Phil Barrington put his arm across David's shoulders and squeezed. "That's alright, David. It's good for college professors to get a little dirty once in awhile." Phil walked out the back door and studied the partially built deck. It occurred to him that building Caren's deck might actually help him with his own deck, a project that he had been judiciously avoiding for almost five years now.

Phil was lost in thought when a deep voice called up to him. "Can I help you?"

Phil noticed a tall, muscular man in his early fifties. He was about six feet two with a wiry body that appeared to have been worked too hard for too long. His gray and dark brown hair was cut short, but there was plenty of it. He wore overalls and cowboy boots that were covered in dried mud. He was carrying a greenish-looking board in each hand. Phil met his gaze. He was intrigued. The thing that was most striking about the stranger was his weathered face and sharp eyes.

Phil's mind raced for a minute. "Are you Mr. Magelby?"

Ben sized him up before answering. "I am."

Phil stuck out his hand. "Phil Barrington. David said that you could use some help."

Ben studied Phil and the clothes he was wearing. He leaned the two boards against the house and wiped his hand on his coveralls before shaking. "Ben Magelby. Glad to meet you. So, exactly how did David rope you into working here today?"

Phil smiled. "Actually, I'm a friend of Caren's. She asked me to come look at David's project and I just got caught up in the spirit of things."

"Are you a teacher?"

"Sort of, I'm a professor at the University of Alaska. Miss Abernathy was my teacher in grade school."

Ben laughed at that. "Yours and everybody else's in this valley. How long has she been teaching?"

Phil squinted. "It must be over thirty years now."

"Well, if you're here to help, grab one of those boards and help me make some cuts. I'll run the saw if you can measure and hold."

Phil grabbed one of the boards and walked over to the saw. The two men worked together for over an hour. Phil enjoyed working with his hands and Ben provided interesting company. At half past three, they stopped and took a break as the Girl Scouts said goodbye, boarded their caravan, and drove off. Miss Abernathy was surprised to see that Phil was still there and covered in sawdust. Phil read her expression and held up his hands, "David told me that Ben needed a little help. What else could I do?" He said it innocently, but it only earned him a confused glare.

About an hour and a half later, Ben's cell phone rang. He spoke for a while and then hung up. He tapped Phil on the shoulder, "Something's come up at the farm. I'll have to take my truck and head home. It's too bad we couldn't finish. We just need a few more boards on top and then I could trim them off. We still have to do the stairs and the rail, but that can wait for another day."

Phil nodded while admiring the deck. "Actually, I think I have the hang of it. If you can leave a few of your tools, I'll finish the top."

"That would be great. Camille can bring my tools home. I'm pretty sure Sarah will want to go with me."

Phil watched Ben gather up his tools when another idea struck him. He gave Ben an earnest look and voiced his question. "Ben, what do *you* think of David?"

Ben smiled and started to answer jokingly, "I wish . . ." He stopped mid sentence. The little joke he was planning to answer with suddenly didn't seem so funny. He wished Camille would marry David. That had been in the back of his mind since the first day he'd worked with the boy. What stopped him from saying it was the realization that he really hoped that might be the case. He had never met a harder working, more sincere and honest young man than David. But Ben knew, from living with the strong-willed women in his household, that if Camille ever heard or even thought that Ben wanted it . . . it would never happen. Ben didn't want to jinx his subtle hope, so he thought better of it and changed his answer. ". . . I wish David were *my* son."

The statement came out more emotional than Ben had intended. He noted the powerful impact that his words had on his new friend. Phil nodded in deep thought and responded thoughtfully. "I think I understand."

Ben shook Phil's hand and thanked him for his help. After that, Phil worked alone for another thirty minutes, completing the top of the deck. He then gathered Ben's tools and arranged them in Tommy's van under Camille's direction. By the end of his contribution, Phil's pants were dirty, his shoes muddy and he was covered in sawdust. He rounded up Camille, Tommy and David and took one last picture. Then Camille insisted on taking a picture of David and Phil together. Phil climbed into his car and rested for a moment. He was tired and he was sure that his muscles would be complaining by morning. But all in all, it had been a good day, a very good day.

* * *

On Monday of the next week, Tommy was outside building the stairs in front of the house while Camille and David worked inside on caulking and paint preparation. There were only two steps from the sidewalk to the front deck, but it was a frustrating task for Tommy since he had cut the boards wrong twice already. He was glad that it was one of those rare days where only he, David and Camille were working instead of the whole town being out there to witness his disastrous carpentry.

Just when he thought he had it, Bill's motley Bronco pulled into the driveway. It was about three in the afternoon. Tommy's first impression was that Bill was a little late getting started. Then he remembered it was Monday and Bill was usually out job hunting on Mondays. Tommy waited to make a sarcastic remark, but Bill never excited the truck. Instead, a young man dressed in new jeans and a dress shirt stepped out. His face was clean-shaven and his hair was only a few inches long. He was almost handsome.

Tommy stared at the anomaly for almost a minute before recognizing Bill, or more precisely, the new Bill. Tommy hopped up on the front porch, opened the front door, and shouted. "Camille! David! Get out here right away. You gotta see this."

Camille and David materialized seconds later. When Bill reached the front porch, Tommy faked astonishment. "Bill, what happened? You look like you've been mauled by the Boy Scouts."

Bill smiled in excitement, "I got a job!"

"Please tell me you're not a school teacher." Tommy pleaded. "I've been surrounded by teachers all summer. It's like I never got a vacation."

"No, no, I applied for a job at the hardware store in town. When they asked me about experience I told them about working on this place, among other things, and the guy just stopped me and asked one question. Did I know Ben Magelby?" Bill glanced at Camille. "I told him that I knew his daughter a lot better. So then he went into his office and made a phone call. It was weird because I could see him talking through the little window in his office and he had this stern expression on his face. I guess he talked to your dad, Camille. When he finished, he was all smiles. He shook my hand and told me that I had the job."

Camille immediately picked up on that. "So David and Tommy, have you learned anything here? Being nice to Camille is a career-enhancing experience."

Tommy rolled his eyes, but David asked Bill a different question. "Did you tell them about being in jail?"

"I wrote it on the application and he read it. I'm sure he knows."

David smiled and stuck out his hand. "Congratulations, Bill. The only problem is that we probably won't see you around here much anymore."

"I can still work Saturdays. But you really don't have that much left to do and the way the town keeps showing up, you'll probably be done in a week."

Tommy couldn't help it. There was still something missing from Bill's story. "So what happened to your hair?"

Bill rubbed his chin. "Oh this? Jim Petersen, the guy who hired me, asked if I would shave my beard since I would be dealing with the public. I went down and got a shave and a haircut before I came out here."

David sighed even though he was still smiling. "Well, we'll miss you. Your carpentry skills have been a life saver."

Tommy didn't say anything. He glanced at the pile of scrap lumber he had made trying to cut the front steps and thought darkly to himself, *Man, ain't that the truth.*

* * *

The next two weeks went by at record pace for Camille. They were mostly filled with painting and caulking, scraping and cleaning. On Monday of the following week, David declared that they were going to try to have everything done by Friday. That made for a blistering pace. The flooring people laid the linoleum and carpet in just two days. Camille set cabinet doors and knobs, while the electricians bounced all over the house placing fixtures, plugs and switches. It was exciting to watch the last pieces come together and by Thursday, it seemed David might be right.

When Friday arrived, Ben woke Camille up early. "Camille, we need to get over to Miss Abernathy's place so that I can be home by the afternoon." Camille rolled over and stared at her clock. It was only a quarter past six. Her dad had obviously been up for over an hour, but it was so early that her face felt puffy.

Still in a fog, she pulled on her clothes and headed down the steps. She didn't bother to take a shower because her dad wouldn't want to wait. Camille dozed in the truck on the way to Miss Abernathy's house. It was seven o'clock when they arrived. She was astonished to see that David wasn't there yet. It was the first time she had ever been there when David wasn't.

Ben climbed out of the truck, went around to the back and dropped the tailgate. The bed was full of boxes: two sinks, a toilet, and a bunch of fixtures. Ben yelled at Camille to come and help him haul them into the house.

* * *

When David woke up that morning he was surprised to smell bacon cooking. He rolled over at his usual time, half past six, and found John up making breakfast. David slipped off his pull-down bed and wandered into the kitchen. He peered suspiciously at John. "I thought you didn't like bacon?"

John smiled. "Good morning." Then he responded. "No I don't much care for bacon or ham, but I know you like it, so it's my treat."

"What's the special occasion?"

John gazed squarely at David. "Didn't you tell me that you were going to finish your project today?"

David nodded. "I think so."

"Then we are celebrating." John turned the bacon in the pan. "Besides, I am going with you today."

David couldn't believe his ears. John had only asked a random question or two about David's work and he had never volunteered to help. The unspoken understanding was that it was David's project and John didn't want to interfere. David screwed up his face.

John sensed David's incredulity. "David, I am very proud of you and what you have accomplished this summer. But to be perfectly honest, I am really quite curious to see it. So if you don't mind, I would like to join you today."

"No problem." David smiled a little, remembering one of John's little lectures. "What was it you used to tell me? Oh yeah, many hands make light work."

* * *

Tommy woke up to a loud banging on his door. "Tommy! Tommy, are you in there? Come on, it's time to get up and get going."

Tommy sat up disoriented and scratched his head. Was that his mother? Why did she care when he got up? Tommy dug under his bed until he found his clock: 8:47 A.M.. *Ow! It's so late!* Then he remembered, he had been up playing a video game until one o'clock in the morning. Tommy shook his head in disgust as he bounded out of bed, unlocked his door, and poked his head out. "Why are you knocking on my door? I thought you had to go to work today?"

Amethyst Anasogak smiled at her son. "I'm taking the day off so that I can come with you. I spoke with Sarah Magelby in the restaurant Tuesday and she said you were going to finish the house today. I've wanted to do something for Miss Abernathy all summer. I need to visit with her today, if I'm ever going to make a contribution."

"Oh," Tommy responded staring suspiciously at his mother. She was all dressed and ready to go and she had that motherly expression on her face. It was unsettling. Tommy slowly closed the door while his mind raced. He wrinkled his face up and gazed into the mirror. *My mother is coming to work with me today.* Then a terrible thought crossed his mind. Tommy began throwing his clothes on. No time for a shower. As he combed his hair he pleaded to thin air. *Please, please, please, don't let Camille be there when I get there. If she sees my mother dragging me along, I'll never hear the end of it.*

Tommy and his mother arrived at Miss Abernathy's house at half past nine. Tommy was surprised to see John there scraping paint and stickers from the windows. When he searched for Camille's car, he was more than relieved to find it missing. A tiny satisfied smile crossed his lips. *One good thing about Camille, that girl loves to sleep in.*

Tommy took a couple of seconds to gather his tools before stepping out of his mom's car. When he finally started towards the project, he noticed his mother standing in front of him, staring at the house. She must have heard him coming because she spoke softly as he stepped behind her. "Oh Tommy, it's beautiful. I can't believe you've done this." Suddenly, she whirled around and wrapped her arms around him. She held him tightly and buried her head into his neck. Tommy felt a hot tear slide down his collar. He stood stiffly like a wooden totem pole, not knowing exactly how to get his mom back to normal.

The moment lingered and Tommy was in turmoil. Just when he was about to tap her on the back, Camille stepped out on the front porch. Tommy gazed at her in horror as she glanced up and saw Tommy's mom hugging him. Camille's mouth dropped wide open. Tommy realized that Camille had no idea who she was. Tommy shook his head in agony and then rolled his eyes upward. *Why, God? Why does this have to happen to me?*

After staring for a few seconds, Camille's cheeks flushed. She dropped her head and walked to her dad's truck to get the propane torch that he'd asked for. She couldn't help stealing looks and halfway to the truck she shook her head in wonder. Tommy was still standing there like a wooden post and that woman was still hugging him. Camille couldn't imagine who it could be. She was a small woman with black wavy hair. She seemed a bit older . . . When Camille reached her dad's truck she recognized Mrs. Anasogak's car instead of Tommy's old van and suddenly . . . it hit her.

A wicked smile crossed Camille's lips. She looked up with pure glee in her eyes and watched Tommy suffer. *So, Tommy boy, the big tough guy, has to have a little morning hug from his mommy,* she thought menacingly. She stopped moving then and just stared at him with her mouth hanging wide open like she was stunned. She could see the pain. Tommy was in agony. Camille stared for almost a minute and then she couldn't resist. She made kissy faces at Tommy until she saw the horror in his eyes transform to murder.

After a few more seconds of humiliation, Tommy had had enough. He gently pushed his mom a little and spoke urgently. "Mom . . . Mom, we better get moving. What exactly did you want to do here today?" He was still scowling at Camille, who had perched herself on the bumper of her dad's truck and was staring at him with that evil smile on her face.

Mrs. Anasogak pried herself away from her son and wiped her eyes. "I'm sorry, Tommy. I don't mean to be so emotional. I just wanted to see if I could sew some curtains for Miss Abernathy. Do you know where she is?"

Finally, Tommy thought in relief, *I have a chance to get away from her.* "Miss Abernathy is probably over in that RV. That's where she's living until we complete her house." Tommy started toward the house, but before he could escape, his mother grabbed his hand and pulled him toward the RV.

Camille couldn't help it. When she saw Mrs. Anasogak snatch Tommy's hand like a toddler, a snicker escaped her lips. Mrs. Anasogak didn't hear it, but Tommy did. Camille watched the color rise in his cheeks as he reluctantly walked toward Miss Abernathy's camper with his mom.

Even with the extra help, the last day turned out to be a long one. Camille, who was the best painter of the bunch, helped her father with the final plumbing. David and Tommy attached rain gutters on the front and back of the house where the porches were. The electricians finished the rest of the fixtures while John cleaned windows and touched up a few paint spots inside.

Mrs. Anasogak went through the house with Miss Abernathy, measuring and discussing the curtains. They finally settled on something for the living room and the bedrooms. They decided that Caren would buy the material and Amethyst would make the curtains at her home. After measuring, Mrs. Anasogak retrieved her camera and took pictures of everybody.

At eleven o'clock that morning, a shiny blue pickup with oversized wheels and a noisy muffler, screeched to a halt in the middle of the driveway. The truck then did a series of forward and backward motions until it came to rest with the tailgate facing the house. The driver of the truck gave the horn three long blasts until everybody was gathered around staring at the obnoxious vehicle. Finally, a tall, brownish red-haired young man stepped out of the vehicle with a mischievous grin on his face. It was Marty Kenley!

Camille instantly narrowed her eyes and started toward him, but her father caught her arm. Ben glowered at Camille until she saw his face and then he warned her with his eyes. Marty marched around to the back of his truck while he addressed the crowd.

"I have an announcement." He glanced at Caren. "Since Miss Abernathy is the person who actually coined the phrase 'an ounce of prevention is worth a pound of cure,' I have decided to donate a little something to the cause here today." Everyone was confused. They looked at each other for a moment and then back at Marty. Marty loved it. He took hold of the tailgate lever on the truck and shouted, "Behold." He dropped the tailgate of his truck with a swift motion and everyone noticed the bright red concrete car stop lying there. David thought it looked a lot like the car stops from the local grocery store, but he didn't say anything.

Marty just stood there glowing in the attention until Miss Abernathy spoke. "Martin Kenley, are you actually giving that to me?"

Marty beamed. "Yep."

"Well, then you better unload it." Miss Abernathy snapped.

The smile faded a little from Marty's face. "Ah, it's a little heavy." Marty surveyed the crowd, his face pleading for help.

Nobody moved for a few seconds and then David nudged Tommy. "Come on. Just think of it as a peace offering."

Tommy scowled at David. He was not in the best mood. Camille had been throwing little barbs at him all day and the rain gutters, which seemed like a really easy thing to do, were more than difficult. He had gooey sealant all over his hands along with four or five little cuts. Grumbling to himself, he stepped forward with David and grappled the car stop. Marty stood there like he was going to watch them unload it until David gave him a severe look.

Marty trudged around to help when Tommy stopped him. "Marty, where have you been all summer?" Tommy smiled and stuck out his hand. Marty automatically shook it. It wasn't until he released Tommy's hand that he realized that it was covered in some kind of sticky glue. Marty peered down at his hand in disgust and Tommy smiled for the first time all day.

The three of them dragged the car stop out of the truck and lowered it gently to the ground. By the time they finished positioning it, everyone except Miss Abernathy had gone back to work. She tapped Marty's shoulder. "Martin, did you come here to work or just deliver your gift?"

"Neither," Marty smiled back. "I came here to harass all your workers and eat free food."

Miss Abernathy sighed. "You always were an honest child, if not obnoxious. How is it that you still haven't put that big brain of yours to work doing great things in this world?"

Marty stared at her blankly. "Why would I want to do that?"

Caren shook her head. "Okay." She peered over at David. "Give him something to do and keep an eye on him." Then she placed her hand on Marty's shoulder. "Thank you for the car stop, Martin. I know you probably meant it as a joke, but at my age, it's comforting to know where the end of your driveway is."

David rubbed his chin while studying the car stop. "Marty, since you brought this car stop for Miss Abernathy, why don't you start by securing it in place with a couple of pieces of rebar? There are a few pieces over there and you can ask Ben Magelby for a hack saw and a hammer." Marty didn't speak. His eyes lifted from David and searched the area until he found the prey he was searching for. Then, he smiled. David could tell he hadn't been lying when he told Miss Abernathy that he was only there to harass her workers. David turned around to go, but an old memory tugged at him. He turned back slowly to face Marty. "Marty," David implored, "don't torture Camille. Who knows? Someday she may be someone very special to you."

David said it more out of reflex than anything he had thought out, but from the look on Marty's face, he could tell he hit a nerve. Marty's mouth came open and he glared at David in horror, "What are you talking about?" His face melted to complete disgust. "You know what your problem is Samuelson? You're weird, just plain weird."

David sighed and sauntered off to continue the rain gutters. The fireworks all started a few minutes later.

Martin Davis Kenley was in an especially good mood that day. It had been a long, boring summer and for the first time since school let out, he was in a position to really irritate Camille. He watched like a hawk through the windows until he saw her approach the front door. Then he put his foot in front of it and when she turned the knob and attempted to push it open, it didn't budge. After a couple of seconds, Camille put her shoulder into it. She really gave it a shove just as Marty removed his foot and stepped out of the way. Camille came flying into the house and nearly fell down. Luckily, she caught herself before she hit the wall.

"Good morning, Camille," Marty smiled at her. "I see you're still practicing ballet."

Camille's face blushed with color and she turned to Marty, squinted, and gritted her teeth. "Don't mess with me today, Marty. We've worked hard all summer and we have a lot to do if we're going to finish today. For once in your life, just try to do something helpful."

Marty looked at Camille like he'd been wounded. "Of course, that's why I'm here." But things just went from bad to worse.

When Ben finished setting the toilets, he told Camille that he didn't need her help anymore. Camille went back to touching up the outside paint where spots of white trim paint had spattered on the yellow house paint. She painted for about an hour and after taking a potty break, she picked up her brush only to discover that the handle was coated in Tommy's rain gutter sealant. It was so sticky that she had to use paint thinner to get the brush out of her hand.

She searched around for Marty, but he was nowhere in sight. Camille was livid. She knew he was out there watching and laughing at her somewhere. At lunch, Miss Abernathy brought pizza in and everybody ate together. When Camille came back from getting a second piece, she took a gulp of her drink and found a rock in the bottom of it. Once again, Marty was, of course, nowhere to be seen.

Marty's reign of terror continued until half past two. Camille had just finished touching up the yellow walls and was rinsing out her brush in the rear water facet. She was concentrating on cleaning the brush when suddenly, she saw something out of the corner of her eye. It was coming through the air and headed directly for her. She jerked her head back out of reflex, but she was too late. The errant projectile hit her right between the eyes and bounced off her head. It rose a foot into the air before doing several summersaults and settling to the ground. Staring in disbelief, it only took Camille several seconds to recognize what it was. When she did, she was furious. It was a moose turd!

Marty was having one of the best days of his life. It was hard not to laugh out loud when Camille's face twisted into anger as she discovered that she was, once again, the butt of one of his jokes. He found the dried moose pellet near the edge of the woods. It was a long shot, but Marty estimated that if he heaved it on a high arc . . . It was poetry in motion.

He watched the feathery missile sail unmolested toward its victim. He knew he should find a hiding spot, but the suspense was too great. He just stood there and stared in disbelief and then, the gods of luck smiled on him. As it sailed through the air, he could tell it was right on target, but when Camille jerked her head back and her golden braids dangled behind; when his little missile connected perfectly with Camille's face and bounced, oh yes, *bounced* off her forehead and landed on the ground, Marty couldn't resist. Camille looked up and the expression of pure astonishment on her face, well, it was too much. Instead of sneaking behind a tree, Marty just started laughing uncontrollably.

Camille heard him. He was off to the side of the house by the forest watching at her. No, he wasn't just watching her, he was laughing. A single thought went through her mind before she bolted. *I'm gonna kill him.*

Marty saw Camille drop the paintbrush and run towards him. He was laughing too hard to think straight. He reacted out of reflex. He turned into the woods and started running himself. It was difficult to run because he was laughing so hard, but he quickly found a game trail and followed it. He could hear Camille gaining on him, but that only confirmed how mad she was and made it all the funnier. He crested the hill and ran down into the gully below. There, he was forced to stop. A small stream blocked his escape route. It was only about eight feet across, maybe two feet deep at the most, but Marty didn't want to get wet. The forest was too dense to run in any other direction. He knew he was trapped, but he also knew that he was eight inches taller than Camille and sixty pounds heavier. So he stopped, gathered his wits, turned his back to the stream, and waited for Camille . . . Camille in all her glorious fury.

When Camille reached the bottom of the gully, Marty was waiting for her. That caught her by surprise. She thought she would eventually take him from behind and tackle him. She rambled to a halt four feet in front of him. He was still laughing. Camille was so angry that her face was red and her fists were clenched at her sides.

"So, Camille," Marty started in an inquisitive tone, "have you seen any of those flying moose that people have been talking about?"

Marty's smug confidence jolted Camille back to reality. She was outmatched. When they were in grade school together she had trounced him several times, but now, he was taller and heavier than her. Even though she was in great shape, Marty was a big, strong boy. A sickening thought seized her. *What am I going to do?*

Camille squeezed her fists a bit tighter. *Just one lucky punch,* she wished. *Maybe, if I can land it on his big pointy nose, it would break and he could have a crooked nose to go with his crooked smile.* Camille edged in a little closer when suddenly, another thought occurred to her---something better.

Camille lunged at him with all her might. She took two steps and brought her hands up under Marty's shoulders. What happened next is something that Marty could not have conceived of. The three years Camille spent exercising with the track team and lifting weights paid off. She caught Marty under the shoulders and lifted him off the ground. With his feet in the air and his balance tipped against him, he was helpless. Then Camille did the unthinkable. She simply extended those powerful arms and sent Marty sailing through the air. Everything went into slow motion. It was a strange dream.

Marty was flying, flying backwards, and then his back hit something. He expected a hard landing on the ground, but instead, he sank into something soft. Then he remembered. It was the stream behind him. It was water . . . cold water. As the sub-forty-degree water surrounded him and immersed him, his expression went from surprise to shock. It was so cold that it took his breath away and when it closed over his face, he thought he was going to die.

Camille just barely stopped before falling into the creek on top of him. She watched his haughty expression fade to surprise and then terror as the cold water snatched his breath away. A vicious smile crossed her lips. She waited for just a second until Marty bobbed back to the surface and gasped for air.

"Perfect!" Camille clapped her hands, turned around, and ran back to the house.

Tommy saw Camille chase Marty into the woods and when she emerged with that giant grin on her face, he was worried. As she approached the house he shouted to her. "Did you kill him?"

Camille glanced over, still smiling broadly. "I wish."

David also saw Camille disappear into the woods. He waited and watched and when Marty didn't show up after about three minutes, he looked up at Tommy with a concerned expression on his face. "Maybe we should go find him. Who knows what Camille did to him?"

Tommy nodded in agreement, but just as they headed toward the forest, Marty emerged. He had an angry scowl on his face and he was wringing moisture out of his shirt. David stared at him in confusion, but Tommy snickered. "What happened to you?"

Marty glared at him in disgust and anger. "I was attacked by a big, ugly . . . no a big, *fat,* ugly bear. I had to dive into the stream to avoid being killed by its bad breath." He noticed Camille staring at him and barked out the last sentence so that she was sure to hear it. Camille just smiled sweetly.

Tommy continued. "You know what your problem is, Marty? You're a little slow. Everybody stopped picking on Camille in the sixth grade after she tackled Bobby Hanson and pushed his face in the mud. Look at her, man. She's in better shape than all of us."

For the first time in memory, Marty didn't say anything. He lowered his eyes and glowered at Camille, but she was in a state of bliss. Marty realized that Camille had gotten the best of him. He was mad. He sneered at her and then he squished up to his truck and climbed in. Everybody stopped working and watched as the wounded Martin Kenley peeled out on the gravel and zipped down the driveway.

It was a rare day that somebody bettered Marty. He had bested almost everyone in his brilliant comedic life. Camille's little maneuver had been a sucker punch. He would get even, no matter what. Everybody had seen him and he couldn't end the feud by giving Camille the upper hand. So as he raced down the road in his soggy condition, he thought and thought about how to even the score. But it wasn't working this time. No, there were far more disastrous thoughts echoing in his head that day.

Marty never had much respect for women. They were weak and pathetic. It was always, help with this or do that. They were irritating that way. They cried and got emotional about stuff. They were soft whenever you touched them. They were dumb, too. Always worried about stupid things that didn't really matter, like how so and so felt and what somebody thought about them. *Morons!*

But Camille was different. That body of hers was molten steel. *Geez,* he thought in amazement, *even her teeth and her hair are strong.* She had picked him up and thrown him into that stream! He couldn't help thinking about her. He couldn't help thinking about her body. What kind of weapon was she hiding under those tight jeans and t-shirt? Marty shook his head, *This is madness.* But in his heart he knew what he really wanted to do. He wanted to go back and pick a fight with

Camille. He wanted to wrestle her to the ground and then he wanted to hold her . . . he just wanted to hold her.

* * *

The day reached its climax with Marty's unusual baptism and dramatic departure. Ben Magelby finished late in the afternoon. He left with his pickup and took Mrs. Anasogak. She left her car for Tommy and Camille. By half past six, Tommy and Camille were also finished. Once they loaded her Ben's tools in Tommy's car, they wandered inside to find David.

"It's done, David." Camille shook her head. "I can't believe we're finished."

Tommy looked around and sighed, "Yeah, I thought this day would never come." Then Tommy furrowed his brow in concentration. "You know what?" Tommy paused to gaze at his two best friends. "This was the best summer ever." Both David and Camille nodded in agreement. No one spoke.

Camille finally broke the silence. "We'll we better head out. I'm supposed to go out with my mom and dad tonight and Tommy has to drive me home."

Camille and Tommy departed and David started gathering his tools into the suburban until he remembered that he needed to caulk the kitchen counter with some colored caulking that Ben had brought. David labored over the task. He lost track of time until dusk settled in. When he finally finished, he noticed John patiently waiting and watching him. He had completely forgotten about John.

John spoke first. "It's getting dark, David. I guess it's time to go."

"John," David grimaced. "I'm sorry. I forgot you were here."

"I figured as much." John smiled. "It's alright, David, I have been enjoying this beautiful home and I have enjoyed watching the care and determination with which you work."

David blushed a little. "How long have you been watching?"

"Oh, about an hour. Besides, after seeing your work here, I have decided that there are a few things I would like fixed at my house."

That made David smile. "I guess I owe you that since I haven't touched the garden this year."

David walked over and dropped his caulking gun into the open toolbox. "I'm finished. We can go now." Then a thought crossed his mind. "John, could you take my tools out to the car? I just have one little thing to take care of."

John nodded. "Of course, I'll just wait in the car."

David wandered through the house one last time. He stepped from room to room, checking for unfinished items and turning out the lights. As he closed the front door, he was overwhelmed by his feelings. He thought he would be relieved when he arrived at this point, but strangely, he felt empty.

He walked over to his little tent and went inside. There, he picked up the blue notebook, opened it, and slipped his house key in the pocket on the inside of the notebook. Two other keys were already in there. Then he walked over to Miss Abernathy's camper and knocked on the door.

Caren Abernathy had watched the day come and go with mixed feelings. She was actually excited to see her new home completed, but she was also saddened to see the work come to an end. In the past, she had been a little lonely in the summers, but this summer had been like a whirlwind. The knock on her trailer door came at half past seven. When she opened it, David stood there holding his blue notebook.

Caren ushered him inside. "What is it, David?"

David placed the blue binder in her hands. "It's done, Miss Abernathy. Your house is finished."

Caren had thought about this moment all summer. It was hard to believe it was here. She had thought of a thousand witty things to say, but none of them seemed appropriate now. Slowly, she took the notebook from David and set it on the tiny table in the RV. She felt her head spin and sat down at the table herself.

David leaned over her and opened the notebook. "The rest of the keys are here in the pocket. Tomorrow, I'll borrow a flatbed trailer from Camille's place. We'll get your stuff from the storage shed and help you move in." David could see that Miss Abernathy was moved. He didn't want this to be emotional. He decided to just slip away nonchalantly. "John's waiting for me in the car. I'd better get going."

Before he could turn around, Miss Abernathy grabbed his hand. "David," her voice was weak and wavered a little. She cleared her throat and began again. "David, sit down." David bit his lip and then he relented. He sat across the tiny table from her. Though there were tears in Miss Abernathy's eyes, she quickly composed herself.

"There is no way I can ever repay you for what you've done here, but I do have something for you." She reached over and picked up an envelope that was resting against the window above the small table. She stared at it pensively as she handed it to David. "Read this."

It was a thick envelope and he noticed it was from the University of Alaska, Fairbanks. It was already open. He reached in, took out the multi-page document, and opened it to the cover page.

Mr. David Samuelson,

It is our privilege and honor to inform you that you have been selected as a recipient of the Samuel Adam's Scholarship for outstanding public service and leadership . . .

David read the rest of the first page, folded the letter, and gazed up at Miss Abernathy. He didn't speak.

Miss Abernathy read the question in his eyes. "I made a special trip to visit an old student of mine. Do you remember

Phil Barrington? He came by to meet you one day and you put him to work!" Miss Abernathy smiled a little. "Anyway, after meeting you and seeing your work, he championed your cause to the scholarship committee. Normally, this scholarship is awarded to only one person a year. The candidates must submit in January and the winner is announced in March, but in your case, and by a unanimous vote, they awarded two public service scholarships this year, one in March and one last week." She paused to let David absorb her words. "David," she smiled, "you're going to college."

David gazed again at the letter in his hand and then back at Miss Abernathy. He didn't know what to say. It was a gift he never expected.

Miss Abernathy continued. "The scholarship is for full tuition and housing. Phil has offered to take you on as an assistant in order to help you with the extra money you'll need for books and other personal items."

David couldn't believe Miss Abernathy's revelation. He had thought about college, but he had never discussed it with anyone. In the back of his mind, he had decided to find a job this winter and try to make enough money to go to school the next fall. He hadn't connected all the dots yet and he wasn't sure if his plan would work, but now, here it was, already complete and lying in his hands in the form of a single letter. David was dumbfounded. He muttered meekly, "But I never even applied."

Caren smiled at that. "Oh, you applied alright. You applied when you excelled in every task you were ever given. You applied when you graduated third in your high school class with a 3.99 GPA. You applied when you built that beautiful home for me and when you brought this community together in a way that no one ever has." Caren peered into David's eyes. "Frankly speaking, David, you will be a great man one day. The University of Alaska will be lucky to count you as one of their alumni."

David was silent for several seconds. He finally found his voice and spoke in humility. "Thank you, Miss Abernathy."

There wasn't much emotion with David, there never was, but Caren knew enough about him to realize that he meant it as few people did. She put her hand on his wrist. "I'll miss you, David. You've been like a son to me." Caren took a deep breath. "Anyway, you have two more weeks before school starts, but Phil wanted you to call him as soon as you opened the letter. You need to notify them of your acceptance and start getting ready. Phil said that you should come early and get yourself oriented before starting. He said you could stay with him for a few days until your dorm is available. When you come to move my furniture tomorrow, we'll give him a call."

David was lost in thought when suddenly he remembered he wasn't alone. "I have to go, Miss Abernathy. John is waiting for me in the car."

"Go on then," Miss Abernathy said briskly, sitting up straight. "I'll see you tomorrow anyway."

David stood and gave Miss Abernathy one last bewildered look before disappearing through the door of the RV. He ran from the house to the suburban. John was sitting in the passenger seat, staring out the window as the Alaskan sun completed one of its long sunsets. When David climbed into the driver's seat he apologized. "I'm sorry I took so long." David set his letter on the dashboard and started to fish the keys out of his pocket.

John didn't change his view. "I have just been admiring your work. It's a beautiful home. I like the yellow color. There will always be a bit of sunshine here in this place."

David stopped fumbling and looked out the window. "Miss Abernathy picked out the color. Funny, she said the same thing. She wanted a bright color to remind her of the sun shining." David reached for the letter on the dashboard and handed it John. "She got me a scholarship to the University of Alaska. I guess I'm going to college."

A tiny smile touched John's lips and he nodded. "She loves you a great deal, David." Then he sat silent for a long time. Finally, he turned slowly and faced David with his penetrating eyes. "There are many who love you, David, in this world and . . . the next."

REFLECTIONS

Chapter 20

David stood in the living room of John's house and studied his surroundings. There was a fine layer of dust on everything, making it obvious that the house had not been occupied for some time. The past four years of his life had been very busy and this was the first time he had returned home since leaving for college. John had written him several letters, but they were all from foreign countries. Perusing the old cabin now, it seemed as if no one had ever lived there.

David gathered the last of his things and smiled, remembering one of John's lessons on cleanliness. He made his way out the door and loaded his belongings into the compact pickup that Phil Barrington had loaned him. He walked around the cabin and took one last look across the clearing. Even the garden plot was overrun with fireweeds. No one had lived there in years, maybe since the day he left. An empty sadness washed over him as he locked the door and made his way to Phil's pickup. He studied the lonely cabin for several minutes before sighing and fumbling in his pocket for the keys. *One last place to visit,* David started the truck and headed down the driveway.

Fifteen minutes later he was in front of a yellow and white house. It had changed little since the day Miss Abernathy moved in. There were only a few flowers now and the paint had weathered some, but for the most part, it still appeared as the day they finished it. David was relieved to see Miss Abernathy's jeep parked up against the car stop Marty had given her. He parked Phil's truck next to it and took a gift from the passenger seat. It was wrapped in shiny white paper with a large silver bow on top. It was a wedding gift.

David took his time walking from the truck to the house. The memories assailed him as he took in every detail and savored the memories of that summer. It had been the most difficult thing he had ever done, but it had been the best summer ever. Tommy had been right in that observation. David arrived at the porch and knocked on the door. There was no answer at first, but when he knocked again, he heard a voice muttering inside. David smiled. He would never forget that voice.

Seconds later, a tiny woman opened the door and gazed out at him in surprise. David had forgotten just how small Miss Abernathy was. She seemed even smaller and frailer than he remembered. Though they had written and called each other several times, this was the first time they had been together since she visited him at the University of Alaska three years earlier. Initially, he had planned to come back home during the summers, but Phil kept him so busy with construction projects around Fairbanks that he never found the time.

Miss Abernathy stared up worriedly into David's face. He could tell she didn't recognize him. "Miss Abernathy, it's me, David."

Her mouth dropped open. "David, I can't believe it. Why, you've grown some."

That was true. Since leaving for the university he had gained another six inches in height and almost a hundred pounds in weight. He was now six feet ten inches and weighed 280 pounds. According to the physical education department, less than seven percent of it was fat.

David smiled. "It's me, alright." His voice was deeper and more resonant than it had ever been.

Caren Abernathy opened the front door and waved him in. "Come in, come in . . . let me look at you." He came into the house and barely missed hitting his head on the doorframe. "What have you done to yourself? Those shoulders of yours hardly fit through my door."

David felt conspicuous under her scrutiny. He had changed a lot from the tall skinny boy that built the house Miss Abernathy called home. During his years in Fairbanks, his shoulders had grown wide and thick. The football and basketball coaches at the university also noticed, but he refused their invitations. David understood his limits and besides, he just didn't have the time. The Samuel Adams Scholarship was one of the best, but he still had to work to make ends meet.

Working construction during the summers put some of those muscles on him, but the real reason that David looked the way he did was because he had found the weight room at the university, his meditation space. It was during a weight training class that he discovered the secret. At the intensity points in his routine, the pain would become great enough to stabilize the shadows in his mind. Those powerful liberating moments gave him a rare clarity that allowed him to examine the world, his life, and his memories, without the crushing threat of the cauldron.

"I found the gym." David chuckled at her astonishment.

Miss Abernathy examined David from head to toe and front to back. She was hardly able to recognize the little boy who used to grace her house every week. He was a huge and powerful man now, but his face still held the kindness that she had come to love, and his eyes . . . his eyes still had that strange cloudiness.

David changed the subject. "By the way, have you seen John anywhere? I haven't seen him since the day I left for college, although he did write a few times."

"No, I haven't seen him since the day he worked on my house." Miss Abernathy shook her head. "Sit down, sit down, David." She pointed to the couch. Then her eyes narrowed as a stern expression crossed her face. "You've gotten so tall that it's hurting my neck to look up at you."

David sat on the couch and placed the present next to him. Miss Abernathy sat in a chair at the end of the coffee table.

"So," she continued, "who's the present for?"

David tapped the package. "This is for Camille. I went by the Magelby's house to drop it off, but I couldn't get anyone to answer the door. I'm sure Mr. Magelby was around there somewhere because his truck was in the driveway, but I didn't want to leave it on the porch. I was sort of hoping that you could deliver it for me."

Miss Abernathy shook her head. "You should stay for the wedding. The whole town will be there and they all remember you." Incredulity crossed her face. "Can you believe she's marrying Marty? I thought those two would kill each other in the sixth grade. I hear that Ben isn't too happy about it. I think Ben always wanted Camille to marry you."

David focused on the fireplace as memories of Camille washed over him. Finally he glanced back at Miss Abernathy. "I love Camille, you know. She and Tommy brightened up a lot of lonely days in my life, but . . . it wasn't meant to be."

"And Tommy," Miss Abernathy continued. "I haven't seen Tommy in a couple of years either."

"Tommy found a job in Hawaii working at a zoo with exotic animals. He sent me a crazy picture of a huge snake wrapped around him. He really looked happy. I think he finally found his niche in life."

"Yes, that makes sense."

David picked up the present and held it in his lap. "Anyway, I have a really early flight out of Fairbanks tomorrow, so I have to get back tonight, drop off Phil's truck, and get to my hotel room at the airport. I'm leaving Alaska, Miss Abernathy. I have a job back east." David frowned a little. "Can you believe it? I'm going to New York City."

"I heard about that. I spoke to Phil two weeks ago and he mentioned that you landed one of the top jobs at a real estate development group out of New York. Phil said they only hired four graduates across the entire nation and you were one of them."

David nodded. "I think they hired me because they needed somebody to keep them safe in the streets of New York."

Miss Abernathy narrowed her eyes. "I bet not. I bet you'll be one of the best in the business and you'll probably be rich and famous out there. My only regret is that you won't be here to build Alaska."

David straightened the bow on the present. "You always believed in me, Miss Abernathy," he smiled, admiring her tiny form in front of him, "my champion."

But Caren wasn't smiling. She had a very serious expression on her face as if she was seeing David for the last time. After a while, she tilted her head down so that David would not see her eyes, "You are very special to me, David."

David felt her grief. He hated to see her sad and attempted to cheer her up. "I tell you what, Miss Abernathy. If you'll take this present to Camille's wedding and give her my regards, I'll fly you out to New York when I get established. You can tell my boss how lucky he is to have me working for him and how great I'm going to be. I'll probably need the help by then."

"I doubt it. *He'll* probably be telling *me* how great you are, but you have a deal. I've never been past Seattle so going to New York sounds like a real adventure."

They talked for several more minutes before David stood to leave. Miss Abernathy gave him a lingering hug and promised to deliver Camille's present. Then he was out the door and off on the long drive back to Fairbanks. He couldn't help feeling pangs of loss and regret. He remembered the first time he had seen this valley from the windows of John's suburban. It had seemed so bleak and barren at that time, but now it was home to him. How he loved this valley, its people, and the memories that he held in his heart. As he turned north on the highway to Fairbanks, he took in the vista of snow-capped mountains that surrounded the valley.

Wherever life takes me, David mused, *I will always have the memory of these beautiful mountains and these beautiful people.* Then he smiled wryly to himself. *I will always be rich.*

MAMMON

Chapter 21

Nicole Mitchell sat behind her tall black desk and surveyed her tiny empire. It was a single fifteen by twenty-five foot room and it was filled with an assortment of chrome, glass, and black leather furniture. A large arrangement of flowers rested near the center of the glass table in front of the sofa. Everything had a place here and everything was in its place.

She was bored today. Most of the time she sat at her desk and read fashion or fitness magazines, but today nothing appealed to her. Unfortunately, she couldn't leave. If the company phone rang, she had to answer it. That was her job. Nicole was the receptionist for Downing & Burkover, a real estate investment company located in the heart of New York City.

Nicole had worked at the offices of Downing & Burkover for just over a year now. Her father, Colton Tyler Mitchell, landed her this job through his association with Greg Downing, the co-owner of the firm. Her father made his fortune building a variety of projects: highways, hospitals, office buildings, factories, you name it; C. T. Mitchell was a fixture in Texas. But when it came to investing that fortune, Colton Mitchell used only a few trusted associates. Several million dollars of his estate had gone to investments with the firm of Downing & Burkover, where those investments had quadrupled in value over the past ten years. Not all of her father's investments had done so well, but enough of them had that Nicole was rich and she would be taken care of her entire life.

Wealth may have been enough for most people, but it wasn't enough for Nicole. Wealth was only a means to the end that burned brightly at the center of her heart; she wanted to be famous and . . . admired. She had the raw ingredients to do it. Nicole was a Texas beauty. As a young girl people had noticed her and she basked in the light of their attention. Through junior high and high school, she had been in so many beauty pageants across the great state of Texas that they ran together as a blur in her mind. She had a list of titles to punctuate her efforts, but what Nicole really wanted was to be in film and be somebody.

With that goal in mind she came to New York City after graduating from a big high school in Houston. Here she attended four years of acting school and now she worked evenings in a Broadway show. She had an agent and was trying to find more acting work, but once she had graduated from the academy, her father insisted that she do more to support herself. He lined her up for an interview with Greg Downing and the rest was history.

It was a great job. The pay wasn't so good, but there were other advantages. First and foremost, there was the employee bonus pool. Last year her Christmas bonus was the same amount as her total income for the year. Secondly, she had a lot of freedom with her schedule. She could get away with leaving early sometimes and not coming in other times. It was a real advantage when she needed to be at an audition or a rehearsal, or when she just needed to get away and meet someone. She wasn't really sure what Greg Downing got out of the deal. If they had three visitors a day at the office it was a miracle; although, the phones rang incessantly when they were closing big deals.

Nicole was a tall, well-proportioned girl with striking features. She had a classic beauty like the old stars of black and white movies. More than one of her mentors had mentioned that she looked like Rita Hayworth. It was always a huge compliment when people compared her to someone famous. Just the thought of being famous could distract her for hours.

Nicole had long, wavy, dark blond hair with gold highlights that accented her blue eyes and perfect smile. Of course, like most beauty contestants, she had had a few artificial enhancements along the way. Nothing too drastic, most of Nicole was the real thing. The only flaw in her movie star image was her height. She was five feet eleven, which made her over six feet tall in a pair of high heels and kept her out of many parts. The majority of leading men weren't tall enough to project the perfect romantic image with her by their side. Whenever her agent told her that this was the reason she missed a part, she would always remember her father's consoling advice: "Oh well, my dear, they grow things big in Texas." Still it was a point of frustration for Nicole.

In the year since Nicole had joined Downing & Burkover, the partnership had changed a great deal. She wasn't aware of the history of that change, but slowly over the last ten years, the sheer number of investments the firm participated in had grown dramatically. Due to that expansion, Hank Burkover and Greg Downing had decided to augment the managerial staff.

Hank took on the task personally. Unfettered by what he labeled, "the chains of marriage," Hank loved to travel and this was one of his greatest contributions to the corporation as it grew. During several business trips that year, he interviewed graduating business students at more than two dozen colleges across the nation. He tracked down standout candidates at the smaller, lesser-known colleges and thereby avoided hiring battles with the big companies for candidates at Ivy League schools. He used his instincts to identify the winners, instead of letting the system do it for him. It was a lot like big game hunting and Hank loved to hunt.

Hank Burkover's recruiting spree resulted in Downing & Burkover's acquisition of four top graduates from business schools across the country. Nicole had met the two young men and the young woman who came in for interviews, but the fourth was from Alaska and no one but Hank had met him in person. The scuttle in the office was that Hank really went up there to scope out good hunting places and finding the fourth candidate was just an excuse.

Hank loved Alaska. He went there every year or two and always had a story to tell about the place. But it was too far away to have the graduate come in for an interview, so they did a videoconference and no one but Greg, Hank and Sam had ever seen the mystery candidate.

When Hank returned from his trip, he commented that he had hired three of the top business candidates in the nation and one grizzly bear. He said that the boy from Alaska was huge and that he was one of the sharpest young men he had ever interviewed. So the intrigue and interest levels were high at Downing & Burkover when David, the Grizzly Bear from Alaska, pushed the buzzer that summer morning and Nicole opened the electronic door latch to let him in.

The creature that entered the reception area that day surprised even Nicole. It was big. Hank hadn't really exaggerated that point. Nicole peered intently over the edge of her tall reception desk as his rack of shoulders cleared the door. He was as tall as the doorframe and his shoulders were almost as wide. He wore an old blue suit that was at least one size too small. Under it was a stodgy white shirt and a tie that reminded her of her grandfather. Nicole smiled and guessed that nobody told David the dress code was casual.

After taking his first step into the office, the mountain-sized stranger examined his surroundings until his eyes fell upon her. Then he approached the desk. He had brown hair, brown eyes, and strong features for a man, but his most striking feature was his white, almost translucent skin. Nicole grimaced. He was so pale the she wondered if he had a skin disease or was under treatment for cancer.

Nicole examined him until David's eyes were upon her. He was about to speak when suddenly, he froze. Instead of saying anything, he just stared at her. It was the most uncomfortable feeling that she had had in years. David's eyes weren't quite right. There was a strange distant haziness about them, even so, they seemed to cut right through her.

After several seconds of discomfort, Nicole took her headset off and stood up. "You . . . you must be David," she stammered. Even when she stood, David towered over her. What was worse, his expression didn't change. He just stared at her as if he was lost within his thoughts. Nicole was always conscientious about her appearance, but under David's relentless scrutiny, she felt absolutely naked. Instinctively, she glanced down and checked her outfit. It was perfect. She thought about checking her makeup too, but her compact was in her purse. Confused and off balance she swallowed hard and gathered her dignity. Finally, she gazed back into David's eyes and reached out her hand. "Hello, my name is Nicole. Mr. Burkover is expecting you."

With the mention of Hank's name, David seemed to snap back to reality. He closed his eyes and shook his head. "I'm sorry. Yes, I'm David Samuelson, the new employee."

He grasped her hand and shook it. She was amazed at how big his hands were and how strong and calloused they were. *If he just graduated from college,* she thought abstractly, *then they must have some strange classes in Alaska.* She extracted her hand and instructed David to have a seat on the couch. Then she called Hank's office and spoke to him quietly so that David wouldn't hear.

"Mr. Burkover, this is Nicole. Your grizzly bear just arrived."

Hank Burkover smiled with anticipation. "Thank you, Nicole. I'll be right there." Seconds later, he bounded down the hall and into the reception room.

Hank Burkover was a big man, but next to David, he seemed small. He shook David's hand before David could get out of his seat and then he patted him on the back as they left the room together.

Nicole watched them disappear down the hallway. She shook her head before replacing her headset. *It's going to be an interesting summer* . . . she thought to herself. Then a roguish smile touched her face . . . *very interesting.*

* * *

David had been in airplanes and airports for almost twenty hours straight before he arrived in New York. It didn't help that he didn't sleep well the night before he left Fairbanks and that the seats were so small on the planes that he felt like a sardine. He noted, longingly, that there were bigger seats in the front of the airplane, but on every flight, his seat was in the back.

He didn't arrive in New York until the morning of the next day. It was still early when he reached his hotel. There, the hotel receptionist explained that he would have to wait until noon before he could get into his room because the previous guests hadn't checked out. Hours later, when he was finally able to settle in, he took a quick shower, unpacked his clothes, and lay on the bed. That turned out to be a big mistake. He woke up at three the next morning, unable to go back to sleep. Not knowing what else to do, he watched TV for a while before deciding to just read his Bible. At six o'clock, he dressed and went down to breakfast. They had a buffet table set up and David made three passes before he was full. The restaurant was empty when he sat down, but by the time he finished, every seat was full.

David climbed the stairs after breakfast and finished dressing. He wore his best suit but after studying his image in the mirror, he bit his lip. He hadn't really noticed it before, but his suit certainly wasn't up to the standards of the other patrons in the restaurant. *Oh well*, he reasoned, *it will get me through the first day*. He brushed his teeth and knelt to say his morning prayers before heading down to find a taxi. By the time the cab made its way through intolerable traffic to the offices of Downing & Burkover, David was actually a few minutes late.

It took him another five minutes to locate the correct floor and office. When he pushed the door bell, he heard an electronic buzzing sound in response. It took him a few seconds to figure out it was the door latch. He pushed open the door and stepped into the office.

It was a beautiful office. Everything was new. There was a large black leather sofa with a matching black leather easy chair, a glass coffee table in front of the sofa, chrome end tables, and a large arrangement of fresh flowers on the table. There was a high desk on one side of the room and behind it was a young woman. David stepped toward the desk and peered over it. His heart stopped.

She was stunning! David stared in awe. They had girls in Alaska, of course, but he had never seen anyone like Nicole Mitchell. Her blond hair fell in flowing waves past her shoulders, caressing her lovely face. When she peeked up at him, her large, shining blue eyes, delicate nose and full red lips mesmerized him. David's mind went blank. He simply stood there staring at her with his mouth hanging open.

The young woman stood to greet him and David noticed how tall she was. Her slender, well-proportioned body was surprisingly athletic. She had perfect, smooth skin, a healthy tan, and a gleaming white smile. A strange thought seized him. *She must be a movie star.*

She spoke haltingly, "You . . . you must be David." He was still staring in awe when she reached out her hand. "Hello, my name is Nicole. Mr. Burkover is expecting you."

At the mention of Hank Burkover's name, David finally snapped back to reality. He shook her hand and apologized for gaping at her, Nicole directed him to sit down and seconds later, Hank came bounding in.

The rest of the day went like a whirlwind. Hank Burkover talked to him about the business and introduced him to several of his colleagues. He explained how the office worked and then turned him over to Sam Cardston. Sam had been with the partnership for about five years and was one of the real contributors. Sam explained the current deals he was working on and the ones that David would be helping with, then he settled David into his office with some documents to read.

Sam's secretary, Darlene, showed up at eleven o'clock. She knocked softly on David's half-open door before letting herself in. "Hello, you must be David. I'm Darlene Romero, Sam's assistant."

David stood as she entered the room and Darlene smiled. She had heard the rumors about how large David was, but when he stood up, even she was surprised. Darlene studied him in curiosity. He was well proportioned with his large shoulders and thick muscles.

She continued. "I'm making a list for office supplies and I wondered if there were any items you wanted."

David's face melted to a puzzled expression. "Well, I think I should be okay. I have a notebook and some pens. My old computer will get here next week, so I guess not."

Darlene narrowed her eyes at him, realizing he did not understand. "Ah . . ." she politely explained, ". . . the other new employees ordered a *new* computer, printer, paper, notebooks, envelopes, staplers, whole punches and business cards. Are you sure you don't need any of those items?"

David froze in concentration before stammering his question, "The . . . uh . . . company provides all that stuff?"

"Yeeees," she answered with a lilt, cocking her head. This was really starting to get entertaining. Then, noting David's embarrassment, a nasty little thought erupted in her mind. *What a bumpkin!* Darlene smiled at a hundred more mean little thoughts, before quickly shaking them off. She decided to just help out for once. "I tell you what, David, I'll get your office up and running if you just pick out a computer. The company has standardized on four different models, but since you'll be traveling a lot, I suggest you get the laptop with the docking station." She stepped up to his desk and opened one of the documents Sam had left him. She pointed to the laptop. "The IT company that takes care of us can get one of these on your desk in two days. Would that be okay?"

David smiled in appreciation. "Yes, that would be perfect."

"I'll take care of it." Darlene turned to head out the door, but before she took two steps, David called out her name. "Mrs. Romero."

Darlene stopped and glanced back at him. "Yes?"

"Thank you."

"You're welcome, David. But do me a favor."

"What?" David questioned earnestly.

"Call me Darlene. And call everybody else by their first names as well."

David's face took on a serious tone. He nodded in understanding. "Okay."

David finished reading almost everything Sam had given him by four o'clock. He was tired and ready to go home then, but since everybody in the office stayed past eight o'clock, he resigned himself to staying late just to conform. Nicole, however, left right at 5 P.M. and one of the other new hires, Richard Hemberly, told him that she was in a play on Broadway.

By seven o'clock David was beat. He stood and gathered his few belongings before heading for the door. When he was halfway to the reception area, Darlene stopped him in the hallway. "David, you also need to pick out a car. The company provides a car for every manager." She peered knowingly at him over her glasses. "I know you aren't that busy yet, so why don't you go tomorrow morning. Just bring me the invoice when you finish."

David couldn't believe it. John's ancient, rusting suburban was the only car he had ever come close to owning and it was more of a liability than an asset. There were weeks when he spent as many hours fixing it as he did driving it. The thought of getting a car of his own was exhilarating. David smiled. *It's like Christmas in June!*

David spent the next morning perusing a myriad of cars at five different dealerships before finally settling on a car that seemed practical, dependable and functional. He worked the salesman over for an hour before extracting the price he wanted. That afternoon he proudly presented the invoice to Darlene. "I got my car." Darlene glanced curiously up at him.

David continued, "I had to haggle with the salesman for almost an hour. Prices seem a bit high here in the city."

Darlene gave David a strange glare and examined the invoice carefully. She found the total at the bottom of the ledger, $9,788 for a used Dodge Caravan. That included taxes, title and license. Darlene couldn't help herself. She laughed out loud.

Darlene's little outburst caught David by surprise. He frowned in concern, "Is something wrong?"

Darlene shook her head, but the smile never left her face. "No, no, it's fine, David. I'll have to get Hank to approve this, but I'm sure it won't be a problem."

David turned slowly and trudged back to his office. Something was wrong. He was sure of it. Darlene wasn't being completely honest.

Darlene knocked on Hank's door and he shouted for her to come in. When Hank saw her face, he could tell something was up. "Darlene," he said dryly, "it's a rare day that I see you smile. What little bombshell are you holding?"

Darlene couldn't help laughing again as she laid the invoice on Hank's desk. "You'll love this."

Hank peered down and read the invoice. It was for a used Dodge Caravan, of all the strange things. Hank's face melted to concern. "Who bought this?"

"Your new farm boy from Alaska thought this would be a good company car." Darlene couldn't resist the temptation. She embellished the story a little. "He said that the passenger door is taped shut and the rear bumper has been stolen, but it's a real gem other than that."

Hank stared at the invoice for a long time while rubbing his chin. A smile suddenly crept across his face and he peered up at Darlene. "Well, I guess it's easier to get the boy out of the farm than to get the farm out of the boy." Then they both laughed. "But he can't drive that around. He'll be the butt of office jokes for years." Hank waved his hand in dismissal. "Take that thing back to the dealer and get him something reasonable."

"Me?" Darlene practically shouted. "Sam has me buried all week with the Pyron deal." Then she thought quickly. "What about Nicole?"

"Fine," Hank nodded, "send Nicole."

Nicole was reading the latest review on a new play when Darlene interrupted her. Nicole glanced up with a touch of anger in her eyes. She didn't say anything, but the expression on her face conveyed her annoyance. The few times that Darlene had come to her desk had resulted in Nicole running errands for her. Those errands had been humiliating to say the least. Usually it was special items for Hank or Greg, or ordering food for visitors and guests. This time Darlene was smiling though, so maybe it was worse.

Darlene waited until she had Nicole's full attention. "Hank needs you to run a little errand for him and I think you might get a kick out of this one."

Nicole sighed, laid down her magazine, and spoke flatly. "What is it?" She hoped her display of minor irritation might dissuade Darlene's enthusiasm, but the smile never left her face. Darlene dropped the keys and invoice on Nicole's counter. "Our farm boy from Alaska went out and bought a used Dodge Caravan for his new company car." Darlene waited a few seconds for the image to fill Nicole's brain. It did. Nicole scowled at the keys on her counter like they were diseased.

"Hank wants you to take the Caravan back to the dealership and select a more appropriate vehicle for David. You can take the rest of the day if you need it."

Nicole didn't really like being bossed around by Darlene, but this was too good to be true. She lifted the invoice, read it, and nodded, "No problem."

"Thanks," Darlene quipped. Happy with herself for escaping the task, she turned and headed back to her office. What happened next became the stuff of legend around Downing & Burkover for years.

Nicole left immediately and was gone all afternoon. The next morning, she drove to the office instead of taking the subway. When she arrived, she was wearing skin-tight black leather pants, a low-cut silver blouse, a black leather jacket and dark sunglasses. She parked in the visitor's spot and stepped out of a brand new gleaming black Dodge Viper. She made a special effort to linger in front of the Viper, hoping someone would notice. It was impossible not to.

Richard Hemberly noticed. He parked his car and was walking across the lobby when he caught a glimpse of Nicole adjusting her hair in the side mirror of the Viper. When she saw him, she waved nonchalantly and walked across the foyer to join him for the ride up the elevator. They chatted and when they finally reached the offices of Downing & Burkover, Richard fished out his ID card and opened the magnetic lock. He held the door for Nicole and then wandered off to the coffee room to speculate about her new acquisition.

Nicole reached the reception area, took off her coat, and sat in her swivel chair. She pulled her purse up and set it on her desk. Searching inside, she retrieved the envelope containing the invoice from the dealership. She grabbed the envelope and keys and headed to Darlene's office. Halfway there she met Michael and Richard coming back to their offices with coffee in hand. Richard smiled at her. "That's quite a ride you showed up in today. Is that yours?"

Nicole stopped momentarily and smiled at Richard. Richard wasn't too bad. He was a little too short for her taste, but he was smart, really smart. She had noticed him ogling her more than once, but he was discrete about it. She was tempted to tell him that the car was hers, but then she realized they would figure it out soon enough. She paused for a second trying to think of an answer that would make her sound important, but before she could get the words out, Michael jumped in.

"How about giving us a ride sometime?" Michael leered at her and spoke forcefully as if he expected her to agree. Nicole couldn't stand Michael. He was a dope and a bore. Every time she went to the break room, he made it a point to show up and chat with her. It was innocent enough, but the way he stared at her was indecent.

Nicole's demeanor soured and suddenly, a vicious little thought came to her. It was one of those perfect moments in life when the truth held more venom than any lie she could conceive. She stared directly at Michael and smiled sweetly. "Didn't you hear?" Nicole opened her eyes wide and tilted her head. "Hank told me to get that for David."

The result was amusing. Richard's face hardened for just a moment and then he snapped back to their pleasant conversation. Fortunately, the effect was far more devastating on Michael. The smile disappeared from his lips and his forehead furrowed in anger and jealousy.

Perfect! Nicole smiled inwardly as she turned and sped past them down the hallway. Savoring the moment, she walked into Darlene's office and dropped the keys on her desk. She smiled and spoke brightly. "Mission accomplished." Then she handed over the envelope containing the invoice. She didn't wait for a response. She turned immediately and headed back to the reception area.

Darlene was suspicious the instant she saw Nicole's smile. She opened the envelope and pulled out the paperwork. Then she gasped. Nicole had just spent $117,488.87 on a Dodge

Viper. She slumped in her chair. Her first impulse was to go down to the reception area and yell at Nicole, but she couldn't really do that. Nicole didn't actually work for her and she hadn't given her any guidelines, so this was her reward.

Darlene shook her head in defeat. She had no choice but to go and explain the disaster to Hank. Worried sick, she took the invoice and keys and headed to his office. This time she knocked softly. When she heard Hank invite her in, she entered and rolled her eyes. "You're not going to believe this." She slid the keys on his desk and laid the invoice in front of him.

Hank read the invoice in silence. His mind began spinning. *How could such a little problem turn into such a big one?* He knew this would send the office into a tailspin and reduce productivity for weeks. He frowned at the paper for almost a minute as his anger boiled; then suddenly, he laughed out loud. "Well," he peered up at Darlene, "we should have known better. If you can't send a boy to do a man's job then you shouldn't send a princess either."

Darlene wasn't smiling. Hank could tell that she was genuinely worried and he understood her predicament. He rubbed his forehead. Once again he was glad he had never married and doubly glad that Nicole was Colton Mitchell's daughter and not his.

"Will David even fit in a Viper?" Hank wondered out loud.

Darlene raised her hands in a show of surrender.

Hank read the invoice again and sighed. "You know what? I don't have time for this." He pierced Darlene with a stare. "Call the dealership and change this to a one year lease and drop the keys on David's desk." He gave Darlene a stern look. "Next year *you* are going to help David get his new car." Darlene nodded.

* * *

The days stretched into weeks at Downing & Burkover. David slid through the mentoring phase with only a few other minor disasters. He quickly came to a fundamental understanding of the business. Although everybody referred to it as D&B or the Partnership, it was actually a privately held corporation. It had been a partnership in the beginning, but Greg and Hank changed that long ago, in order to share ownership with their best and most valuable employees.

The company started in real estate leasing and management. It grew quickly in the beginning, due mostly to Hank and Greg's ability to find and close big deals. Some of the biggest were huge leasebacks in which they fabricated corporations to purchase power plants and lease them back to the utility companies. Those deals sustained the company for years until federal regulations changed to disfavor the arrangement. During that period they had taken on investors and through a careful and targeted set of REITs, they were able to establish the real foundation of D&B. The timing was good for the REITs. Most of them returned anywhere from 200 to 400 percent over the five years they were in existence.

Always impeccable with their timing, Greg and Hank sold several of those properties at peak value. These successes had two effects on Downing & Burkover. First, they generated a huge bubble of cash, which was now the object of the current investment search and second, they created an extremely loyal clientele who were constantly pressuring the partnership for more investment opportunities.

Both of these forces were in motion when Hank visited universities across the country and recruited what he called, "the best and brightest business graduates available." After bringing them on board, the middle men, like Sam, trained them while Hank and Greg gave them incentives in the form of a generous bonus program. Within six months, they were all pounding the streets of America to find investment opportunities that matched the recipe Greg and Hank had formulated for success.

By the beginning of his second summer, David had become an expert. He helped Sam Cardston with the Gedding Building in downtown Boston. It was a good deal. There had been better, but this would be a cash cow in two years and would perform well for years to come.

David grew to have great respect for Hank and Greg. Besides working hard, they were honest with their clients and generous with the staff. Of course, all this success was making them very rich men, but David sensed that wealth was not the object of their ambition.

In November of his third year, David found a little gold mine. It was an old telephone building with a nostalgic facade and it was in one of the best locations near Washington, D.C. It was being sold as part of a restructuring plan for the phone company that was suffering from extreme competition. David organized a package on the building that was very favorable to the partnership. He knew he could get it for a song because its current application was generating little revenue, but David had a better idea. If he could change the interior to commercial use, it would lease at much higher rates. He backed up his hunch with a hundred pages of research on lease and occupancy statistics from surrounding buildings.

It was a home run. In eight months the lobby and top floors were remodeled and with just half the building in service, it was already returning a profit. David received a hefty finder's bonus and, although he didn't spend much time thinking about it, the digits in his bank account would have made him one of the wealthiest men in the Mat Valley.

Thus was the situation at D&B when Nicole received the summons to bring coffee to Hank's office. Angela, Hank's usual secretary, was out on vacation. When she set down the tray, Hank handed her some papers to copy. She noted, with interest, that they were discussing bonuses. She purposely left the door ajar when she slipped out to make copies on Angela's machine. What she read on those documents intrigued her. David and Richard's bonuses were $400,000 each. When Nicole returned with the copies, she heard Hank mention David's name again. She couldn't resist. She stopped four feet from the door and listened.

"Okay, okay," Greg surrendered, "you were right about those new grads you brought in. Every one of them has made a contribution."

Hank smiled. He loved being right when he took a risk. It didn't always work out that way and he was a smart enough businessman to realize it, but when it did work, *Ah*, it was so sweet to hear the ever-conservative Greg Downing admit it. Still fishing for a few more compliments, Hank went on. "And David?"

"Uncanny insight. He's a natural."

Hank loved it. "He's just extremely intelligent."

Greg nodded for a moment but then disagreed. "No, it's more than that. Actually, Richard is probably the most intelligent of the bunch. He is so thorough and methodical about his approach, but David has something far rarer; David has vision."

Hank thought about Greg's observation and then nodded in agreement. "You're right."

Both Greg and Hank were silent for a few moments and then Greg voiced what was on both their minds. "It would be a serious problem to compete with either of them if they ever left the partnership."

Hank peered up at Greg. "Then it's time?"

"Yes, it's time. Let's give Michael and Amber 100,000 options each."

"And Richard?" Hank raised his eyebrows.

Greg gazed up at the ceiling. "What did we give Sam on his fifth anniversary?"

"Hmmm, 250,000."

Greg tilted his head and peered at Hank. "Then let's give Richard and David 250,000 each. I hope that's enough of a leash to keep them here."

Nicole sucked in her breath. According to the rumors, Sam's options were now worth over five million dollars. Nicole suddenly remembered what she was doing. She ambled forward and knocked on the partially open door. Hank waved her in. Nicole dropped the papers on Hank's desk and left without saying a word, but her mind was working overtime. She had always liked David in a way. He was polite and even friendly, although still a bit of a farm boy. He stared at her now and then, but she was used to that. What was weird about David was that he had never really parked himself at her desk and hit on her. Almost all the other new hires had given it a try. She didn't mind really---in fact when people stopped paying attention, it was far worse.

Maybe, Nicole thought, *maybe it's time to be a little extra friendly.* After all, hadn't her dad always said, "If you want to catch the really big fish, you have to use the right bait." Nicole hesitated. She had an on and off boyfriend, Brett, who was a fellow actor. He was really handsome and had a wry sense of humor, but that relationship wasn't really going anywhere. Nicole debated how to deal with the situation for a while and then she just shrugged her shoulders. *Oh well . . . I guess it's off again.*

Then another thought bludgeoned her and her smile disappeared. *Maybe the reason that David has never paid any attention to me is because he already has a girlfriend.* She'd never seen David with anyone and she'd never heard any such rumors, but there was some logic to the assumption. The thought slowed her for a few seconds until an image of David with another woman marched across her mind. By some inexplicable logic, it made David even more attractive. A wicked smile crossed Nicole's face. *Whatever,* she thought to herself, *there's only one way to find out.*

The next day Nicole sat at her desk spinning her plot. She needed an excuse; some reason to capture David's attention and interest. It took her almost an hour to figure something out, but finally a workable plan materialized. At eleven o'clock, she sauntered down the hallway and knocked on his door.

David was talking on the phone, so Nicole opened the door a little and waved at him to let him know she was there. David glanced up in surprise. He waved her in and motioned for her to have a seat while he finished his phone call. She sat in the chair in front of his desk and studied him for a minute. He was huge, even his hands were extra large. She knew, from her interactions with him, that he was intelligent, but he had just a little haziness in his eyes that made it seem like he wasn't quite all there. Luckily, he had gotten a little sun since he arrived. He no longer seemed sickly pale like the first time she saw him. Still, he needed a good tan. *Not a problem,* Nicole schemed, *it's a lot easier nowadays than it used to be.*

David finally completed his conversation and turned to face her. "Good morning, Nicole." He studied her for a few seconds and then tilted his head. "What brings you down here?"

She dove right in. "David, I uh . . . need a ride over to midtown to pick something up. Any chance you're going that way sometime today?"

David nodded. "Sure, I can take you right now if you're ready."

Actually that wasn't exactly what Nicole had in mind. She bit her lip and scrambled to mend her plan. "I, uh…I can't leave the desk right now. How about lunch? Can you take me around noon?"

David squinted and nodded slowly, "I think so."

Nicole flashed David one of her radiant smiles. She rarely used those around the office. "Thanks. Just come by my desk."

* * *

David wasn't quite sure what to make of Nicole's request. Parking was difficult in midtown during the day. It was much easier to catch a cab or take the subway. Still, Nicole had asked . . . At half past twelve, he finished up his last documents, grabbed his coat, and headed down to the reception area. Nicole was there talking on the phone. David made sure she noticed him and then he sat on the couch and waited. Nicole finished her conversation and called Darlene to tell her she would be out for awhile. She stood behind her desk, stared out at David, and smiled radiantly.

"Ready?" David asked.

"Yeah," Nicole grabbed her purse and stepped from behind her desk.

David peered at her curiously, "Don't you need your coat?"

Nicole had plotted this through all morning. She had a coat in the closet next to the break room, but she had her eye on a full-length black leather coat downtown. It was terribly expensive, but it made her look like a rock star, so that was that. "No," she batted her eyes and answered sweetly, "that's why I need a ride. I was hoping to get a new winter coat." She peaked up at him with her most innocent look.

David took off his coat and draped it over his arm. "Here," he said, handing it to her, "you can wear mine."

Nicole grimaced. It was a nice wool overcoat, but it was so big that it looked like a blanket on her. She shuddered a little at the thought of looking like a homeless person. She was about to refuse and then she thought better of it. "Thanks, David, if you're sure you'll be okay."

"Not a problem," David replied. "Remember, I'm the guy from Alaska." He smiled and helped her into the coat. Nicole could tell it was a genuine smile. She laughed a little inside. David was such a Boy Scout. It was refreshing in a way and so different from the jaded negative circle of friends she normally associated with.

They rode the elevator down to the garage together and walked to David's car. Nicole's expression soured when David pressed the automatic door opener and the vehicle's door locks clicked. It wasn't the black Viper she had picked out. *What a shame that Darlene made him trade in his Viper for a LeBaron.* Nicole sighed. *Ah well, at least it's new.* When they reached the car, David opened the door for her. *Boy Scout!* Nicole thought in irritation, but she smiled anyway. David climbed in the driver's side and together they made their way out of the parking lot.

"So, Nicole, where is it you need to go?"

"Macy's in midtown. You know, it's at the corner of 34th and Broadway." Actually, David didn't know, but Nicole rattled off a few more directions and David sped off to midtown.

When they reached the intersection, David peered over at Nicole. She blinked her long eyelashes and something stirred inside of him. There was no doubt that she was the most beautiful woman he had ever known. She was wearing a tight tan sweater shirt and a moderately short black skirt with high-heeled black leather boots. Her golden hair was cut in layers this winter, giving her a wild appearance.

Nicole picked up the conversation. "So what do you do in your spare time?"

David concentrated. To be honest, he didn't have much spare time and what spare time he did have was dedicated to taking care of his apartment and working out. Occasionally he sampled some local entertainment, but most of it wasn't to his liking. David answered honestly. "Oh mostly I just take care of my personal stuff and work out. How about you?"

Nicole thought about shifting to her life, but she still didn't have the answer she was searching for. "You must do more than that. Don't you have any friends or family around here?"

"My friends are all trudging through three feet of snow in Alaska right now and my family . . ." David sighed as his face fell a little, ". . . well, I don't really have any family."

Nicole sensed the sadness in his response. Curiosity bubbled inside her, but Nicole decided not to pursue it. She was pretty sure she had the answer she needed. David wasn't seeing anybody. He was always so honest, she was sure he would have told her by now. She decided to change the subject. "How about entertainment? Do you ever go to shows or movies?"

He shook his head. "I've been meaning to, but I haven't found the time yet." He thought for a moment and then queried her. "Got any recommendations? Michael told me that you're an actress."

Nicole beamed at the title. For once her feelings were genuine. *So*, she thought happily, *he did notice me, at least enough to ask Michael about me.* She glanced out the window and then back at David. "I love theatre. That's why I came to New York when I did. I studied acting at the New York Academy for Arts and I've been in plays ever since." She was still smiling. "If I could make a living at it, that's what I'd do all the time. Unfortunately, it doesn't pay that well, so my father helped me get this job with the partnership."

David nodded in understanding. "Colton Mitchell?" He connected her to a list of investors he had seen in the documents Sam showed him.

"C. T. we call him." Nicole returned the conversation back to herself. "Anyway, my real goal is to make it into film. I have an agent working for me, but so far no luck." She debated telling David the source of her acting problems and then decided to forge ahead. David was so tall that she was sure he would understand. "You know what my real problem is?" She blinked her long eyelashes. "I'm too tall."

It was really hard to be with Nicole and not fall in love with her. David smiled a little. "Well, I guess that rules out acting for me."

"It's not the same for men." Nicole blurted. "Tall men are pretty popular in acting. In fact I wish you had the lead in my play. Then I might have a shot at the female lead."

David laughed inside himself. He had never been good at anything but telling the truth. He could only imagine what a disaster it would be for him to act like someone else.

They reached the department store in short order thanks to Nicole's directions. David pulled up to the front door and Nicole smiled at him. "David, could you just wait here for me? I'll only be a minute." She took off David's wool coat and laid it on the seat. "I won't be needing this."

David nodded, "At your service."

Nicole disappeared inside the store and David waited for forty-five minutes. Of course, Nicole did have a coat in mind when she went into the store, but then she got sidetracked because they had a new series of colored leather jackets that intrigued her, especially a red one that made her look absolutely wild. After a half hour of equivocation, she stuck with the long, tight-fitting leather coat because it looked best with her boots.

She hadn't meant to take so long and she was a little worried that David would be mad when she returned. She peeked inside the window to see his expression before opening the door. Fortunately, he was still there and still unperturbed. He smiled at her as she climbed in. She was about to apologize when David interrupted her. "That coat looks . . ." and David tilted his head approvingly, ". . . *very* good on you." Nicole loved it.

"David, I'm sorry I took so long." She grimaced, "I got a little sidetracked." Then she smiled. "Macy's is uh . . . sort of a dangerous place for me."

David nodded. "Well it was worth the wait."

Nicole regrouped. She had finally come to the real reason she had taken David on this wild goose chase. "David, I really appreciate this. Could I buy you lunch?"

"Oooh," David furrowed his brow in loss. "I already pushed my meeting with Sam back to two o'clock. I don't think I should make him wait any longer."

Nicole was instantly mad but mostly at herself. Why had she dawdled so long in Macy's? Now she wouldn't have a chance to have lunch with David. Normally she would just wait for another opportunity, but she was already into this plot over $700 and she didn't want to be uncertain about where she stood. She decided to take a chance, a big chance. "How about dinner sometime?"

David was surprised. Nicole had been polite to him but had never shown any personal interest. It seemed a little forward that she would ask him to dinner. He thought about it for some time before realizing that he hadn't been on a date in two years. The pause was pregnant. When he glanced over at Nicole, he could tell she was nervous. "Sure. How about tonight?"

Nicole let out a silent sigh of relief. She didn't like rejection and she was good at avoiding situations that might end up that way. Then she remembered her schedule. "Not tonight." She bit her lip. "I have a show tonight. How about Monday?"

"Monday would be my pleasure, Nicole." David raised his eyebrows. "I'll make you a deal. Since you know New York better than me, you pick the restaurant and I'll drive."

* * *

So it began, David and Nicole went out together several times over the winter. Their relationship was hindered by both of their busy schedules and the fact that David was out of town most of the time. The business worked that way. Everyone searched and researched opportunities across the U.S. Each of them had different cities or areas where they were considered the experts, but when a deal started to come together they would all converge on that city until the project was completed.

In March, David returned after working on a deal that Richard was putting together in Miami. When he came into the office that morning, Nicole was waiting for him. She was wearing a provocative black lace dress that fell just short of her knees. The dress had a low scooped neck that emphasized her strong collarbones and perfect skin. At first glance, the dress appeared to be see-through lace, but as you got closer you could see the tan fabric beneath it. It had a stunning effect. Nicole stood and smiled when David entered. "Welcome back, stranger."

Even though they had been dating for almost four months, they were careful not to broadcast their relationship around the office. They hadn't actually discussed this. It was more of an unspoken agreement between them. David smiled back. "You look terrific, Nicole. It's great to be back in the city."

That afternoon, Nicole called him just before leaving work. "I'm leaving early tonight because I have a rehearsal. What are your plans tonight?"

"Ow," David winced, "I was hoping to have dinner with you."

"That will work if you don't mind going a little late. Rehearsal gets out at eight. We could go after that."

"Sounds great."

"Pick me up at the theatre and we'll go straight from there." She smiled. There were days she liked David and days that she didn't like him as much, but she had to admit that right now, she was happy he was back in town. Somehow life seemed a little brighter when David was in town.

David worked until after seven o'clock and by eight o'clock he was driving through the theatre district. He found a parking place as close to Nicole's theatre as he could and then walked the three blocks to the entrance. As he made his way through the streets, it dawned on him that in the three years he had been in New York, he had never seen her play. Minutes later, he was at the entrance. He could tell they were finished rehearsing by the number of people pouring out into the street. Hoping he wasn't late, he made his way through the crowd asking for Nicole. He finally spotted her talking with a couple of cast members near the stage. David smiled when she saw him. Nicole smiled back and waved him over.

When he reached the stage, he stopped next to her and she introduced him to her friends. "Marlita, Carl, this is David. David, this is Marlita and Carl. They're in the play with me."

Marlita scrutinized him. "So this is the young executive you've been talking about?" David nodded politely and then he slipped his left arm around Nicole's slender waist and pulled her next to him. "Man, Nicole, he's a big one."

David shook Carl's hand and smiled at Marlita. "Just what stories has Nicole been telling you about me?" He peered worriedly at Nicole and furrowed his eyebrows. "Maybe you and I should sit down alone somewhere so that I can hear a few stories about Nicole." Marlita smiled wickedly and glanced at Nicole.

Nicole narrowed her eyes at Marlita and gave David a fierce expression. He ignored it and hugged her. It was always a thrill to hold her, even if it was only for a second or two. Nicole glanced around nervously and then hugged him back stiffly. David let go and as Nicole's eyes met his he reached down and took her hand. He never took his eyes off her, but spoke to Carl and Marlita. "Nicole and I were headed out to get some dinner, if you two would like to join us . . ."

Carl smiled at Marlita who nodded "yes" and then looked back at David. "Sure, we'd love to. In fact, if you're up to it, we've been waiting for a chance to visit a little seafood place across the river. Neither one of us has a car. Are you driving?"

"At your service."

The four of them walked the three blocks back to David's car. Though Nicole was obviously tired, David noticed that she smiled the whole way. The drive across the bridge wasn't extraordinary except for the fact that they went to Jersey. Nicole gave David a concerned glance as they drove through the sprawling buildings on the Jersey Shore. Finally, they reached an area that was mostly industrial. Carl told David to turn right and they drove to the end of a small peninsula. There, at the edge of the water, was a restaurant that appeared to have been constructed out of old planks from a torn-down dock. The parking lot was almost full and music boomed through the open doors.

David stepped from the car and absorbed his surroundings. The place was saturated with the smell of the sea and diesel oil. As he raised his eyes, he noticed that directly to the east, across the Hudson River, was Manhattan. North and west of the restaurant, a tall apartment building filled his view. It was built almost at the edge of the water. There was a large swimming pool between the restaurant and the apartment building, but it seemed to be out of service. It was hard to tell in the dark.

David walked around the car and was about to open Nicole's door when she let herself out and gave him a "don't embarrass me" sort of expression. David understood. Nicole didn't always appreciate being taken care of, especially around her friends. David smiled to himself. Everything was so complicated with Nicole. He looked away from her so that she wouldn't see the little smile on his face and then, as she closed the door, he took her hand in his. As they walked to the restaurant together, David glanced back at the apartment building. He was taking in the scene when he noticed a large sign close to the building. It looked like a "For Sale" sign, but it was facing the parking lot in front of the building and David couldn't read the letters from his angle.

They entered the restaurant and waited at the bar for several minutes before being seated. Nicole, Carl and Marlita all ordered something to drink, but David never drank. He just ordered a Perrier instead. The wait turned out to be entertaining. Carl and Marlita were great company. Being a native to North Jersey, Carl was a fountain of knowledge about the Jersey shore and New York City. He told story after story about growing up in the harsh environment of the city's shadow. Marlita, on the other hand, was from Southern California and she also had all kinds of stories. But Marlita's best stories, and by far the most entertaining, were the ones about Nicole. Together they kept David and Nicole laughing until the waitress came to tell them their table was ready.

The restaurant turned out to be every bit as good as Carl bragged it up to be. The selection of seafood was great and, having grown up in Alaska, David loved seafood. Nicole wasn't quite as high on it, but she ordered some of the crab cakes the waiter recommended. After ordering, Carl turned the discussion to one of their co-actors who had recently gotten a job with a new play that was opening at the beginning of the summer. David tried to pay attention, but his mind kept drifting to the apartment building next door. After a few minutes, he excused himself and wandered outside.

It turned out that the name of the restaurant was Poseidon's Kitchen at Pearl Point. David walked across the parking lot and studied the large sign. It was definitely a for sale sign. It was big enough, about fifteen feet high, ten feet wide, and resting six feet off the ground on two large posts. David took mental note of the real estate company promoting the sale. The apartment building was only partially occupied and the pool was indeed empty. Judging from the cool breeze he felt coming off the river, David deduced that it probably wasn't a good spot for a pool.

David walked behind the apartment building and along the Hudson River to the back of the restaurant. There was a dock behind the restaurant and slips for several small ships. He lifted his eyes and took in the scene. It was a picture frame view of the skyline of New York and it was beautiful. Looking around, he imagined the possibilities. His observations coalesced into a vision as an idea formed in his mind. *This place has potential. Maybe . . .*

David made one last perusal before slipping back into the restaurant. When he reached to their table, Nicole gave him a worried look. "You were gone for quite a while. Where did you go?"

"I just slipped outside to take in the view. The skyline of Manhattan is beautiful from here. I'll take you out the back when we leave. You can see it for yourself." David sat down and noticed that his salad was waiting. "Besides, the building next door is for sale."

Nicole smiled. "Still working, huh?"

David nodded. "I couldn't help it."

Marlita studied David intently. She was silent for a several seconds and then a mischievous expression crossed her face. "What is it you do exactly? Nicole told me that you make boatloads of money, but she never explained how."

Nicole glared at Marlita and for the first time, David noticed that she was blushing.

David glanced up from his salad. "Real estate investment and/or development." David attempted to explain. "I work for a group of very successful people who buy buildings and modify them so that they will be more effective in the markets where they are situated. From there, we usually rent them out for several years and finally sell them. Business has been great over the past few years, but most of the genius behind the success belongs to the two co-founders, Hank and Greg."

Nicole piped up. "But David is one of their rising stars. They take pretty good care of him."

David nodded in agreement. "Hank and Greg are very generous with their employees."

Carl stared at David. "Is it just here in New York or all over?"

"We search all the U.S. markets but mostly on the eastern seaboard. I've been out of town in Miami most of this month working on a deal down there."

Marlita couldn't help it; her curiosity was just too great. She blurted out her next question. "So how much do you make at this?"

David's eyes widened and the warmth disappeared from his demeanor. Salaries and other compensation were strictly confidential. Hank had been quite clear on that. The employees of D&B were very intelligent and very competitive people. It would create a terrible distraction if anybody knew anything about anybody else's salary. David recovered quickly. After a moment of awkward silence, he smiled wryly at Marlita and shook his head. "You'll have to ask Nicole that question in private. She knows as much about salaries as anyone."

Nicole smiled knowingly and was about to comment when dinner arrived. David was hungry. He concentrated on finishing his salad and then started in on his salmon. It was delicious. It was poached in some kind of vegetable combination with pistachios and a spicy sauce. Carl had been absolutely right about the place, it was definitely worth the drive.

The rest of the evening was uneventful. They got back to Manhattan after eleven o'clock and drove across to the east side to a large apartment building where Carl and Marlita departed. David then drove Nicole to her apartment. Neither one of them spoke. Instead, they traveled in silence, luxuriating in each other's company. For once, Nicole was in a good mood and that made David happy. She had smiled most of the night. Still, he was careful. He was never quite sure how Nicole felt about him.

When they arrived at Nicole's apartment, David leaned over as if to exit when Nicole stopped him. When he turned to see what the problem was, she pulled him close to her and gave him a kiss. David closed his eyes and drank her in. He loved her smell and the smoothness of her skin. He loved her wild hair and her beautiful blue eyes. He wanted the moment to last forever.

Nicole released him and looked into his eyes. "Why do you do that?"

"Do what?" David responded in confusion.

"You know," Nicole gave him a flat expression and then realized that he didn't know, "open my door, hold my hand, push in my chair . . . treat me like a child. You don't have to do that."

David nodded. "I know."

Nicole was still staring at him. She shook her head. "So why do you do it?"

David shrugged. "I guess I'm old-fashioned. I grew up most of my life without a mom or any sisters, so women are sort of magical to me." David thought for a moment about Camille, but then he shook his head. *Camille doesn't count.*

Nicole continued. "It makes people think you're a Boy Scout, you know---like you're a farm boy and you aren't very smart."

David frowned. In retrospect he could see Nicole's point. "I know," David nodded, "well . . . I guess I am a bit of a farm boy." David smiled.

Nicole's expression went flat. She studied David like she was seeing him for the first time and then she slowly shook her head. "No," she spoke quietly. "I don't think so."

David came in early the next day. After finishing up a few details from the Miami project, he left at ten o'clock. He drove back across the river and up the freeway to Pearl Point. There he spent the next two hours examining every detail of the apartment complex he had seen the night before.

The building seemed sound and the location was good. David had a premonition. Somehow, he knew it could be a good deal, depending on the price and a few other factors. For once there was plenty of parking, always a nightmare in New York.

The location was good in Jersey because it was accessible from either of two freeways. But the commute to New York was a tough one because of the industrial neighborhoods you had to crawl your way through to get to the tunnels. In addition, both the accessible freeways were clogged during rush hour. Suddenly, an idea occurred to him. He spun quickly and stared at the old docks behind the restaurant. *Maybe* . . . David's mind was racing. He wasn't sure. It was an unusual idea, but it could be the deciding factor. He needed a little help. He pondered for a moment and determined his course of action. *Hank and Greg will know.* The thought made him smile.

David walked to the end of the parking lot and surveyed again at the entire project from the entrance. He pushed time forward until he could see it in his mind. It was completely renovated and the warehouse on the south side of the marina was gone. In its place stood a second apartment building. The whole thing sparkled and every parking spot was full. David blinked his eyes and the vision disappeared.

By Friday, David had all the information he needed. Although not for sale in the package, the restaurant and marina were owned by the same company as the apartments, more commonly known as Pearl View Apartments. The real estate agent was sure the seller was motivated enough to sell both. The warehouse and marina were not big enough for the larger container ships and were only used occasionally by their current owners. David knew he would have to pay a premium, but he was sure he could get those as well.

Late Friday morning, he walked down to Hank's office and, seeing Angela at her desk, asked if it would be okay to disturb Hank. Angela gave David a quick nod and he knocked on the door.

"Come in," was all David heard from the other side. As he entered, Hank smiled at him. "David, it's good to see you again." Then, thinking quickly, Hank teased. "I send you to Miami for a month and you still don't have a tan." Hank laughed. "That's a good thing . . . a very good thing."

"Good morning, Hank," David sat down in the chair in front of his desk. "Yeah, Miami wasn't as much fun as I thought. Richard is quite the task master."

Hank was still smiling, "That's good news, too." Then his expression melted to something more serious. "So what can I do for you?"

"Well," David's brow furrowed in dark concentration, "I think you need to have seafood for lunch today."

Hank stopped smiling. "I usually just have Angela bring me a sandwich from the corner. Is there something special about this seafood?"

"I think so, since there is a good chance you'll own the restaurant in a few months."

Hank caught on and raised his eyebrows. "Around here? We haven't done anything in New York in almost four years."

"Not quite." David glanced out the window. "It's across the river in Jersey. But I think you're going to like it."

Hank smiled and stood up. "On second thought, seafood sounds great today."

On the way to Pearl Point, David laid out the entire project. Hank whistled when David divulged the pivotal idea, a commuter ferry to New York. Hank confessed that it was out of his league, but Greg could probably help. Greg had a lot of influence in the city since he had supported more than a few candidates; several of whom were now in office.

They surveyed the site for almost an hour before lunch. David kept explaining and Hank kept nodding. Everything made sense. The view was incredible, but there were some firsts here---ideas that lay outside the ever-successful formula that Hank and Greg had developed over the years. Fortunately, Hank was not timid. He liked having a little adventure in life and he loved the idea of owning a marina. Although he didn't really understand much about it, the possibilities seemed fascinating. *Who knows?* Hank mused to himself. *If the business keeps growing the way it has been, maybe the*

- 216 -

company could buy a yacht. Hank knew that Greg would never go for it, but it was something to think about.

After lunch, they talked all the way back to the office. Hank indicated that he would discuss it with Greg that afternoon. He was pretty sure that Greg would give the okay for David to assemble a bid package. Then they would discuss how to structure the deal and when to pull the trigger. Hank told David to be ready to come down to Greg's office on a moment's notice.

The call didn't come until half past five and David didn't get much accomplished before then. He was so nervous rehearsing what he needed to say that everything else evaporated from his mind. It wasn't that he was afraid of Greg, he just didn't know Greg as well as Hank and he didn't want to disappoint Hank in front of Greg. When he reached Greg's office, both men were smiling and he could tell that Hank had already sold Greg on the idea. Still, the first words from Greg were a little rough.

"A ferry," Greg gazed at David in disbelief. "You want a ferry to the city? Do you have any idea how much wining and dining it will take to get permission for such a thing?" Greg gave Hank a sour expression. "And I will have to do most of that work myself, since my backwoodsman partner has no tact or patience for dealing with our magnificent city government."

David put on his most timid face. "Just a small ferry, sir." Both Hank and Greg laughed out loud. Then David gave Hank his most serious expression. "Did you tell him about the amusement park?" Greg's face dropped for a minute and then he noticed Hank was chuckling.

Greg shook his head, realizing that David was pulling his leg. "No, he didn't mention the amusement park, but Hank has this ridiculous notion that he might get to park a company yacht there. Let me tell you right now that we are not going to buy a yacht."

David was confused for a second until he put the pieces together. Hank hadn't mentioned a yacht to him, but it was so in character with Hank's way of thinking that it wasn't hard to believe.

Greg finished the conversation. "Let's give this a whirl. David, you put the deal together and see what it will cost us to get the warehouse and the marina. Since you found this one and you seem to have the vision of what it will be, Hank and I have decided to give you the lead on the project."

David smiled. It didn't get any better than that. He would be calling the shots on this one and if it was successful, it would have a huge positive impact on his bonus and options. Hank was studying him and nodding. David smiled at Greg and responded politely. "Thank you."

Greg sighed and stared out the window in the direction of Pearl Point. "You've earned it, David." Then Greg looked back at David. "Now go hit a home run for us."

The next four months swept by like the water over Niagara Falls. David worked fourteen-hour days for the entire time. Sundays were the only exception. He never worked on Sundays but spent his time studying the Bible and enjoying the sights of the city. He found a few hours here and there to be with Nicole as well. Having a local project was a big plus for the relationship.

By the end of July, the deal was ready. The three of them, David, Hank and Greg, sat in the offices of Trans-Continental Realty. All the real work had been done at this point. The only thing left was to sign the paperwork and transfer the money, but nothing was ever simple when you were spending almost $300 million. It wasn't the largest deal that Downing & Burkover had done, but it was in the top ten. When the excitement was over, David called Nicole to tell her the good news. "We closed on Pearl Point today. Let's go out and celebrate."

"So you're one of the big boys now." Nicole almost laughed.

"Something like that. Of course if it's a bust I will be one of the big bums, but I don't think so. This looks pretty good to me. Only a few unknowns left."

"Did Greg get the private ferry thing with the city?"

"Yeah, it was difficult, but not unheard of. There are actually quite a few private ferries, although permits are always a problem."

"So," Nicole answered pensively, "how do you want to celebrate?"

David was silent for a minute before answering. "You know what? I've always wanted to go swimming in the ocean. In Alaska if you fall in the ocean it means death. There is no other way to describe it. Either you get stuck in the mud and drown, or you die from hypothermia within minutes. Sometimes it's hard for me to imagine that a person can actually swim in the ocean and enjoy it."

Nicole grimaced. Swimming in the ocean in California would be great, or even Texas, but swimming in the ocean around here was definitely not on her list of things to do. Probably the Jersey shore was best, but she had heard rumors that medical waste turned up on Jersey beaches regularly and she couldn't imagine anything worse than stepping on somebody's used syringe.

Rather than just say no, Nicole decided to deflect her answer. "How about going to a play with me? Carl's friend joined that new play in the spring and it opened at the beginning of the summer. So far it's getting great reviews."

"You're on," David said. "When would you like to go?"

"How about tomorrow night? I get Wednesday off."

"Okay, I'll pick you up at half past six on my way home from work."

Wednesday night found David and Nicole together and headed down to the theatre district. It was always a challenge to find a parking spot, but Wednesday night wasn't so bad. They parked about two blocks away and walked together. It was a hot muggy night in New York and the evening breeze was just beginning to take the heat out of the air. When they reached the theatre, there was a long line at the will call window.

Laura Downing had planned to see the new Plutin musical for months. She had seen his last play five years earlier and had thoroughly enjoyed it. The tough part was to get a night free on Greg's schedule, but she finally managed it. The limo pulled in front of the theatre promptly at 7:30 P.M.. As it came to a stop, Laura stared out the window at the two tallest figures standing in line. She nudged Greg.

"Isn't that your receptionist?"

Greg leaned over Laura's lap and peered through the window. "I think so. It's hard to tell from the back."

"Who's that big fellow she's with?"

Greg noted that Nicole was holding the hand of the rather large fellow. It was really hard to tell because they were both studying the billboards on the side of the theatre. Greg started to answer, "I can't tell," then David turned slightly and Greg saw enough of his face to recognize him. "No," Greg muttered to himself. He sagged back into his seat and spoke in concern. "That's David, the big kid that Hank hired from Alaska. You remember him from the Christmas party."

"Oh yes," Laura smiled, "he's quite a handsome young man."

"And dating Nicole," Greg shook his head. "I had no idea."

Laura opened the door. "We'd better go say hello."

Greg and Laura slipped out of the car and walked down the line. Neither David nor Nicole noticed them until they were standing behind them on the sidewalk. Laura tapped Nicole on the shoulder. "Nicole, how are you?"

Nicole froze for a second before dropping David's hand nonchalantly and turning. "Mrs. Downing and Greg." Nicole smiled back at both of them. "Are you here for the show?"

"Yes," Laura went on, "I just love Alex Plutin's musicals." Then Laura peered up at David. "And this is David?"

David stretched out his hand and shook Laura's. "Hello, Mrs. Downing. We've met a couple of times." He nodded at Greg. "Good to see you."

Laura took both of Nicole's hands. "How's your father doing? He was so kind to us when we visited Houston last year."

Nicole smiled at the mention of her family. "Dad's doing great, although he's slowing down on the construction business. He claims he wants to control his time and money instead of having them control him."

"Good advice," Laura nodded. "Maybe I should have him talk to Greg." She gave Greg a side glance, but Greg didn't notice. He was lost in concentration, staring at David.

Nicole and David stepped forward as the line began to move. Laura Downing took one step with them. "Well, we'd better get to our seats. It looks like the show is sold out."

They headed off to the entrance and Laura whispered to Greg as they walked. "They make a lovely couple. They're both so tall." Greg never responded.

They next morning, Greg was stewing in his office when Hank wandered in. Hank made sure Greg noticed him and then he spoke. "You look glum today."

Greg glance up from his desk, put his hands behind his head, and leaned back in his executive chair. "They say misery loves company, so . . . " Greg gave Hank a flat expression, "close the door and pull up a chair."

Hank's expression immediately went sour. He reached back and flicked the door shut as he sat down in front of Greg. "What is it?"

Greg leaned forward. "It may be nothing, but . . . I saw Nicole and David at the theatre last night."

"So?"

"They were holding hands."

"Oh," Hank smiled, "so we have a little romance blossoming here at the office. You can't blame the boy, you know. Nicole's quite a piece of eye candy."

Greg shook his head. "This is where you missed out on corporate education 101. There *are* some things you can learn by working for a big company."

Hank gave Greg a puzzled look.

Greg continued. "If it gets serious you're going to lose one of them."

Hank's smile melted to a frown. There was a pause as both men's eyes met. They stared at each other for over a minute before Hank ground out the next words. "Well, I can tell you which one it will be."

There was serious heat in Hank's comment, but Greg just shook his head. "You don't get to choose."

"Yes, I do." Hank muttered it through his clenched teeth. "I'll just fire Nicole today and that will be the end of it."

Greg was still shaking his head. "They'll both quit then."

"So, Mr. Oracle, just what *can* we do?"

Greg sighed and blew out a breath. "Hope and hedge. The best outcome would be if the whole thing blows over without a whimper. But judging the situation from what I know about David, I would say he is going to fall head over heels for Nicole. If we get really lucky and if Nicole has a brain, she'll marry him and spend all his money. David will be here the rest of his life trying to make enough to keep her happy."

Hank wasn't smiling. "And if we aren't that lucky?"

"Hmmmm," Greg nodded, "if we aren't that lucky she'll break his heart and he won't be able to stand this place. In big companies, people transfer to a different department or even a different office. That might be a possibility if we open a new office in Boston or D.C."

"I need him here working on the Pearl Point project. So what else can we do?"

Greg nearly winced at Hank's angry expression. "You need to hedge, otherwise this whole thing could end up in your lap. Why don't you bring Richard in to play second to David? Just in case."

Hank shook his head again. "Richard is too busy with Miami and he wouldn't like the assignment anyway."

"What about Michael?"

Hank frowned. Of all the college grads he had hired that year, Michael had turned out to be the closest thing to a disappointment. He was a good worker and spent plenty of time at the office, but he never made any original contributions. He was more of a support person who was good at pinning down the details once the big decisions were made. Still, it was a good idea. It might help them both in the long run. *Only one problem,* Hank thought sourly to himself, *if David leaves, I'll be stuck working with Michael.* Hank nodded in surrender. "Alright, that makes sense."

Hank trudged slowly back to his office. On the way there, he scowled through the wall in the direction of Nicole's desk. He muttered quietly to himself. "If David goes . . . you go."

David was with Nicole again on Saturday and then on Wednesday. Half the fun of going out with her was seeing what outfit she would wear. David wondered at times if he would ever see her wear the same outfit twice. She had never done so on a date, although he had seen a couple of repeats at the office.

On Friday he gave her a call to see what her schedule was like for the weekend. "Nicole, how would you like to get together this weekend?"

Nicole recognized David's voice, "Sure, I'm busy every night, but I have Saturday morning off. I don't have to be at the show until five in the afternoon."

"Let's go down to the shore. I really want to go swimming in the ocean."

Nicole frowned at the idea. "It's so far away, David." She tried to dissuade him. "They have a pool at my apartment. We can go swimming there if you want."

David sensed Nicole's reservation. He didn't understand exactly what her problem was, but it was now obvious to him that Nicole had issues with swimming in the ocean. "Nicole, I really want to swim in the ocean at least once in my life and I don't want to go alone. I'll pick you up early if you want. We'll have plenty of time to get there and enjoy it for awhile before coming back." David waited for a response. The other end of the line was silent. He knew that Nicole was thinking. Finally he resorted to pleading. "Please, Nicole, I really want to experience swimming in the ocean and it won't be any fun without you."

Nicole pondered her situation. She hated the thought of swimming in a polluted ocean, but there were some upsides. She would finally get a glimpse of David with his shirt off and she could improve her tan and get David started on one. Then Nicole remembered the designer bathing suit she purchased last fall. She had paid almost $400 for the thing. That was way out of her budget, but it was so incredibly gorgeous that it made her look like a goddess. She just couldn't resist. She hadn't yet had a chance to wear it. *I'll go, no problem and I'll wear my new suit. I just won't get in the water.* She frowned. It wasn't the best solution, but it was a workable one.

She sighed into the receiver, "Okay," then drawled out the words, "if you really want to go, but it won't be hot enough until noon so why don't you come by and get me between ten and eleven?" Nicole went silent for a second and then a devious thought seized her. "But," she smiled naughtily, "since I'm doing this for you, you have to make me a promise."

David smiled. He couldn't believe he had actually gotten his way. "Anything, my dear, you only have to ask."

Nicole couldn't think of anything specific at the moment so she just wrote herself a blank check. "You have to do what I want sometime, no questions asked." She smiled and thought wickedly. *Maybe I'll take you shopping with me one Sunday. That will be a real test of your devotion.*

David responded quickly. "It's a deal."

On Saturday David woke up at 5:30 A.M. and went to the gym for his workout. While most people dreaded working out, it was a David's favorite time. He loved freeing his mind from the cauldron and the dark thoughts shrouding it. It was here that his mind was clear enough to allow him to examine his past and plot his future.

Today, he was especially excited. Swimming in the ocean had been one of the big things on his checklist. Going with Nicole just made it that much better.

The rest of the morning went quickly. When he arrived at Nicole's building, he called her on the cell phone. She told him to come upstairs and help her pack all her things down to the car. When he reached her apartment, he was a little surprised by the volume of equipment Nicole needed just to go swimming. Even so, David never complained. As always, Nicole looked fantastic. She was wearing her big sunglasses and a brightly colored halter top with a matching wrap skirt.

David packed down the ice chest and the umbrella and made a second trip for the beach chairs. Nicole followed with a medium-sized duffle bag full of clothing and makeup. He shook his head when he finally got it all stuffed in the trunk. *No wonder Nicole doesn't like going to the beach.*

Nicole gave David directions for Monmouth Beach. It was one of the closest locations and supposedly nice this time of year.

It took thirty minutes to get off the island and another hour to get to the beach. It was crowded and David had some trouble finding a parking spot. Luckily they were there before noon so the worst of the crowd hadn't yet materialized. David extracted Nicole's heavy duffle bag while Nicole retrieved her large umbrella. Together they lugged there bounty down to the beach and after a ten minute search, Nicole finally found a place away from all the kids running back and forth.

David pitched the umbrella and Nicole watched their belongings while he went back to get the rest of her stuff. By the time he returned, she had removed her tank top and skirt and was standing there in her two-piece swimsuit. When she saw David, she walked over to help him carry the chairs and ice chest the rest of the way.

David opened his chair and let his eyes linger on Nicole. She was stunning. The bathing suit she was wearing was sky blue and had a slight sheen to it. The top piece was made of delicate horizontal pleats that gathered to a golden ring in the center of her chest that was open and revealed her beautiful smooth skin beneath. The bottom piece was also layered with delicate horizontal pleats that gathered to a larger golden ring. That ring rested upon a span of tightly stretched blue material that dipped slightly at the center. Both the top and the bottom were edged with a fine gold braid. The sky blue material stood out starkly against Nicole's tanned body.

As David stared in awe, something powerful stirred within him. Suddenly a hollow feeling opened in the pit of his stomach. The urge to seize Nicole his arms nearly overwhelmed him.

David let out a sigh and looked away. Behind Nicole, he noticed that the three teenage boys who had been kicking a beach ball, stopped in place and were staring at her. David swallowed hard. His mouth was dry. As Nicole struggled to open the second beach chair he reached over and touched her hand, lacing his fingers between hers. She glanced over at him and he noticed her big blue eyes under her sunglasses. David shook his head. "Nicole, that is the most beautiful bathing suit I have ever seen."

Nicole smiled. "You like it?"

David wasn't finished. He continued staring into her eyes. "And you," he spoke from his heart, "are the most beautiful woman I have ever known."

Nicole felt it. It was like sunshine washing over her on a cold winter morning. David never lied, but when he spoke like that, it was as if her heart opened and the words raced through her whole body. She leaned forward and kissed him on the lips. It felt so good. Pulling her head back, she let out her sigh and then something strange happened. A powerful feeling of warmth washed over her. It was mesmerizing. She felt her skin tingle and when she glanced down, she noticed goose bumps on her arms. She shook her head and her senses returned. "Thank you."

David finished unfolding the chair and took off his t-shirt. Nicole was impressed. David's torso and chest were rippled with muscles and his arms were just as impressive, but he needed a tan badly. Nicole shrugged, *That's part of the reason we're here.* She smiled at him. "Been working out, I see."

Nicole's words startled David. He hadn't realized that she was watching him. "Oh yeah," he nodded indifferently, "every day when I'm not traveling."

Nicole noticed a lady with two little children watching David and smiling as he removed the rest of his shirt. It made her mad. *Already taken, lady,* she thought spitefully. *Better keep your wandering eyes on your kids and not my young executive.*

When David took off his sweat pants Nicole gasped. She had never seen a bathing suit like the one David was sporting. After staring in horror for several seconds, she guessed that it was some kind of grunge wear. Finally she couldn't suppress her curiosity. "What *is* that?" Nicole pointed disgustedly to David's trunks.

David followed Nicole's gaze to his cutoffs. "Oh, this is just a pair of my old work pants that I made into cutoffs. I didn't have time to buy a swim suit."

Nicole squinted in despair. "No, I mean all those colored spots and those white lumps all over it."

"Oh," David responded, "these were an old pair of painting pants I used when I worked on people's houses." David smiled until he noted the expression of disgust on Nicole's face. "The white lumps are caulking and all the colors are different paints I used . . . " It suddenly dawned on David that he wasn't making the situation any better. He changed the subject. "Come on, Nicole, let's go swimming."

"Go ahead, I just want to work on my tan today."

That wasn't exactly what David had in mind, but he decided not to press Nicole any further since she didn't seem to approve of his improvised swimsuit. He ran down the beach and right out into the surf. It was a bit chilly, but nothing like the lakes and streams of Alaska. He loved the feel of the sand squishing between his toes, the lapping of the waves as they slapped against his chest and ultimately washed up on the shore. He swam out for quite a while and then he heard the lifeguard shout at him with his bullhorn. David swam back until his feet touched the sand. It was exhilarating.

The teenage boys who had been kicking the ball on the shore were now playing some kind of keep away game. He noticed several children playing near the edge of the water. They were making sand castles and every few minutes, he would see them throw a little sand at each other when their mothers weren't watching. David's eyes traced the beach until they settled on Nicole. She was sitting in the chair rubbing lotion on her body. Hands down, she was the most beautiful woman on the beach that day. He still couldn't quite believe that she was with him.

At one o'clock, David sauntered up the beach and sat in the beach chair next to Nicole. She shook her head. David was smiling like a big kid. Nicole wondered if she would ever be able to get the farm boy out of him. Then she wondered if she really wanted to do that. He was so honest and straightforward. It was so different from most of the people she associated with.

"What's for lunch?" David asked.

"I made my specialty," Nicole laughed. "Tuna fish sandwiches."

"Sounds great." He opened the cooler and took out two sandwiches. Handing one to Nicole, he unwrapped the other. Nicole sat up in her chair and studied David carefully. His skin was so white that she hadn't noticed it at first, but now she could see the scar on his right leg. It started at his ankle and went up his leg until is disappeared under his cutoffs. She had already noticed the scar on his forehead, but somehow, that didn't bother her. In fact it made him seem more masculine.

Nicole touched David's leg. "What happened here?"

"I was in an accident on my bicycle when I was eight years old. I got the scar on my forehead from the same accident. My folks were really worried. My mother later told me that everyone thought I wouldn't make it, but she always believed I'd get better. She said she had a dream about me. She said I was a grown man in the dream."

"You never talk about your folks. What was it like growing up in Alaska?"

David stopped eating and gazed up from his sandwich. Nicole studied him in fascination as that distant hazy look filled his eyes. His brow furrowed in concentration. "My folks passed away when I was nine. John found me and took me to Alaska.

"Who was John?"

David had never answered that question before. He paused for almost a minute before answering briskly, "My guardian." David could tell from Nicole's puzzled expression that he had left the question unanswered.

Nicole was pondering David's answer when a strange word came into her mind, *Orphan.* She shook it off. *No, that can't be right.* But the longer she thought on it, the more she realized the truth. David was an orphan. Nicole couldn't imagine such a plight. Her parents had played a huge role in her life. Even now, they were a constant influence.

Nicole's thoughts expanded and she wondered what else she didn't know about this big, strong, farm boy from Alaska. David finished his sandwich and wolfed down some potato chips. Then he drank a soda pop and was on his feet. "Come on, Nicole, come swimming with me."

"David," Nicole whined, "I really don't want to get wet today. Just go without me. I like watching you frolic in the water." Then she chided him, "But don't get the lifeguards all upset---they'll kick us off the beach if you keep swimming out too far."

David ran off into the surf again. The ocean was an experiment in physics. He tried everything: body surfing, swimming, diving; you name it. It was the most alive he had felt in years. By two o'clock, he realized that Nicole was running out of time. He needed to get her back home in time for her to get ready for her play.

When he eyed her on the beach, he noticed that she had dozed off in her chair. It was just too tempting. Slowly he snuck back onto the beach and right up next to her. She never woke. A mischievous smile crossed his face as he stood over her.

The first thing Nicole felt were her sunglasses lifting off her head. She was just starting to wake when two strong, cold, wet arms slipped under her and lifted her out of her chair. The next thing she saw was David's smiling face while she was bounced along the beach in his arms. Shaking the cobwebs out of her mind, she realized that David was wading through the water. Then it dawned on her.

"David," she shouted at him as crossly as she could, "don't you dare."

But David was standing in waist-deep water and laughing. Suddenly, with an almost effortless flick of his arms, Nicole was in the air. She sailed five feet through emptiness and then her back hit the water. The cold water engulfed her, stealing her breath. For a second, she couldn't believe that David had done it. Then, as her feet finally found a solid perch on the sandy bottom, her anger boiled over. She wanted to rise right up out of the water and start screaming at him, but she was afraid that her little flight and splashdown might have separated her from her swimsuit. She adjusted the top piece frantically and then she raised her head above the water and started shouting. "David, you . . . " Nicole was livid, ". . . I told you I didn't want to get wet."

David was laughing so hard that he didn't realize how angry she was. He finally calmed down enough to divulge his rebuttal. Nicole wasn't quite as beautiful with her hair wadded to her head and an angry scowl on her face. "You told me you'd go swimming with me."

Nicole didn't even respond to David's rationalization. She marched up the beach and walked over to her chair. David followed her and handed her a towel. She didn't accept it, but clawed through her duffle bag for one of her own. David was still laughing until he finally realized how angry she was. She wouldn't even look at him. He was immediately sorry.

"I'm sorry Nicole, I just couldn't help it."

Nicole didn't acknowledge him. She dried herself, found her sunglasses and donned her halter-top. Then she wrapped her skirt around her hips and started walking toward the car. "Just take me home," she muttered.

David walked to the car with Nicole and let her in. It was hot and stuffy inside, but she rolled down the windows and sat in there anyway. David went back two more times to retrieve all the paraphernalia they had brought to the beach. By the time it was all packed, he was sweating as well. He didn't bother putting on his t-shirt and sweat pants before climbing into the car.

While fishing for his keys, he noticed that he had a white line across his chest where he had been carrying one of the chairs. Nicole noticed it too. She pushed her finger into his bicep. It left a white print behind.

"You're burnt to a crisp." Nicole practically spit the words out at him. "Didn't you put on any sun block?"

David's face melted to confusion. "What's sun block?"

Nicole shook her head while staring at the floor mat. "You are such a dumb farm boy. Don't you know anything?"

David didn't answer. He could tell that Nicole was too mad to reason with. He started the car and made his way out to the main road.

It was a long ride home. Nicole stared out the passenger window without speaking a word. They rode the elevator in silence until they reached her apartment. Then, Nicole flung open her door and raced inside. David followed her and propped the apartment door open before it could close. He then made three trips up the elevator carrying all the things Nicole had brought. Nicole never appeared or said a word to him. He could hear her showering in the back, but he just left everything in her living room, closed the door, and walked glumly down to his car.

David hadn't felt that bad since Camille tackled him at the track meet. Everything had been so wonderful. Too good to be true, really, and he had messed it up by throwing Nicole into the water. *That was dumb,* David thought in despair, *if I could just live that moment over.* But that wasn't the end of David's problems.

By evening, David was in pain. The sunburn that Nicole has so viciously pointed out to him was most severe on his back and shoulders. His face wasn't far behind and by Monday morning, it all started to peel. He went in a little late to work hoping to catch Nicole alone in the reception area. When he entered he noticed the top of her head behind the tall desk and tested the waters. "Good morning, Nicole."

Nicole didn't answer. She gazed up from her desk and frowned when she saw him.

David walked slowly across the reception area, stopping halfway to the hall door. "Any chance we could talk?"

Nicole didn't respond or even raise her head this time. She just pretended that he wasn't there. When David reached to the hall door, he opened it and started to go through. Then he stopped and let the door close without entering. He was silent for almost a minute, thinking very hard about what he might possibly say, when he heard Nicole speak derisively, "Lobster boy."

David turned around and peered at the tall desk. He noticed the top of Nicole's head. She was still staring down. Finally he spoke. "If it makes you feel any better, I've been in pain all weekend."

That got her attention. Nicole glanced up with surprise on her face. She hadn't realized that he was still there. She stared back down at her desk.

David gathered his thoughts. "I am really sorry Nicole. Please forgive me." He paused, hoping that no one else would come in. "The truth is, I just wanted to hold you in my arms." Nicole never moved or spoke. All David could see was the top of her hair behind the tall desk. He finally sighed and trudged through the hallway to his office.

When the inner door clicked shut, Nicole let out a sigh. Then she smiled a little. Actually, it did make her feel better to know that David had suffered all weekend. What was making her miserable now, was how she felt inside.

When David had picked her up at the beach, several things went through her mind. The first was fear. She had always thought of muscles on men as "just for looks," but when David flicked her five feet into the air, she realized how strong he was. He could just as easily have snapped her back. In fact, he could do anything he wanted to her and she would have no control. That stark realization made her admit to herself that, for the first time in any relationship, she wasn't completely in control. She had never felt that way about any of her other boyfriends and . . . she was afraid.

The thing that bothered her most, however, was the fact that something inside of her was melting. She was starting to lose sight of the ambitions that had given her life purpose. Nicole lifted her hands and studied them. They were trembling. They had been fine until David walked through the door.

There were other worries too. Nicole knew that David really cared about her. Saying you were sorry wasn't something that she heard very often in her family. Everybody just did what he or she could get away with. She couldn't remember every hearing her father apologize for anything. But David was different. He really cared and when he spoke his apology, she felt it. It was all she could do to keep from running over to him, wrapping her arms around him and letting him squeeze her again with those powerful arms. She was still trembling.

Nicole didn't know how she could feel this way. She had dated several men. There were even a few that she had been intimate with, but this was different. She had never before felt such powerful emotions. She had to stop it; she had to slow it down; she had to catch her breath and get her bearings. Maybe it was the right thing, maybe it wasn't, but she needed time to figure it out.

The rest of that week went by without much fanfare. David came in every morning and said hello. Nicole never responded. She knew she had to say something before long, but she just didn't know how to climb out of the box she was hiding in. When the weekend came, she was lonely and miserable. On Sunday, she had to attend Carl and Marlita's wedding by herself. It was a big occasion and all of the crew from the play was there. When she gave Marlita a hug in the reception line, Marlita asked her about David. Nicole was tempted to tell her the truth, but quickly decided against it. Instead, she simply told her that he was out of town.

Nicole stewed all night after she returned home from the wedding and finally decided that David's punishment was over. She wanted to call him just to hear his voice, but that was too forward. She knew she could walk down to his office and end it, but if she was too obvious, he would figure out just how whipped she was. Nicole cursed silently to herself.

She hated all the head games. It was three o'clock in the morning before she figured out her tactic. She would just say hello back to him when he walked in the office on Monday. If he looked at her, she would smile a little bit. *That should do it,* she thought happily. Then she shook her head and rolled her eyes. She wasn't sure. *David is such a farm boy. I might actually have to talk to him first.* "Whatever," she murmured aloud in disgust.

DESPAIR

Chapter 22

David had a dream. He had dreams all the time, but something bothered him about this one. He was standing on the Jersey side of the Hudson River, admiring the New York skyline, when he felt a tremor or explosion. Riveting his attention in that direction, he saw a building shaking in distress. It was a tall building . . . a familiar building. Suddenly, to his surprise and horror, the building buckled. The side closest to the river seemed to fold in upon itself. Then, at about one-third of the way up, the top of the building began collapsing into the bottom.

David watched in slow motion as the walls shattered and fell. Seconds seemed to stretch into minutes as each floor of the building collapsed into the one below it. He could see the windows exploding level by level, belching out swirls of dust and glass as they disappeared. The process accelerated until a huge dust cloud rose into the breeze. In his dream there was no sound, only silent demolition. Still, he knew people had died. The sun was just beginning to illuminate the sky and the parking lot was full of vehicles.

The dream stuck with him through his workout and breakfast. He hadn't really gotten a good look at the building before it collapsed, but it was familiar. And the view . . . the view was familiar too. David closed his eyes and retraced every detail: the building, the parking lot and the view across the river. There was another building to the south, but that building was new. He could tell because the landscaping was new. Then his mind's eye concentrated on a seemingly insignificant building east of the disaster. Oddly enough, it was a small, old wooden structure. David froze, his stomach churned as sweat beaded on his forehead. He recognized the little wooden building with sickening clarity. It was Poseidon's Kitchen. The building that collapsed in his dream was Pearl View!

David didn't bother going into the office or even calling that morning. Instead he headed through the traffic and across the river. It took almost two hours in the congestion until he caught sight of Pearl View. It was still there, calm as any other morning. Nothing had changed. He parked his car and rested his head on the steering wheel. A measure of peace returned to him. *It's still here. It was only a dream, but* he wasn't so sure. It didn't seem like the jumbled imaginings of his unconscious mind.

Throughout his life, David had seen another type of dream, dreams that became reality. John called them visions. Those dreams kept coming back with greater and greater clarity. They always carried a message and it was always important. David had come to trust those dreams and his heart was telling him something terrible. This was not a dream. It was a vision.

David spent four hours examining Pearl View that morning. It was impossible to tell that there was anything wrong with the building. There were no cracks visible from the outside, no noticeable settling or even cracking on the inside. There was no evidence the foundation was shifting. It was Pearl View, the same steady old building it had always been, but David could not clear the knot in his throat.

At three o'clock that afternoon he finally climbed into his car and drove back to the office. He needed help. There was something wrong with Pearl View. It was something subtle which would require an expert's consideration. He rolled to a stop in his assigned parking place and made his way up the steps. He slid his magnetic card across the reader and opened the door. He was concentrating so hard that he never looked up until he reached his office. Placing his briefcase on his desk, he flopped into his chair and sat there in deadening silence, trying to arrange his thoughts. Every time he went over it in his mind; he perceived more and every time he perceived more; it was worse.

Exasperation brought a wave of despair. *How can I explain this to Hank?* David imagined the conversation. *Hank, I had a dream and I believe that Pearl View is going to collapse some day. I would like your permission to spend hundreds of thousands of dollars to find a problem that may be uncorrectable or cost millions of dollars to correct.* David pondered a hundred scenarios, but there was no way out of his dilemma.

By five o'clock that afternoon, David knew he had to act. He walked down the hallway to Hank's office, waved hello to Angela and knocked on Hank's door. Hank yelled for him to come in and when he entered the office, Hank sensed something was wrong. David's face was more serious than he had ever seen it. Hank smiled anyway.

"David, what's wrong? You look like death warmed over."

David grimaced. "I, uh . . . I think there may be a problem with Pearl View."

Hank sat up, immediately serious. "What kind of problem?"

David felt Hank's eyes pierce him. "I believe Pearl View may have structural defects."

Hank was genuinely puzzled at this point. "Why do you say that, David? We paid those assessors and engineers a fortune to examine it. They gave us a clean bill of health."

David groaned inside himself. "I . . . have a feeling."

Hank studied David for almost a minute and then, to David's complete surprise, he started laughing.

Hank read the confusion in David's eyes and answered his unspoken question. "Ah, you've got the 'I can't believe I bought it' blues." David's confusion only deepened. "I have to admit it took you longer than me. I remember the first time I spent a hundred million. I was so excited about closing on the property that I didn't really weigh all the work involved. When I figured out what I'd gotten myself into, I was sick for a week. It's anxiety, David. Your mind is figuring out the scope of the project ahead of you and you're reacting to the stress." Hank shook his head, still beaming at David.

"Take some time to catch your breath and then take each problem one at a time. You aren't in this thing alone and you didn't make this decision alone."

David pondered Hank's insight for a few seconds and then let out a sigh. *Maybe Hank's right.* The week of the closing had been extremely stressful and since that time, he had found a lot of little problems that he wasn't really on top of.

Hank continued. "Keep working and the anxiety will pass. Before you know it, everything will be coming together like clockwork."

David nodded. "Maybe . . . maybe you're right, Hank. I'm sorry to have bothered you."

Hank laughed again. "It's okay, David. Actually it's a good sign that you care so much. For what it's worth, Greg and I believe that the Pearl Point project is going to be a home run."

David nodded his head, turned slowly and ambled down the corridor to his office. He anchored his mind on Hank's advice and tried to forget his terrible dream, but the sickening foreboding that had plagued him all morning did not fade. He spent the rest of the afternoon and evening catching up on the work he had failed to complete that morning. He didn't leave the office until eleven o'clock. He had not eaten since breakfast. When he arrived at home, he had a bowl of cereal and went to bed. Sleep never came.

By five o'clock the next morning, David realized he had a serious problem. He could not close his eyes without imagining Pearl View collapsing. Surrendering to his dark fears, he donned his gym clothes and drove over to Pearl Point. As the first rays of the sun touched Manhattan, he turned his tortured gaze upon the building. Nothing happened. He waited till eight o'clock, when the sun was up well above the point he had seen in his dream, still nothing. He sighed in relief and slipped back into his car. *Not today.*

David made his way through the miserable traffic back to his apartment. It was eleven o'clock before he was showered, dressed, and headed for work. He fasted that morning because his stomach was still churning from worry. It was after noon by the time he reached his office. Work was impossible. He attempted several tasks, but his mind was still fixated on Pearl View. "This is madness," he muttered.

He thought long and hard for the next four hours. If Hank was right, then all of this was anxiety and there was nothing to worry about. But if Hank was wrong; if the lives of a thousand people were lost due to his inaction, David knew he would never be the same. He had to know.

David exploded into action. He studied every form of building and structural testing he could find on the Internet. He spoke to five offices and made three appointments to go over procedures and techniques with testing companies. He didn't leave the office till ten o'clock that night, exhausted and starved. Once again, he had not eaten all day. On his way home, he stopped in a diner and ordered a hamburger. Even though he was famished, he could only eat half of it.

That night when he undressed, his mind was heavy with worry. He was too tired to think clearly. When he knelt beside his bed to pray, he was uncertain. He finally bowed his head and pleaded. "Father, please protect Pearl View and watch over the souls that live there. Please give me time to figure this out." As he climbed into bed and pulled the covers up over his chest, he felt peace flow into him. It strengthened him and allowed him to close his eyes. *Not tonight.* He thought reassuringly. *It won't collapse tonight.*

The next day David had two meetings with structural engineers before he arrived to the office. During those interviews, he learned of a number of defects that could affect buildings. The catastrophic issues had their roots in foundation and support column problems. Luckily, there were new nondestructive tests that would identify those problems, but they were expensive.

David made a decision. He would perform nondestructive testing on the building at his own cost. A vertical sample of the complete building would cost between $120,000 and $200,000. There was no way to ask Hank for the money. He would simply have to pay for it himself and try to schedule it without anybody really noticing what he was doing. If Hank was right, there would be no results worth mentioning. But if he found something, then he would have proof he needed to convince Hank that they had a problem. David bit his lip. This course of action was contrary to Hank's orders. He suspected that Hank would be angry, but there was no choice here; people's lives were at stake.

David opened the door with his security pass and went straight across the lobby to the hallway. He needed to make several more phone calls and talk to at least one more engineer before settling on a contract. It was his own money he would be spending this time, so he was careful. The supply was limited.

* * *

Nicole was exasperated. David came in late Monday and never looked up. She could tell he was preoccupied. He slipped through the lobby like a man on a mission. It was like she didn't exist. The thought made her livid. She stewed at her desk in sullen silence. By the time she left work, she had pretty much concluded that she hated David. She decided she was never going to talk to him again. Unfortunately, she had the night off, and when she ate her dinner alone in the silence of her apartment, she thought better of it. She knew she was in a bad mood from lack of sleep and she also knew that she had avoided him the week before, so what did she expect?

On Tuesday Nicole was ready. When David came in, she stared right at him to see if she could catch his eye. She failed.

However, this time she saw his face and from the expression on it, she guessed that something was terribly wrong. She could tell that he was worried and afraid. It softened her heart when she realized he was suffering. She wondered if he was upset over her and that thought made her want to run down to his office and give him a hug. She resisted.

When David came in Wednesday he appeared less afraid but still totally absorbed and worried. Nicole decided that she had had enough. She was tired of playing cat and mouse when nobody else was playing, and she was terribly curious about what was going wrong in David's life. Nicole surrendered in exasperation. David was torturing her and he didn't even know it. She debated how she could approach him all morning and finally decided on a direct one. She crept down to David's office just before leaving that day. The door was open about a foot and she could see him studying something on his computer.

Nicole took a deep breath and let out a sigh. She pushed open the door, stepped into his office, and closed it behind her. David heard the door latch and stiffened in his chair. He sat there for a second before swiveling around. When he recognized her, surprise filled his face and he smiled. "Nicole." The word was filled with warmth.

Nicole smiled back weakly. It was the first time she had seen him smile in almost two weeks and it filled her with hope. She leaned against the wall and collected her thoughts. "David, I'm not mad anymore. I just need a little . . . " Nicole pursed her lips, "time."

David nodded in understanding but did not speak.

Nicole continued, "You look so unhappy and worried lately. What's wrong?"

"I'm having some problems with Pearl View, but," David smiled at her, "if you're talking to me then things are definitely getting better."

Nicole shook her head. David was still a farm boy, but it was fun to be able to make him so happy.

David tilted his head. "Would you like to have dinner this week? It's been pretty lonely eating every meal in solitude."

That's for sure, Nicole concurred. Then she made a hurt expression. "I'm busy this week, but I'll let you know when I get a break. We'll do something . . . special." She gave David a sly look as she turned and headed out his door.

Nicole couldn't believe how happy she was. It was stupid, really. Nothing had changed, but it seemed so important that David noticed her, that he hadn't given up on her, and that the possibilities were still alive. She must have been smiling too much because a stranger in the elevator tried to strike up a conversation with her on the way down to the ground floor. She was polite, but that was all. She stopped smiling until she reached the front doors. Then she smiled all the way to the deli, picked up a sandwich, and ate it on the way to a shoe store she had spotted the week before. It was a wonderful day.

The next three days were miserable for David. He hated going behind Hank's back, but he scheduled the preliminary tests Pearl View anyway. The first would be a foundation scan and then a vertical test. Three support columns on every floor all the way up. David was a little shocked when he received the estimate: $154,000 plus change. It seemed crazy to spend all that money in the hope that this would be a complete waste of time. He remembered that he had built Miss Abernathy's house for half that amount. At least the results would be almost instantaneous and there would be little damage to the building.

The best thing about that week was Nicole. David smiled when he thought of her. She made it a point to say good morning to him and smile every time he walked by. *Sometimes,* David thought wistfully, *it seems like everything would be alright if I could just hold her again.* Late Thursday, he was staring at the phone and waiting for news, when it rang. The sound startled him because he was concentrating so hard.

"David Samuelson speaking."

He heard Nicole's smooth voice. "Is that David the farm boy or David the lobster boy Samuelson?"

He laughed. He loved Nicole when she was in a good mood. She was right, too. No matter how bad this week had been, he was way too serious. He was about to ask why she called when another idea struck him.

"Nicole, would it be okay if I came up to the front, held you in my arms, and kissed you with all my heart?" He said it flatly, like he was ordering takeout.

The line was silent for several seconds before he heard Nicole respond with the tiniest lilt, "Maybe."

David smiled. Nicole was the most complex human being he had ever known. He was never quite sure where he stood.

Nicole was distracted by David's comment but not detoured. She had called for a reason. She didn't have a break in her schedule, but her cast was gearing up for its one-thousandth-performance celebration. That was a milestone for any production and they were going to celebrate with a black tie gala at one of the big hotels downtown. It was such a big event that Carl and Marlita had arranged for their honeymoon to end in time for the festivities. Everyone who was anyone would be there and Nicole didn't want to go alone. She also didn't want to go with farm boy or lobster boy, so she'd cooked up a plan to get her young executive to the gala in full regalia.

"Listen," Nicole dove in, "when I went to the beach, you promised you'd do something for me sometime."

David thought quickly, "Oh . . . yeah, I remember."

"Well, we're having a big cast party next Friday night at a hotel downtown and I want you to escort me."

David smiled, "I would love to, Nicole."

Nicole bit her lip. "Next week on Friday before the party, I want you to visit a friend of mine at the tanning salon and let her give you a makeover."

David squinted for a second. This didn't sound good. He blurted out his reservation, "I thought makeovers were for women." David grimaced, realizing his mistake. He regretted his response.

Nicole was instantly mad. *This is hopeless,* she smoldered.

David recovered quickly. "I'm sorry, Nicole. I guess a promise is a promise. I'll do whatever you want."

Nicole reined in her feelings. "Great! I really appreciate it, David, and who knows? You might actually enjoy yourself."

Nicole rattled off the instructions and David took notes while strange mental images flashed through his mind. He was to meet Elaine, Nicole's hair stylist, at the tanning salon in midtown at one o'clock on Friday the following week. She would get his tan fixed and then do his hair. After that, she would help him pick out a tuxedo. Once he was dressed, he was to rent a limo and be on his way by 6:30 P.M.. He was to pick Nicole up at seven o'clock making them fashionably late to the gala by 7:30 P.M..

As a last comment Nicole added, "And, David, could you pay Elaine for everything?" Nicole frowned when she said it. She knew it was a bit much, but she could always bring up her swim in the ocean and blame David for ruining her designer bathing suit. That was a little underhanded since she had actually been able to save it by showering the salt water off and drying it on a hanger. Luckily, she never had to make her case. David simply agreed.

Nicole was excited. She was curious to see how well Elaine could shine David up. He had all the raw ingredients. He just didn't know how to put the ensemble together. As for her, Nicole had been saving a beautiful black lace evening dress for the night. It cost a fortune and it was scintillating.

First there was the tight-fitting top, cut diagonally with a single shoulder strap over her left shoulder. Then there was the asymmetrical cut across the bottom of the dress. It came up high over the left thigh, dipped to a point between her legs and back up on her right thigh. The dress would have been scandalously short, but it was covered with black metallic beaded lace that swept down irregularly to her knees. When the light caught her legs, you could see through the lace and it had a dramatic effect.

To top it off, Nicole decided to dust off her strappy black sandals. She had purchased them on a whim and had never worn them. They had three-inch heels which, when added to the wild hair she was sporting, made her almost six and a half feet tall. Nicole smiled. Even with three extra inches, David would tower over her. They would be the talk of the evening, a different species from the rest of the attendees.

* * *

When David arrived at work Friday morning, he noticed that his message light was blinking. He tossed his briefcase on the desk and grabbed the phone. It was Salinger Engineering. The message was long and detailed, but David understood the information. His heart sank. The results were generally good except for one column on the 8th floor. The results from that floor showed something that might be a problem.

The 8th floor, David thought quickly. Pearl View had 27 stories. The 8th floor was a third of the way up. A shiver went through him. In his vision, Pearl View had buckled at a point roughly one third of the way from the ground. David's face was a mask of concentration as he picked up the phone to call Salinger Engineering. He asked for Mark Eliason who was the chief technician on the job. After three transfers, he heard a familiar, "Hello."

David was not in a good mood when he spoke. "I understand that the Pearl View building had some issues."

Mark was silent for a moment. "That's the apartment building in Jersey?"

"Yes," David answered.

Mark was silent for several seconds as he typed on his keyboard and scrolled his mouse. He finally found what he was searching for. "Looks like we had one hit, some kind of porosity problem in a column on the eighth floor. We did three columns on that floor and the other two were fine."

David was silent, thinking deeply for a moment. "How serious is the problem?"

"The degradation isn't too bad. If it's just one column, I wouldn't worry about it. However, if you have several bad columns close together, it could be dangerous."

"How's that?"

Mark answered thoughtfully. "Sometimes porous concrete can lose strength, even disintegrate under the right kind of stress. If the columns around it are secure, the structure tends to compensate for the weak member before catastrophic failure occurs."

David concentrated on Mark's analysis. "What causes this?"

"Who knows?" Mark responded thoughtfully. "Bad mix, freezing, curing issues, it's hard to tell at this point. If you do a core sample and a chemical analysis we would know more."

David sighed at all the uncertainty. *What do I do now?* He had to know more. He knew that Hank would kill him for this, but he also knew that lives hung in the balance.

"Mr. Eliason, do you still have your equipment on site?"

"Yeah."

"Test every column on the 8th floor and test any columns that might be affected on the 7th and 9th floors. If you have to go through walls to get to it, I don't care. I need those floors tested and I need them tested soon. I'll take care of any tenants you need help with and clean up when you're finished."

"Every column? Don't you want to do a little spread sampling first?"

"No," David answered. "I may not have time for that."

Once again, David had to wait. Even with the equipment on site, it took five more days to get the personnel back in place and get the building tested. In addition to all that anxiety, Nicole was too busy to see him until the gala Friday.

It was a miserable week. When Salinger Engineering finally finished testing on Wednesday, Mark Eliason gave David a call.

"Mr. Samuelson?"

"Yes."

"Mark Eliason here with Salinger engineering. We have the results on your building. We had to go through a few walls to get to the support columns, so you've probably had some complaints."

David was well aware of the damage to the building. He had heard from three angry tenants himself. Luckily he had Michael working on it. They would rebate a month's rent to each and get the problems cleaned up shortly.

"So," David inquired, "any more damaged columns?"

"As a matter of fact, yes." Mark Eliason paused and David heard the click of computer keys. "The good news is that there are only eight columns which seem to suffer from the porosity problem. The bad news is that they are all together in a row on the north side of the building."

David weighed Mark's implications, but he lacked the experience to reach a conclusion. "How dangerous is it?"

"We'd have a better idea if we could core sample a couple of them and do a finer analysis, but in general, the building will be okay, unless it is subjected to stress."

"Like an earthquake." David interrupted.

"Well, we don't have many earthquakes around here, but that would definitely do it. My guess is that columns on the north face of the building would buckle and the top would collapse into the bottom. It would be catastrophic. Of course New York is not a high risk earthquake zone, so none of the buildings are built for serious earthquake. Probably a lot of them would come down in a quake." Mark paused. "Still, if it were me . . . I wouldn't live there."

David was in agony on the other end of the phone. Mark had just described the dream that had run through his mind a hundred times in the last three weeks. At that moment, it seemed to David that everything in his life hinged on the next question. David spooled out his inquiry in trepidation and anxiety. "Can it be fixed?"

"Oh yeah," Mark responded with casually. "There are several companies in the city that can correct this. Usually they go in before the buildings are inhabited, but I'm sure they can work around your tenants."

David let out half a sigh of relief, but the other half of that relief depended on the next answer. "Any idea what it might cost?"

Mark was silent. "I really hate to give an estimate like that. The cost can vary greatly depending on the way the column is engineered into the building, which contractor you get, and how busy he is."

"Please Mr. Eliason," David pleaded, "I just need a ball park number."

Mark heard the desperation in David's voice. "Don't quote me on this. If you get a fair price, it would probably be somewhere between four to six million."

David let out another sigh of relief. It was a lot, but not prohibitive. David closed his eyes and gave a silent prayer in thanks. There was a way out. Then he spoke to Mark again. "Alright, can you document the data and send me a report? I need it as soon as possible. I have a big sales job here inside my company and I'll need all the evidence I can get."

"I can send you a copy of the preliminary report. It's not much more than a statement of work and a collection of images. I'll write up a conclusion in it to reiterate what we discussed and courier it over to you. You should have it by 5 P.M. tomorrow. I'll include the bill for our services as well."

David grimaced. He'd forgotten about that. He wondered what the final testing was going to run him, but before he hung up, another question occurred to him. "Mr. Eliason, can you recommend someone to repair the building?."

"No," Mark responded immediately. "We aren't allowed to recommend repair services. You can imagine what a conflict of interest that would be. Years ago we lost a very expensive lawsuit over that, but if you think it'll help, I'll include a list of city approved construction companies that you can contact. Of course this is not an endorsement of any of them, and I'm not sure if they're approved in Jersey, but at least it will get you started."

David expressed his appreciation before hanging up the phone. He sighed once again as a great burden lifted from his shoulders. *It can be fixed.* Then he thought about explaining all of this to Hank. It was going to be tough, but at least it made sense now.

David received the report at half past four the following day. He was a little disappointed when he examined the data. The difference in the images of the good columns and the bad ones was hardly distinguishable. The conclusion helped a lot, especially since it showed the location of the eight columns on the north side of the building. He reviewed and fussed over the document for almost an hour before deciding to take action.

David stood, rolled up the report and headed down to Hank's office. It was well past six o'clock, but he knew from long experience that Hank would still be there. Hank wasn't married so he almost always worked till ten at night. He worked hard and played hard. If he wasn't out on some adventure somewhere, he was in his office.

Angela was already gone so David knocked on Hank's door, breaking the silence. A moment later he heard Hank's rough voice. "Come in."

David opened the door and poked his head in. "Hank, may I interrupt you for a minute?"

Hank lifted his head and David flinched. Hank's expression was flat and angry. Something was wrong. He glared at David with a scowl on his face. "What is it?"

David reconsidered his plan. It was obvious that Hank was in a bad mood, but he decided to forge ahead anyway. "I've been running some tests on Pearl View. There's a

problem, but . . ." David held up his hands, ". . . it's fixable."
David placed the report on Hank's desk. "I had the columns
in the building tested from top to bottom and found a
problem on the eighth floor. When the engineers tested the
eighth floor they found eight adjacent columns that have
structural deficiencies." David peered up from his report to
get a read from Hank. Hank was staring at him with murder
in his eyes. David swallowed and opened the report. "As you
can see here, most of the columns . . ." David stopped
talking. Hank had not moved. He was still sitting in his chair
staring.

David lifted his eyes again and studied Hank. Their eyes
met. And then, the storm that was brewing inside of Henry
Walton Burkover, exploded.

"Who in the hell do you think you are?!" The words were
spoken with such venom and hatred that David recoiled,
slumping back in his chair.

"I told you that this was nothing; that you needed to
move on and forget about it." Hank paused and the veins in
his neck stood out. "Next thing I know, there is some
moronic engineering company kicking holes in the building
and pissing off my tenants." Hank picked up a stack of emails
on his desk and shook them.

David trembled in confusion. *How did he know?* The
answer suddenly materialized in his mind, *Michael,* Michael
had no doubt told Hank everything that was going on at Pearl
View. He noted with a glance that the emails were from
Michael.

David swallowed to stabilize his voice. "There's a
problem with Pearl View." David started in again. "If we
don't do something about it, people will die."

Hank bellowed in frustration. "What in the hell are you
talking about? Pearl View has been there for thirty years with
absolutely no stress or foundation problems. We had an
engineer go through it with a fine-toothed comb. David,"

anger and frustration boiled in his voice, "there's no problem with Pearl View!"

Hank bit off his words with such force that he was shouting. David felt cornered and threatened, but he kept his head. "I've tested the building Mr. Burkover," David pointed to the report on Hank's desk, "There are eight damaged adjacent columns on the eighth floor."

David was about to show him the pictures when Hank stood up and batted the report off his desk. He hit it so hard that it flew across the room and thudded dully against the plate glass window. "That is a crock!"

Hank never took his eyes off David and David never felt more exposed. Sitting there without his expensive and carefully extracted evidence, there was no way to take a position. He searched desperately for the right words to say. How could he convey the urgency of the situation? Closing his eyes, David could feel the heat of the cauldron in the back of his mind. Once again, he was trapped, there was no way out.

David's hands curled into fists and he stood to face Hank. Though he had never thought of himself that way, he was an imposing figure. He was eight inches taller than Hank and probably sixty pounds heavier. But Hank Burkover was like a locomotive out of control. He had given David specific instructions and David had gone behind his back to do exactly the opposite.

Once again, David stabilized his thoughts and found his voice. His voice deepened and he bit off his words with certainty. "I have seen it fall."

Hank's fierce expression changed slightly to one of partial confusion. He lifted his hands and shook them at David. "What are you talking about?"

"In a dream." David's voice was low and grave. "There is an earthquake or an explosion; Pearl View buckles at the eight floor and collapses on itself." David paused recognizing the absurdity of his statement. Hank had left him with no other defense. "I have seen it in a vision."

The expression on Hank's face shifted from anger to revulsion. His nostrils flared and the veins pounded in his neck. His bitter words came out harshly. They were absolute. "You . . . are . . . mad!"

David didn't speak. There was nothing left to say. Both men stood there staring at each other for almost a minute. Both men realized that they had lost something precious that day. Their relationship would never be the same. Hank gazed down at his desk. "I'll give you one more chance, David. I don't ever want to hear about this subject again."

David sighed and lowered his head in defeat. His thoughts started racing. *There must be something, some way to change this.* But nothing materialized in his mind. Facing the reality and understanding the magnitude of his failure, David turned and walked across Hank's office. There was an ominous feeling to his heavy steps. When he reached the door, he opened it and departed without looking back.

* * *

Elaine Kaminsky was nervous. She normally worked in her shop on Fridays, but Nicole had talked her into this crazy ordeal. She was supposed to meet Nicole's boyfriend, David, at the tanning salon, get him a tan, a hairdo, and help him rent a tuxedo for her gala tonight. Elaine didn't like the idea from the start, but Nicole had been Elaine's best customer, best tipper, and friend of sorts since they met four years ago. Still, Elaine's anxiety persisted. Part of her trepidation came from Nicole's insecurity over this crazy escapade.

Elaine arrived at Quick Tan ten minutes ahead of schedule and seated herself in the lobby. She was praying in her heart that David would be a nice guy, because if he was even the least bit mean or upset, then she was bailing out. She had devised a plan B which was, basically, to run away. She made a point to arrive at the salon early so she could get a good look at Nicole's boyfriend before he recognized her. If she felt threatened in any way, she would slip out before being recognized.

At 1 P.M. the doorway darkened and a huge young man stepped through. He was almost seven feet tall. Nicole hadn't mentioned that he was built like a football player. He had brown hair and brown eyes with a little scar over his left eye. There was no mistaking him. It was David.

Elaine took one look at his face and bile filled her stomach. He was not smiling. He was not happy. Elaine groaned in despair. *Why did I let Nicole talk me into this. I have enough problems without getting mixed up in Nicole's stupid high maintenance social life.* Elaine was only five feet two and barely a hundred and ten pounds; David looked like a monster to her. She had only studied him for a second when a terrifying thought seized her. *He's upset.* Elaine felt like crying. She decided to make a run for it, but as she turned her head look away, David caught her eyes and spoke questioningly.

"Elaine?"

"Y. . . yes."

"David Samuelson." He held out his hand. "I guess Nicole sentenced you to babysit me for the day." His smile helped relieve Elaine's distress. When she shook David's hand, it engulfed hers like a whale swallowing a fish. "So," David's expression went flat, "how do I get a tan in one day? I tried it once before and I wasn't very successful."

"Oh," Elaine responded nervously, "you'll see." She walked with David to the counter.

It took about an hour. The attendant led him to a changing room where he donned a tiny paper swimsuit and tucked his hair under a swim cap. Then he waited for twenty minutes until a beautifully tanned girl with blond hair led him to a booth where he was sprayed with tanning mist. It was humiliating to be so exposed in front of a complete stranger, but she acted like it was nothing. She led him back to another private room where he waited another thirty minutes for it to dry. That room had a mirror and when he gazed into it, he was shocked to see that he had a perfect tan.

Elaine was nervous. David wasn't very happy when he went into the tanning booth and now he looked perfectly miserable coming out. The tan was perfect, but she could tell he didn't really think of it as an improvement. As they walked from the tanning booth to her hair salon, she attempted to make the situation more comfortable by keeping up a constant conversation. This was a professional necessity for any hairdresser, but for Elaine, it was also a nervous tic. Usually her clients interacted with her, but David's mind seemed elsewhere. His hard expression never changed and he never spoke a word in the four blocks they walked together.

Since David didn't know where Elaine's was taking him, he followed a step behind her. She was going a little fast because she was nervous and the tanning salon had taken longer than she expected. She had trouble making her way through the streets because she kept turning around to engage him in conversation. To make matters worse, David was so tall that it was killing her neck to look up at him.

She was in full discussion when they arrived at Prince Street where her salon was located. As she approached the intersection and took what she thought was the last step, her right foot never hit the ground. She had miscalculated where the sidewalk ended and the road began. Instead of landing on solid ground, her foot slipped off the edge of the curb. She stumbled forward and swung her other foot forward to balance herself. Unfortunately, the heel of her right pump landed in a drainage grate, pinning her foot and completely throwing her off balance.

Elaine went down hard. She flung her purse out and attempted to catch herself with her hands. Unfortunately, she was too twisted to get her hands in front of her. Her elbow slammed onto the pavement and then her shoulder. She managed to fall sideways enough so she didn't land in the center of the street, but that motion twisted her ankle. As if all that wasn't bad enough, the curb was filled with some kind of sticky fluid and the right side of her outfit was soaked in it.

Elaine lay there frozen for a second and then the pain in her elbow and ankle blossomed. She turned her head slightly to see David. He was staring down at her like she was an idiot. She sagged in despair. She was so embarrassed that she hung her head as her eyes burned with tears.

David never said a word, never asked, never opened his mouth. He stood there frozen for a moment and then he stepped over Elaine, knelt down in front of her, and lifted her in his arms. Elaine was even more embarrassed then, but she was also amazed. It was like he was picking a bagel up out of the gutter. There seemed to be no strain or effort in his actions. He carried her across the street to a bench where two boys sat watching the whole thing.

David addressed them forcefully. "Excuse me boys, could I borrow your bench? My friend has taken a little tumble."

Both boys jumped up and David sat her on the bench. Then he ran back to retrieve her purse and the shoe she had caught in the grate. A minute later he returned and set them beside her. "Are you alright?"

Elaine nodded. Her ankle hurt a little, but it was her elbow that she was worried about. Worst of all, her face was bright red with embarrassment. David knelt in front of her and gently took her foot in his hands.

"Does this hurt?" He moved her ankle slightly and put a little pressure on it.

"No, that doesn't hurt much, but my elbow is sure sore."

David took Elaine's hand and gently lowered and raised it. "How about that?"

"I guess it's okay too."

David disappeared into a corner grocery store and emerged with several paper towels. He gently wiped the liquid off Elaine's shoulder. It would leave a bad stain for sure, but at least it didn't smell.

"I'm so embarrassed, David. I hope you won't think of me as a total klutz."

David smiled for the first time. "You are a very kind person, Elaine. Nicole is lucky to have you as a friend. I'm sorry I'm not more of a conversationalist today. I'm having a lot of problems at work and it has preoccupied me."

Elaine smiled. *He is so sincere.* She glanced up the street towards her studio. "We'd better get going. We're running a little late."

David nodded and then, to Elaine's complete surprise and horror, he stooped over and lifted her in his arms again. Elaine protested. "No, no, you don't have to carry me. I can walk. I'm sure."

"You're so light, Elaine. This is fun. Could you humor me a little? I haven't had any fun in weeks."

Elaine wanted to object out of dignity when a stray thought stopped her. *What will my friends at the salon say when they see David carrying me?* Elaine worked with a lively bunch of women and she could only imagine what responses she would get when they saw her in David's arms. It would provide a wonderful backdrop for future conversations. Elaine chuckled. *It is kind of fun.* A big smile broke out on her face. "Okay," she said, "anything for Nicole."

David pulled Elaine close to his chest. She set her purse and shoe on her stomach and wrapped her arms around his neck. Then he carried her the three blocks to her salon. Every eye was upon them as they passed.

Elaine was amazed. It seemed so effortless for David. She was actually sad when they reached her shop. David smiled the whole way. He never broke a sweat. When they reached the front door, he lowered her and held her arm while she put on her shoe.

As they entered, Debbie, one of the other hairdressers, shouted to her. "Elaine, I thought Nicole asked you to do her boyfriend's hair not marry him."

"David gave me a lift because I fell down."

"Are you alright?"

"Yes, I'm fine but," Elaine lowered her voice and winked at Debbie, "don't tell David that. He carried me for three blocks and it was sweeeeet!"

Debbie glanced at David and whistled. Then she whispered back to Elaine. "Nicole is gonna kill you!"

Elaine took David to her station and organized her equipment. Once he was seated, she lowered his chair until the back of his head was in the sink, then she sprayed warm water in his hair and shampooed it. It was pretty short so it didn't take long. She lathered it down twice, being careful not to wash off any of his new tan. Then she dried his hair and raised the chair.

Elaine mussed with David's short hair for over an hour. She set up four different styles. Each time she would ask him what he thought, and each time, he would gaze at himself in the mirror and say something like, "It looks pretty good. Are we finished?" After the fourth time, Elaine realized that he was just being polite.

Nicole told her to add some highlights to his hair and make it stand up, but Elaine couldn't do it. She settled on darkening it and making it fuller with some wave. Then she darkened his eyebrows to match. David looked amazingly good. He reminded Elaine of a Greek God and he looked more mature and masculine than he would have with highlights or spikes.

Since she didn't end up highlighting his hair, they finished early. From there they took a cab to the tuxedo rental shop. Together they poked around for about an hour until Elaine settled on a Cordova-style tuxedo. The lapels were broad and shiny. It was double-breasted and very open in the front, revealing David's large chest. She was able to find a fitted shirt that seemed to mold to David's body and pants that emphasized his small muscular waist. Once she finished with the matching bowtie, she studied him in the fading sunlight.

He was handsome and ooooh so masculine. *I'm in love*, Elaine thought dreamily.

David wasn't smiling much and it worried her. Ever since he set her down in the salon he seemed unhappy. She suspected it was probably because of his work, but it made her nervous. She glanced at her watch. It was only a quarter past six. Since the limo wouldn't be by for a half an hour, they had time to kill. David figured as much and as they finished the tuxedo fitting he leaned over and whispered to her. "I'm starved, Elaine. I left straight from the office and didn't get any lunch. Could we get a bite to eat?"

Elaine was relieved. "You stay here. I'll go get us a couple of sandwiches and be right back." After talking to the tuxedo people, Elaine sped down the street a block to a deli where she purchased two sandwiches. She had an ulterior purpose in leaving David behind. She telephoned Nicole while she was waiting.

Nicole was in her own dressing dilemma. She frowned when her cell phone rang and debated whether or not to answer, but when she noticed Elaine's name on the caller ID she flipped it open in concern. "Hello, this is Nicole."

"Hi, Nicole." Elaine tried to sound perky.

"Elaine," Nicole forged ahead. "How's it going? I've been so curious about you two."

"Well, I finally got him ready. I didn't put any highlights in his hair because he looked better without them. But," and Elaine paused for effect, "he is gorgeous, girl, and so polite. You are soooo lucky!"

Nicole didn't answer. A broad smile filled her face.

"Anyway," Elaine continued, "there's one thing I wanted to mention." Elaine gritted her teeth. She knew how Nicole hated bad news. "He doesn't seem very happy. He told me he was having some problems at work, but I don't think he likes being dressed up. Whenever he sees himself in the mirror he looks away kind of disgusted." Elaine sighed. "Anyway, I wanted to let you know. Maybe you can cheer him up a little when you see him."

The smile evaporated from Nicole's face as her temper flared. *Dumb farm boy,* she thought. Here she had made all these arrangements to make him look like somebody and he gets all moody. Then, remembering how upset he had seemed at work, she thought better of it. *Maybe I pushed too far.* Nicole felt guilty. She tapped her fingernails on her teeth nervously. *Well, I'll just have to make it worth his while.*

Elaine heard the silence on the other end of the phone and hoped that Nicole wasn't mad. That girl had a temper to be sure, but Elaine was trying to help her out. Nicole answered back pensively. "He did have a tough week, but I'm sure everything will be okay. Thanks for the heads up, though. I'll try to cheer him up a little when I see him." They said goodbye and Elaine picked up her order.

David and Elaine ate their sandwiches in silence. It had rained that morning, but it was shaping up into a beautiful evening. When the limo arrived David smiled flatly at Elaine. "I guess it's time to go." He took an envelope out of his wallet and handed it to her. "Nicole said this would cover everything." Elaine opened the envelope and found a check made out to her for $700.

Elaine nodded. "It's more than enough. Thank you, David. I really enjoyed being with you today."

The limo driver opened the door and David climbed in the back seat. He waved goodbye to Elaine as they sped away. Twenty minutes later, he was at Nicole's apartment. He flicked open his cell phone and called.

"Hello, this is Nicole."

"Miss Mitchell," David responded regally, "your coach has arrived." He paused for effect. "We are a few minutes early. Would you like me to come up and escort you?"

"I'm ready. I'll be down in a second. Wait there for me."

David stepped outside the limo to wait in the evening breeze. Three minutes later, Nicole appeared at the entrance to her apartment building. When his eyes traced the figure of her beautiful athletic body, he stopped breathing. Nicole was stunning. She was wearing a pair of black high-heeled sandals that made her taller than he remembered and her hair looked like a lion's mane, but what really stopped his heart was her black party dress. It clung tightly across the top of her body with a single strap over her left shoulder, then it flowed down to her knees. But it didn't completely cover her. The lower part of her dress was made out of some kind of beaded sheer lace. He could see Nicole's beautiful long legs beneath it.

David felt something primal awaken inside him. An emptiness opened in his stomach as desire burned in his veins. He swallowed and wet his lips. "Nicole . . . you are a dream."

She didn't speak, but walked up to him, wrapped her arms around him and kissed him with all her might. David held her tight. It was a long, lingering kiss. When their lips parted, Nicole never let go. Instead, she smiled up into his eyes and spoke a single word, "Yes."

David smiled. "What was that for?"

"Well," she squeezed him a little tighter, "you asked me if you could come down to my desk, hold me in your arms, and kiss me with all of your heart. The answer is yes."

David remembered. He had been teasing at the time, but now he was glad he said it.

"Besides," Nicole went on, "you look fantastic tonight."

David let go of her. Stepping back he opened the door and held it for her. "Shall we go?"

Nicole climbed in the car and David followed. She leaned forward and spoke to the driver. "Since we're a little early, could you take us down through the theatre district? I want a peek at what's playing."

Nicole sat back in her seat and took David's hand in hers. She gazed curiously into his face. She couldn't believe he was the same person. Elaine had transformed David into a movie star and Nicole loved it. But there was something more than what Elaine had done to him. David's eyes were different. He wasn't smiling, so that hazy farm boy look was gone. Instead, the anxiety and concern in his eyes made him seem fiercely intelligent. It reminded her of a warrior preparing for battle. Tonight would be her night. Nicole knew it. It would be impossible to miss David. He was so tall and so big and so serious that they would be the talk of the town. Everyone would stare at them.

They drove around for forty minutes, checking out the different theaters. Nicole pretty much knew what was showing, but it was always interesting to check out the posters.

They pulled up to the hotel a few minutes after eight o'clock. It was lit up like a cruise ship and loud music was pouring from the lobby. When they stepped out of the car, Nicole adjusted her dress before catching David and straightening his bow tie. Then she inspected his jacket and slicked down a loose lock of hair. She smiled at him approvingly and took his arm. Together they walked through the hotel lobby and into the ballroom.

It was exhilarating. David was so big that everybody turned to see who he was. Nicole pulled him to a halt at the entrance and stood there. David was not smiling. His eyes narrowed as he peered into the dark room. He looked absolutely menacing. She watched in total bliss as the eyes and faces of her friends and associates turned toward them. They found David first and after measuring his size and intellect, their gaze fell on her. Nicole radiated.

After thirty seconds that would last for an eternity in Nicole's mind, Marlita waved to her and she started David in that direction. Everybody spoke to them as they passed. David said almost nothing. He stood straight as a soldier as Nicole held onto his arm and greeted everyone in their path.

The night was magical. Nicole spoke to everybody who was anybody in the play. She even had a chance to meet a couple of successful agents. Her director and producer both made it a point to come and say hello. She danced every slow song with David and, other than trips to the lady's room, she made it a point to be next to him the entire night. David hardly smiled all night. It added to his mysterious air and between all the attention they were getting, Marlita and Carl told them about their honeymoon cruise through the Caribbean during hurricane season. They had a great time, in spite of a storm chasing them.

As the night wore on, David grew quieter and quieter. Nicole didn't really mind since it was her party and she was the center of attention. In fact, it was better that way. David seemed so fierce and intelligent when he was quiet that Nicole loved it. The farm boy from Alaska was gone.

Nicole's magical evening slowly came to a close around one o'clock. She had drunk more than usual and she was starting to feel it. It wasn't enough to affect her judgment, only her mood. She had enjoyed herself immensely and she felt more secure than ever because she had David, the warrior king, beside her.

Nicole closed her eyes and imagined she was a queen, the object of everyone's attention and admiration. No one could harm her. No one could *be* her. She was beside David, holding his hand. *Safe hands*, Nicole thought. David never drank, never lied, never deceived. He was secure, steady and stable like a rock. Then another thought struck her. *Safe hands*. Nicole peered up at David wickedly. *Tonight* . . . Nicole smiled mischievously. *We'll see how safe those hands are tonight.*

They took the limo back to her apartment. Nicole held David's arm tightly and rested her head on his shoulder the whole way. Every once in awhile she would glance up into his face and shake her head. He looked soooo good. He could have been a famous movie star and the night wouldn't have been any better. When they reached her apartment, David exited ahead of her and came around to hold the door for her. *David never changes*, she thought, but it didn't matter tonight.

Together they walked to her building and Nicole buzzed her way through the security door. They took the elevator up to her apartment on the fifth floor. When they reached her door, she gave David another hug and a lingering kiss. As their lips parted, Nicole slid to David's side. She ran her hand under his jacket and threaded her fingers under his shirt. She gazed up into his eyes.

"I don't ever want this night to end, David." She raked her fingers across the rippling muscles of his stomach. He was trembling. She smiled slyly and spoke softly to him. "Stay with me tonight."

David lowered his head and closed his eyes. She felt his body shake even harder. He let out a long sigh and his face tightened in concentration. Then, he spoke a single word. It rose from a place inside of him that she had never sensed before. His voice had never been deeper and the sentiment that filled it was more powerful than any moment they had ever shared together. She felt the word rise from the center of the earth, pass his lips, and echo into the empty hallway.

"No."

Nicole couldn't believe her ears. She stared into David's face in shock. His eyes were closed. He stood frozen in silence for a few seconds. Then he carefully extracted her hand and let it drop to her side. He opened his eyes but never looked at her. Instead, he stared past her to the elevator. The doors were still open. He walked down the hall and climbed in. He never looked back.

* * *

David was sweating like an athlete. He could feel his heart beating and his hands wouldn't stop trembling. He couldn't close his eyes without seeing her and feeling her soft skin against him. The images that filled his mind were vivid and powerful. Desire burned through him, threatening the very essence of who he was. It was all he could do to walk away, but in the end . . . he did. He clenched his teeth in determination. *I will not surrender to this.*

David stared at the back of the elevator and pushed the button for the ground floor. He didn't turn around until the elevator doors closed. When the doors opened on the first floor, he made his way out the front door and climbed into the limo. He gave the driver the address of his apartment and slumped back against the seat. He had to regain control.

Strangely, it was the cauldron that helped him. It was the only image his mind could hold that was stronger than Nicole's. He concentrated on it. He concentrated on the endless burning of the embers, on the dark fear and sorrow it held, and using that powerful anchor, he pushed the image of Nicole from his mind. It was almost impossible. His mind clung to the vision of her and him together. It was intoxicating. His hands were caressing her soft skin. She was kissing him. Her warm breath was upon his neck . . . "Stop." David said the word aloud and the limo driver turned around and gave him a strange look. David quickly apologized. "I'm sorry, I was thinking about something else." David peered down at the floor.

When they arrived, he paid the limo driver and trudged up the steps to his apartment. He went straight to the bathroom and turned on both faucets in the bathroom sink. When it was full, he stuck his face in the water and then, raising it up, he gazed at himself in the mirror. It wasn't him. The man staring back at him from the mirror was handsome. He wore a beautiful tuxedo with a pleated shirt and tiny round black buttons. He had a perfect tan and his hair was dark and moist.

David groaned. He took off his clothes and climbed into the shower. He washed himself for almost thirty minutes. When he was finished, his hair was back to normal and his tan was not so dark, but he still didn't recognize the image staring back at him from the mirror. Something was different.

What should have been the best night in his life, had been the worst. Nicole was so beautiful and the gala was as lavish as anything he had ever attended. But every time he met a new person, he wondered. *Did that person live at Pearl View? Would that person live at Pearl View when it collapsed? Would that person know someone at Pearl View when it collapsed? Would that person curse him in the next life, when he came to understand that David knew the building would collapse and didn't do something to prevent it?* He shuddered. How could he stand before God and answer for his life if he were responsible for the deaths of so many?

Then another voice rose in his head. He had done everything he could. He had spent almost $380,000 of his own money to identify and isolate the problem. He had told Hank in the clearest of terms what would happen and why he believed it. He had risked his career on it but in the end, he didn't have the ability or the authority to fix it.

Then there was Nicole. Her image was seared his mind. All night long he was drawn closer and closer to her. Holding her hand, holding her body as they danced. She had been so happy, so loving, so . . . willing. When he held her in front of her apartment, he knew that if he could lose himself in her arms for one night, that it would be gone. He could forget about Pearl View and, for once in his life, he could be like everyone else.

The cauldron burned with intensity. David's fragile peace was shattered. He walked back and forth across his room, pacing and pacing in the vain hope that some solution would materialize. It was an impossible dilemma. At half past three, he crossed the room one last time and dropped to his knees. He clasped his hands and lowered his head. He knelt there in silence for minutes, pouring through the thoughts that haunted him. Finally, these few words left his lips.

"Father, I don't know what to do. Please Father, help me find a way . . . help me to save Pearl View."

He rose slowly from his knees and climbed into bed. He turned off the light and stared at the ceiling until his eyes adjusted to the darkness. He could barely make out the image of the ceiling fixture. David's mind was racing, measuring every path. *What can I do? How can I stop this disaster?* Nothing came to him, but as David peered at the subtle light highlighting the edge of his curtains, a strange thought struck him.

New York was always awake, always alive. It was impossible to be in complete darkness anywhere in the city. There was always a little light no matter how hard you tried to seal it out. Sometimes you just had to let your eyes adjust, but there was always a way to see. A sliver of understanding illuminated David's heart. *There is a way.* Hope filled him. Like a soothing blanket, it flowed through him, stabilizing him against the despair that threatened to swallow him. He closed his eyes and clung to the tenuous calm within him. Minutes later, he drifted off into a fragile sleep.

DELIVERANCE

Chapter 23

R ay Campbell stared at the file on his desk. "McMurray Estate" was written in heavy black ink on the tab. *How long has it been?* He thought searchingly. *Ten . . . no, more than fifteen years since this first came to my attention. Poor David and Helen.* Ray had been a member of the Methodist congregation and friends with the old pastor years before it happened. Actually, he had been his bookkeeper. Ray rarely thought about it anymore. It was the saddest story he'd ever known and Ray was disturbed by it. It challenged his faith. David McMurray was one of the most honorable men Ray had ever met and yet, life had dealt harshly with the McMurrays.

David McMurray had two daughters, Rachael, who lived at home and Catherine, whom he'd known as a little girl. Catherine married a roofer and eventually moved away to California. They had four children. There had been a terrible accident. Catherine, her husband and three daughters perished in a fire. The only survivor was their little boy, David. Rachael had flown out immediately at the request of the authorities and arrived in time to speak with her sister one last time. A friend brought the little boy to the hospital hours before Rachael arrived. He took one glance at his dying mother and bolted into the streets of Sacramento. He was never seen or heard from again.

The tragedy destroyed the family. David and Helen searched every inch of Sacramento and even organized a national campaign to find their grandson. There was a lot of crying and praying the first few months, but after a year passed with no sign of the boy, most people gave up. The old pastor didn't, however. He always believed that his grandson was alive and no one could convince him otherwise. He worked with police and detectives for years to find him, but it was all in vain. His wife passed away in her sixties and the old minister wasn't far behind.

Their only surviving daughter, Rachael, continued the cause. She searched for her nephew diligently until she was diagnosed with cancer. Then she carefully liquidated all the estate and consolidated it into a trust for him. The estate was significant because the old pastor had judiciously invested in companies that he knew the managers of personally.

After her father died, no one but Rachael believed the boy was alive. Rachael held that hope to the end. Ray still remembered her final instructions to him. "You'll find him one day, Ray. Be sure to give him the material I've prepared for him and tell him that we never forgot him. Tell him that we always loved him."

That was six years ago and Ray Campbell still had the estate in his care. He told Rachael that a lawyer could better handle this kind of thing, but Rachael insisted. She told him that he was the only person her father trusted and therefore, the only person she trusted. They formalized the trust and Ray became executor. Rachael died a year later. Ray hadn't really done anything with the case since.

Sunday night, as he was getting ready for bed, the thought occurred to him that he should probably do another search. He had long since given up hope of ever finding the boy, but he felt obligated to keep trying in honor of the old pastor and their friendship. Ray was doubtful. It would be a miracle if he were alive and another miracle if he were using his real name. What was it? Ray racked his brain until the name popped up. *David . . . like his grandfather, David Samuelson.*

Monday morning Ray pulled out the McMurray file and gave Barbara, his secretary, instructions on how to proceed. She was to do a search on the name David Samuelson in the white pages, yellow pages and general Internet. If that didn't turn up any interesting results, they would jingle the authorities again and see if they could get a hit on the social security records.

Barbara worked all morning. Like before, the search turned up over a hundred matches, most of which had already been catalogued. The remaining new hits were easily eliminated by age, but there were three new real candidates. It was always a long shot, but to be sure Ray told Barbara to contact every one of them in person. She would verify their names and birthdays but no other details. If it was even close to a match, Ray would make the final call.

This was a little tricky. The old minister's estate was worth almost two million dollars. You couldn't call and tell people that two million dollars was waiting for them if they were the right David Samuelson.

By two in the afternoon, Barbara had narrowed it down to one real candidate. She left the information on the corner of Ray's desk. Ray slid the folder over until it was directly in front of him. He peeled the yellow sticky off and studied the phone number on it. *This one's in New York City.* His curiosity piqued and he dialed immediately. After three rings, a deep voice answered. "Hello, this is David Samuelson."

Ray cleared his throat. "Hello, my name is Raymond Campbell. I'm working in conjunction with a family who is searching for a missing person." Ray paused to see if there were any questions, but the phone was quiet. Ray continued, "Would you have any information on a Catherine Samuelson?"

It was, of course, a trick question and Ray expected a quick dismissal, but this time there was nothing. He waited several more seconds and then, suspecting the line was dead, he spoke again. "Hello ah . . . Mr. Samuelson . . . are you still there?" Ray was about to hang up when David's deep and penetrating voice filled his ear.

"Catherine Samuelson . . . was my mother."

Ray's mouth dropped open in shock and disbelief. *It can't be . . .* A thousand questions suddenly burst in to Ray's mind but he quickly regrouped and continued his investigation. "Do you know how we can get in touch with her?" It was another trick question and, once again, there was a long pause. This time, however, Ray waited with anxious hope. When David answered, his voice was grave.

"I'm sorry, Mr. Campbell. My mother, Catherine, and my father, Joseph, passed away almost twenty years ago."

Ray was dumbfounded. *It's him.* The thought left him speechless for several seconds. "Mr. Samuelson, it is extremely important that we meet. Is there any chance you could come to Atlanta this week?"

"No," David responded without hesitation, "I'm in the middle of a large project. I'm afraid it will be quite some time before I can get down there."

Ray nodded in understanding. "Well, if I can get to New York, would you have time to sit down with me?" Ray added intensely. "I assure you, this will be well worth your time."

"I'll make time," David answered firmly. "Thursday or Friday afternoon this week would be good. Let me know and I'll pencil in an appointment for you. What is this regarding?"

"Your family, David." Ray was smiling now. "This is about your family."

Ray made an appointment for Friday afternoon. He wanted to ask David the question that was burning in his mind. *Where have you been for the last seventeen years?* But he knew he needed to wait until he could meet with him in person. He had to have one confirming look at this specter to know if he was real. They exchanged contact information and Ray wrote down the directions to David's office. After setting the phone on its base, he leaned back in his chair and gazed blankly at the ceiling. His mind reeled. *Rachael and the old pastor were right! They never gave up and they were right. It's a miracle!*

* * *

David was miserable. It was one of the slowest, longest weeks in his life. He spent every day working on Pearl View, but the cloud of doom that hovered over the project was impenetrable. Then there was Nicole. He tried not to think about her. He knew she probably hated him by now.

Monday he received the phone call from Atlanta. He'd set up a meeting with a Raymond Campbell for Friday afternoon. Mr. Campbell seemed so excited when David answered his questions, but David was not encouraged. Their conversation touched something raw inside of him and the cauldron had been burning more intensely all week. David's mind drifted back again and again to that conversation, but each time he started down that road, the cauldron would nearly overpower him. *Somehow*, David thought darkly, *they are connected.*

Friday at 1 P.M., Ray Campbell buzzed the door outside the offices of Downing & Burkover. He was surprised at the height of the tower and how plush the office was where David worked. Ray reasoned that whoever this David Samuelson was, he lived in a far different life than his conservative family had. The receptionist was a beautiful girl and she initially seemed quite cordial, but when Ray told her that he was there to see David Samuelson, she peered back at him like he had leprosy. She lowered her head, jerked her thumb over her ear, and said sharply, "Down the hall to the left."

It unnerved Ray that the mention of David's name evoked such an unpleasant reaction. The McMurrays had been such polite and friendly people. He couldn't imagine their son being any different. *Oh well*, Ray thought in annoyance, *this is New York after all.*

Ray noticed David's nametag on the door as he approached. He stepped in front of the open door and peered inside. What he saw startled him. There, sitting behind a beautiful mahogany desk, was a huge young man. He wasn't doing anything. He was sitting quietly, staring at the top of his desk in deep concentration. There was nothing in front of him. Ray hesitated and then knocked softly. David glanced up and, seeing Ray in the doorway, he stood. "Come in. You must be Mr. Campbell."

Ray nodded politely and was relieved when David smiled. He shook David's hand and then had a nagging doubt. David was huge. *How could Pastor McMurray be related to this monster?* Ray brushed the thought away. He was here. He had to finish what he started.

"David Samuelson?"

"Yes."

Ray sighed. "I would like to show you a few pictures. Could you tell me if you recognize any of these people?" David studied him with an intense expression as Ray opened his briefcase and took out an envelope. After shuffling through the documents for a few seconds, he held up a picture of the old pastor. "Is this person familiar to you?"

David peered at the picture momentarily and then back at Ray. It made Ray uncomfortable to fall under that piercing stare. "That's my grandfather, David McMurray."

Placing the picture on the desk, Ray wiped his forehead and brought out another picture. "And this?"

"That's my Aunt Rachael."

Ray placed the second picture on the desk and pulled out the final one. *Maybe* . . . a little warning voice said inside his head, *maybe this isn't such a good idea.* Ray took a deep breath and studied the picture of Catherine. A revelation suddenly burst forth in Ray's mind. It was obvious. David had his mother's eyes. Ray carefully laid the last picture on the desk.

The reaction was palpable. A ragged breath shuddered from David's lips and every muscle in his face went taunt. Then his eyes changed. Those disturbing eyes that had been so penetrating, suddenly became fierce. Fear gripped Ray and a haunting thought seized him. *What have I awakened?* But it quickly passed. David's eyes softened as he studied the picture. He was silent for a long time. When he answered, his voice was hardly more than a whisper. "That's my mother, Catherine."

Ray cleared his throat and sat up straight. "David, I have known your family for over twenty years. Your grandfather was my dear friend. When your mother and father died seventeen years ago, it nearly killed your grandfather. He and your Aunt Rachael spent years searching for you. They never gave up. They always believed that you were alive and that you were in God's hands somehow."

Ray realized that his voice was tight and his hands were shaking. *This is much harder than I imagined.* "Unfortunately, the sorrow of losing your family took its toll on both of them. Your grandmother passed away ten years ago and your grandfather died a year later. Your aunt lived on and continued to search for you for years, but six years ago she was diagnosed with cancer. A year later, she died as well.

Ray paused to let David absorb the bitter news. "Before Rachael died, she liquidated your grandfather's estate and consolidated the proceeds into a trust in your name. She appointed me executor until I could find you. I nearly gave up, but last Sunday something prompted me to make one more try and, well, here I am."

David didn't speak. His eyes were riveted upon Ray. Ray continued. "Anyway, the estate is worth almost two million dollars and it belongs to you, David. There is also a storage unit in Atlanta with some personal items that Rachael wanted you to have, or at least see. Oh and . . ." Ray bent over and pulled his briefcase up into his lap. He opened it and took out an old photo book. Laying that on the desk, he pulled out a weathered enveloped. ". . . She also wanted you to have these." The envelope was addressed simply "To David."

David gazed at the photo book and the envelope as if they were dangerous. "Thank you, Mr. Campbell. This is very difficult for me, as you can imagine, but I know my family would want me to remember them."

Ray took another document out of his briefcase. "This is the trust that your aunt set up. As you'll see, once we establish your identity the trust belongs to you and you can do with it as you wish. Here is an accounting of the assets. It's mostly CDs and bank deposits along with some stocks and bonds. It would be best if you could come to Atlanta. That way you could see the contents of the storage shed and we could fill in the paper work with the help of my attorney. If you'd like I . . ." but Ray couldn't finish the sentence. His throat tightened and he had to stop. It was all so academic when he was staring at the files in his office. But now, seeing David and seeing the effect it was having on the McMurray's only survivor, was too much. The sadness came crashing through. He blinked back his tears. "If you'd like, I can show you where they are buried. They're all together, even your family. They bought a plot for you as well."

David nodded his head and then lowered it. A minute passed in silence. Finally, David sighed heavily and rubbed his forehead. "Okay. I'll try to get down there in a week or two. Maybe I'll spend the weekend there."

Ray didn't know what else to say. He stood and reached out his hand. David stood and shook it. "David, it is truly an honor to meet you. Your aunt and grandparents were some of the finest people I ever knew. You will never know how happy it would have made them to know that you received your inheritance."

David didn't respond. Instead, he stared tenuously at the photo book, the letter, and the trust papers on his desk. A million thoughts went through his mind, but nothing drifted to his lips.

Ray nodded and headed for the door. He knew the important part was over, but the one question that plagued him early this week, still haunted him. He stopped at the door.

"David, this isn't important, but I'm so curious. Where have you been all these years? Why couldn't we find you?"

David glanced up at Ray, his mind spinning with questions. *How can I explain? Where should I start?* After reflecting upon all his possible responses, he decided to keep it simple. "An old man found me and took me in. We traveled for a long time and then settled in Alaska, in the Matanuska Valley. He raised me like his own son."

Ray's mouth fell open in disbelief. "That's kidnapping! What was his name? We should turn him in to the authorities." Then he reconsidered. "You say he was old. Is he still alive?"

"Yes, I'm sure he's still alive. But he didn't kidnap me. My mother sent him to help me. He was a very special person."

Ray was confused. Some old man had taken David and raised him like a son. Normally there was some kind of abuse or mental illness associated with something like this, but David seemed perfectly well adjusted. He sensed that David held this person in high esteem. Still, Ray smelled a rat. The old man had lied to David. His mother couldn't have sent him.

"David, your mother was dead. She couldn't have sent him."

David looked down at the picture of Catherine on his desk. "I know," David's eyes shifted from the paperwork to stare directly into Ray's, "but she did."

* * *

Twenty minutes after Ray Campbell left his office, David left as well. It was only 2 P.M., but the day had been so unproductive that it didn't matter. His mind was lost in the past now and those memories only fueled the cauldron. He gathered the photo book, the trust, and Rachael's letter, and loaded them in his briefcase. Then he carried it slowly down the hall, through the reception area, and out to the elevators. Nicole was at her desk. He felt the strings pull in his heart as he passed by, but he didn't know what to say. In fact, not a single word had passed between them since the night of the gala.

When he arrived at his apartment, he placed the briefcase on the kitchen table and went to his bedroom to take a nap. Sleep never came. Finally, with anxiety tearing at his heart, he went to the kitchen, opened the briefcase, and reached for the photo album. His first impulse was to look at the pictures, but as he touched the front cover, Catherine's image flooded his mind and he froze. The cauldron flared. David ground his teeth to brace against the onslaught. He let the photo album slip back into his briefcase. His heart was pounding. It felt like someone was sitting on his chest. *Fear*, he thought in silent recognition. *This is fear.*

He had faced so many difficulties in his life. He couldn't imagine anything worse than what he had already been through, but there it was. He was afraid of what was in that photo book. David bit his lip, examining the book without touching it. *It's one tiny book, paper and plastic with a few colors.* He reached for it again and stopped. *No. Not yet.* He swallowed and took the envelope from the briefcase, cut the seal, and opened it. The letter was yellow and brittle where it was folded. He unfolded it carefully and studied each word with intensity.

Dear David,

If you are reading this letter then my prayers have been answered. We have searched now for almost twelve years trying to find you. We never gave up. We always believed that our Lord and Savior was looking over you and taking care of you. Sometimes our faith was a little thin, but our hope always survived. Part of the reason that we always believed was because of something that happened to your grandmother, Helen.

After the loss of her daughter and grandchildren, and when the intense initial search for you yielded nothing, your grandmother became distraught. She stopped getting out of bed and I believe that she willed herself to die. It nearly destroyed your grandfather. He poured every ounce of his soul into the search for you; believing that if he could find you, he could save his wife.

One morning when your grandfather and I got up, your grandmother was cooking breakfast for us. We couldn't believe it. She was thinner and more frail than ever, but she was happy again. Neither of us dared say anything. We dressed and sat down at the table like nothing had ever happened. After we said the prayer, she told us that there was something she needed to say.

She told us that she had seen your mother in a dream. She said that Catherine was very busy and very happy. Your mother told your grandma not to worry about you and not to search for you anymore. She said that you were in the care of someone that God had sent and that you were safe for the time being. She said that it had to be like that. There was no other way.

At first your grandfather and I worried that maybe she was having hallucinations. We worried that she might relapse. But her faith was so strong that she simply recovered. She always said that she missed all of you, but she knew without a doubt that she would see her daughter and her grandchildren again.

Your grandmother's faith helped to heal us, David. When we saw that she was happy and that life went on for her, it helped us to continue. Eventually we believed enough to stop spending so much time searching for you, but, partly because of her dream, we never gave up completely.

Now there is something I want you to know, David. You were never alone. All those years you were away from us, we still loved you. You were named after your grandfather and you come from a wonderful loving family. Our lives may have been shattered, but our faith burned ever so brightly. We know that we will see you and your family again. And even if we are dead when you get this letter, you should know that we love you, and we are watching over you.

You know, your grandma always set a place for you at Thanksgiving. Every year on your birthday and at Christmas she bought you a gift. I have kept most of those items and some other family keepsakes in a storage unit in Atlanta. Whenever you are ready, Mr. Campbell has the combination.

There is one more thing that I have to tell you. I debated writing this for some time because I wasn't sure that your mother understood what she was saying at the time. But now that I have had time to ponder her words, and partly because of Grandma's dream, I believe that Catherine was right.

When the authorities notified me that your family had been in an accident, and that your mother was in critical condition, I went immediately to Sacramento. You were there a few hours earlier and I have wondered so many times, how our lives would have been different if only I had gotten there before you. But it was not to be.

When I arrived at the hospital, I went to your mother's side. She was so heavily injured that I wept when I saw her. I felt bad for all the little mean things I had said or thought about her, but I realize now that they were not significant. Catherine knew I loved her. She woke briefly while I was at her side and even though she was in terrible pain, she was thinking of you. She spoke your name and then asked me to tell you the following. These were her last words, David, and they were terribly important to her because she struggled against all her pain to get them out. So, I will let her last words be my last words.

You are someone very special, David. You are a messenger from God.

Love,

Rachael

David folded the letter and put it back in the envelope. Then he laid the envelope on top of the photo book. He spent the rest of the day doing laundry and cleaning the apartment. It was already pretty clean, but he couldn't think of anything else to do. Every few minutes, he would glance at the photo book. It was still there, but somehow he wasn't ready.

Saturday started with a workout and then a long walk around the city. It took almost all day and it helped David to clear his mind. While he walked he thought about Rachael's letter and her words seeped into his heart. At dusk he had recovered to a degree and he smiled. *I have a family, people who care about me.* When he arrived home that evening, he poured himself a glass of orange juice and sat down in front of the kitchen table. The photo book and letter were there, exactly where he had left them. He took a large drink, removed the letter, and opened the photo book.

The first picture was of him smiling and standing next to a towering pine tree in California. David remembered how happy he had been and why not? Everything important was still intact in his life. The next pictures were of Grandpa David and Grandma Helen. There was a picture of his Aunt Rachael and then he turned the page. There they were, his whole family, standing in front of their old house in Atlanta.

The cauldron flared to life in David's mind. He closed his eyes and tried to calm the raging beast, but it had little effect. He closed the book and thought about abandoning his efforts, but David had to see the rest of those photos. He wanted to remember. He needed to remember. He opened his eyes and opened the book to the page his finger was holding. He made a conscious effort to study each face in that picture: his father, Joseph, Helen, Elizabeth, Rachael, himself, and his mother, Catherine. There was a new bicycle parked in front of everyone. *Grandpa must have taken this at my birthday party.*

The rest of the pictures were various scenes from Atlanta. There was even a picture of them standing in front of the minivan before heading off to California. David remembered that day. It had been a sad day and he remembered something else. His mother had sung to them. David's breath caught in his lungs. The cauldron was burning with more intensity than it had in years. There was no escape.

He closed his eyes and composed himself before gazing at the last picture. He finally found the courage and opened the book to the last page. It was different from the rest, taken with a digital camera and printed on computer paper. It showed a row of grave markers, one of which was covered in flowers. David counted them, there were eight and on the picture was written in black marker: "Rolling Hills Cemetery." Behind the row of headstones was a huge weeping willow tree next to a tiny brook.

David noticed that there were a few blank pages at the end of the book. He sat the book down and went into his bedroom. From a box on top of his dresser he pulled out four additional photos. The first was a picture of Camille and Marty from her wedding invitation. It was in black and white, but Camille looked so happy that David loved the picture. The second was a picture of Tommy in a flowered shirt and a straw hat with a huge snake wrapped around him. The third was a picture of Tommy, Camille and himself standing together in front of Miss Abernathy's new house. The last was a picture of Miss Abernathy, John and himself standing in the same spot. It was the only picture he had of John. He studied it for almost a minute and smiled. He carefully placed those pictures in the unused pages of the photo book.

The cauldron burned in David's mind that night and he hardly slept. He woke up several times and drank a glass of milk, but it didn't help. He rose at six o'clock on Sunday and started to read his Bible. He never questioned why he did that. It had been John's custom and he had simply adopted it. He was reading that morning from Romans Chapter 8 when his eyes stopped on verse 28.

> And we know that all things work together for good to them that love God, to them who are the called according to his purpose.

Light filled David. The words *all things* seemed to lift from the page and then an idea occurred to him. He scrambled to his briefcase and pulled out the trust account. He studied the numbers on the list of assets: a total of $1.7 million. If he added that to the $1.4 million that he had saved over the four years he had been at the partnership and his options . . . Yes! David rushed to the box on top of his dresser. He took out his option agreement. Almost 200,000 of them had vested. They were worth $2.2 million. David added it up . . . over $5 million. It was enough!

He smiled. His mind cleared as the pieces began to fall into place. It was like a giant jigsaw puzzle, but now . . . now he could see the final picture. David lowered his head in silent prayer. "Thank you, Father, I see the way. Please, my only prayer, Father . . . don't let Pearl View fall until I can finish."

That night David slept like a baby---ten hours from eight until six. When he went through his workout that morning, the weights felt like feathers. He made it to work by 7:30 A.M. and made his first call. Unfortunately, Ray Campbell wasn't in yet. So he left a message and took out the final report from Salinger Engineering. At the end of that report was a list of city-approved construction companies.

David worked like a tornado. He lined up seven interviews in the next three days and three on-site inspections with engineers from those companies. He noticed that Michael watched everything he did at Pearl View, but he no longer cared. David called and spoke directly with several construction managers who had worked with each of these companies. One name kept coming to the top, McClintock Consolidated.

McClintock Consolidated specialized in high-rise construction and had been successful in restoring several old buildings. More important to David, however, was the fact that they were a family business and had a reputation for being honest, although not necessarily the most economical. On Thursday, Jason McClintock, grandson of the founder, Herschel McClintock, met with David at his office. Jason was a serious man. Almost fifty years old and balding in spots, he sported a heavy mustache and had sharp eyes. Although he was only five feet six inches tall, he had a commanding presence.

David showed Jason the images of the columns and after an hour's discussion, they drove across to Jersey and inspected the building together. Jason dragged a ladder up to the eighth floor. Once David pointed out the suspect columns, Jason climbed up his ladder, peeled back the dropped ceiling, and disappeared into the rafters. Thirty minutes later he emerged and jumped back down the ladder.

"Not too bad. I can give you an estimate in writing next week."

"I need it tomorrow, but you can give me a verbal."

"What's your hurry?"

David shook his head. "It's a long story."

* * *

Ray Campbell couldn't believe that he was back in New York. He had never visited there before last week and now he was on his second visit in as many weeks. His flight was on time that morning, so he ended up with a few extra hours before his three o'clock appointment with David. David, he mused. The name seemed to glow in Ray's mind. He still couldn't believe the boy was alive.

David had called him Monday and asked him to come to New York by the end of the week. He said the meeting was urgent. Ray didn't know what to think. He cleared his calendar and made arrangements. When he arrived in New York it was only one o'clock in the afternoon, so he took a cab and toured the city for a while. He spent an hour wandering through the big department stores before purchasing a small gift for his wife. His taxi pulled up in front of the building where David worked at about five minutes to three. Luckily, Ray knew where he was going this time and David's company was only on the fourth floor. When he walked in, he asked for David. The receptionist gave him the same cold glance before directing him through the inner door.

Ray was headed down the hallway when he noticed David sitting in a conference room with a tough-looking middle-aged man. Ray could tell that the man was a severe person. He had a few patches of hair on his head and a large mustache. He was leaning over some papers and explaining something to David. Ray knocked and entered. "David, are you ready to see me or do you need to finish here?"

David motioned for him to come in. "No, this is the meeting. Raymond Campbell, meet Jason McClintock." Jason stood and shook Ray's hand and the three of them sat around the table. Ray noted that David seemed concerned but confident. "Jason is bidding a job for me. The partnership has a building that needs some critical repairs in order to be safe.

There are some structural problems that Jason's company has expertise in repairing."

It all seemed interesting, but Ray couldn't understand what it had to do with him.

David noticed the confusion on Ray's face. It was time to drop his bomb. "Gentlemen," both men looked up at him, "about two months ago, this partnership purchased the apartment complex and marina at Pearl Point. They made this investment under my advice and counsel and I am currently responsible for making the investment profitable. Part of that success will come from a second building we are planning for the site, but we plan to keep the current building as well. Unfortunately, the existing building, known as Pearl View Apartments, has structural flaws that could make it unsafe in the event of heavy vibrations."

David paused. He didn't quite know how to explain the rest of his predicament. He decided to come to the crux of the issue. "No one else in the partnership believes there is a problem. The building is twenty-nine years old and we did a full inspection before we bought it. There is no settling, cracking, or any other external evidence to cause someone to believe the building has a problem.

"But upon more thorough inspection by a specialized engineering firm, I have discovered that eight columns on the eighth floor are flawed and must be replaced to make the building safe." David fell silent as he gathered his thoughts. He peered up at Ray. "Since I am the only person who shares this conviction, I have decided to fund the reconstruction myself."

David watched his associates in concern. Jason McClintock was the first to react. He focused his sharp eyes on David as a frown covered his face. Then there was Ray's astonished look. David continued before either one of them could object. "After inspecting the site, Mr. McClintock informed me that his company's bid to repair the building is $5.7 million with possible cost overruns of up to twenty percent." David studied Jason's concerned face. "According to my preliminary calculations, I don't quite have enough to cover that, but my hope is that with your help, Ray, we can figure out what is available and determine if there is any way that it might be enough to engage Mr. McClintock's company."

Jason scowled. David could tell that he felt he was being cornered. "How much are we talking about?"

David met his eyes. "If I add my personal savings, my stock options, and the inheritance my family left me; I estimate around $5.3 million."

Jason slumped back in his chair while glaring at David. He was clearly unhappy. "It's not enough. You need to get your company to fund this."

David spoke flatly. "That will never happen. If the partnership is involved, nothing will be done, eventually Pearl View will collapse, and . . ." David hesitated, studying the proposal in front of him, ". . . people will die." Then he raised his head and peered through the walls in the direction of Hank's office. He spoke gravely. "My time is running out, gentlemen." David glanced back at Jason. "It comes down to the three of us, in this room, today." Jason flattened his mustache in annoyance.

Ray had been quiet for as long as he could stand it. "This entire conversation is absurd!" He nearly shouted. "David, you are not responsible for the property of your company. There is no legal basis for them to force you to use your inheritance to fix their building. My advice to you is to quit today. File a grievance with the company or the city and walk away from the whole thing. It's their building, their decision, and their problem. At least that way you'll have saved your inheritance and you'll have washed your hands of the responsibility."

"I can't do that."

Ray was angry. He couldn't imagine that the foolish and stubborn young man sitting across the table from him was related to the McMurrays. They were soft-spoken, careful people who spent their lives in preparation to make his life better. Ray glared at David. "I won't allow this. After your family died in the accident, your grandparents spent their lives searching for you. They loved you. They saved everything for you. They made every preparation for you. When they died, they turned it all over to me and I have watched over it and taken care of it because they were my friends. They were my friends! I will not allow you to throw everything away because you are being manipulated by your corrupt employer."

David lowered his head, but Ray continued his tirade. "If I let you follow through with this madness you will have nothing. Everything your family saved, everything they wanted you to have, will be gone. Your grandfather used to sit in my office and daydream about you. He wondered what you looked like, how tall you'd grown, if you were happy. He lived for the day that he could see you and he died with the hope that you would one day receive this inheritance. Now you are throwing it all away. It's like erasing him from the face of the planet---like he never existed!"

Ray stopped shouting and the room fell silent. All eyes were on David and inside of David, the cauldron was burning out of control. It seemed like everything was caving in on him. The pictures from the photo book kept turning over and over in his mind: his grandparents, Aunt Rachael, his family. David closed his eyes and the last photo in the album appeared in his mind, the picture of the eight headstones. When Ray yelled that it was like they were never born, he watched in terror as the headstones disappear one by one. He ground his teeth and moaned, "No!"

They weren't gone! David could still see them in his mind and in his heart. They were there every time he closed his eyes, every time he hoped or dreamed. Every time he looked into the mirror, he could see them staring back at him and at night, he could sometimes hear his mother singing that quiet song. David had to get control. He was slipping over the edge to a place he could not go. He shuddered as a ragged breath seeped from his lungs. Every muscle in his body went rigid. He was on the edge of snapping when suddenly . . . there was a snap.

Pain, David thought in surprise. Pain exploded from his right hand and radiated through his body. He realized without opening his eyes that the crystal tumbler he was holding had snapped under the pressure of his crushing grip. The shards of glass cut deeply into his palm, driven by the unrelenting pressure. It stabilized him. He used the pain to push the cauldron back. He took a second breath and his mind cleared. The images that haunted him began fading. Soon, the picture of the cemetery returned to its original view. When the image of his grandfather's grave returned, he lifted his eyes and stared directly at Ray. He spoke the first words that came to his mind. He spoke through gritted teeth, his voice deep and menacing. "I still bear his name."

Both men stared at David in astonishment. They were frozen in their seats like caged animals. They felt those words and the power behind them. David's fierce eyes were fixed upon Ray. Ray lowered his gaze to David's clenched fist and the puddle of blood accumulating beneath it. David followed Ray's eyes and realized that he was making a huge mess and needed to do something quickly. Jason moved first. He reached behind him and gathered a stack of napkins sitting beside the coffee pot. He handed the napkins to David, who dropped them onto the spreading pool of blood. David released his hand and several shards of blood-stained glass and the bottom of the tumbler dropped onto the table. He then took several napkins, shoved them into his right hand, and closed it into a fist. He wiped the bottom off his hand with another napkin before looking around the room. "If you'll excuse me for a moment, gentlemen, I need to tend to this. I'll be right back." His voice was back to normal.

Both Ray and Jason nodded as David headed out the door of the conference room. David realized he couldn't tend his wounds by himself. He hesitated for a moment and then poked his head into the reception area. "Nicole?" It startled her. She glanced up in surprise. "I've cut my hand. Could you help me for a minute?"

* * *

When David left Nicole at her apartment on the night of the gala, she had been dumbfounded. She stood there several minutes telling herself that she didn't understand what David said, that he was teasing her, that he had gone down to let the limo know he wouldn't be needing him. After ten minutes, she began to lose hope. Sick with the loss, she went into her apartment and closed the door. Even then, a part of her still expected David to knock and rescue her. He never did.

By the time an hour passed, the full realization of her situation crashed in upon her. David really had said no. He wasn't coming back. She removed her shoes and lay in bed still wearing her party dress. Then, for the first time in years, she cried. She was angry; she was worried; she was sad. She kept rolling the whole evening over and over in her mind, but she couldn't figure out what had gone wrong.

It was a circular madness that she could not escape. First she would reason that she had pushed him too far. David had been uncomfortable with the whole thing: quick tan, tuxedo, big party, it had all been too much. When she thought like that it made her sad and she would come to the first conclusion. *I'll call him in the morning and apologize.* But then her mind shouted in protest. *It isn't fair!* David said he would do it and she was trying to make him look better; make him somebody. Then the anger would well up inside her. *I was trying to help him.* Her brow would furrow as her fury boiled over and she would reach the second conclusion. *No, I'm not going to call him. This is all his fault. He'd better call me and apologize or it's over baby . . . it's all over.*

Then her mind would twist again. She had at last seen David's potential. He was gorgeous. *And his eyes,* Nicole thought longingly, *they were so powerful and intelligent.* That made her sick. The stalemate brought her to the third conclusion, do nothing. But she longed to see David again, longed to be in his arms, longed to gaze into his eyes.

Nicole finally fell asleep around five in the morning. She woke up at eight o'clock with a terrible headache. She hung around her apartment all morning hoping the phone would ring. It didn't. At three in the afternoon, she called her director and told him that she was too sick to be in the play that night. He told her he understood. Then he complimented her on how great she looked with her friend at the party. Nicole didn't say anything, but when she hung up the phone, she started crying again.

She slept a little better Saturday night, but when she woke up Sunday, she didn't feel like doing anything. Instead, she sat by the phone all day watching TV. She told herself she was taking a day off, but every time the phone rang she jumped. By 5 P.M. she couldn't stand it any longer. She had to talk to someone. She called Marlita.

Marlita answered with a laugh and Nicole could hear Carl joking with her in the background. Nicole thought about hanging up, but after a moment's silence, Marlita noticed Nicole's name on her caller ID and coaxed her on. "Nicole, is that you?"

Nicole sagged on her end of the phone. When she spoke her voice broke. "Marlita."

Marlita heard the pain in her voice and answered in alarm. "What's wrong, girl? You sound upset."

Nicole closed her eyes and whimpered into the receiver. "I need to talk to someone."

"I'll be right over."

"No, I need to talk to you, but we can just do that on the phone. I'm sure Carl doesn't want you out of his sight."

"Nonsense. Carl has had enough of me for a few weeks. He could use a break. I'll be there in an hour."

Nicole felt better when she hung up. Marlita was such a good friend. In some ways, Nicole was upset that Carl had married her. They both seemed so happy though. Nicole couldn't begrudge her that happiness. When Marlita buzzed from the entrance, Nicole let her in the building. A few minutes later she was knocking on Nicole's door. As soon as she saw Nicole's puffy face, she gave her a big hug and they went in and sat down on the couch together. Nicole turned off the TV and related the whole story. She didn't leave out anything. It was like confession and she wanted to make sure that she got everything out, so that she wouldn't have to go over it again. She even mentioned the fact that she had gotten Elaine to get him a tan and a "do" before the gala.

Marlita listened quietly then shook her head sadly. She took both of Nicole's hands in hers and revealed the only answer that made sense to her. "Oh Nicole," Marlita almost sobbed, "He's probably gay."

Nicole stared at her in disbelief, "It can't be . . ." but she never finished the sentence.

Marlita explained. "All the really gorgeous ones are gay these days. David probably really likes you and he probably wanted to have a relationship, but when it came right down to it, he couldn't. That's the way it is for those guys. Women just don't turn 'em on."

Nicole's head sagged against her chest. She still couldn't believe it, not the farm boy. Then an image of a bunch of perverted hillbillies went though her mind. Nicole shuddered.

Marlita stroked Nicole's arm. "Wasn't David raised on some farm in Alaska? It's really cold and dark all the time up there. What do you think they do all winter long? There probably aren't even very many women up there."

They talked for hours after that. By the time Marlita left, Nicole was feeling a lot better. She wasn't quite sure she believed what Marlita was saying, but she was convinced that it wasn't anything she had done wrong. Still, she felt a terrible sense of loss. *If David is gay, maybe*, she wondered, *maybe there is some program that can help him get straight.* Then she shook her head in disgust. *No way! If David is gay, I don't want anything to do with him.*

Come Monday morning, Nicole was back to full strength. She arrived at the office right on time and she was ready for David. When he came in she was going to burn holes in him with her eyes. He hadn't called her, hadn't explained anything. He disappeared Friday night and ruined her weekend. He was a dumb, ignorant, gay puke and she was going to let him have it, if his eyes every met hers again. Unfortunately, David didn't come in at his usual time on Monday morning. It wasn't until ten o'clock before she realized that he was already in his office. She didn't even see him that day. It didn't matter. She glowered at him every day when he came and went. She was angry with him and she wanted him to know it.

By the second week, however, she was tired of it. David seemed to be in the middle of something really serious. He was out of the office most of the week and he never even glanced at her, not ever. It made her sad, but she decided she would avoid him the same way he avoided her. She acted nonchalant whenever he came and went, but she couldn't help watching up every time the door opened. *Is it David? Will he look at me? Will he speak to me?*

Then it happened. On Friday, two weeks to the day that he had ruined her life, David poked his head in the reception area and called out her name. "Nicole, could you help me?" It startled her so badly that she froze for several seconds. She tried to burn holes in him with her eyes, but he never looked up into her eyes. She could see that his hand was injured. He was holding back the bleeding with some napkins. She thought about snapping back "No," but changed her mind and followed him dutifully back to the coffee room. When she arrived, David was standing over the sink, rinsing his bleeding hand under the tap. It was then, after two dismal weeks of confusion and pain, that he finally spoke to her.

"Thanks for helping me, Nicole. Could you get some tweezers out of the medicine cabinet? I think I have some glass fragments in my hand."

Nicole opened the medicine cabinet and found a sterilized pair of tweezers. She popped them out of the little box they were in and handed them to David. Then she watched as he dug the tweezers into his bleeding hand and flicked out tiny pieces of glass. It was a gruesome sight and would have made almost anybody squeamish, but Nicole had seen it all before, thanks to the deep-sea fishing excursions she had shared with her father. On more than one occasion, she had had the disgusting pleasure of digging fishing hooks out of him. She had even dug one out of herself once.

David set the tweezers down and rinsed his hand. Then he clenched his fist. Apparently he hadn't gotten all the fragments because he grabbed the tweezers again and started digging into his palm. Nicole flinched a little. She could only imagine the pain that was shooting through his hand and arm. But he kept digging, rinsing, and clenching until he seemed satisfied. Then he rinsed his hand off thoroughly.

"Nicole, could you get me some of those gauze bandages and one of those wraps?"

Nicole plucked them out of the cabinet. She took the bandages out of their sterile packs and handed them over. David pressed them into his palm and then held his hand out for Nicole to wrap it. She draped the end of the bandage over David's palm and he held it in place while she wrapped the bandage around his hand. She stared at his face the entire time trying to catch his eyes, trying to let him see how angry she was. He never looked up.

Nicole couldn't stand it any longer. The anger boiled over inside her and she bit off her words with such bitterness that she surprised even herself. "David," she smoldered, "are you gay?" David froze for several seconds before slowly lifting his head. When Nicole saw the fierce intelligence in those burning eyes, her heart pounded.

David was afraid. He knew if he gazed into Nicole's eyes, the fire would ignite again in his soul. It had taken every ounce of his self-discipline to avoid her, to avoid sweeping her in his arms and losing his life to her. Now he had no choice. He had to look at her and he had to answer her. He had avoided the situation too long and he knew from the anger in Nicole's voice that his silence had been a mistake.

David took a long and cleansing breath. His emotions were at the brink. Something inside of him was screaming, begging him to reach out, take Nicole in his powerful arms, and hold her. He trembled as he reigned in his thoughts. When he finally spoke, his words were deep and powerful.

"Every time I gaze upon you . . . my flesh burns." His words hung in the air between them. He was staring into her eyes now. His voice filled with emotion. "I long to hold you as I have never held anyone in all my life."

Nicole felt it. David's nostrils flared and the heat of his passion washed over her. It was magnetic and intoxicating. There was no question here. David was not gay! But his answer left so much confusion in her mind. *Why then?* She wondered until the thought found its way to her lips.

"Then why didn't you call me? Why didn't you talk to me?" Nicole paused to gather strength. She wanted to be strong and tell him how wrong he was. It was no use. She couldn't hold it back. A single, silent tear slipped from her eye and ran down her cheek. "Why didn't you stay with me?"

David saw the tear trace down her cheek. He felt the pain and anger in her voice. He couldn't bear it. He closed his eyes, took a step forward and seized Nicole in his arms. It was a powerful embrace.

All the air went out of Nicole. *No, no, no,* she thought in protest, *this is not going to happen.* She stood there rigid, defiant, she would not, could not, let this happen again. Then something magnificent happened. From every point where

David was touching her, a wave of heat flowed through her body. It started unexpectedly and spread like sunshine touching her skin. She couldn't resist. She went limp, letting her body flow into David's, sagging against the pressure of his powerful hug. It felt so good. It was like being healed from the inside out. Finally, in complete surrender, she wrapped her arms around his waist, rested her head on his shoulder, and let the warmth saturate her. She had never, in all her life, felt like this. Her emotions soared from the depths of depression to inexplicable joy. She luxuriated in it.

They stood holding each other in silence for almost a minute. Then, with his head next to hers, David whispered his answer. "We are from two different worlds, Nicole. I cannot find peace in yours and . . . you would never be happy in mine."

David fell silent but continued his embrace. He wished that the moment would never end. Nicole felt David trembling.

"I'm sorry, Nicole. I'm sorry I hurt you. But I can't do this. Whenever I touch you, I feel my soul slipping away. That can never be. Many things are sacred to God, but none more than the lives of His children and . . ." David paused trying to find the right words, words that would explain without offending, ". . . the creation of that life."

David released his embrace and Nicole stepped back. She gazed into David's eyes and saw the loss, the sorrow, and the love in those eyes. She didn't understand everything David had said, but she knew that he believed it wouldn't work. David lowered his eyes and finished wrapping his hand. He turned and headed out the door to the conference room without speaking.

Nicole was stunned for several seconds before her brain started working again. Her mind was in a tailspin of images as she made her way from the break room and sat down at her desk. There was nothing wrong with David. He loved her. He loved her like no human being had ever loved her. It was physical. Oh yes, it was physical! But it was more than that, it was in his mind and in his heart, his---soul. That was what was so powerful and unique about it. Something inside of her had awakened as well. It was a place that she had forgotten existed. It had always been there, but it had been quiet for a long, long time. Then, from that innermost place, a powerful thought soared to her consciousness. *What would it be like to live in the light of David's love . . . every day?*

* * *

When David left the conference room, both Ray and Jason were left alone to stare at each other in shock. The scope of the course David wanted to take was clear. His commitment to that destructive path was even clearer. Both men felt the conviction in his voice and, what was worse, they had seen it in his eyes, those terrible eyes. Jason was the first to recover. He turned around and searched in the cabinet behind him. From there he pulled out a new stack of napkins. He opened the stack and, taking the trash can from next to the coffee table, he went around to where David had been sitting and cleaned the water and blood from the table.

"Can you believe this madness?" Ray asked.

"Oh, I don't know if it's so mad."

"It's not David's responsibility. His company needs to step up and do this."

"They don't believe there's a problem."

"Well, maybe there isn't a problem," Ray glared back. "Maybe all of this is in David's head."

"David is convinced there's a problem."

"Okay, you're the building expert. You've seen the building. Is there a problem?"

Jason narrowed his eyes in concentration. "It's a tough call. There's definitely something different about those columns, but whether it's enough to cause a collapse . . . I don't know. One thing is certain, however; eight flawed adjacent columns is something to worry about."

"So you protest to the company, file a complaint, blow a whistle. You make sure everybody knows about the problem and knows whose responsibility it is to fix it."

Jason fixed Ray with his stare. "And if it doesn't get fixed?"

"Well, then whatever happens isn't your fault."

"So, now we're back to where David is." Jason shook his head. "Think about it. If you knew those people were going to die and you had the power to stop it, would you give everything you had, including your inheritance, to save the lives of a thousand people that you don't even know?"

Ray glared suspiciously at him, but Jason just continued. "Not me, I wouldn't do it. I'd do exactly what you said and I would be noisy about it so that everybody knew where I stood. That way, if something really bad happened, I couldn't be held responsible."

"Exactly," Ray nodded. "And that's what everyone would do."

"Not everyone." Jason's voice trailed off to a whisper. "There are people out there who give everything to help their fellow man. Some strange names come to mind when you think about it: Mother Teresa, Albert Schweitzer . . . Florence Nightingale."

Ray's mouth fell open. "Surely you aren't comparing David to those people!"

"I don't know, but this much I do know. If I was dead and had a grandson who was willing to give up everything he owned to save the lives of people he didn't know . . . money wouldn't be an issue."

Neither Jason nor Ray spoke for the next five minutes. When David finally entered, he spoke gravely. "Gentlemen, I apologize for the delay." He seemed oddly sad and distracted. "How can we make this work?"

David's question hung heavily in the air. Both men stared at him in silence. David sensed their mood and made his way to his seat. He noted that the mess he had made earlier was gone. He was about to restart the discussion when Jason interrupted him. "We've worked it all out, David. I'll take the job and guarantee it for $5.3 million, but since I'll be taking a risk on the implementation side, I can't afford to take a risk on the payment side. So I won't begin until I receive the full payment of $5.3 million in advance. If I don't get the whole thing by December, I'll refund everything you've sent me and, well," Jason shook his head, "the deal's off."

Ray peered at Jason and nodded in unspoken understanding. "If it's what you want, David. I'll liquidate the trust and send the funds to Jason before December."

David let out a sigh of relief. "That's what I want, Ray. That's what I want." Then he turned to Jason. "I will liquidate my accounts next week and hand deliver the first part. I'll bring you a cashier's check for about $1.4 million."

Ray broke eye contact with Jason. "You still have a problem, David." David expression melted in concern. "The trust is divided into three parts to avoid taxes, but if you cash in your company options, the government will want about forty percent."

David nodded. "I realize that. I'll need a little cooperation from D&B as well. I'm going to try to get the partnership to cash out my options by sending Jason a check directly instead of through me."

"That will work." Ray agreed.

Jason flattened his mustache. "Remember, David, if I don't get everything by December, you get it all back and the deal is off. Is that clear?"

"I understand." Then David voiced his real concern. "I hate to wait so long."

"We have projects underway that will keep us busy into November. That's the best I can do."

They worked together for the next twenty minutes ironing out the details. Ray brought out a stack of paperwork for David to sign. By 5 P.M., they were finished. David thanked them both as they left the conference room and then he sat there alone. The next thing he had to do was the hardest of all. David swallowed and said a quiet prayer. "Please Father, be with me."

David picked up the tentative bid that Jason had given him, opened his briefcase, and withdrew a sealed envelope. It was bulging with papers. Rising from his chair, he walked down the hall to the storage room. This area was generally the domain of the secretarial pool, but no one was there. He made a copy of the bid Jason had given him and then he made the long walk down to the end office in the hallway. It was a door David was well familiar with; it was Hank's office.

The outer room was empty and David surmised that Angela was out on an errand. He walked past her desk to Hank's inner office. The door was open. David stopped to collect his thoughts before knocking on the casing.

"Come in." Hank's words came out in a normal voice, but when he realized that it was David, his eyes narrowed and his lips compressed. David stepped through the door and closed it. Then he turned and met Hank's glare. Hank said nothing as David walked across the room and sat in the chair in front of his desk. David could feel the anger and mistrust in Hank's penetrating eyes. *No doubt,* David sighed, *Michael has told him everything.*

David took a deep breath before beginning. "I'm leaving the partnership."

Hank's expression did not change immediately. He sat there staring at David with his angry eyes for several seconds before an expression of disgust crossed his face. He spoke gravely. "I guess so."

"I've made arrangements to have the flawed columns at Pearl View replaced, but I need your help."

Again, Hank did not speak but simply stared at David as if he wanted to bite his head off.

David continued. "I have contracted McClintock Consolidated to make the repairs. Since the columns are all along the north wall, only about twenty tenants will be affected. The work won't begin until December, so Michael should have plenty of time to move tenants around before constructions starts."

Hank never reacted. He sat stock still staring at David with dark hateful eyes. David laid a copy of Jason's bid on the desk and withdrew his hands. He half expected Hank to bat it off, but Hank never moved. He never lowered his gaze.

David went on. "The cost of the restoration is $5.3 million. I have made arrangements to pay for the construction from my own funds but---this is where I need your help." David dropped the bulging letter on Hank's desk. "These are all the options that I have received from the partnership. They are currently worth about $2.2 million. I need all of this to complete the construction."

Hank's eyes traced a path from David to the envelope on his desk and then back at David. "You know the drill. The board of directors sets the value of the options every three months. Since this is still a private company, we will only repurchase them based on funds available."

David sighed. "That won't work for me. If you pay me directly for the options, I'll have to give half to the IRS. Instead, I would like the partnership to send the funds directly to McClintock. I'll surrender the options to you and since they haven't been exercised, they'll expire in seven years anyway. You can keep them in your drawer and the company's liability will simply disappear. Everything that you send to McClintock will be a write off, so, in the end, it should be better for the partnership as well."

There was another long pause. "And this is what you want?"

David let out a sigh. "That's what I want."

Hank shook his head in surrender, "Okay."

David felt a tremendous weight lift off his shoulders. He closed his eyes and bowed his head in exhaustion. Still, he knew he had one last bitter cup to drink. "My employment agreement states that I have to give you two weeks notice. Do you want me to finish out the two weeks?"

"No." Hank answered immediately.

David sighed. "Then this is it."

Hank shook his head. "What a shame. What a terrible waste. You could have been the best."

David peered carefully at his would be friend. Only three weak little words left his mouth, "I'm sorry, Hank." But Hank wasn't listening anymore. It was as if he were staring through him to the empty chair behind David. David stood. He hated the feeling that he had betrayed his friend. There was no other way to describe it. Before he turned to leave, he made his final gesture. "For what it's worth, I will always think of you as a friend." David reached up slowly and extended Hank his unbandaged hand.

Hank looked at David's hand and then back at David. He spoke curtly. "That means nothing to me." His words were so laden with contempt that David peered into his eyes to see if they held the same feeling. They did.

Hank swiveled his chair so that his back faced David and gazed out the window. David lowered his outstretched hand and trudged to the door. He hesitated before opening it. *There must be something I can say, some way I can explain.* Nothing came to mind. As he wavered there, Hank spoke his final word. "Goodbye."

David exited slowly and headed to his office. It had been as bad a day as he could ever remember. He wondered if it felt like this to be on death row. It was dark humor, but strangely, the thought made him smile. In his office he took the few personal items that he had and collected them in his briefcase. Then he took his car keys, office key, and desk key and laid them on the desk. He perused the office that had been his home for four years one last time. It was hard to believe it was over. He had ended almost exactly where he started.

David walked down the hallway toward the exit. He felt Nicole's presence in the reception area. He didn't dare look at her. He was afraid. His heart pounded. He knew that he loved her. He knew that he wanted her more than anything he had ever wanted in his entire life, but he also knew it could never be. His pace slowed. He couldn't leave like this. He had to say something. He stood a few inches from the door and stopped.

A part of him wanted to ask Nicole to come with him. He wanted to be with her, every day and every night, forever. But he had told her the truth when he had admitted that they were from different worlds. Still, the ache was in his heart.

David found his voice and spoke quietly. "Nicole, I'm leaving the partnership." He tried to find other more comforting words that would soothe the empty ache he felt. Nothing came to mind. He slowly opened the door and spoke the only word he could think of . . . "Goodbye."

* * *

Nicole was in turmoil. From the moment she returned to her desk, she had done nothing but ponder and review her relationship with David. She blocked out everything else. In all her life, she had never felt as badly as she had over the past two weeks. She had dated so many different men. Many of them had been more handsome than David. All of them had been more sophisticated. Nicole smiled to herself. None of them had been bigger. Only a couple of them had dumped her and after she thought about it, she was glad they did. But it was so different with David.

Frustratingly, this had been the least physical relationship she had had since high school and yet, she felt absolutely violated. It was as if David had poured through every part of her being, every memory in her head, and decided that it wouldn't work. Nicole felt like she had fallen from the world's largest roller coaster and lay dying in a heap on the ground.

Her thoughts drifted to the moment David held her in his arms in the break room. The warmth that had flowed through her body was still with her and she knew, more than if she had heard it from his lips, that he loved her. She kept rolling that thought around and around in her head, trying to tie it off into a conclusion, but she couldn't make it coalesce. One question kept resurfacing. It was the one question that she couldn't seem to answer. *What is so special about David? Why do I care?*

At that point, David entered the reception area. She followed his every step, hoping beyond hope that he would look at her and say something, anything, and at the same time, fearing that he might. But he didn't look, and he didn't speak, at least until he reached the exit. The world stopped for Nicole. Her heart raced when he hesitated at the door. The words that passed from his lips came in slow motion because her mind was spinning so fast. They didn't make any sense.

"I'm leaving the partnership."

Nicole's mind blanked. That couldn't be right. Everything was upside-down today. She knew from the sessions she'd overheard that Hank and Greg thought David could do no wrong. It was impossible to imagine that he would leave. What about the money? If David's situation was anything like Sam's, his options would double in value every year. Nicole was stunned. The realization hadn't completely washed over her, when she heard his last word. "Goodbye."

It wasn't goodbye like I'll see you tomorrow. It was goodbye like forever. David was leaving.

Panic seized her. She had to understand, *Why?* Somehow she knew if she understood the answer to that question, she would understand everything. *Why is David so different? Why do I care so much? Why, why, why?*

Nicole closed her eyes and thought back to the night when he had left her at her apartment; when he had said no. The word had been so low, so powerful, and so absolute that it was like something waking up inside of him. It was part of him really. It was always there, always guiding him. It was strength like no other person she had ever met. It was that part of David that had touched her, that thing inside of David that controlled him and guided him. She hadn't understood in the beginning, but now, the pieces began to fit.

There was something like that inside of her, too. There was a part of her that didn't really care what she looked like. It wanted to love people and help them. It wanted to trust and believe everything. It was that little girl who used to play dolls endlessly with her friends. The little girl who sat on her father's knee and believed all those ridiculous stories he used to tell. David had touched that part of her. He had awakened it.

For an instant, everything froze in Nicole's mind and then, the puzzle fell into place. Something inside of her was untainted by the world. It was perfect and beautiful and it loved without limit or reservation. David had awakened that part of her and it loved with complete abandon. It loved David.

The thought assaulted her. *That's why*, she realized, *that's why I love him.* Nicole couldn't believe her own thoughts. Aside from her mother and father, she had never told a single person that she loved them because she was honest enough with herself to admit that she didn't, but now it was clear. She whispered the words softly to herself to be sure. "I love you, David." They filled her. The warmth she had felt in the break room returned with force.

Then from the same place that David had awakened within her, she felt new words form in her mind. They were powerful and compelling words.

Follow David! Surrender your life to him.

Nicole stood. She slipped on her sandals, grabbed her purse, and took a step toward the door. It was already closed, but she knew David was still in the hallway waiting for the elevator. She knew there would be no turning back. Whatever David's world held, it would be her world now. She took a second step and another thought stopped her. *David has lost his job. He'll be poor.* She shook her head violently. *David can get another job and if he doesn't . . . oh well. Daddy has plenty of money.*

She took another step and another thought blossomed. *You were going to be an actress. You were going to be famous.* Nicole gritted her teeth in defiance. *I'm too tall and it's getting old anyway.*

She touched the door with one hand and a third thought bludgeoned her. *You won't be special anymore. You'll be just like everyone else.* An image rose in her mind. It was a familiar face. It was the harried face of her old friend Tammy Miller.

Tammy and Nicole had done everything together in high school. They had gone their separate ways in college and to Nicole's utter disgust, Tammy married at the end of her second year of college. During Nicole's final year at the Academy she went back to Houston to visit her family for Christmas. Through a casual conversation with some of her old friends, she discovered that Tammy was back in town. Nicole called her to see if they could get together and catch up. Tammy agreed, but on the morning they were supposed to meet, Tammy cancelled. Upset, Nicole traced down Tammy's address and knocked on the door anyway. When Tammy opened it, Nicole was alarmed. Tammy had changed.

Tammy apologized for breaking their date and, after a moment's hesitation, let Nicole in. Tammy was still in her bathrobe, but even wrapped in that bulk, Nicole could tell that her friend had gained at least twenty pounds. A diapered noisy boy ran circles around the sofa while a baby's terrible screams echoed from the back bedroom. Before sitting down, Tammy went into the bedroom and picked the tiny girl up.

Then she sat down across from Nicole, opened her bathrobe, and began nursing.

Tammy shook her head in exasperation. "This is my little girl Jennifer. She was up all night with colic. I really wanted to see you, Nicole, but I didn't get any sleep last night and I can't turn Jennifer over to a baby sitter while she's sick like this."

They only talked for a few minutes before Nicole left in shock, sickened by Tammy's dreadful plight. It was like she had died. There was no fun or excitement in her life anymore. The Tammy that Nicole remembered, the Tammy that used to be so attractive and fun to be with, was gone. No one would notice her now. She was invisible. It was day after day of kids, work and drudgery. Nicole made a vow that day. She promised herself that she would never fall to Tammy's fate. No matter what, people would always notice her; she would always be admired; she would always be envied.

Nicole froze at the door. She could finally see the precipice she was about to step off. She stood transfixed for almost a minute and then she reached her conclusion. She lowered her head and muttered quietly, "I can't, David . . . I can't live like that."

Nicole slumped over and rested her head against the metal door. She stood there for minutes until Darlene poked her head inside the reception area. "Nicole!" Darlene sounded upset. Nicole glanced up in surprise. "Are you still here, girl?" Nicole studied Darlene face. She seemed angry, but Nicole had no idea why. Darlene glared at her like she was an idiot. "Answer the phone! It's been ringing off the hook all afternoon. Where have you been?"

The command startled Nicole back to reality. She took her hand off the door and headed back to her desk. It was past five o'clock already. She decided to finish work and reconsider her options that evening. But as she returned to her duties, the warmth that she felt when she thought about

David diminished. Nicole didn't realize it then, but she had already made her decision.

* * *

David walked slowly from the door of Downing & Burkover to the elevator. He was alone. Emptiness seeped into him as the events of his life seemed to swirl about him. He had lost everything really and yet, there was peace in his heart. His only real regret was Nicole. David knew he loved her. A tiny smile crossed his face as he arrived at the elevator and waited. Even with all Nicole's complex rules and requirements for life, there was something beautiful inside of her, something that he had come to love, *But,* he thought sadly, *it can never be.*

It took almost five minutes for the elevator to arrive and when it did, it was strangely empty. The door opened with a hiss, David stepped inside, and pressed the lobby button. As the familiar feeling of weightlessness overcame him, he bowed his head and spoke softly. "Thank you, Father. Thank you for helping me to save Pearl View."

The elevator didn't stop until it reached the bottom of the building. David exited and headed for the doors as if it were the conclusion of a normal day. When he stepped out of the lobby and into the street, he noticed it was a beautiful evening. Although his apartment was at least a two-hour hike away, he decided to walk. He didn't have a car anymore and, frankly, not much money either. *Maybe,* he thought amusingly, *walking isn't such a bad idea.*

It was an interesting walk home and David enjoyed the sights of the city as he went. It was especially fascinating to watch New Yorkers emerge from their busy working lives and try to get home quickly to their busy nighttime lives. The sun set as he rounded the final turn onto the road where his apartment was. It had been a longer commute than he had estimated. As he walked down the street to his apartment, he noted abstractly that some of the streetlights were out or didn't come on. It was much darker than he remembered. Then, two blocks from his home, he felt it.

It was coldness. It was darkness. It was hatred. The coldness seeped into David's heart and he staggered to a stop. Terrible memories and fear gripped him as the cauldron burst into brilliant flames in his mind. *Run*, was the only clear thought that materialized. His muscles went rigid. He took a step and then he stopped. *No!* David shouted inwardly.

He could feel it now. *Hate*, David thought silently, *this is hate in its most primal form.* The foreboding weight of it pressed against him, threatening to cut him off, threatening to destroy him. The source of darkness and hatred was so personal and so intense that David suddenly realized it was behind him and to the left. It was standing at the edge of the alley that went behind his building, staring at him, willing him to die.

The cauldron flared to life and David stopped. There was no escape. He could conceive of only one way to stabilize himself against the fear that threatened to drown him. He knew it was wrong, but he had to push back the cauldron's abyss. Slowly, reluctantly, he closed his right hand into a tight fist. Pain shot up his arm as the wounds he had acquired that day reopened in his palm. Using the pain to stabilize himself, he found the tranquil space at the center of his fear. Then he straightened himself and turned to face the source of hatred that poured out against him. David opened his eyes half expecting to see the evil that stalked him, but there was nothing there.

He spoke forcefully. "I will not run again."

There was a brief flare of hatred. David felt the coldness shoot through him as his lungs constricted and his heart stopped beating, but the presence did not linger. Seconds after it began, it ended. Light flooded back into the space where he stood. He was alone.

David walked the last steps to his apartment in silence. He was more exhausted than he had been all week. He stood at the boundary between two worlds, but there was nothing left in this one. There was only the path forward into the future and the unknown. David took a deep breath and let out a long sigh. *Tomorrow,* he nodded in submission, *tomorrow I will begin again.*

ALONE

Chapter 24

D avid stood in front of his apartment window and gazed at the bustling city below. Beside him were two large suitcases that contained the sum total of his worldly possessions. It had been a long and lonely month since he left the partnership.

In the first week after his departure, he emptied $1.4 million from his various bank accounts and delivered it to McClintock Consolidated. It was his portion of the funds he had promised for the repair work at Pearl View. He still had $40,000 left, not including the two weeks' severance that Downing & Burkover had generously sent him.

Initially, he had hoped to stay in New York City. He began that process by combing the newspapers, tracking down employment, and interviewing with job search agencies. It was a time-consuming and difficult process. Soon, however, the realization of what he had lost became clear. His job, his life, had been a fairy tale compared to how the rest of the world lived. He might find another job, but the opportunity to make millions of dollars in such a short time, would probably never happen again.

Other firms made investments similar to the partnership, but David was an unknown entity to them and without a personal introduction or a recommendation from Hank, it would be impossible to reach and influence the appropriate people. The process was gradual, but he arrived at the disappointing conclusion that, while he could find another job, he couldn't make sufficient income to live in New York City and live well.

Armed with that knowledge, he broadened his search to other metropolitan areas. He researched the cost of living in many of them and came to the conclusion that living almost anywhere was cheaper than the Big Apple. He was tempted to go to Atlanta because of the information Ray had given him, but then the dreams started.

It was the same dream and he had it three times over a period of several weeks. It never made sense even though the dreams were vivid and always identical. In that dream, he was running in the desert, climbing up a stony hill. He was in terrible danger. Someone was chasing him. On top of the hill was a house of sorts, more like a one room cement shack. There was nothing around it. It sat alone at the top of a steep slope on a ridge in the middle of nowhere. It was abandoned.

In his dream, David climbed desperately to escape whatever was chasing him. When he reached the top of the hill, he rounded the cement shack to the far side to avoid his pursuers. There was a door on the far side and when he opened it, something very important was inside. David always woke up at that point. David believed the dream had some significance so, after seeing those images three times, he changed his job search tactics. He narrowed his search to cities in the southwest, cities that were set in the desert.

That left Phoenix, Albuquerque and Dallas. He wasn't sure if Dallas was actually a desert area, but Nicole had said so many fond things about Dallas that he was curious to see it. The other thing that attracted him to Dallas was apartment rent. Dallas was a cheap place to live, a third of the cost of New York and there seemed to be more jobs in Dallas than most places. Since Dallas was also on the way to Albuquerque and Phoenix, David decided to start there.

After scanning the online version of the Dallas newspaper, he found several openings for accountants, business managers, and controllers. He researched real estate investment companies, but they didn't have any postings and, to be honest, he didn't know enough about the real estate community in Dallas. There were several postings with big companies in fields like telecommunications, consulting and retail, but David was used to so much autonomy that he just couldn't imagine working for a conglomerate.

He finally stumbled upon a listing for a controller with a construction company. The position captured David's interest because it bridged his two areas of expertise. David called the number in the paper and was eventually able to make a connection with the owner. They set up a casual interview.

David worked out a deal with his landlord in New York. There was a waiting list of applicants, so the apartment would be immediately occupied, but he ended up forfeiting his deposit. Near the end of the month, Jason McClintock sent him an email indicating that Downing & Burkover had sent a little more than the $2.2 million he promised. Jason also indicated that Michael had contacted him and was running the project from the partnership's end. The only part that was missing was his inheritance and David knew that Ray would eventually take care of that. By the end of the month, every loose end was tied down and David's sojourn in New York came to an end.

David sighed as he gazed out his apartment window; it was time to go. He drew his apartment key from his pocket and left it on the kitchen counter. Then he picked up his suitcases and made his way to the street. Thirty minutes later, he was sitting at the terminal in Penn Station.

It was October in New York and it was cold. The clouds were thick overhead and the rain came in a slow drizzle, exacerbating the dreary setting. He had chosen to take Amtrak instead of flying because he wanted to see the country, but it was so gloomy out that he wished he had chosen otherwise. It hadn't occurred to him how lonely train stations could be.

He still ached inside whenever he thought of Nicole. *Perhaps*, he thought over and over, *there was another way.* But he could think of no other outcome that brought the slim peace he now enjoyed. Then there was the cauldron. It was always there, always waiting like a deadly animal to pounce on him at his weakest moment.

"Well," David spoke softly just to hear his own voice, "there's always tomorrow." David smiled at a little boy bundled up in a big coat and sitting in a stroller. *Life,* he thought as he watched the squirmy child roll past. Then he remembered something his mother used to say. It seemed strange that those words would come to him now, but he recalled that those words had often buoyed her in the worst of times. He could still hear her soothing voice and the introspective way in which she would say it. "David," she would stare at him with her most serious expression, "you must never give up. Where there is life, there is always hope." It was still hard to think about her, but the pictures Ray had left and Rachael's letter helped ease the sorrow.

David reminisced about his life and the strange twists and turns it had taken. Then he shook his head. His stay in New York had ended disastrously. *How did I end up like this?* The thought was introspective and emphasized his failures, but in spite of the weather, the loneliness, and his financial shipwreck, David had a feeling---more of an impression really. He peered at the train in front of him and his thoughts coalesced. *There is something out there for me . . . something good.* David smiled.

For more information come visit us at:

www.guardianofheaven.com

About the Author

Mark Barratt was born on St. Patrick's Day, 1956. He grew up in Alaska, one of five children whose inheritance included the loving example of hard working and noble parents.

After graduating from high school he served as a Christian Missionary in South America where he witnessed firsthand the faith and endurance of God's children in a country torn by revolution. Upon returning he obtained a master's degree in engineering, married a country girl, and began a family of eight children. As a consequence of his work, he has traveled to almost every continent of the earth and worked with people of many faiths, including four years with the charismatic, energetic people of Israel.

The Guardian of Heaven is based upon the extraordinary prophecies found in Revelations 11:3-12. It is the work of a lifetime. The development of this story spans four decades and includes the values and ideals of Christians from six continents. Although set in the future, the characters that compose this story come from the lives of biblical heroes, historic reformers and everyday people across the globe. Their examples of courage and faith are the wellspring that has inspired this journey into the prophecies, places and faces of Christianity.

Made in the USA
Las Vegas, NV
17 December 2021